His Wicked Lady

By
Sharon Drane

SKY LAKE
LOST

1

KIT

Eerie stillness blew in with the girl. It smelled like a storm coming.

I was hunched over another sheet of disappointing numbers when my ears popped. The air felt damp and heavy and carried the faint scent of roses down my hallway.

Lights flickered. A chorus of startled beeps rang out from other offices. I thought, *flowers can't grow in a place like this.* And then, everything went silent.

The building held its breath. I held mine.

Something was here.

Those who didn't know better ran for the locked front doors. The generators thudded to life before anybody got out. The building sighed, the power chugged back on, and the usual stink of fear, chemicals, and cafeteria food fell down like a curtain.

But I still felt it—crackling in the walls. Something new.

I didn't know what it was, only that it had to be coming from somewhere—from *someone.*

Someone who could shift the atmosphere of the whole building.

Someone who could light up my machine and give me my life back.

My machine and I lived in a closet. It smelled of bleach and mildew. I waged constant war with the black mold that crept up the walls. I couldn't close the door all the way without making myself dizzy, but it was big enough for a small table and two chairs. At night, I pushed the furniture to one side and unrolled a camping mat, and I slept under a soft quilt that made me feel more or less homesick, depending.

It wasn't much, but it felt like enough when I still thought I could make my machine work. As hope left me, it became less. I'd given up my freedom, my son, my chance to make a difference in the world, for what? A pulsing hunk of metal and unrealized potential.

Foolish. A mistake I could not fix with my tools.

I kept my sanity by walking the halls. Pacing my cage felt like a more accurate description, but it was something I could do.

Since I always walked, no one noticed me searching for the stillness.

No one noticed me anyway. I was a clown in a sea of lab coats in my long skirts, smiling and singing to myself, and people stop paying attention when everything you do is a little off. They looked right through me. There are benefits, as I always told my son, to being an outsider. It gives you a certain kind of freedom.

I kept my routine the same—a quick stop in the cafeteria for a cup of coffee and two chocolate covered donuts, then 45 minutes of brisk movement.

Only my goal changed.

There weren't many places to look. An unlucky newcomer would be taken to one of the basements or the hospital, and a luckier one would be in the dorms. That meant three, maybe four, days of walking.

The basements were locked. It was just as well—I could feel the horrors that lurked underneath me, and I had no desire to meet them.

The dorms felt as blank and empty as ever. Only the smell of microwaved food indicated any life at all, and the only energy I felt there was loneliness.

That left one place to search—the hospital.

I returned to the dorms twice before resigning myself to it.

The stillness went into the hospital, so into the hospital I would go.

The air changed as I crossed the boundary between "office" and "hospital." It felt dark in spite of the glaring lights. Cold. Wet. Not like a hospital at all. *This is a place that should have teeth*, I thought, as I left one world and entered the other.

It was like a fairy-tale forest. I couldn't see the wolves, but I knew they were there.

I shivered and pulled my shawl tight. I hoped I was the witch in this story, and not the princess. Princesses walked a hard road, trapped in towers, at the mercy of evil kings. Witches, on the other hand, had curses to play with and knives in their boots. They smelled magic in the air, and they could *use* it.

"Focus," I whispered, clutching my shawl. "This is not a story. It is your life." A hard thing to remember, when you are living in a nightmare.

The hospital was a maze, and every choice I made felt wrong. I heard screaming but never got closer to it. Room numbers changed without logic, and caution tape and "wet floor" signs blocked every other turn I tried to make. I quickly went from *searching* to *lost*.

They say you should stand still when you're lost, but that only works if someone is looking for you, so I kept moving. Hoping and losing hope and hoping again.

Pain and fear seeped under every door, and I whispered prayers as I walked. I imagined myself wandering like this forever. The lost saint of the hospital. There were worse fates.

And then, I felt it. Something new and different and *wonderful.* The hairs on the back of my neck stood up and my nose tickled, halfway to a sneeze. This wasn't stillness, not exactly. It was fast, spinning like spiderwebs in the air. And a sound spun with it, almost a song.

It could be anything, I told myself. *A radio, maybe.* But it didn't feel like a radio. It felt like a current, pulling me down the hall.

"Where are you?" I asked, and the strange energy lifted the folds of my skirt. A breeze brushed my face, and it smelled like roses.

I was the witch and this was the magic. Finally.

Barriers blocked every path but one.

The door was propped open with a pair of sneakers and the door said 231 even though the one across the hall said 17. Inside, a young man lay in a bed, so many tubes running in and out of him that I couldn't tell where he ended and the medical equipment began.

And next to him a girl, singing.

And all around her that fast, spiderweb energy glistening like spun sugar in the air.

My hands flew to my cheeks and my shawl fell to the floor and I felt, for the first time in months, like there might be a way out, after all.

Johnathan Everett told me I could leave as soon as I finished my machine. I had already signed the contract by then, a mistake that dawned on me slowly, then all at once when the screens came on for the first time.

I thought I knew what I was doing. Everett Research & Consulting funded all kinds of groundbreaking research—even the "woo-woo" kind I did. But under the surface, it was a labyrinth of illegal and immoral experiments.

Not so different, I thought, believing myself quite sophisticated, *from any corporation.*

But ERC *was* different. Horrifying things came out of its labs. People disappeared. I should not have gone near it.

My pride made me blind.

But I did not think I would pay with my life. And then the screens came on, and I learned the truth about the shot they jabbed in my arm when I arrived, and the floor fell out from under me. What had I done? If my machine didn't work, I would be at his mercy.

His mercy. Ha. He showed no one mercy.

When Johnathan told me I could leave if I gave him a working machine, I felt better, because I knew my machine would work. The thing I didn't count on, the thing that kept me in my closet-office and away from my son for one year, then two, was the difficulty of finding anyone with enough power to activate it.

And here she was.

As I watched the girl singing in her shining web, I forgot to breathe. She was hanging between worlds, the air around her so charged that I could feel it. Bright and strong and wild. Tears sprang into my eyes—happiness, relief, *awe*. A rush like the sudden drop of a rollercoaster whooshed through my belly.

I felt intoxicated. If the power went out, I would have run for the front door, even though I knew the generators would beat me to it.

I wanted to drink buckets of that feeling.

But I wasn't hunting for a feeling. I was hunting for the *source*. And I'd found it—the illusive thing I'd been trying to measure for my whole career. It swirled so thickly around the girl that I could see it, swooping and flashing and leaving its glowing residue in her dark hair.

Her hands were clasped, but it wasn't a prayer. She wasn't begging for anything. She *was* the thing. She would light my machine like fireworks. Joy bubbled up inside me, so unfamiliar that I mistook it for panic at first. I felt her energy like sparks in my own fingertips.

I was going to be *free*.

And then, she looked up.

A tangled head of dark curls framed a pale face. Her cracked lips trembled around a beautiful, heartbreaking note. Glassy eyes passed over me, looking somewhere beyond, or somewhere else altogether.

She was exhausted. She was in pain.

She was a *child*.

And then, the thing I only realized later—if I could see the magic rushing around her like a whirlpool as she sang, so could Johnathan Everett.

I was the witch. And she was the princess. And I would have given her the knife in my boot, if I had one.

The girl had the hazy look of a person deep in meditation—she was there, and also not there, a state I knew not to interrupt. The young man in the bed appeared to hover, shimmering, also not entirely there.

"Where are you, little one?" I whispered, carefully tucking a lock of hair behind her delicate ear. "Somewhere better than here, I hope." Grief and love, for the son I might never see again and this girl in front of me, made me ache.

The girl shivered, but didn't stop singing. The words, I realized, weren't a song at all. She was talking to the man. When she paused for breath his lips moved in answer, their conversation riding a sad, wandering melody. Wherever they were, they were together.

I left my second donut next to her, still thinking of my little boy, who wasn't so little anymore. He always woke up hungry.

I couldn't help the girl without risking Johnathan's attention, so I went to Damia. Damia worked in a room with a desk, a couch, and her own coffee maker on a long counter in front of the window. The ERC equivalent of a corner office. It was presumptuous of me to barge in with a demand, but I had a feeling about her.

I wanted to grab her and shake her and say *be more than this*.

"What are we going to do about the girl?" I asked. I learned a long time ago that people will often accept responsibility for a problem if you act like it already belongs to them.

"Do about her?"

She didn't look up from her papers, so I covered them with the palm of my hand. She raised her eyes reluctantly. She was giving up. Soon, she'd be no use to me, like the others, and I felt heavy with the peculiar grief I always felt when I saw Damia's inner light dimming.

"You have access to her," I explained, because Damia visited the hospital every week, armed with questions devised by scientists who were curious about all the wrong things. A waste of her talents, I thought, but what did I really know of her talents? I only had a feeling about her. "You can ask what she needs. Help her."

"No one can be helped once they're here." Damia shook her head and pulled her papers back. "You know that, even if you're not ready to admit it. Go invent time travel and prevent her from coming in to begin with. That's your area, isn't it?" She lifted the papers and smacked them down decisively to end the conversation.

I laughed. A person couldn't do what I did without growing a thick skin. "Maybe you're right. But there is still value in trying." *It keeps us human*, I wanted to say, but I didn't know if Damia would find that persuasive. "Bring her some blankets and pillows," I suggested. It wasn't much, but it was a start. "Talk to her. Ask what her name is."

Her name was Grace. I heard the sick young man say it in a voice that broke my heart, and I didn't even know him.

Damia nodded. She was a docile zombie, able to follow my instructions but not understand them, and I wondered how long it would be until I became one, too. But as I left the room, I saw it—clouds flitting across her forehead, her hand rubbing the back of her neck. She hadn't given up—yet. She would help little Grace.

I would help little Grace.

The knowledge slammed into me so hard that it left me gasping in the cold hallway outside Damia's office. I could not take my freedom at a little girl's expense. Even if she could power my machine.

Even if it meant I never saw my son again.

I clutched my chest with both hands as a familiar, burning pain squeezed my heart. My son. He *needed* me.

But so did she. I couldn't betray her.

I closed my eyes and hugged myself, waiting for the pain to give my body back. Angry tears ran down my cheeks. I found the magic. The way out. And I couldn't take it.

A thousand arguments howled through my skull, but there was no denying the whispering voice of my soul.

She is important, it said. *Keep her safe.*

2

GRACE

David and I left Sky Lake together for the last time the summer I was eleven.

I didn't know it would be the last time. Or that most endings are written in invisible ink—seen only from the future. I thought I had a lifetime of Sky Lake summers ahead of me. A lifetime with David.

He carried his guitar and a half-empty backpack. I dragged a heavy suitcase. I knew I could find my way back to Sky Lake, but I still picked up handfuls of rocks every time we visited. Insurance, warming on the windowsills, promising that I'd be home next summer.

Sky Lake wasn't an ordinary place, but I didn't know it. For the first six years of my life, I thought all gardens bloomed in the winter and all hot springs healed paper cuts. It didn't seem strange when my grandmother gave pebbles from the lake instead of directions. Sky Lake was just home.

I assumed I could stand under any full moon and feel the light fill me up like shiny silver syrup. That I could put my hands on any patch of earth and feel it buzz up my arms like bees. That the stars would sing me to sleep wherever I went to bed.

I took Sky Lake completely for granted until my grandparents died and I had to move across the country to San Francisco to live with my brother.

David was only nineteen, and his boyfriend, Bobby, just twenty-three when they got stuck with me. They never treated me like a burden, but they didn't have to. I turned their lives upside down. They planned to have kids someday, not to have one left on their doorstep like a stray kitten. But I had no one else—our mother died before I was old enough to remember her, and David and I never knew our fathers.

David and Bobby tried to argue privately, but I heard everything in the one-bedroom apartment where I slept on an air mattress in a curtained section of the living room. Bobby wanted to send me to cousins who hadn't spoken to my grandmother in decades. "Real grownups," he called them, with houses and kids and careers. But David wouldn't consider it, and Bobby loved him, so they replaced the air mattress with a real mattress and tried their best.

David put his music career on hold and took me back to Sky Lake for four weeks every summer. "It's not negotiable," he'd tell Bobby, who objected to these trips.

It was the only thing they fought about. Even though Bobby didn't know David when our grandmother caught him with a boy in the hot springs and kicked him out for good, he held the memory close. As far as Bobby was concerned, my grandmother poisoned the house and the lake and every tree in the forest. He wanted no part of it.

"We need to keep her in touch with her roots," David always said, and I pretended not to hear the tremble of superstition in his voice. He knew Sky Lake wasn't an ordinary place, and he didn't think I was ordinary, either. He brought me back like an offering to some old god he didn't quite believe in. *See, she's fine, I'm taking care of her.*

Every summer, we got on a plane and flew back, just the two of us. I loved it. Without Bobby to enforce the rules, we stayed up late for meteor showers and only washed dishes when we ran out of surfaces to stack them on. We swam at midnight, daring each other to touch the moon's shining reflection. We lived on junk food—frozen pizzas, pop tarts, salt-and-vinegar potato chips, chocolate ice cream straight from the tub—for days at a time, then attempted elaborate recipes that inevitably failed, requiring late-night runs for takeout. We wore our most comfortable clothes and rarely put shoes on at all.

I measured my life in summers instead of birthdays. The summer David taught me to dive off the dock. The summer we picked enough wild strawberries to make a pie. The summer David built a stage out of four big rocks and an old board that sagged in the center, and sat outside for hours listening to me sing.

I loved to sing at Sky Lake. It was like nothing else in the world. As soon as the first notes spilled out of me, I was whole again. Knit back together by the sound of my voice bouncing off the lake and climbing the trees and ringing along with the stars.

My voice felt like magic pulled straight out of the earth, and I basked in the spotlight of my brother's attention—two miracles that I took completely for granted, as children do.

When I was seven, I asked David if I could sing with his band. "I know I'm too young now," I clarified, when he didn't immediately say yes. I had just finished performing every song I knew the words to, and several I didn't really know the words to, and I can't imagine how he stayed the whole time. "But someday, when I'm older."

"Maybe." He smiled with his mouth, but not his eyes, and it scared me— David always smiled with his eyes. "It won't feel the same to sing somewhere else." He looked at me like I was a spider on the shower wall that might know how to jump. "Here you're... grounded. Connected to... all this." He swung his arm to encompass the forest and the lake and the lazy bees buzzing around the yard. "It'll be different out there. It might be... painful. Or... dangerous." He spoke slowly, like the words were too big for his mouth.

"You mean I won't be any good?" I wanted, more than anything, to be *good*.

"No. You'll be good." He leaned back in his chair, considering. "You *are* good. You have the power of this place in you." He smiled, and it was a real smile this time. "And that's a gift. God knows I wish I had it." He ruffled my hair and I felt the scratch of his calloused fingertips on my forehead. "But gifts can be… tricky."

He squinted at the lake, flashing gold under the late afternoon sun. We called it Sky Lake because it glowed robin's egg blue on nice days and turned into a bowl of stars on clear nights, but it didn't have an official name. You couldn't even find it on a map.

"We'll figure it out," he said, to it more than to me. "When you're older. Right now, how about if I teach you to play my guitar?"

Later, I wished I had pressed him for more, but I was young and easily distracted. It never occurred to me that someday, I'd be out in the world, singing, and David wouldn't be there to answer my questions.

Afternoon gave way to evening and mosquitos bit our ankles and I stayed on that stage, the rich, mysterious hum of the forest pouring out of me like magic.

Our second-to-last summer at Sky Lake was so persistently wet and miserable that even the mosquitos gave up on it. The house, which normally felt far too big for the two of us, seemed to shrink. My stage sat forlornly in the yard, soaked and rotting. The garage flooded. The water heater broke. We ran out of popcorn.

Anyone else would have cut the trip short, but David didn't think like other people. Or, he was too superstitious to take me home early. Either way, we stayed.

One gloomy morning, he woke me up at sunrise. "How strong do you feel?" he asked.

I wasn't very strong, and to be honest, neither was he, but I never said no to David's projects. I showed him my muscles, and he laughed, and we spent the morning huffing and puffing and shoving the old piano from its dignified place in the hallway to the middle of the formal dining room. "Better acoustics," David gasped, when it finally sat where he wanted it. "And better energy. That hallway has ghosts."

He spent the rest of the vacation teaching me how to play. Once I knew a few simple melodies, he ordered me to make up a new one. "I'll be back in an hour to hear it," he said, and retreated to his room. He must have been desperate for a little peace and quiet and privacy after all that time cooped up with me, but he never said so. He just gave me songwriting assignments, increasing the difficulty a little bit every day to keep me busy.

The displaced dining room table stayed in the yard for the next twenty-five years until I finally came back to clean up. When I saw it there, I missed David so much that I wished the hallway really *did* have ghosts.

But I'm getting ahead of myself.

I've tried, a million times, to remember our last trip to Sky Lake, but the details are lost in everything that came after. I'm sure the sun shined hard enough to close our eyes. I'm sure the lake turned silver under a full moon, and the roses bloomed big and bright and their perfume blew into the house and made us both wake up sneezing. I'm sure we played the piano and reconstructed my stage and ate ready-bake cookie dough without baking it. We must have hiked in the woods until our feet ached, had picnics in the meadow, and floated in the little red rowboat.

But I don't remember any of it.

At the time, it must not have seemed remarkable.

I remember locking the door the morning we left, my pockets full of rocks, David in the driveway with his half-empty backpack hanging off him. "You really don't need to take so many," he said, eyes dancing with suppressed laughter as my heavy suitcase bumped down the steps. "You'll always be able to find your way back. It's in your veins."

I knew that was true, and I also knew he would lift my rocks into the overhead bin without complaining, and both of those things made me feel safer than I should have.

We didn't speak in the car. David looked forward to returning at the end of our summer trips, and I didn't, and we protected each other from our feelings. I would have given anything to stay at Sky Lake where I had David all to myself, instead of going back to San Francisco where I had to squeeze into the edges of his life. But I would never say that. Not when he already sacrificed so much for me.

We sat in the back of the plane and I entertained David with funny observations as passengers made their way to the bathrooms. He said, "You should be a comedian," laughing so hard he had tears in his eyes, and I thought I'd burst with pride even though I didn't want to be a comedian. I still wanted to be a singer in a band, like David.

I remember my suitcase thumping up the narrow staircase where a dozen different cooking smells competed for dominance. Our smell—Bobby's thick, garlicky tomato sauce—hung heavily outside number ten. David took a deep breath. It smelled like home to him, just like the pine and roses of Sky Lake smelled like home to me.

I thought David was joking when he collapsed that night. His eyes rolled back, and he shook, and I said "David, stop it," because David liked to play jokes. I didn't realize he was serious until he hit the floor. It wasn't that David wouldn't pretend to fall down—my brother would do anything for a laugh. It's that a body doesn't fall that way when a person is in charge of it.

"I made him laugh really hard on the plane," I tearfully confessed to a nurse in the emergency room. "Could that be it?"

But that wasn't it. And neither were any of the other things they looked for. He didn't have a blood clot or a tumor or a disease the doctors could see in the blood they took. I started to wonder if Bobby might be right about Sky Lake. Maybe rejection lingered in the walls, poisoning David as he slept in the room where he spent so many miserable nights.

DEDICATION:

To all the social workers, volunteers, therapists, law enforcement officers, and advocates who work in the field of family violence. No one who hasn't experienced what you do knows how hard your job can be. Thank you for your dedication to helping those who need it.

I want to give a special *thank you* to actor Robert Stevens, who performs in the Austin, Texas area. An excellent, classically trained actor, it was one of his character shots he shared on Facebook which gave me the idea for the character Gareth Grayson. Thanks, Robert, for helping me to create a fascinating villain.

Robert is a brilliant onstage villain, but he is a wonderful kind-hearted man in his real life. Now that's an actor!

As always, thank you to Salt Run Publishing, LLC, for publishing my work.

To my editor, thank you for all your hard work. You're incredible.

To my readers, bless you.

AUTHOR'S NOTES for *HIS WICKED LADY* ...

The third novel in the *Touch the Sky* series, *His Wicked Lady*, is the story of Baron William Hargreaves and his tempestuous relationship with wealthy American Caroline Burgess.

William was the 12-year-old brother in *Touch the Sky*, a rebellious, rock-tossing boy. By the time the action picked up in *Swept Away*, he was a 34-year-old Baron, as stodgy and stiff-lipped as they come. His niece, Lisette, teased him unmercifully about his attraction for Miss Burgess. He refuted her accusations and began to torment the self-assured American heiress.

In *His Wicked Lady*, Caroline comes into his life, although he makes her an object of ridicule at every ball and gathering. Criticizing her gowns, her ideas, her attitudes, he is the darling of the British aristocracy. He will say anything to deny the growing attraction he feels for her.

They begin to grow closer as she helps his family deal with his niece, Lisette, the daughter of Celeste and Sheridan from *TOUCH THE SKY*. She is drawn to an unscrupulous fortune hunter, elopes with him, and pays the consequences. He is an abusive husband.

Caroline runs a settlement house back home in Philadelphia where she works with abused women and their children. With her help to the family, Lisette finally comes home.

I write stories of strong women healing from adversity. This is the prevailing theme for each of the three novels in the *Touch the Sky*. My hope is that this story will reach someone who can relate to the situations.

I know how hard it is to leave an abusive relationship, but it can be done.

You can do it.
All it takes is the first step to seek help.
When you are ready, take the first step.

It will put you on the path to the rest of your life.

His Wicked Lady
Table of Contents
PART I

RULE BRITANNIA

PART II

YANKEE DOODLE DANDY

Part I
Rule Britannia

Chapter One

His pompous laughter assaulted her ears. "I say, where did you find such a dress, or should I say *mess*? I thought even in America one would know such a garish garment would be ridiculed." His hand touched the immaculate cravat at his throat as he sneered at her, one supercilious eyebrow raised.

Other voices joined his in rousing derision, although his was the only one that mattered to her.

"Really, Miss Burgess, where is your fashion sense?" Lady Afton looked through her lorgnette. "Baron Hargreaves, you are right in your assessment."

Caroline straightened her shoulders and lifted her chin. *I will never show them how they hurt me.* "I am not one to follow anyone's dictates but my own." Her voice sounded calm, untouched by their slurs.

"You will never find a husband if you do not conform to proper fashion and etiquette." Lady Afton snapped her lorgnette closed and looked at the surrounding crowd of the elite, her face a study in malicious triumph.

Caroline pretended to consider the dowager's words before she replied. "I did not come to London seeking a husband. Yet, in spite of what you may think of my personal style, I am hounded by fortune hunters seeking my hand at every gathering." She sighed. "Pity so many of you squandered your family assets. What a burden it must be for you to send your sons after me in pursuit of my wealth." With a regal nod, she turned to go and looked over her shoulder. "You face a losing proposition. I do not need your aristocratic men, any more than I need another carriage horse. My father can buy and sell the queen herself and still be wealthy."

"Well, I never . . . ." sputtered Lady Afton, her face crimson, glancing at her son, Everet "Yes, I can understand why you have not. I bid you a pleasant evening. I am burdened with other invitations." With the final

1

salvo, she glided out of the room, leaving their small minds behind her.

She heard the murmuring voices to the end of the hallway. Never slowing her steps, she marched to the grand double doors of the elegant townhouse. While she waited for the maid to bring her cape, she looked at the doors before her. The gilt paint trimming the cream-colored doors peeled in places. Caroline pursed her lips at the sight.

Like so many of these pretentious London fools, their chic facades are cracking. No wonder they want my money. They must maintain their illusions, keep their benighted world intact. For most of them the artificial show is all they possess of their former glory.

The young maid brought her royal blue cape trimmed in white fox. She wrapped Caroline in the garment and curtsied. "Is there anything else I can do for you, my lady?"

"I'm nobody's lady." She smiled at the girl, reached into her reticule and gave the young woman a handful of coins.

"Oh, no, ma'am, I couldn't take your money." The maid tried to hand it back to her.

Caroline took the girl's hand and closed it over the coins. "Please keep them. Are you happy here? Are you safe working for these people?"

The girl glanced at the scowling butler. "I . . . I . . . ."

"How would you like to work for me? I need a good companion. What do you say?"

With one last frightened look at the butler, the maid smiled at Caroline. "Yes, please, Miss Burgess. I'd be honored to work for you."

"Then it is settled." She put her arm around the girl's shoulders. "Come along, we can send for your things later, if you like. I will buy a new wardrobe for you in any case."

"Oh, thank you, ma'am, thank you."

Caroline turned to the butler. "See her things are packed. They had better all be there when my servants come for them. If anything is missing, you will answer to me. Understand?"

With a mocking smirk, the butler nodded and gestured to the open doors.

The women hurried out to the waiting coach.

"By the way, what is your name?"

"Jayne Murchie, ma'am."

"You needn't call me ma'am. Call me Caroline."

"Oh but I couldn't. It isn't proper."

"Didn't you hear, Jayne? Neither am I. Here we are." She let the girl enter the coach first, climbing in afterward.

She passed the fur lap robe to the shivering young woman, as she leaned out the window.

"Take us back to the house, Harrison."

The coach rolled smoothly forward.

"You aren't going to another social engagement?"

Caroline smiled at her new companion, completely wrapped in the fur. "I couldn't take any more of those awful people tonight."

"You don't know how awful they truly are."

"When we're settled and warm, I want you to tell me what frightened you so at their house."

Jayne bit her lip and nodded.

Caroline looked out the window at the passing buildings looming out of the gas lit darkness. All she could picture in her mind were the glacial blue eyes of William Hargreaves.

I would be attracted to my greatest critic. Why can't I forget him? Why do I dream about him night after night? I must be an idiot.

She shivered as she pictured images from her lusty dreams of the red haired baron. In her dreams, his eyes didn't mock her. They held a different expression when he focused their power on her, making her melt with desire.

She covered the catch in her breath with a cough. "We should be home soon."

William glanced around the room. The assembly became dull, a dead bore after the departure of Miss Burgess. He frowned as he looked over the gathered aristocrats. The same faces stared at each other, their dreary

3

bovine eyes wandering around the ballroom. Chatter assaulted him from all sides, with the occasional laugh that clanged too loud as its flat tones insulted his ears.

Miss Burgess stole the energy, the very life of the *soiree* left with her. He paced the edges of the huge chamber, working around to the other side nearer the exit.

William envisioned Caroline as he walked. Truth be told her gown flattered her. The rich dark blue set off her burnished hair, making it shine like polished gold. Her eyes nearly matched the gown in intensity. The white fox trim around the hem of the full skirt spoke of her wealth. He cleared his throat like a member of the House of Lords preparing to orate.

Perhaps the gown was becoming, however far too bright and too rich a color for a young unmarried woman. A young woman should wear pale colors that confirmed her status as an unwed lady.

He reached up with both hands and grasped the lapels of his evening coat. He set his chin at its most stubborn angle as he retained his rigid pose.

She is a most uncouth American, one who is not suited for the British aristocracy. I would never wed such a woman. She would never fit in my circle. Her flaunting of convention would be a lifelong burden.

Out of his peripheral vision, he recognized the Countess Bloomsbury approaching with her daughter in tow. He turned to greet the pair. Watching them, he could not help comparing Lady Jessamyn, a pale blonde dressed in a light blue gown appropriate for her age and station, with the departed Miss Burgess.

As he bowed over Lady Jessamyn's hand, he noted the insipid tint of her gown leached the color from her face. Unbidden, the image of his vibrant adversary came to mind, so full of life and fire.

Stop this instant. The American is a brazen hussy, no match for a Baron from a fine distinguished family.

"Such a pleasure to see you this evening." He bowed with perfect manners. "May I have this dance, Lady Jessamyn?"

The chit stood dumbstruck until her sharp-faced mother prodded her in the back.

"Of course you may, Baron Hargreaves," she whispered, sank into an unsteady curtsey, rose, and held out her hand.

He led her to the floor where they twirled among the other dancers in silence. He tried to speak to her, but she did not respond.

I say, she's either too awed by my grandeur, or she's counting the steps.

When the music stopped, he bowed and took her back to her mother. Walking away with his society smile, he moved as far from her as possible. Across the room, he stopped and checked his watch.

Damn when will this boring stiff-necked agony end? He pocketed the timepiece and stood staring at the mass of familiar faces, seeking the one he knew he would not find.

Chapter Two
Burgess House

"That will be all, Mrs. Arnold. It's late, please seek your rest." Caroline smiled and kissed the well-padded housekeeper on her cheek.

As the older woman shut the door behind her, Jayne whispered, "Is it true she came with you from Pennsylvania?"

"Of course, we'd be lost without her. Since my mother died when I was twelve, Mrs. Arnold helped raise me."

"Some of the fine folk here employ nannies to bring up their children, too."

Caroline gestured to the soft loveseat. "Please sit down, you look tired."

"Yes, ma'am, I am tired."

"How many hours did they make you work at the Afton home?" Caroline disappeared behind a changing screen.

"May I be of help?" Jayne rose from the comfortable seat.

Caroline's head appeared from behind the screen. "No need, I've been dressing myself for years. Sit back down and relax."

The young woman looked around in confusion and sat once again.

"I should probably tell you I'm independent."

Jayne looked down with a smile on her weary face.

Caroline came out from behind the screen tying the sash on her dressing gown. She walked to the dressing table and shook the pins from her hair. "Ah, that feels much better." Picking up her hairbrush, she moved to sit in the chair nearest to Jayne. She began brushing her hair with rhythmic strokes. "Would you like some tea or some chocolate, perhaps?"

"Oh, no thank you, I am not thirsty."

"You didn't answer my question. How many hours did they require you to work at your last position?" She put down the brush and riveted her attention on her new companion.

Jayne shrugged her eyes evasive. "Only twelve to fourteen hours, they were more generous than most in that way."

"So what kept you from sleeping?"

"How did you know?" The new servant looked up. "I mean . . . ."

Caroline touched Jayne's hand. "It's all right, you can tell me. Your position here is secure."

"Oh, ma'am, you don't know . . . you don't know at all."

"Who hurt you?"

"Everett, their oldest son." Jayne looked away, her voice faint as she dabbed at her eyes. "He said I had to, if I didn't let him, I'd be dismissed with no reference. No one would hire me then."

Caroline's lips twisted into an ugly scowl. "Did you tell him no?"

"Many times, but he just laughed and said I didn't have anywhere to go. He said he could have me whenever he wanted."

She covered her face and wept harder, sobs shaking her slim body. "And then when the baby was coming, he brought in this horrible woman."

"What happened?"

Jayne wiped her nose with the back of her hand, gulping uneven breaths. "She gave me this bitter drink and made me swallow all of it." Chewing her lip, she looked at Caroline. "It must have worked because I lost the baby."

The American pulled her into a hug. "You don't have to worry. You're safe here. No one will ever hurt you again."

Jayne's sobs grew in intensity while Caroline held her and stroked her back.

"Cry all you want. Get it out of your system. This is the beginning of a new life for you. Let go of the past."

The smaller woman pulled back. "Thank you again, Miss Burgess. But how did you know? Has it happened to you? I don't mean to be impertinent, but . . . ."

Caroline smiled down at her. "You aren't impertinent. I volunteer at a settlement house for women and children back home in Philadelphia. Many of the women who come there tell similar stories. I recognize the signs of abuse."

Jayne nodded. "It would be better if I left, so my shame doesn't rub off on you."

"Nonsense, you have no shame. Everett Afton is the one who should be ashamed."

With a sniff, his victim looked down at the floor. "He'll never admit it. He told me so. He said no one would ever believe me."

"Well, he's wrong, isn't he? I believe you. In fact, I'll put him on my list." She took Jayne's hand and led her out of the room and down the hall.

"What list?" The shorter girl nearly ran to keep up.

Caroline opened the door to another bedroom. "Here you are. Do you think you'll be happy here?"

Jayne walked into the room, her mouth wide with wonder. "This can't be meant for the likes of me."

"Why not, don't you like the color?" Her employer gestured at the soft rose walls.

"It's beautiful, but it's for a young lady, not for a servant."

"You are a young lady as of now. Everyone is well treated in the Burgess house. Look, I see Mrs. Arnold laid a nightdress on the bed for you." She walked to the washstand. "There's fresh water here, too. Will you be comfortable?"

Jayne spun and looked at the room before sitting on the side of the lofty bed. "Who wouldn't be?"

Smiling, Caroline went to the door. "Very well, then, I'll let you get some sleep. Call me if you need anything." She started through the door and looked back. "The door has a lock and key. Lock it behind me if you like, although no one will bother you."

"Wait, Miss . . . ." she stopped when she saw her employer shaking her head. "Uh, Caroline, what did you mean by a list?"

Her hand on the doorknob, Caroline smiled at Jayne once more. "I keep a list of wrongdoers, so I know who needs to be taken down a bit. I don't take bad treatment of women lightly. I get even."

As she closed the door, her expression kind, she nodded to her new companion.

"Goodnight, Jayne, sleep well."

Chapter Three
Brenham House

"You should have seen her, *Maman*." Lisette paused, her teacup halfway to her lips. "I never saw anyone like her before, not even Aunt Mimi's relatives. Miss Burgess took down the *Ton* with a few well-chosen words."

William scowled at his plate filled with kippers and eggs. "She is a brazen thing." He attacked the kippers, slashing them with his knife. "She does not belong in society. No one cares about her rude opinions."

"Why are you upset?" Celeste looked at her brother. "What is it about her that bothers you so?"

He sighed. *I don't want to have this conversation. It is not worthy of my attention . . . You don't really believe such nonsense, you know. Everything about Miss Burgess draws your notice. But you must staunch this unrealistic interest. It would never work between the two of you. She's given Lisette enough gossip fodder as it is . . . .*

Celeste cocked her head as she watched her brother's apparent inner dialogue. "William, did you hear me?"

His glanced in her direction. "I am sorry, I became lost in thought."

"You didn't answer my question. Why should you care what Miss Burgess does or says?"

His face heated. He pushed back his chair, rose and tossed down his napkin. "If you will excuse me, I must be about the business of my estate."

"You did not even taste your breakfast. Would you like to have something sent to the study?"

He marched out the door. "I lost my appetite." As he walked into the corridor, he heard Lisette's triumphant musical laughter and growled.

At Afton House, the morning filled with tension. Everett attended his

10

mother by her decree in the morning room.

"You sent for me, *Mamá*?"

Her lips pursed, she gestured for him to sit. "We must discuss a very unpleasant situation."

"What do you think I did now?" He smiled as he sat. "Whatever it is, I'm certain it is of little consequence."

Her stare cold and accusing, Lady Afton paused before speaking.

He fidgeted in his chair. "What is it? What are you going on about now?"

"Do not dare take such a tone with me, I am not only your mother, I control the purse strings until you reach the age of thirty, in case you forgot."

"I well remember because you threaten me with cutting off my allowance each time you are displeased. Get to the point, I have an engagement later." He studied the cuffs of his coat sleeves.

She slammed her palms on the desktop as she rose. "You've done it now. We lost the Burgess fortune. How could you? What did you do? I counted on her money."

He sighed. "It isn't my fault. You're the one who made her angry, remember?"

"Did you know she took the little Murchie slut out of the house? Miss Burgess hired her on the spot according to Merriweather. What say you now?"

He stretched his arms and yawned. "It isn't of any importance. I grew tired of her, anyway."

"You ignorant fool, you take after your dim-witted father. What if Miss Burgess finds out what you did?"

"What if she does? I'll deny everything. Surely she'd take my word over a servant's."

Lady Afton took a deep breath. "Has it occurred to you the strategy will not work with the American?"

"What does it matter? My prospects are good with the other young ladies who are out this season."

"Are you fond of anyone in particular?"

He grinned. "Lisette St John is a pretty thing. Her father, Viscount Brenham, is on the Queen's Privy Council. Will she meet your expectations?"

Lady Afton sat down and smiled. "Yes, she will, you are a clever boy indeed. There was talk of an inheritance her mother rejected years ago from her French aristocratic family. It falls to Lisette, if I recall. Can you bring her to heel?"

"Do you doubt me? If she won't comply willingly, I'll compromise her if I must, so her only choice will be to become my wife."

His mother nodded. "Your plan should succeed. Beware as you pursue her, Viscount Brenham would make a formidable enemy. We could be ruined if you anger him."

He stood and kissed her on the cheek. "No worries, *Mamá*, I'll take the silly little fool before she even knows what I'm about."

Chapter Four

Caroline stopped in the doorway. "Are you certain you don't want to accompany me?"

"You know I don't belong at such an affaire." Jayne shook her head.

"Well, then I'll stay here and keep you company." She flashed her brightest smile, "Shall I?"

"Indeed you will not, Missy." Mrs. Arnold, summoned by the butler, came striding to the door. "You've never backed down from any challenge. You are expected at this shindig and you won't disappoint them."

Caroline sighed. *It's no use. I cannot get out of going.* She nodded and walked out the door. "I will tell you all about it when I come home."

In the carriage on her way to Lord and Lady Hampton's musicale, she leaned against the cushions. Her escort, Cousin Barton, looked out the window, ignoring her. *Just as well.*

I suppose Baron Hargreaves will be there. It is inevitable we will meet at these gatherings. Perhaps I can successfully avoid him tonight. I'm so tired of this whole war we seem to fight.

The sumptuous townhouse was lit with glittering lights in polished sconces. The usual crush of the elite filled the fashionable rooms. Caroline stood in the entry as the maid removed her cape.

"I've fulfilled my part of the agreement tonight." Barton bowed to her, his eyes on the line of gentlemen heading for the card room.

"Yes, you are dismissed. If I wish to leave will you be able to find your own way home?"

"Of course I will." He took her hand and pecked it before rushing away.

She stood watching him go. *It's for the best. If I were ever to encounter a situation I could not handle, you would be no use to me.*

She walked into the salon where the night's musical selections would be performed. Nodding to the people she passed, she moved to a seat on the end of an aisle.

A footman came to her and offered her a glass of champagne. She took it with a smile.

She sighed and sipped the sparkling wine. If it weren't for her father's business connections she would never appear at another function again. The chatter of the growing crowd flowed around her like chickens clucking. *Why do these people think they are superior to the rest of the world? I've not seen much to recommend them beyond their colossal self-importance and arrogance.*

"Are you here unescorted, Miss Burgess?"

Shoulders clenched in dread, she turned to the speaker hoping it wouldn't be, but alas, it was. "Baron Hargreaves." She nodded to him.

"I ask again, where is your escort? If you are in attendance alone it is a terrible breach of propriety."

She stood and met his eyes with bravado. "Why are you so interested? My actions are none of your concern."

He cleared his throat, sounding years older than he appeared. "I only do what any responsible man of means would do at finding a young lady without her chaperon."

Her laughter silenced the din of the horde. "How thoughtful of you, I must admit your sudden concern is refreshing." She smoothed the wide skirts of her elegant cream-colored gown. *Leave me alone, can't you?*

"I did not mean to offend you."

"You needn't worry about me. My escort is in the card room indulging in his favorite activity."

His face tinged red, William bowed. "Very well, then, I wish you a good evening." He turned, his body stiff and unyielding.

"Don't you wish to criticize my gown, my hair, something you find unworthy?" She called after him, not caring the entire mob listened with rapt attention.

He turned back and moved his glance from the top of her head to the satin slippers peeking from beneath her skirts. "I congratulate you. Miss

Burgess, for once you are dressed as a proper young lady."

She watched him walk away in silence. After he disappeared through the throng, she breathed once more. *Imagine that, tonight I look like a proper young lady. I shall take pains to remedy his opinion. He mustn't be nice to me. I might not be able to control myself, might do something I will regret.*

She glanced around at the mass of people as they scrambled for seats. *The entertainment appears to be imminent. Good, the sooner it's over, the quicker I can leave.* Patting her upswept hair, she looked in all directions.

Baron Hargreaves led his niece, Lisette, to a chair near the back. As they settled to watch the evening's recital, Everett Afton presented himself with a bow.

Dear Lord, what is that slug doing with them? Doesn't her uncle suspect he would not be a proper companion for his niece? She shook her head and dared to keep watching.

Everett smiled, his handsome face alight with interest as he moved to sit on the other side of the beautiful Lisette. Caroline pursed her lips as genuine concern swelled within her.

Looks to me like he and his mama know there is no chance of winning my fortune, so they've moved on to the next victim.

"Ladies and Gentlemen, honored guests, I am pleased to present this evening's entertainment . . . ."

Drat the luck, Lady Hampton would choose to begin the program now. Caroline turned to face the front. *I must speak to the Baron after the recital is concluded. He must be informed what danger lies ahead for his niece.*

I don't want to speak to him, but Lisette's future is at stake. I wouldn't want her to be under the heel of such an arrogant monster.

The recital dragged on for what seemed to be hours. When the final young lady played her last note and took her bow, Caroline looked back to see Baron Hargreaves, Lisette, and Everett exiting the room in a jovial group.

With no apparent rush, she followed them into the grand salon. People greeted them as she circled their party.

"Miss St John, may I compliment you once more on your skill at the pianoforte? I've never heard anyone play Mozart any better than you did this evening." Everett bent over her hand and lightly brushed his lips on her flesh.

I hope she isn't already smitten with that viper. It will be harder to stop him.

"I must agree." Caroline inclined her head to Baron Hargreaves as she joined the group. "Your skill surpasses any other young lady of my acquaintance. How long have you studied?"

Lisette smiled at the praise. "I began when I was a small girl. I love music so even to practice is a joy for me."

A trio of other debutantes with their escorts surrounded them, capturing Lisette's attention.

Good, I can draw the Baron off for a bit of private conversation. She scanned the room and found a vacant corner.

"Baron Hargreaves, may I speak to you on a confidential matter?"

His voice equally soft he bent toward her. "I cannot leave my niece."

"If we move to the corner to our left you will be able to see her and the people around her. I wouldn't ask this of you if it were not a matter of importance."

His brows drew into a frown. "Very well, we can speak for a moment." He crooked his elbow to take her arm.

They walked to the empty corner. "Now what is it?" His voice though still low pitched sounded impatient, demanding.

"I wanted to warn you about Everett Afton."

"Did he scorn you, reject you, or make fun of you?" His tone sarcastic, his glanced at his niece before returning his gaze to his companion.

"It is nothing like what you suggest. I was informed of his mistreatment of a young woman formerly in service to his family. I also endured his ardent pursuit of my money."

William's blue eyes flashed in momentary anger. "Did he hurt you?"

He grabbed her arm.

"No, I did not give him the chance. However you're hurting me now, please release my arm."

His face grew red as he dropped his hand. "Forgive me, it was not my intention."

She flicked her wrist. "It is of no consequence. I want to warn you for your niece's sake. He's a bounder, a cad, and a cynical user of women." She took a deep breath and rushed on. "I've met his type before. Believe me, he is dangerous and does not have Miss St John's best interest in mind."

He cocked his head as he looked at her. "Why would you want to help a member of our family? What will you gain from this?"

"I understand our relationship is contentious at best. It is not for you but your niece I tell you what I discovered. Back home in Philadelphia I work with a group who assist women who have suffered abuse. We often help them begin new lives free of the cruelty they endured before. The women come from all levels of society."

He looked at her for a moment and then spoke in a respectful tone. "It sounds to be honorable work, Miss Burgess. I thank you for the warning. By informing me of Afton's exploits, you may save Lisette from a life of pain. I will see he is discouraged from his pursuit of her."

She nodded with a tentative smile. "You are welcome." *Why can't I meet his eyes?* "I best let you return to your party." She curtsied and started to walk away.

"Caroline." He sounded breathless. "I will not forget this. Our family owes you a debt of gratitude."

"I . . . ."

"Well, here you are." Lisette's laughing voice interrupted. "What are you two doing in *tête-à-tête* away from the rest of us? Are you professing your vows of love?"

"Seems that way to me." Everett's smile was sarcastic.

"Nonsense." Caroline drew on her cynical persona like a well-worn cloak. "We passed the time indulging in our battles of propriety. I declare I took this round, Baron. Assemble your ammunition for our next skirmish." She nodded to the group and sauntered out of the room.

I must stay away from William. No good can come of a close association. One of us will come away wounded. I doubt it will be him.

Chapter Five
Brenham House ~ Lord Brenham's Study

"How well do you know Everett Afton?" William asked the question in a neutral pitch.

Sheridan frowned, "Not very well. I believe he and Drake were at Cambridge together but they are not close. Why do you ask?"

"He seems interested in Lisette. I noticed she received a calling card this morning from him."

"Her tray filled with calling cards today, according to her mother. Why are you concerned?"

"I was told he is a fortune hunter who is careless with the reputations of women."

"A serious accusation indeed." He put down his coffee and looked at his brother-in-law. "Is the source of this information reliable or could this be an attempt to discredit Afton?"

"Given our adversarial relationship, I'd say she would rather do anything than speak to me in private. I'm certain she is telling the truth." He gazed out the window. "I believe her."

"Don't tell me." Sheridan chuckled. "Miss Burgess told you about Afton, didn't she?"

"Yes, but it doesn't mean she spoke anything but the truth." He leaned forward. "I watched Afton with Lisette afterward. I think Miss Burgess is correct. He is too anxious to please. Moreover Lisette seems to dote on him after only one evening together."

"My daughter is no fool, but she is young, not used to the games some men play. I don't want her learning of such things." He stood.

"What will you do?"

Sheridan took William's arm. "Come along, we are going to drop in on her informal afternoon gathering. I imagine he will be there. I'll know

19

what he's about."

The sounds of merry laughter greeted their approach to the salon.

"How amusing, Miss St John, a walrus indeed," came the man's voice.

Sheridan, his hand on the doorknob turned to William. "Do you recognize his voice?"

"Yes, it's Everett Afton."

Throwing open the door, Viscount Brenham entered the salon, Baron Hargreaves at his side. "You are enjoying a lively discussion." He smiled at the assembled young people.

"It is Lisette, sir, who made us laugh." Afton smiled at the confident young woman. "She said," he chuckled once more, "Prince Albert reminds her of a walrus with his mustache. Isn't she witty?"

The room erupted into giggles once more. Sheridan looked at William and cocked his head toward Afton holding Lisette's hand.

She smiled at her admirer, her eyes shining.

"Such talk may be amusing in private, but I hope my daughter has the good sense not to mock the monarchy in public." His voice stern, he delivered the warning. "It is not appropriate for the daughter of a member of the Privy Council to ridicule the Prince Consort."

"Oh, Father, we are only talking. What harm can a bit of humor be? No one will be hurt."

"In the right circumstances such insolence toward the Queen's husband could be considered treason. I ask you to refrain from indulging in such nonsense in the future."

She waved him away with a shrug of her shoulder. "I never knew you to be such a stodgy old man." Lisette leaned toward Afton until their foreheads almost touched. Laughing, they shared a look.

Sheridan glanced at William before speaking. "It is time for your guests to leave. Good afternoon, ladies and gentlemen, I'm certain you understand Lisette must return to her studies."

Afton did not move. "Surely you do not include me in your orders."

"Yes, I do. You are not welcome here."

"Father, how dare you?" With an adamant expression, Lisette rose. "I am a young lady entitled to entertain guests in our home."

"As your father I am entitled to determine who is suitable for you and who is not. You do not know Afton well. You do not know his reputation."

"What reputation do you mean? Who told you lies about my friend?"

"They are not lies, Lisette," William responded. "My source is unimpeachable."

Afton narrowed his eyes. "Never tell me you heard malicious tales from the Burgess bitch."

"You listened to her? Well of course they are lies." Lisette stood and stomped her foot. "How could you believe such drivel? Everett told me how she chased after him, determined to take him for her husband. He refused her. Of course she would spread falsehoods about him. She is a woman scorned."

Sheridan stared at Afton. "Leave my home or must I have you ejected? You are not to come here again, nor are you to approach my daughter at any venue. Do you understand?"

His face set and red with repressed rage, Afton nodded and left the room without a backward glance.

"Father how could you? Wait until I tell *Maman* what you did." She stomped past him with a derisive sniff.

His voice ironic, Sheridan turned to William. "That went well."

Later the same afternoon, Celeste sat with William in her husband's study. "Lisette is upset, but she tends to be impulsive. She swears Everett is a most upstanding young man."

"Miss Burgess does not agree. She told me an ugly tale about Everett and the maid she hired away from Lady Afton."

"My daughter insists such a tale could not be true. Are you certain we can trust Miss Burgess? Could this be a ploy to win Afton for herself?"

William guffawed in the manner he once had as a schoolboy. "I'm sorry, CeCe, but if you ever saw Afton with Miss Burgess you'd know she has no interest in him. Moreover, what need does she have for his minor title? She doesn't like the arrogance as she calls it of the aristocrats in London. Her father is wealthy several times beyond most of the *Ton.* What would she gain by such an alliance?"

"Do you believe her motive is to spare Lisette, nothing more?"

"Yes, if you knew her as I do, you would not doubt her intention. She is plain-spoken to say the least."

Celeste stood and walked to the window staring at the afternoon sun. "I'll invite Miss Burgess to my theatrical afternoon next week and judge her for myself."

He shook his head. "You invited Gareth Grayson, didn't you? How can Sheridan allow you to consort with those actors? It isn't proper."

Her eyes flashed as she looked at him. "Sheridan does not *allow* me. I do what I wish."

Putting his palms up in front of his face, he surrendered. "I'm sorry I misspoke."

"You should be. Gareth Grayson is the Impresario and director of the Richmond Shakespearean Society, founded by Sheridan's father when my children were young. Don't you remember?"

"I remember the man strutting about spouting Elizabethan English looking like a fool in trunk breeches and stockings."

"He is a talented actor. His portrayal of Macbeth won praise from everyone in the *Ton.* The Prince Regent himself lauded the man's ability."

"And we all know how astute the Prince Regent was known to be."

"No matter, he recognized a good actor when he saw one." She turned to leave. "You'll see Miss Burgess will have a wonderful time. Mr. Grayson is an enchanting man."

I am not jealous. What do I care who entertains Miss Burgess? His fists clenched as he walked out of the room.

Chapter Six
Brenham House

"Miss Burgess, what a pleasure it is to meet you at last." Sheridan held her hand in his. "Welcome to our home."

She inclined her head in greeting. "It is an honor to meet you."

The introductions continued as William observed. *I don't think this is a good idea. No telling what she will say.*

Lisette's expression grew cold when her father led their guest to her. "Miss Burgess." She gave a brisk nod of her head and turned away, the epitome of bad manners.

Celeste glared at her daughter with a raised eyebrow and walked with their guest to the salon. "I am so happy to have you here. We're expecting Gareth Grayson, the Shakespearean actor and director. I expect this will be an entertaining evening. He is an interesting man and a lively guest."

"How wonderful, Father and I saw him in Macbeth last month. We both love Shakespeare and spent many snowy nights at home reading his plays aloud." She laughed. "Between the two of us we play all of the parts."

"I hope you will honor us with a reading. Here we are at the salon. Please sit where you like."

Caroline chose a brocaded chair and sat with grace, spreading her sage green skirt.

She's sitting next to my chair. Did Celeste plan this? William glanced around but saw nothing suspicious on his sister's face. Shrugging, he moved to a chair across the circle as far from his nemesis as he could get.

You were honest when you told me about Afton, but I cannot afford to become too acquainted with you. It would never do at all.

Later when the impresario arrived, William watched in consternation as the handsome gentleman chose the seat beside Caroline. As he watched with a sour expression, the pair spoke to each other with animation.

She's only just met the man. How can she be so animated with him? She's touching him on the arm and laughing. She never acts like that around me.

William sat with his arms folded and a shuttered expression, puckering his lips.

"Will you read a scene with me, Miss Burgess?" Grayson's deep voice reverberated in the room.

"I would love to if you will allow a rank amateur to read with you."

He looked at her with a rakish grin and a raised eyebrow. "Something tells me you will surprise all of us with your ability."

"Thank you." She did not meet his eyes.

Oh for heaven's sake. One would think he was a king at the very least with the amount of deference she shows him, humph. William folded his arms across his chest and glowered at the pair.

"Shall we start with this passage?" Grayson showed her a section in the script.

"Yes, that will be fine."

He moved his chair closer to hers. Smiling, he looked into her eyes. "Are you ready?"

She nodded.

He began to read, his baritone ringing through the room. "If I profane with my unworthiest hand this holy shrine, the gentle sin is this, my lips, two blushing pilgrims, ready stand to smooth that rough touch with a tender kiss."

Speak a bit louder, why don't you? I doubt they can hear you in Scotland.

Caroline's voice, in response, became musical as she read. "Good pilgrim, you do wrong your hand too much, which mannerly devotion shows in this. For saints have hands that pilgrims' hands do touch, and palm to palm is holy palmer's kiss."

She read the passage quite well. I am astounded.

The impresario gazed into her eyes. "Let's try another scene, shall we?" He turned a page. "I would like to hear you read this one, if you will?"

She glanced at the scene. "Certainly, it is one of my favorites."

He no longer read the passage. Instead, he gazed at her as he spoke. "Lady, by yonder blessed moon I vow, that tips with silver all these fruit tree tops."

"O, swear not by the moon, the inconstant moon, that monthly changes in her circled orb, lest that thy love prove likewise variable."

"What shall I swear by?" He leaned closer to her.

She looked into his eyes, the page before her forgotten. "Do not swear at all. Or if thou wilt, swear by thy gracious self, which is the god of my idolatry, and I'll believe thee."

The room pulsed with awe-filled energy. After a moment, Sheridan shook his head as if to awaken.

"Oh I say, you are wonderful. Brava, Miss Burgess."

"How beautifully you spoke those lines." Celeste smiled at her guest.

"Indeed you did." Grayson touched her hand. "I have not beheld such an exquisite Juliet in many years."

Caroline looked down, her cheeks pink. "We read this play often at home. It helps to pass the long cold nights."

"Would you consider auditioning for our company? I know it isn't considered proper for a lady . . . ."

"I'm an American, not an English lady. I say why not? It would be fun."

Oh Dear God, no, she will ruin her reputation forever. "It would be more than simple fun. You would be destroyed by the *Ton*, banned from their entertainments, forever a pariah."

She looked at William with sparkling eyes and a wide grin. "You provide me with even more incentive to audition for the Shakespeare Company. Do not look so condemning. I may well not be asked to join."

William stood to tower over her. "Your reputation will be shredded by the audition. To even consider this is so far beyond the pale . . . ."

She jumped to her feet, her fists knotted at her sides. "You have condemned everything about me since I first appeared at a *Ton* function. According to you I have no taste, no style, and no worth." She paced away from him.

He ran his hand through his hair. "You should be grateful to me. I only tried to help you make your way in our complicated society."

"You cannot be so delusional. You criticized me at every function I attended and most of the ones I did not. Do you think aristocrats do not gossip? I'd wager I heard every remark you ever made about me. Does it sound like you tried to help?"

"Blast, I never meant . . . ."

She hung her head and seemed to withdraw. "I ask your pardon, Viscountess Brenham for creating a furor in your home. Thank you for your kind invitation." She nodded to Celeste and Sheridan. "I believe it is time to make my exit."

Grayson rose. "I will see you home, shall I?"

"Thank you, I accept your kind offer." Her eyes sparkled with tears when she turned to go. "Goodnight to you all."

Lisette sneered at her. "And good riddance to you, this is what happens when trash is brought into our home. You may have all the gold in America but it doesn't make you a person of quality."

"Enough!" Sheridan roared at his child. "How dare you insult an invited guest in my house?" He took Caroline's hand. "I am sorry for the behavior of my foolish daughter."

"It doesn't matter. She is quoting the gossips. I've heard it before."

"It matters to me. I will not have her behaving in such a manner." He turned to Lisette. "You will apologize."

"I will not. Why should she be indulged because her father is well-heeled? It doesn't make her acceptable. Why can't you see?"

Sheridan frowned as he looked at her. "This isn't like you. It must be Mr. Afton's influence. He sinks deeper in my estimation. You will never see him again."

She started to protest but he put his hand up.

"I've heard enough from you tonight. If you won't apologize, go to your chambers."

Lisette tossed her curls. "You cannot stop me from seeing whomever I wish. I will tell every member of the *Ton* how you prefer this low-born whore to your own daughter."

"Devil take it, you will never see the scoundrel again. And if by some chance you do, you may tell him I will disinherit you if you marry him. You will learn how much he loves you when you tell him."

She stood before him her mouth open in stunned silence.

Sheridan's expression cold, he rang for the butler. "Weston, please escort my daughter to her room, and lock her inside."

"Very well, my lord." The butler bowed and guided Lisette out of the salon.

With a final nod to the remaining family members, Caroline left on the arm of Grayson.

William looked at the devastated remnants of a once-congenial evening. *I cannot believe she left. But I must never show anyone I care. This is for the best. I will not see her again.* "I knew nothing good would come of having Miss Burgess here." His tone was pompous.

Celeste whirled on her brother. "What is wrong with you? Tonight you behaved in a most abominable fashion. You were not always such an obnoxious prig. I cannot believe you treated our guest in such a way."

"My behavior? Do you not see she started it?"

"She did nothing of the kind. You spoke hurtful words to her. How can you be so cruel? Don't you remember what it was like to be outside of society? I do." She narrowed her eyes. "That's it, isn't it?"

He grasped the lapels of his coat and assumed his familiar stance. "I do not understand what you mean."

"Yes you do." Celeste spoke in a soft voice. "You're terrified to lose your place in society once more. You're attracted to Miss Burgess and frightened. That's why you do all in your power to push her away." She shook her head.

"What utter nonsense." William turned and strode out of the room.

Sheridan put his arm around his wife's shoulders. "You are correct in your assessment, my dear. No wonder he is so determined to push his lady away."

Chapter Seven
Hyde Park

"Oh, Everett." Lisette nudged her horse forward. "I thought you weren't coming."

He reined in his horse beside her. "Please forgive me, I was engaged elsewhere when I received your note." He swung off his gelding.

"Who were you with?" Her voice suspicious she looked at him.

He laughed. "Why so petulant? I went to a business meeting for my mother, that's all. I came to you as soon as I could." He dropped his horse's reins and reached up to her. "Come, let me help you."

With a moment's hesitation, she glanced around to see if they were alone. Satisfied no one could see them, she slid down into his arms.

"That's better, sweetheart." He looked into her eyes. "Tell me what is worrying you so?"

Father is wrong. Everett loves me. I know he does. He looks at me like a hero in a novel looks at his beloved.

"Last night I grew so livid in my own home, Father sent me to my room."

His blue eyes crinkled at the corners and deep dimples appeared around his faultless lips. "What did you do to make him angry?"

She shook her head and moved away. "I didn't do anything wrong. My father is besotted by the Burgess woman and believes her over me."

"In what way?" His voice became lower, less jubilant.

"Do you know what that woman did? She read Shakespeare with Grayson. He asked her to audition for his company and she agreed. Can you imagine such a shocking exhibition?"

"I am appalled." He put his hand to his muscled chest. "Why did your father become upset with you?"

"I called her out for the slut she is, the graceless lump. My father took

29

her side."

He released a breath. "Perhaps he meant to be a good host or he felt sorry for her. She is a shocking incompetent in social matters."

Lisette gazed into his eyes. "It was more than that. He claimed you are a bad influence on me. He said I would never say such things if you and I were not acquainted."

"And, what else?" His voice sounded rough, all merriment gone from his eyes.

She waved her hand. "It is nothing, I am certain. He didn't mean it."

"What did he say?" His voice lowered still, until she strained to listen.

"Very well, if you must know, he threatened to disinherit me if I married you."

"Oh he did, did he?" His face stern, he no longer resembled a romantic hero. He turned his back to her.

She frowned as she watched him. "He would never do such a thing. He was angry, he will come around."

He turned back to her, his face smoothed into pleasing lines. "How can you be so certain?"

She shrugged. "Father's temper can be fierce. But he's quite reasonable inside. When he knows you as I do, he will relent." She moved to him and smiled up into his eyes.

He put his arms around her, drawing her close to his body. "If you're certain, I will hold you to it."

Breathless at his nearness, she watched as his head lowered to hers, his golden curls catching the sunlight. Stretching up on her toes, she met his lips halfway, sighing when he kissed her.

Oh my goodness, the novels are right. Kissing the man you love is incredible. I love the feel of his strong arms, his hard body pressed into me, and the taste of his lips. Now I am positive I love him and he loves me.

Later after he parted from the infatuated Lisette, Everett ran up the stairs of his family's townhouse. "Mother, where are you?"

"In my sitting room," came her strident reply. "Where else would I be this time of day?"

"We've got a problem." He sat in one of the chairs.

"By all means, do sit and tell me what is wrong." She cocked her head and raised an eyebrow in sarcastic glee.

"I mean it, there is an impediment to our plans. Lisette's father threatened to cut her off if we marry."

"Perhaps you should look for another young lady."

"No, she's already ripe for the taking. Does he hold sway over her inheritance through her mother's side?"

"I don't see how since he decided not to seek it when they married. My understanding is the money reverts to her daughter."

He stood and began to pace. "I wish we could be certain before I take the necessary steps. I'd hate to come away empty-handed."

"Yes, we need the money. We could all live quite well off such a princely sum." She pursed her lips. "I have an idea. Do you remember your father's solicitor, Herr Braun?"

"Do you mean the man from Austria?"

"Indeed I do, he returned to Austria and now practices his profession in Vienna."

"You think he could help us?"

"Why not? For a nice fee, of course, I'm sure he would be willing to investigate. He can make inquiries about the status of the funds and what Lisette would need to do to claim her inheritance."

"What if they don't believe she is an heiress for the money?"

"Piffle, you worry for nothing. Her mother's status was well-documented in the broadsheets of her day and in the evidence of the subsequent trials. They will be glad to give Miss St John the money."

He grinned down at her. "I hope you're right."

She preened in her chair as she smiled at her son. "Mother always knows best. Now off with you while I write the necessary missive to Herr Braun. In the meantime, keep your Lisette enthralled. By the time we're finished, she will beg you to marry her. We will all live in comfort for the rest of our lives."

31

He leaned down and hugged her. "Mother, I love you. No other woman in the world can compare to you."

She patted his hand. "See you remember those words. Now leave me in peace and go plan your seduction of the St John chit."

He rubbed his hands together in anticipation. "I'll plan a seduction like she's never seen. She won't ever suspect it's all for her money until we're married and she cannot escape."

Chapter Eight
Richmond Theater

"Brava, Miss Burgess, you gave an excellent reading." Grayson stood and applauded. One by one the other members of the company looked at each other and stood.

Are they standing for me or because he did? Why they're doing it doesn't matter, don't try to understand their motives. They're standing for me, how wonderful.

At the side of the stage, Jayne smiled at her as she applauded as well.

"I think we've found our Juliet at last. Excellent." He walked to the edge of the stage and extended his hand. "Come along, Miss Burgess, we have much to do." He led her down the stairs. "We open in three weeks. Do you think you will be ready by then?"

Will I be ready? Is this really happening? She took a deep breath. "I know the part, so the lines won't be a problem."

"Good, learning lines is the biggest hurdle for a fledgling actress in such an important role." He led her to a plump woman with bright red hair. "This is Mrs. Shaughnessy, our costume mistress. When we finish here I want you to go with her so she can take your measurements."

With the cast assembled, they read through the entire play. When she was not engaged in the scene, Caroline watched the others. *I wonder if I will be as confident when we perform before an audience.*

While the director critiqued the performances of the other actors after the rehearsal, Caroline looked around the theater. The gaslights at the foot of the stage flickered and smoked. Phantom scents of previous casts as well as audience members mingled to create a unique bouquet.

I sense the energy of all the people who have performed here. This place is filled with their essence like nowhere else.

After her session with Mrs. Shaughnessy, Caroline was dismissed for the evening. Leaning back against the cushions of her coach she sighed. "Isn't it astonishing? To think I'll be playing Juliet next month, for all of London to see."

In the darkened coach, Jayne's expression was difficult to read. "I hope you know what you're doing." Her voice sounded concerned.

"Ah, Jayne." Caroline reached across and took her companion's hand. "This will be a grand adventure. After my treatment by the aristocracy here, it will be magnificent to be respected for who I am, not pursued for my father's fortune."

"Those very people will scorn you now. You'll be an actress, someone who isn't received in their homes. They may come to see your performance and may even love you onstage, but your days of waltzing at their galas are over."

Caroline tossed her head as she felt her throat constrict. *All I can see is William's disapproving face.*

An errant teardrop slid down her cheek. "No matter." Her voice sounded brittle in its forced gaiety. "I shall be admired and accepted in a way I never was at their social functions."

"But, ma'am . . . ."

"I will be fine. I never wanted to stay in England. After my lark, we shall sail back home where life is different." She smiled at the memory. "I look forward to showing you the glories of my country."

"What about your father, does he know what you did tonight?"

"Of course he does, I would never do this without his consent. He's all for it, says I'll be the most admired Juliet in the history of the play. Besides, he's had his own tussles with the English. He'll be ready to return home when we are."

Jayne's voice sounded uncertain. "Do you still plan to take me to Pennsylvania when you go back?"

"I would never leave you behind. You will live a whole new life there, far beyond your expectations. You'll see. We'll both leave our pain behind us in England. It won't follow us to the United States." She leaned forward toward her companion on the other seat. "It would not dare."

Lisette spoke with animation behind her unfurled fan. "And did I tell you? My brother Drake has seen the playbills all over London. Her face is plastered on walls all over the city. The brazen thing, to think she was after my uncle."

Millicent Pryor shook her chestnut curls. "I shiver to think she actually attended my birthday ball. Well, she will not appear at any of the best homes now. No one would invite her."

"If she tried to gain entry she would be barred at the door. Oh, I'd like to see that." Lisette rocked with laughter as her companions tittered with her. "Arrogant American, she thought her money would gain her acceptance but we the true elite showed her how mistaken she is."

The sound of peals of female giggles drew William to its source.

Lisette, I might have known. She is no doubt making fun of Miss Burgess once more.

He shook his head as he watched the five young ladies circled on the edge of the dance floor, no doubt to vilify some unfortunate female's reputation.

Straightening his lapels, he strode to his niece. "Young ladies, you make an inappropriate spectacle tonight. It is not proper for you to be so open with your behavior."

Lisette greeted him with a lifted eyebrow and a sardonic sneer. "Don't tell me you of all people would advise us to avoid the topic of the scandal Miss Burgess is making."

"She is beneath our notice, put there by her own behavior." He cleared his throat. "Someone else will be a new topic of tittle-tattle and Miss Burgess will be forgotten."

"With her picture posted all over town, I doubt it." Lisette looked at her companions, causing them to nod and titter.

He paused and assumed a stern expression. "She is no longer a fit topic for young ladies to discuss at a large gathering. You draw dire attention with your chitchat. The *Ton* may question your behavior if you do not stop this."

35

He leaned down and whispered in her ear. "Do not give your father more reason to censure you and forbid you to leave the house."

"Father would not do that . . . ."

"You know he would. It is your reputation you risk, your position in our society. You must be careful of your actions and guarded with your words." He bowed to the group and moved across the room.

Millicent hesitated a moment before she spoke with an avaricious gleam in her eyes. "What is your uncle talking about? Is your father displeased with you?"

Lisette tossed her blond curls. "My father still thinks of me as a child. He does not accept I am a woman grown." She smiled at her assembled friends. "He objects to the man I wish to marry."

"Who is it?"

"Do tell us who you mean."

"Tell us, please . . . ."

They circled around her, pressing in from all sides.

Go away, can't you see I don't want to talk about it?

She turned within the circle, seeking escape. Across the room, she saw Everett laughing as he caught her eye.

I wish I could run to you, but we agreed to be cautious, not trip our hand too soon.

"Ladies, I am sworn to secrecy." She turned to face her friends. "When the time is right I promise I will tell you. Until then, you mustn't ask me to reveal his name."

As the other girls turned to bedevil another unfortunate lady with their ridicule, Lisette watched them go.

She glanced at Everett and cocked her head. He bowed in response and turned away to talk to his male companion.

Drat, I want your attention. She pursed her lips and lifted her foot to stomp. Awareness of their surroundings stopped her.

All the busybodies here are hoping to find something on a prominent person. Very well, I'll follow your orders, Everett, but not for long. If we can't announce our love soon, I will take matters into my own hands.

Chapter Nine
Brenham House

"Drake, I did not hear you come in last night." Celeste offered her cheek for his kiss.

"I came in late, *Maman*. With the ship unloaded and a respite until our next sailing, there's little to do but seek amusement."

Sheridan chuckled. "Be careful what amusement you seek. London is a dangerous city as you well remember."

"Are you hungry? Cook can prepare something for you, if you like."

Drake poured a cup of tea from the remnants of the buffet. "Tea will be enough for now."

With a rattle of the broadsheet he held, Sheridan looked at his son. "Sounds to me as if your evening included a visit to a tavern."

Drake sat at the table, holding the warm cup of tea. "Yes, we went to three taverns as I recall. You know what seamen are like when they are in port."

"Have you had any word from Miss O'Halloran?" Celeste's eyes filled with concern.

"No, other than she is still at their estate in Ireland. She manages to get an occasional note to me. Her father does not plan to return to London any time soon."

No one spoke for a while. None of them had any words of comfort for Drake.

Sheridan looked at his son. "Do you remember a man of your age named Everett Afton?"

"That bounder, why do you ask?"

"He's taken a fancy to Lisette. What's worse, she thinks she is in love with him."

Drake shook his head. "Father you have to put a stop to her

foolishness. I knew him at Cambridge. He's a womanizing drunkard, spending every sixpence on drink and . . . ." He stopped as he looked at his mother.

"It is all right. I know what you mean." She smiled at him. "Then you don't think he's a suitable marriage prospect for your sister?"

"No, I don't mean to slight my sister, but he is after her money, I would swear an oath he is."

Sheridan nodded. "I think so as well. I already told her I would disinherit her if she is silly enough to wed him."

"Your decision should cool his ardor. He'll move on to someone else."

"Your uncle saw them together at recent society events. They are always discreet. Still, they find an out of the way corner to speak urgently to each other." Celeste looked at her son. "We think he hasn't given up on her."

"I could speak with him, if you wish. We were never great friends but we moved in the same circles."

"Could you find out his plans concerning your sister?"

"Yes, I should be able to question him without any problem."

"Please," began Celeste, "don't embarrass her. She is too full of herself but inside she is sensitive, easy to hurt."

"Don't worry, *Maman*, I will be careful with her delicate sensibilities." He kissed her cheek and moved toward the door. "I have some appointments today I'd best be about."

Drake retrieved his hat and walked out to the street.

Where would I find Afton this time of day? No doubt he's still abed.

"Baron Hargreaves, you honor us with your presence at our little at-home today." Lady Winslow tittered and wiped her moist face with a delicate handkerchief.

"The honor is mine, my lady." He bowed over her hand and moved to take the hand of her daughter. "Lady Antoinette, what a pleasure to see you again."

The ill-fated young woman inherited her mother's tendency to corpulence. She blushed as he bowed over her hand.

"You're looking lovely today as usual." He focused his eyes on the mustache on her upper lip, beaded with sweat.

"Thank you," she whispered, her eyes anywhere but on his.

He nodded and moved to a chair in their circle.

"Oh, have you heard the latest about that Burgess woman?" Lady Winslow leaned forward, an expression of malevolent delight in her eyes. "She is actually going to tread the boards at the Richmond Theater. Can you believe her lack of propriety? What would the late Duke have said about her appearing on the stage in the theater he founded?"

"I believe she will appear in the role of Juliet. When Grayson heard her the first time, it was at one of my sister's gatherings. I heard Miss Burgess read part of the dialogue. She is talented, to be sure."

"Never tell me you accept her rash decision."

He paused a moment. "I do not approve of a young lady doing something so improper. However, we must remember she is an American. Perhaps it would be accepted there."

A general outcry arose from the women present as the men lounged on the edges of the group with salacious smiles.

No doubt they all hope to see Miss Burgess in scanty attire and care not a whit for her acting skill.

Lady Winslow rapped his knuckles with her fan to gain his attention. "The late Duke of Richmond was your guardian, was he not?"

"Yes, he was the guardian for my two sisters as well."

Her fan prodded him once more. "Surely he would have objected to this wicked display in his theater company."

With deliberation, he moved her fan off his leg with two fingers. "He loved the plays of Shakespeare which is why he created the company. I rather think he would be enthralled with her performance." He rose and addressed the group.

"If you will excuse me, I must take my leave of you." He bowed once more to his hostess. "Why don't we compose a guest list to attend opening night at the Richmond? Then you may judge her for yourself."

He left the room without a backward glance.

"Oh, Antoinette, did you hear? Baron Hargreaves invited us to the theater with him. I told you he was interested in you . . . ."

The voice faded as he moved down the corridor to the front door. He shivered at her words. *The woman I care about is the pariah we will be there to observe.*

Chapter Ten
Whitechapel

"What the hell do you think you're doing, St John?" Afton's hoarse voice questioned the man who stood in the doorway.

Drake made no attempt to mask his disapproval of the scene before him. Afton was twisted in dingy sheets with a prostitute, by the look of her, both of them sleeping off a drunken evening.

"I ask again, what are you doing here? Did you come seeking me in your fine captain's coat?" Afton sneered at his visitor, pushed back his hair, and struggled to sit up. He did not bother to cover his nakedness nor that of the woman moaning beside him.

"You are not changed from our days at Cambridge." Drake leaned against the doorjamb. "Still up to your old ways, I see. Do you even know her name?"

Afton's grin was lopsided as he slapped the woman's bare behind.

"Owww," she mumbled as she snuggled deeper into the pillow. "Give off, can't ya?"

"I don't need to be introduced to her to purchase her wares."

"What you do is no concern of mine." Drake stood straight and moved into the room. "In only one case do I care about your plans. What are you planning to do with my sister?"

Afton looked away, his face closed, evasive. "Who told you I have plans for Lisette?"

"The two of you may think you're being clever and hiding your relationship from the members of our set. You are mistaken. Everyone knows you are planning to marry her."

"Everyone knows more than I do. For the present, I have no desire for a match with your sister. She is safe from my wicked intentions. Now get out, leave us alone."

Drake walked up to the bed. "What everyone knows is your family is in dire need of funds to maintain your current position in society. You are seeking to marry well to replenish your coffers."

Afton's face grew dangerous. "You are unwise to threaten me, St John. I always repay an insult."

"Will you tell your mother? I am not afraid of her or you." He turned to go. "Oh, and by the way, my father is serious about cutting off Lisette if she marries you. If you follow through with your plan, she will come to you with nothing. Think of that while you laze away the day."

At the door, Drake turned back. "You've grown soft in your indolence. The life of a seaman, even the captain, is a hard one. I am no longer the boy you once defeated."

"No, no, Caroline, do not read it like a dispassionate sonnet." Gareth leaned over her as she lay atop the faux funeral bier. "This is the man you love to the depth of your soul. His death is the greatest loss of your life. Give me the line again and make me believe it."

She blinked up at him as he hovered above her. His eyes bored down on hers with an intense expression. She squirmed under his scrutiny.

Surely his zeal is created by the wish to coax the best performance from me.

Not convinced by her thoughts, she concentrated on becoming the distraught Juliet as she found her young husband dead beside her.

Taking a deep breath, she sat up and looked at the actor who lay beside her. She picked up the poison vial.

"Poison I see hath been thy timeless end. Happily some poison doth remain." She mimicked swallowing after raising the vial to her lips. "O churl, drunk all, and left no friendly drop to help me after?" She collapsed on the actor's body.

"No, no, no." Gareth's voice filled the theater. "You muffed the line and I still don't believe you." He looked out at the assembled cast.

"Rosalind, come up here please and show Caroline how it should be done.

"Of course." The older woman sprinted up the steps to the stage, "If you will pardon me, Miss Burgess." She waited until Caroline moved off the bier and jumped up to take her place.

After a moment's pause, she looked up with tears flowing down her cheeks, "O churl, drunk all, and left no friendly drop to help me after?" Her voice filled the theater with anguish as she collapsed, sobbing.

The sounds of her cries echoed in the silence of the stage.

Gareth looked at her. "There now, do you see the difference? What did she do that you did not?"

Caroline wiped the tears of empathy off her own cheeks. "She wept."

"Not only did she weep, she used her whole body to express her pain. Can you do that?"

Oh dear, how can I weep on cue? "I'm not sure I know how," she began.

"All right, perhaps I expect too much of an untrained actress. The rehearsal is dismissed for the evening for everyone but Miss Burgess. Please be here by two o'clock tomorrow afternoon, prepared to rehearse the entire play. We open in ten days, ladies and gentlemen."

Caroline watched the rest of the actors gather their things and leave the theater. *What will I do if I am unable to please him? Will he release me from the cast?*

Gareth spoke to the stage manager and released him. "Go along now Edwards. I will see you in the morning."

"Right you are, Mr. Grayson." He walked up the aisle and through the door.

Caroline watched as Gareth approached her. "Now, as for you, lovely lady." His voice was compelling, soft as molten caramel.

What is he doing? He's coming a bit too close. She stepped back.

"You must put yourself in my hands," he crooned, as he reached for her. He led her to the bier and lifted her upon it. His hands stroked the sides of her torso.

"All you need to do is let go of your fear."

"I'm not sure what you want." Her voice breathless, she quivered in

43

his hands.

"Trust me, let go of your inhibitions, clear your thoughts." His deep voice vibrated through her, stealing her fear, softening her resolve.

"Caroline, I will not hurt you. Reach for your feelings, they will guide you."

His big hands reached around her and stroked her back in long strokes. "Calm your trepidation, you are safe with me."

He urged her down on her back as he murmured to her. "There now, your spine is more flexible as your alarm leaves you."

He brought his palms to her shoulders, still gentling her with his voice and touch. He swept his hands over her breasts and her waist, stopping on her corseted abdomen.

"The core of your being reflects your emotion. We reach for the emotions of the character we portray in our foundation. The truth of our being lies there."

He moved one hand to the joining of her legs. His hands moved between her legs and cupped her most intimate place.

She jumped to feel his hands there. *I should stop him, this isn't proper.*

She took a deep breath to speak and quaked under his touch.

His hands rubbed circles over the center of her being.

"Don't think, just feel. Let the heat of my hands take away your inhibitions. Feel the warmth of the power I bring to you. Inhale deep hold it, and exhale, releasing all fear as you do."

Heat radiated throughout her body from the energy emanating from his hands. As the warmth flowed through her, she felt his power.

I've never known any sensation like this. I feel as if I am floating on a wisp of a breeze. My eyes are so heavy. Why can't I open them?

After an indeterminate period of time, his voice came once more.

"Now, the man lying next to you is your true love, the only man for you. You wake and find him dead, lost to you forever. Feel what that is like."

At the thought of losing William, pain, the likes of which she never experienced coursed through her. *How can I bear this anguish? How can I go on?*

"Are you ready?"

She found the strength to nod.

"Very well, begin."

Sitting up, she mimicked finding Romeo beside her. She did not think, did not reason, she spoke the lines from her heart.

"What's here? A cup, closed in my true love's hand? Poison, I see, hath been his timeless end."

She drank out of the empty cup only to hurl it away. "O churl, drunk all, and left no friendly drop to help me after?"

She paused and pictured Baron Hargreaves lying beside her. "I will kiss thy lips. Haply some poison yet doth hang on them, to make me die with a restorative."

Oh William. She leaned down to kiss him.

Her eyes filled with tears. "Thy lips are warm."

Oh, no, he cannot be dead, he must not.

The tears overflowed her eyelids.

"Lead boy, which way." Gareth spoke the lines.

She jerked at the noise and looked around.

"Yea, noise? Then I'll be brief. O happy dagger, this is thy sheath. There rust and let me die."

She plunged an imaginary knife into her chest and collapsed on the bier.

No sounds echoed in the theater. Then a strong hand pulled her up to a seated position.

"Much better, Caroline. We'll make an actress of you yet."

Gareth pulled her to him and crushed her lips beneath his own, his talented hands gripping her derriere.

Chapter Eleven
Afton House

"Everett, Herr Braun sent splendid news." Lady Afton smiled in triumph. She waved a piece of parchment before him.

"What does he say?"

"The inheritance is intact and waiting for Lisette or her husband to claim it."

He reached for the parchment. "Let me see it."

Lady Afton watched her son read, his mouth forming the words as he stumbled through it.

"There, are you satisfied? At last we can live in the style which we deserve."

He looked up and smiled, releasing a long held breath. "This is the best news I've had in a long time."

He slumped down in the chair, his eyes seeing the future.

"We can restore the country house, travel, and buy anything we desire."

His mother ripped the paper from his hands.

"We can do all of those things after you secure Lisette St John as your wife. What are you planning to do?"

Rubbing the bridge of his nose as if thinking was a difficult chore, he pursed his lips and sat in silence.

"Well, what do you say? How will you accomplish the task?"

"I will seduce her, take her, and then suggest we marry. The ploy should work well. She's already in love with me. I'll make her burn for me."

"I trust you will not bungle the task. We cannot claim the money until she is your wife. Herr Braun already informed the trustees you are to wed."

He shrugged his handsome face cold in its insolence. "Don't worry so much, *Mamá*. I never fail at seduction."

Drake watched his sister as he approached. She sat among the roses of their mother's garden.

"What are you reading?"

She put the book down and frowned up at him, "My favorite book by Miss Austen, why do you ask?" Her tone sounded a touch belligerent.

He sat on the bench opposite her.

"Just wondering what brings you out here today." He looked around. "I believe these benches are the ones Aunt Mimi and Elijah used during their courtship. It is a romantic spot."

"I suppose it is. Why are you really out here?"

He shook his head, his smile rueful. "I never could hide anything from you."

"No you couldn't. I ask again why are you here with me? What do you want to say?"

"How well do you know Everett Afton?"

She turned away with a sigh. "Not you, too. I am sick of lectures about him."

"We were never close as lads but I knew him. His character is weak. He is lazy, always looking for the easy solution."

Lisette shrugged. "Perhaps love will change him. It can work miracles in people."

Drake nodded his tone sarcastic.

"Yes, it certainly worked well for me."

She rushed to him and hugged him. "I'm sorry. I did not mean to disparage your pain. I know how much you miss Bridget. It's so unfair of her father to keep the two of you apart."

"He doesn't think I am a good influence for her."

"Isn't it the same case with Everett and our father? Are you helping him by telling him tales of my love's schoolboy pranks? I thought you, of all people, would understand how I feel." She flounced away from him.

He rose and followed her, touching her shoulder. "Our situations are not the same. He is a cad, a user of women. I saw him recently with a woman who plies her trade on the street."

"Perfect twaddle." She flipped her palm toward him. "Everyone knows a man has needs. He'll stop such behavior when we're married."

"You think so, do you?"

"I know so." She whirled back to him. "You do not understand the depth of his feelings for me."

He folded his arms and looked down at her. "And you do, I suppose? How do you know the depth of his feelings?"

"Everett told me, that's how I know. He loves me. He said he's never loved anyone else like he loves me."

"I understand he loves your money."

"Ha, you think you know him? He is already aware Father threatened to disinherit me if we marry. Everett told me he does not care; he wants to marry me anyway."

His brow furrowed as he considered the news. "Why would he want to marry you without your fortune?"

She flew at him and punched his jaw. "What a terrible thing to ask. Am I not worthy of someone's love? Am I so terrible no one would want me without the inducement of a well-padded dowry?"

"I didn't mean to insult you, Lissi. You don't know Everett Afton like I do. He doesn't do anything unless he will gain from it. You must trust me when I say I know him better than you do." He stood cupping his jaw as he flexed it.

Her eyes welling with tears, she looked up at him. "You should trust me to know my own heart. Your use of my childhood nickname tells me you see me as a child, not a woman. The fault in your logic lies in your refusal to admit I am no longer a child."

"Lisette." He reached toward her. "Please listen. I don't want to hurt you. I want to spare you pain."

"You're too late with your apology. I'm done with you." She turned and marched toward the house.

"Stubborn, little imp, why won't you listen?"

Chapter Twelve
Richmond Theater

"Excellent rehearsal. Congratulations ladies and gentlemen, tomorrow night will be a stellar performance."

Gareth smiled at the cast.

"I'm so happy I took no notes for any of you. If our opening night is as good, this will be the best production of *Romeo & Juliet* ever seen in London."

"Go on, say what you really mean." The actor playing Friar Lawrence laughed, his face red-tinged and jolly.

The cast members smiled in weary triumph.

"I admit I was an ogre during rehearsals, but look at the result." Gareth glanced around the circle. "Now off with all of you. It's time you went to bed . . . and I mean to sleep, no philandering until after our debut."

Caroline saw the stage manager grin as he glanced from Gareth to her.

"The same goes to you, Gareth." He winked at her.

Her face heating, she glanced away. *I don't need anyone to encourage him. He's hard enough to discourage as it is.* He had continued with the *calming* exercise. Thankfully, he never removed any of her clothing to touch her bare flesh.

I imagine he will insist on stripping me next.

As the other cast members scattered to their dressing rooms, she waved goodbye to several of them.

"Are you ready to go home?" Jayne stood beside her.

Caroline jumped and touched her chest to calm her breathing. "I didn't hear you. When did you walk up beside me?"

"I didn't mean to startle you. Shall we go to your dressing room? I laid out your clothes so you can change."

"Yes, let's do, it's time I went home."

She hurried away with her friend. *I don't want to be trapped here with Gareth.* She quickened her pace.

She dressed and walked to the carriage in ten minutes. She sat breathing deeply when the door shut and the carriage started forward.

"When will you tell me what is wrong with you?" Jayne leaned toward her from the opposite seat.

"Why do you think anything is wrong? I am in a play, which promises to be a success. I should be happy."

"But you're not, don't bother to deny it. I am well acquainted with you after the weeks we have spent together. Has Grayson done anything he shouldn't?"

Caroline sighed and looked at Jayne in the darkened coach. "He makes me feel things I don't want to feel for him. It's as if he controls me when he is giving me my 'calming exercises,' as he calls them."

"Remember what you told me. You have the right to say no."

"I don't want to hurt his feelings. He took a chance on casting me."

"And look how well the opportunity turned out for him. If you give a memorable performance, he will take most of the credit, just you wait."

"I'm sure he will. Thank you, Jayne, what would I do without you?" She grinned at her friend as the carriage stopped. "Come along, Mrs. Arnold will have supper ready for us. I'm famished, aren't you?"

"I'm not the one who was emoting on stage all evening."

"You're very kind to put up with this 'wicked' actress."

They walked up to the house arm in arm.

Lisette peered through the misted darkness.

"Everett, are you here?"

A gloved hand covered her mouth as she was pulled backward against a hard body.

"Let me go!" Her words sounded garbled through her captor's hand. She twisted against him, fighting to break free.

"Easy, Lissi, it's me, calm down and I'll uncover your lips."

He released her, smiling, the meager gaslight glinting on his perfect teeth. "Why did you jump? Were you afraid I was a foul despoiler of women?"

"Why did you frighten me so? I ought to walk away and never speak to you again." *How dare he treat me this way?* She turned her back to him.

"Now, now, Love, I was only teasing. I would not do anything to frighten you. I am sorry my little joke failed." He turned her around to face him and tilted her chin upward.

"Let's begin anew, shall we?"

His face came nearer to hers until he kissed her.

"I don't suppose you deserve my anger." She grinned up at him with her hands on his muscled chest.

He wrapped his arms around her, drawing her closer. "I should say not. Can't a chap even say hello to the woman he loves?"

I could stand like this forever. I feel so safe, so well loved. She sighed and leaned her head against his chest.

His chin rested on the top of her head as he held her for a while.

I hear his heart beating. Never has anything felt so wonderful.

Enveloped in his scent and warmth, she sighed in contentment.

"Darling." His deep voice rumbled against her ear. "How would you like to get married tomorrow night?"

"Really, do you mean it?"

"You know I mean it. We can elope with no one able to stop us."

She pulled back from him. "But how will we arrange to get away? Miss Burgess' silly play opens tomorrow night. I am engaged to attend in my Uncle William's party."

He preened like an overconfident rooster. "I can be a clever fellow, don't you think?"

"What are you planning?" Smiling in spite of her misgivings, she looked up at him.

He wrapped her arm through his as he escorted her out of the alley. "I implored Drusilla Edwards to help us."

"She's a silly old woman. How will she help us?"

He chucked her under the chin. "Now, now do not disparage our benefactress. Tomorrow she will send an invitation to you to join her party for the performance. Your family cannot refuse such a well-respected dowager. They will never suspect it is your means to escape your father's dictatorial mandates. She will call for you in her barouche and speak to your father before you leave."

"Why would she help us?"

I am not certain this will succeed. What if they come looking for me in the theater?

"She is helping two young people achieve their destiny. At least, those were her words."

"How will she explain my absence at the performance?"

"Now we're getting to the clever part of the plan. You will never make it to the theater. After the performance starts, a note will be delivered to your father saying Miss Edwards was taken ill. The note will be written by you."

Lisette shook her head. "I don't think he will believe I am helping an elderly lady. He thinks I am nothing but a capricious child incapable of any compassion."

Everett's grin grew wider. "This is the best part. When the invitation comes tomorrow tell your parents you wish to help Miss Edwards to show them how sensible you can be."

Her brow wrinkled as she thought of the scenario. "I will be convincing, sincere." She smiled at him. "You're right, you are a clever fellow."

He puffed out his chest. "I'm clever enough to win a beautiful lady like you for my wife."

The chimes of the clock tower rang the hour.

Lisette looked up at her fiancé. "The hour grows late. I told *Maman* I was walking in the garden. I'd best go back to the garden gate in case someone comes to look for me."

He captured her hand. "Kiss me first." His tone demanded rather than asked.

She giggled and tried to push him backward.

"I must go home."

With a growl in his throat, he forced her to him, kissing her with bruising lips.

She tried to break from his arms. "Please I must return to the house."

His hands clenched her arms as he looked at her. In the dim light, his expression frightened her. *He looks like a stranger bent on evil.*

She pulled back once more and he released her. He took her hand and bent over it, kissing it with faultless grace. "Until tomorrow evening, my love. I will not wait to make you mine."

She smiled at him, turned, and hurried through the gate, closing it behind her. When she turned to look back at him, Everett was gone.

Uneasy, she picked up her skirts and sped toward the safety of the house. *It is the darkness of the night that frightens me, nothing else.*

Her mother awaited her in the back parlor as she entered the French doors from the garden. "Did you enjoy your walk?"

She rushed to hug her mother. "I did *Maman*. It's so beautiful out there even at night among your lovely flowers."

"You sound just like your Aunt Mimi." Celeste smiled at her.

"Have you heard from her at all?"

"No, but I'm not worried." She reached out and smoothed her daughter's blond waves around her face. "She is safe with Elijah. We trust him to protect and love her."

"Do you wish for me to find a man like him to take care of me?"

Celeste touched her face. "It is my dearest hope, *Cherie*. The time grows late. Tomorrow evening will be a long night with the debut at the Richmond. Run along to bed. You need your rest. *Bonne nuit*."

"*Bonne nuit, Maman*." She paused and looked at her mother, taking a last look at her.

No telling how long it will be before I see her again when Father finds out about my marriage.

"No dawdling, Lisette, you need your sleep tonight of all nights."

Indeed I do, Maman.

Chapter Thirteen
Brenham House

"Drat." Lisette pouted, as she read the note the butler brought her.

"What is it?" Sheridan frowned at his daughter.

She sighed. "I so wanted to attend the opening tonight in Uncle William's party, but Miss Edwards wants me to attend with her."

"Drusilla Edwards?" Celeste looked up from her own letter. "I didn't know you were acquainted with her."

"We met earlier this season at the . . . musicale. She was most complimentary of my skill on the pianoforte."

"Do you want to attend with her tonight?"

"She is older and in need of attendants. I would like to assist her if you will permit me."

Sheridan and Celeste exchanged glances. "Very well, it sounds a worthy way to be of service to her." He smiled at his daughter. "You amaze me with your attitude. Perhaps there is hope for you."

She smiled and ducked her head, as if shy. "Oh Papa, I'm not so bad, you know."

"I'm beginning to agree."

William and Drake stopped their card game to listen to the conversation from across the salon.

"So you prefer an old woman's company to mine?" His grin contradicted his words.

"Sounds like it to me." Drake's expression matched their uncle's.

"I warned you not to be so stodgy. The ladies do not respond well to such an attitude."

Lisette tossed her head. "I've seen one lady who responds to it. Why do you think I'd rather attend the boring play with Miss Edwards than watch you in rapture over your Juliet?"

His face reddened. "She is not *my* Juliet or anything else. It should prove to be an entertaining evening. I imagine she will be ridiculed for her audacity in treading the boards in front of London's elite."

"She'll certainly be a beautiful heroine."

Drake smiled as he looked at the cards he held.

"If I were a free young dandy, I would be haunting the stage door with flowers and jewels."

Secure that her plan had worked, Lisette turned to her mother. "What does Aunt Mimi have to say?"

Celeste laughed. "She learned how to swim. The boys and Elijah are all fine. The big news is she expects another child."

"Another one?" Lisette shuddered. "How many children will she have?"

"As many as she and Elijah want, I suspect." Sheridan read his letter, putting an end to the conversation.

"Is everything prepared?" Lady Afton's expression spoke of her anxiety. "There must be no blunder. She must not know your true intent until after you have wedded and bedded her."

"*Mamá,* I know what to do."

"Yes, but will you do it with finesse? Or will you stumble ham-handed and ruin everything?"

"I promise you she will be happy tomorrow morning. I will see to it."

She looked at him with a raised eyebrow, her eyes cynical. "Remember, she is a well brought up lady, not one of the Whitechapel whores you prefer. You must treat her gently with thoughts of her delicate sensibilities."

He shrugged, "All women are the same between the sheets."

"Have you ever bedded a virgin before?"

"Not that I recall, but what difference does that make?"

She shook her head with pursed lips. "You cannot do anything to make her distrust you or hold you in contempt. We could still lose the inheritance after your marriage if she does not agree."

"What are you trying to say?"

"Keep her happy, you dolt. Win her and our path to her fortune will be secure. Don't treat her badly. I mean this. Don't use your fists on her. Remember what is at stake."

"Don't I get to have my amusements?" He whined like a small boy.

"Of course you do." She laid a consoling hand on his shoulder. "*Mamá* never lies to you."

"When do I get to do what I want?"

She smiled at her son, never caring how twisted he was. "When all of her gold is in our possession you may do whatever you want with the obnoxious little flibbertigibbet. It will serve her right for all her supercilious ways, as if the granddaughter of a convicted traitor belongs among the best people."

Alone in her chamber, Lisette packed a small valise with a few of her clothes. She put in a dress, fresh "unmentionables", and her best nightdress. She smiled as she folded the latter garment, her hands smoothing the lavish lace. *I wonder if Everett will like me in this.*

She looked in the mirror and touched her reddened cheeks. *Just think, tonight I will be a married woman, with my perfect love as my husband.*

Her reflection grinned back at her with shining eyes. *I will leave the room of my childhood behind tonight.*

She circled the chamber, stopping to pick up bits and pieces from her young life. With a sigh, she put each object back in place. *I don't have enough room to take my things with me, lest my parents grow suspicious.*

"Ah, Claudine," she whispered as she picked up a battered rag doll whose yarn hair matched the color of her own. "I will come back for you one day, I promise. Surely, Everett and I will have children with yellow hair. My little girl will like to play with you."

Wiping a tear from her cheek, Lisette closed the valise and sat upon the bed, waiting for the summons she expected when Miss Edwards arrived.

Tonight will be the happiest night of my life.

Chapter Fourteen
Richmond Theater

William stood aside as Sheridan led Celeste into the family box. The chatter of the gathered crowd filled every corner of the huge theater. He smiled, trying not to grimace as Lady Winslow sailed past him with Lady Antoinette in tow.

"I will brook no refusal tonight. You simply must sit beside my daughter." Lady Winslow's voice sailed out over the rail to the audience below. "Come along, Antoinette, do not dawdle."

She should provide a distraction at least from Caroline's performance. Keeping his sigh silent, he sat beside his companion of the evening. He nodded to her though she would not look at him.

I would be bored within a week of our engagement should I be so foolish to ask for her hand. He turned to look at the stage below as the gaslights in the theater were extinguished.

The footlights were lit as the orchestra played a plaintive sonata. By the time an actor walked out on the stage, the chorus of "hush," "they're starting," and the simple "shhhh," ceased.

As he looked around at the rest of the audience, William saw the people leaning forward in eager anticipation.

They will revile Miss Burgess with unending delight. She will be the topic of discussion at every soiree for the rest of the season. He shook his head and folded his arms across his chest, not wanting to admit he cared.

"Two households, both alike in dignity . . . ." The actor's deep voice filled the theater to the rafters.

William was drawn into the story in spite of his resolve. When the curtain went down and the gaslights lit for intermission, he blinked as he realized the how much time had passed his notice.

"Brenham." Lady Winslow's grating voice scraped William's ear. "I understand Grayson met Miss Burgess at your home, did he not?"

"Indeed she did." Sheridan's expression reflected his good manners.

"She is surprisingly suited to the role of Juliet. I thought before the play began she would be terrible, a rank amateur."

He smiled at the braying woman. "I heard her read the night she met him. Grayson insisted she audition for the role. I knew she would be excellent in the part."

"She must be descended from *show people*." With an ugly frown, she looked at William. "You were correct in your assessment of her, my dear Baron. Acting onstage is the proper place for Miss Burgess."

I must get out of here for a moment or two. I cannot take this woman any longer.

His face frozen in his society smirk, which passed for a smile among the elite, he rose and bowed to the ladies. "I know you must be parched and desiring some refreshment. I'll call for some, shall I?"

Lady Winslow reached across her silent daughter and touched his arm in the manner of a coquette, unbecoming to a woman of her age. "Such a lovely idea, such a thoughtful gentleman you are. Thank you for your kind offer."

With a nod of his head, he left the box, exiting to the crowded corridor beyond. He waded through the gentlemen escaping as he did. Finding a footman, he stopped and requested the necessary refreshments for his family and their guests.

"Excuse me, Sir did you say you are in the Richmond box?" A messenger bowed to him.

"Yes." William scowled at the young man.

"I have a message for Viscount Brenham. Will you take it to him?"

"Certainly." He gave the young man a coin and turned back to the entrance of their box.

"Sheridan, I've got a message for you."

He took the message and read it. "Lisette is not here. Miss Edwards became ill." He looked at Celeste. "She did not seem to be ill when she came to get Lisette."

"Perhaps she took a chill in the evening damp. She is quite old."

He shrugged. "Our daughter writes she will stay with Miss Edwards tonight to look after her."

She touched his arm as she smiled up at him. "Perhaps Lisette is gaining maturity. This is the first time I've known her to prefer helping someone else rather than attending a social event."

He took her hand and brought it to his lips. "I believe you are right."

A discreet knock at the door announced the arrival of the wine and cakes William ordered. As everyone was served, the music began from the orchestra once more, signaling the play would resume.

William sat beside Lady Antoinette again and nodded to her. She paid attention to the sweet cake in her hand rather than him.

It's just as well. I don't have to make another effort to speak with her. He sipped his wine. *Odd about Lisette wanting to help Miss Edwards, I thought she could not abide the woman.* He shrugged as he turned to the sound of the curtain rising on the stage.

The settling crowd grew quiet as all attention focused on the play.

I don't remember seeing a performance in which the audience sat in rapt attention like this. There is no chatter, no laughter, how strange.

Like the other members of the crowd, William leaned forward, intent on hearing every line.

By the time the death scene was portrayed, audible sniffles filled the smoky air, followed by sobs as first Juliet and then Romeo died for their love.

William glanced around at the women in the Richmond box. Every one of them, including Lady Winslow, wept into their fine lawn handkerchiefs.

"For never was a tale of more woe, than this of Juliet and her Romeo . . . ."

The crying grew louder from the audience.

With his mouth open in awe, he looked back at the stage as the curtain call began.

Polite applause greeted each actor until Caroline Burgess stepped to the center and curtsied with grace.

She made a beautiful Juliet in the footlights, wearing a pale pink gown that flowed around her form in the style of long ago. Her long golden hair hung loose to her waist.

A crashing ovation filled the building as it echoed off the walls. Caroline bowed once more as the applause continued.

Grayson walked down stage and held up his hand for quiet. *What the devil is he doing?* William watched, mesmerized, with everyone else.

Grayson bowed to Caroline and presented a huge bouquet of flowers to her. He turned to the audience.

"Tonight we are privileged to witness the birth of a brilliant star, Miss Caroline Burgess!" He proclaimed with a flourish.

Another wave of cheering swept over the crowd as they rose to their feet.

William gazed at Caroline, his expression bewildered. *I've lost her . . .*

.

Chapter Fifteen

"I now pronounce you man and wife." The vicar smiled like an older cherub, his blue eyes twinkling. "It is time to kiss your bride, Lord Afton."

Lisette looked up at her husband. *We are truly married. I cannot believe my husband is so handsome.*

She smiled and began, "What . . . ."

Everett crushed her to him so hard it knocked the breath out of her. His kiss bruising as he ground his lips against hers, she stood still in shock.

His eyes gleaming, he pulled back from her. "Did I hurt you, my darling? I did not mean to." He wrapped his arm around her shoulders. "Come along." He dragged her with him down the corridor of the empty church and out into the night.

Running to keep up with his pace, her breath came in short gasps. "Where are we going?"

He swept her up in his arms. "You're too slow, my silly girl, we're going to our wedding night."

Without saying another word, he opened the coach door and tossed her inside. "Take us to the Pearl, Rogers."

He climbed inside and sat beside her. Pulling her to him, he renewed his assault.

I have to make him stop. She pushed against his chest in an attempt to back away from him.

Everett laughed and pulled her tighter to him. "Now is that any way for a wife to behave? You're mine now. I can do anything I like to you."

"Oh no, you cannot," she panted in outrage. "At least have the decency to wait until we are in our room."

"Don't you dare tell me no." He hovered above her, reeking of sweat and ale.

"Why are you treating me like this? I thought you loved me." Her strength faded as she continued to resist.

"Of course I love you, I married you, didn't I? If I didn't care, you'd get much worse." He pushed her skirts up to her waist.

"No, I will not be taken in a coach like a common jade." With the last of her strength, she pulled her skirts back over her legs.

His face ugly, he growled at her. "So that's the way it's to be, is it?" As his eyes sparked menace, he sneered at her. "This is your doing. I wanted to treat you decently."

He pressed against her, flattening her body into the cushions.

"Then do so, don't be cruel to me."

His fetid breath covered her face as he drew back his fist. "You need a bit of taming, my sweet." His leering face frightened her.

His cold blue eyes stared at her in contempt. His left hand on her throat, using the full power of his right, he punched her in the eye.

She saw stars dancing around her head.

Dear Lord, what have I done? He is going to kill me . . . .

Drake rushed down the corridor of his home. "Father, where are you?"

"In here, Son." Sheridan's voice came from his study.

Out of breath, Drake shook his head as he stood in the entrance to the room.

"I've just been to see Miss Edwards. Lisette isn't with her. She didn't spend last night with her."

"Then where is she?" His father scowled back at him.

"According to Miss Edwards, she eloped with Afton last night."

"She did what?" Sheridan rose and pounded his rosewood desk. "How could she be so foolish?"

Drake collapsed into the wingchair. "I should have known she was up to something from the way she spoke to me the last time we were alone together."

"Why would he want her? Surely he knew I would cut her off completely."

"He knew because she told him. There has to be something else."

"Perhaps he will relent, though I doubt it." Sheridan sat back in his desk chair as if his old leg wound ached.

"Afton has a wretched reputation with women. I've seen him beat a prostitute almost to death."

His father's face paled. "Surely he would not treat his wife in such a manner. I've known men who were rough with women of the streets yet treated their wives like the most fragile porcelain."

"We can always hope."

"Why are you so serious?" William stood in the doorway.

"Lisette eloped last night." Sheridan sighed.

"Never tell me it was with Afton?"

Drake nodded. "He's the one."

"Do we know where they are?" William looked at Drake.

"No, we have no word of their current whereabouts."

"Your pardon, milord." Weston stood behind William. The baron stepped aside for him.

"A dispatch has been delivered for you from the Emperor of Austria."

Sheridan waved his hand. "I will read it later. Our family matters take precedence."

"The emissary is waiting to discuss the message with you personally. The Emperor wants an immediate answer."

"Oh very well, show him in here." Sheridan dismissed his butler with a wave of his hand.

"William, take a seat. I'm sure this matter is of little importance and easy to handle."

A colonel resplendent in a dragoon uniform strode into the room. "Colonel von Sellers, at your service." He bowed. He handed a dispatch case to Sheridan. "I was instructed to deliver this to you and no one else."

"Have a seat, Colonel while I read what you've brought."

Drake watched his father's face as he read the letter. His expression grew angry, his face flushed red. "Did his majesty say who had given notice regarding his intent to claim the Chemay legacy?"

"He said it was your daughter's fiancé, my lord."

Chapter Sixteen
Burgess House

"I never saw so many flowers." Caroline laughed as she spun around in the salon. Gifts from her new admirers filled the room. "It reminds me of a wedding."

"Or a funeral." Jayne's musical voice sounded light with irony.

"Let me have my moment in the sun. It's been so long since I've been treated this well." Caroline smiled at her companion. "Can you believe this display?"

"Like everything else about the English elite it's overdone, dreadfully garish, don'tchaknow." Jayne lifted a fake lorgnette to her eyes and assumed an aristocratic sneer.

"You should be on stage instead of me." Caroline moved to read the card on the next bouquet.

"I'll leave such shenanigans to you." Jayne perched on the arm of a chair, watching her friend dancing from one gift to the next.

"I like it better behind the curtain. I can watch the play unseen, makes the choice of gown much easier than being among the audience members."

"And you can flirt with Jack."

Jayne's mouth opened in shock. "I . . . I don't know what you mean."

"Oh yes, you do. You two are quite the item backstage. The cast is all talking about your *tête-à-têtes*."

"I never had a . . . whatever you said. We just talk sometimes."

Caroline hugged her. "I approve with my whole heart. Jack seems to be a good man, as well as a handsome one."

"He is both and he is very kind to me. But we could never . . . I mean, how could I tell him about what happened to me?"

"Your Jack will understand."

Jayne's face pinkened. "He's not *my* Jack. We're just friends."

"Why don't you accept his friendship and see how your acquaintance develops? In time you may grow closer."

Jayne looked away. "If only I could be sure . . . ."

"You need to heal. Time will give you the insight you need."

The salon door opened with a thump. Gareth strode into the room, a satisfied smile on his face. "Am I disturbing you?"

Jayne inclined her head to the impresario. "Excuse me, Sir." She scurried out the door.

"You made an impressive entrance." Caroline indicated a chair. "Please sit, should I ring for tea?"

He waited for her to be seated and then took the chair she offered. "I won't be staying long. There is much to do." He reached across and took her hands in his. "Our run is extended by popular demand. Your set is begging for tickets."

She withdrew her hands and folded her arms as she looked at him. *Say what you want, can't you? I am not comfortable being alone with you.*

"I am not considered a member of their set, far from it."

He shrugged. "Your status no longer matters one way or the other. The Queen has requested a special performance to be given for her court."

He stood and paced in excitement. "Do you understand what an honor this is? I waited a lifetime to receive the recognition you got in one night. There is no stopping us. We shall be the most popular performers in London for years to come."

She looked down before answering. "I do not plan to remain in London for years to come. I will return to America when the current production concludes."

"You don't mean that." He dismissed her words with a wave of his hand.

"What say you to our staging *A Midsummer Night's Dream* for our next production? You would make a lovely Titania. You will be required to shed your modesty as the Queen of the Fairies. The character is usually dressed in diaphanous fabric." He leered at her. "You will be lovely, a sight to behold."

"I won't be here for the production." Her voice was quiet, resolved.

"You cannot be serious. You would give up the most promising career I have ever seen?"

"Yes, I would, without a second thought." She stood and faced him. "I never envisioned any career. What need do I have for money? The run of this current production will give me all the adulation I could ever want. There is no reason for me to remain here after it ends."

He stood in silence, observing her, a cold gleam in his eyes. "Very well, I see you will need persuading."

He bowed to her. "Please arrive on time this evening. We have a full house."

She nodded to him. *When have I ever been overdue?*

After he left the salon, she stood rubbing her arms, as a chill shook her.

He does not own me and he never will. I wonder what he will do when he realizes he cannot control me.

"I demand to see my daughter." Sheridan stood in the doorway of Afton House with Drake and William behind him.

"I'm sorry, my lord, I have my orders to admit no one." The aged butler bowed.

"I suggest you step aside." Viscount Brenham's voice carried authority. "As her father I have every right to see her."

"Let him in, Webster." Everett stood beyond the entry with a satisfied smirk on his face.

"I'm certain my little wife will be glad to see her papa."

"If you have hurt her . . . ." began Sheridan.

"What will you do, old man? She's my wife in the eyes of the church and the law. You cannot take her back."

"We'll see about that." Sheridan glared at the cocky younger man.

"Lisette," Everett yelled up the staircase. "Come down here, your papa wants to see you."

"What is all this commotion?" Lady Afton came from the back of the house, stopping with a shocked expression as she recognized Sheridan.

She recovered her poise.

"Why, Viscount Brenham." She extended a shaking hand. "What a pleasant surprise to see you."

"I am not here on a social call. I want to see my daughter."

She backed up from him, as if intimidated by the expression in his eyes.

"Baron Hargreaves, it is always a pleasure to see you." Her hand clawed in agitation at her throat.

William nodded to her without smiling or saying a word.

She was a party to the elopement, probably gave her son the idea to do it. Caroline spoke the truth. I should have been more forceful trying to convince Lisette not to believe Afton.

"Hello Father." Lisette, her face bruised and pale, walked with an unsteady gait down the staircase. "I did not expect to see you today."

In a soft voice, Sheridan called to his child. "Come here, please, I'd like to hug you if you wouldn't mind."

His expression grew flinty as she neared him.

William, determined to hold his outrage, said nothing as he looked at his niece.

The scoundrel blackened her eye, as well as split her lip. The way she moves indicates unseen injuries. Afton is a brute who deserves to be shot for this.

Sheridan enfolded her in his arms in a careful embrace. He held her for a moment before speaking. As she backed away from him, he lifted her chin.

"What happened to your eye?"

"I . . . ." she hung her head. "I wasn't looking where I was going and ran into a door."

"And what about the cut on your lip?" his quiet voice prodded.

"In the dark last night, I tripped entering our coach. It's nothing, it will heal soon."

She glanced back at Afton, trembling so hard, her upswept hair bounced on the back of her neck.

"Lissi, did your husband mention plans to take you to Vienna?"

With a startled expression, she gazed up at her father. "How did you know? We are going to Vienna for our wedding trip."

"And did he tell you the purpose for the journey?"

"I suppose to see the city?"

He put his arm around her shoulders and pulled her to his side. "Will you tell her, Afton, or shall I?"

The groom sneered in triumph at his father-in-law. "Yes, we are going to claim her inheritance. Why else would I marry such a silly little fool? It wasn't for her conversation."

Drake raised his fists and charged Afton. "Why you . . . ."

"No," Lisette screamed, breaking away from her father. "I love him. I won't allow you to hurt him."

"Move away from him," Sheridan commanded.

Lisette walked to stand beside her husband. "My place is with him. I am his wife." She looked at her father. "What is this talk of an inheritance and why did I never learn of it?"

"You didn't know you were related to the late king of France, did you, my pet?" Afton smiled down into her eyes.

"No. I knew my grandmother was from Paris."

"Your great-grandmother was second cousin to the king, a member of the Chemay family. She left an inheritance for your mother, which she never claimed. The Emperor of Austria holds your fortune."

"I received an envoy from the Emperor today asking about the legitimacy of the claim." Sheridan frowned at Afton.

"Did you verify I am your daughter's husband?"

"Of course not, how am I to know if you are or are not?"

Everett shrugged, his eyes filled with conquest. "It's not important. I will carry the necessary papers with us to Vienna."

He squeezed his wife with a damaging grip. "We'll enjoy our voyage, won't we?"

She smiled only with her lips, her face pale and her eyes filled with pain.

"Lisette, come home with me." Sheridan voiced a command.

"No, I will not. I made my choice. Besides, I want to go on our wedding journey." She glanced at Everett, as if asking permission. "If you will excuse me, Father, give my best to *Maman*, won't you?"

She turned and proceeded up the stairs and out of sight.

"There you have it, Papa." Everett grinned at him. "She prefers her husband to you."

Lady Afton glanced at her son. "Everett, it is not wise to alienate Viscount Brenham. You must apologize and show him the proper respect."

"Why should I apologize for besting their benighted family? I am getting the gold, no one will be any better than me."

William shook his head. "The fortune is all you want, isn't it?"

"What else should I want? Women are all the same. It doesn't matter which one you marry. It's the wealth I want."

He turned to go upstairs but stopped on the riser and turned to look at William. "I was angry with you for costing me Caroline Burgess. I would have brought her to heel eventually. Her fortune is massive, but I understand Lisette's is much better." He tossed his head. "It's much more satisfying to have your sister, especially after Caroline took to the stage. I hear she is a great actress. Maybe I'll be back in time to see her next triumph and visit her backstage."

"If you hurt my sister again," Drake growled, "you'd best watch your back. I will see you get what's coming to you."

"I'm quaking with fear." Everett laughed and walked up the stairs. "There's nothing any of you can do. Ta-ta, gentlemen, I'll deal with you after I've seen the Emperor."

"Viscount Brenham, I must apologize for my son. He is high-spirited and passionate. He will be a fine husband for Lisette. We welcome your daughter to our family." Lady Afton held out her hand.

Sheridan's lip curled in contempt.

"Lady Afton, I am certain you are the person who informed your son

71

of the Chemay inheritance. He's too stupid to ferret out the information on his own."

"No, I would never do such a thing. Why I am shocked . . . ."

His eyes grew cold as he glared at her.

She became silent, watchful and wary of his reaction.

"I take no leave of you. This is not over, I promise you. If my daughter is hurt again, you will answer for it as well as your son." He gestured for William and Drake to follow him, stopping at the door. "I will bring the full fury of the Queen upon you, if I must. She will not countenance your son's brutal behavior."

Chapter Seventeen

Caroline tied her horse to a tree and walked to the edge of the pond. *Out here, I can almost believe I am back at home.*

She turned in all directions, taking in the views. "At least I am free to be myself in the park. No one expects anything of me, no fans or dandies follow me begging for attention. Performing was a lark at first. Now I long for privacy and the chance of being unknown."

She shook her head. "I went from being the rich brash American sought after by all the fortune hunters, to the bold actress, no longer welcomed by the gentry. Quite a ride. Have I only been in England six months? Seems much longer." Without thinking, she bent and picked up a handful of small stones.

Focusing on the smooth water, she frowned and tossed the first rock, laughing aloud when it skipped three times across the surface. "I'm out of practice. I used to be able to skip at least five times."

Choosing another stone, she sucked her lower lip in concentration and let the smooth rock fly. "One, two, three, four, come on you can do it, five!" She danced a little jig.

"Very impressive." A familiar voice spoke behind her.

She turned with suspicion on her face. "I thought it was you. What social dictum have I broken now?" She glared at Baron Hargreaves. "Ladies are not to toss stones in the morning?"

He surprised her by laughing. "I suppose I deserve such a comment." He walked to her.

"You deserve more than that and you know it. Care to have a competition?" She held out the remaining rocks in her hand.

"Are you sure you know what you're doing? I am considered quite the expert on rock tossing, have a long history of such activity." William grinned at her.

"Aha, I love a good challenge. Let's put your expertise to the test, shall we?"

He backed away and shook his head. "I have one rule. I collect my own stones. You might give me a defective one on purpose to make me lose."

She bowed to him, chuckling. "By all means, collect your own specimens. The banks around the lake are littered with likely candidates."

He gathered his rocks and turned to her. "I didn't think I would find you alone in a place like this."

"No one expects to find the actress outdoors in the broad daylight. We're all supposed to be night creatures. Besides, this is not the fashionable time of day for the ladies and gentlemen to stir from their comfortable homes."

"I suspect you're right about them. Most of them are still lounging in bed."

Stepping to the edge of the pond, he scanned the water. "You're certain you are up for this?"

"Bring it on, Redcoat. This Yankee can take you."

"Ladies should always go first." He bowed to her.

"Oh go on, none of your friends can see you. I'll allow you a practice shot or two."

"If you insist." He turned back to the water and tossed his first missile. The rock skipped six times.

"That was just a lucky shot. Toss another one. I want to see you do it again."

"Whatever you wish, Miss Burgess." He sent another stone over the lake and watched as it skipped six times.

Her mouth dropped open. "No fair, you're an expert. You hid your abilities from me. I cry foul!" She began to laugh. "I sound absurd, don't I?"

"I will coach you, if you like. Let me see you toss the next one."

"All right." She looked back at the water, pulled back her hand and sent the rock flying. It skipped four times and disappeared beneath the lake's surface. "Drat."

He moved to her. "Here, let me take your hand. You are locking your wrist, which limits the momentum."

He moved his strong fingers over her hand and wrist, flexing them.

I feel his energy deep in the pit of my stomach. Her breath quickened as she gasped and started to withdraw her hand.

"No." He spoke in a soothing tone. "I won't hurt you. Move your wrist as I showed you."

"All right." Trembling she turned and tossed the stone into the pond. It skipped five times and sank.

"Try it once more and remember the wrist action you need."

She nodded and brushed off his nearness while she focused on her task. This time, the stone skipped six times.

"I did it! Oh thank you!" Without thinking, she hugged him.

He held her a moment and pulled back to look into her eyes. "You're quite welcome. I'm glad I could teach you to skip stones."

"I already knew how. You helped me improve my technique." She tried to break away from him, but he held her tight.

"Miss Burgess, I wanted to thank you for warning me about Everett Afton and my niece."

"You needn't, I could never watch such a thing unfold without warning the woman. In the case of your niece, she detests me. I knew she would never listen to me."

William broke the embrace, took her arm and led her to a shady patch. "Would you care to sit and talk for a bit?"

"Why not, I have no pressing engagements elsewhere." She sank down among the wildflowers and settled her skirts around her.

He sat beside her and stared out at the trees and plants surrounding them. "I suppose you've heard?"

She nodded. "Yes, I heard they eloped." She sighed. "I hope she doesn't regret her rash decision."

"I believe she already does. We went to see her and found her bruised, battered, and walking with difficulty."

Caroline squeezed her eyes shut and grimaced. "Oh Lord, he didn't waste any time, did he?"

"No, he showed his true colors on their wedding night."

She turned to look at him. "What are you going to do?"

He looked into her eyes. "What can we do? You're the expert in such matters. How can we get her away from him?"

She took his hand in hers. "Until she's ready to leave him, she won't. Chances are she will return to him if you abduct her and take her home."

"Then there's nothing to be done." His voice caught on his words.

"I didn't say that. You can let her know you love her. Tell her she is always welcome back home. Don't criticize her or blame her for the trap she fell into. She's young, unknowing how some men can be."

His hand clenched hers. "She is learning her lessons now."

"I know, but you must believe she will return home. If you let her know she has a haven, when she's ready she will come back. Be strong for her, it's the best way to get her home where she belongs."

He hugged Caroline once more. "I owe you so much, beginning with an apology for the way I've treated you."

She returned his embrace. "Let's start over as friends, shall we? Forget the past and move forward from today."

"I'd like that, Miss Burgess."

"Why don't you call me Caroline?"

Chapter Eighteen
Brenham House

"Thank you, Miss Burgess, for your wise advice." Sheridan gripped Celeste's hand. We only wish we watched Lisette with more care. We never should have let her slip away from us."

"You could not keep her locked in her room. Don't berate yourselves, you are wonderful parents. No one wants to believe their daughter could be lured away from her home and family."

"May I call you Caroline?" Celeste's beautiful face was drawn and haggard.

"Of course, please. I would like it if everyone in your family would do the same."

Their conversation continued. The topic remained Lisette's rash action, which culminated in her marriage.

"We should have taken the inheritance years ago and given it away so it would not be a temptation to future generations." Celeste wiped the tears from her cheeks.

"We couldn't know this would happen." Sheridan held her close, easing her head on his shoulder.

"The money is tainted with evil." She burst into renewed sobs. "So many people already died because of it. My father, my mother, even my grandfather died as a result of his greed for the fortune."

William's expression scornful, he turned to his sister.

"The curse will finally rest on Afton, where it will do the most good. He deserves all the pain coming to him."

Celeste sniffed. "I wish I could believe what you predict."

"Don't worry, CeCe." William touched her hand. "You'll see he'll suffer the vengeance he is due."

Sheridan appeared anxious to change the subject of discussion. He smiled at Caroline. "I don't believe we've congratulated you on your performance in *Romeo and Juliet.*"

"You're very kind." She ducked her head.

"I hope I haven't offended you."

She smiled at him. "No, I'm not upset by your words. I still am not comfortable taking praise."

"Well, you'd better get used to being honored. You are the most talented actress I've ever seen."

"Thank you. It is most kind of you to say so."

William leaned back in his chair and watched her face with a grin. "So what will your next play be when this one closes?"

She shrugged. "I don't think there will be another play for me."

"Why not, you're the talk of the gentry. Everyone agrees you are an exceptional talent."

She turned away to avoid his eyes. "Gareth approached me about playing Titania in *A Midsummer Night's Dream.*

Celeste nodded. "You'd be perfect in that role even though it's so different from Juliet."

"The play might be amusing to do. It's such a wonderful comedy with beautiful lines and foolery. But I don't think I want to appear in another play."

"Surely you don't care what these stiff-necked aristocrats say?" Celeste's tears had dried as she focused on her new friend.

"Oh, no, it has nothing to do with the society folks here."

"I didn't think it did." William grinned at her. "I saw you express your blunt opinion of the members of the *Ton* at the Afton ball."

"Yes, you did." She smiled back at him.

"So why don't you want to act again?"

She grimaced. "It's Gareth. He is trying to persuade me. I don't like his means of persuasion. Besides, I experienced the thrill of performing in the theater before audiences. I don't have to do it again."

William's face became serious his eyes cold. "How does he try to persuade you?"

"He calls it *calming exercise*. He touches me and tries to take my will away. He makes me uncomfortable."

"I don't care what he calls it, he must stop. I will see to it." He stood as if to charge after an enemy.

"Really, William, I gave him too much power over me. I can stop it. Don't bother about it."

"No, I can't let you be in danger from him. He is known as an accomplished seducer of women."

She stood to face him. "It is not your responsibility to protect me. I can take care of myself."

"No, it's too dangerous. I will not allow you to do such a thing."

"What do you mean you will not 'allow' me to take care of my own business? Who do you think you are, Baron Hargreaves?

"I'm the man who . . . ." He stopped and glanced around the room at his family members. "I . . . ."

"Struck dumb, aren't you?" Caroline taunted him. "You should be for mouthing such foolishness."

She tossed her head at him and turned to bow at her hosts. "Thank you for the lovely evening. It's time for me to seek my coach. I hope to see you again soon." With a second bow, she ignored William and swept from the room.

He hurried after her. "Caroline, please wait . . . ." his voice disappeared down the corridor.

Celeste looked at Sheridan. "In this one thing, Lisette appears to be right. They are falling in love."

Sheridan chuckled as he drew her to him. "She'll lead him a merry dance. I recognize the symptoms."

Chapter Nineteen
Afton House

On the floor, Lisette touched her swelling cheek, tears sliding down her ravaged face.

"How many times do I have to tell you?" Everett loomed over her, his expression contemptuous. Are you a fool? Never say no to me again. You will not like the consequences." He started walking toward the door. "You are such a mess. Clean yourself and get dressed. I don't want you now. You've put me right out of the mood."

His hand on the doorknob he turned back to her.

No, don't come back. Please don't hit me again. She did not move. She could not. Frozen like an animal caught in a trap, she did not breathe, awaiting her fate.

"You're a pathetic excuse for a woman, let alone a wife. If it weren't for your fortune I would simply snap your neck and be done with you. Don't do anything else to upset me and I might spare your life after I get your gold." He turned and walked out of the room, slamming the door behind him.

She waited at least a minute before she moved, listening to his fading footsteps. *Please don't come back, not now.* She curled into a ball, protecting her sore abdomen he'd kicked with his booted foot.

I must not anger him further. He might well kill me. I must be a better wife and obey him. I cannot languish in my chamber. I must be up and about when he returns.

Groaning with the effort, she got to her feet and rang for her maid. *Dear Lord, that hurts.*

The stagehand looked at Caroline, his hands on the curtain's rope, his eyebrow lifted in unspoken question.

She shook her head. "I think two curtain calls are enough for tonight." She let the huge bouquet she carried drag on the floor as she walked.

"Whatever you want, Miss. It seems a shame not to go once more when they're still cheering out there."

"I'm tired tonight. I just want to go home. They'll stop soon enough without encouragement." She passed him and touched his shoulder. "Thank you for your consideration."

"Anything for you, Miss, you're not like every other actor in the cast. You don't put on airs."

"Thank you for the compliment. My life isn't focused on the theater. I have other concerns beyond the stage. Perhaps that's why you think I'm different."

Jayne waited in the narrow gas lit passage leading to the dressing rooms. "Good job tonight, as usual, Caroline." She took the bouquet of flowers and moved aside.

"Thanks, I'm just glad the performance is over. I'm weary, more so than usual."

"Are you all right? You're not ill are you?" Jayne followed her into the dressing room, shutting the door behind them.

"No, I'm not sick." Caroline sighed. "Acting in this play has been fun, but I am ready for it to close."

"I know what you mean. It was exciting at first, but the glamour wore off for me, too. At least I've got Jack to keep me company while you're onstage."

"How is Jack?" Caroline turned to her friend with a smile.

"Well, he . . . ." Loud knocking on the door stopped her conversation.

"Caroline, I need to speak to you," Gareth called.

She sighed. "Yes, all right, come in."

Jayne stepped aside as he strode into the tiny room.

"You're not needed now." He pushed her toward the doorway.

"I do not take orders from you." She stood her ground and looked up at him.

Caroline looked down to hide her smile. "It's all right. We won't take long. Go ahead and make sure our coach is outside."

With a sniff in the direction of the impresario, Jayne left as instructed.

"I'm glad to find you alone." His voice slithered over her skin like swamp water.

When will you ever learn I'm not interested in you? I never could be. When he put his hands on her shoulders, she shook them off. "What do you want?"

His voice dropped to an intimate level. "I thought we should talk. We haven't discussed our plans for the next production in a while."

Ignoring him, she picked up her hairbrush and brushed the glitter powder out of her tresses. "There's nothing to discuss. My mind is set. I will not appear in another play."

His hands back on her shoulders, he leaned toward her. "I can make you see reason."

The devil you can. I'm no longer intimidated by you and will give you no more power over me. She slammed the brush on the counter.

"I told you I will not do it. The case is closed. Do not ask me again."

"You don't understand what you refuse. We could make a fortune. You could be a star in London for years."

Taking a deep breath, she stood and faced him. "There is nothing you can say or do which will give you what you want. A fortune? Why should I care? I already have a fortune."

"But you will disappoint your many admirers."

"They'll get over it. Someone new will come along and I will be forgotten."

"We could rule the world of the theater."

She poked his chest. "You mean YOU could rule the world of the theater. That is your aspiration, not mine."

"But . . . ."

"No." She stopped him. "I don't want to hear any more. You must accept my decision. I will not act in another production. My stage life is over."

His face flushed dark red.

For a moment, she faltered. *I hope I haven't pushed him too far.* She waited in silence for a moment. "Please leave, I want to go home."

"Very well." He bowed stiffly. "We will resume our conversation at a later time."

"Don't bother, my answer will not change."

"We'll see." He walked out the door and disappeared down the corridor.

She slumped against the chair. "Give it up, can't you?"

Chapter Twenty

Drake stood on the deck of his ship, the newly commissioned *American Eagle,* the first steamship of the Foster Shipping Line. "Promise me you will check on Lisette from time to time."

William nodded to his nephew. "She and Afton left for Vienna a few days ago. But I will see her as soon as they return."

"I want to kill him for mistreating her." Drake pounded his fists together as he looked out over the harbor. He turned to his uncle. "Why did she marry him? She isn't a fool, far from it."

"She thought they were in love, poor girl. Bounders like him will say anything to get what they want. He paid extravagant attention to her until your father put a stop to the courtship."

"I'd like to stop Afton permanently."

"You may not have to take the trouble. Word is Afton has a growing crowd of unhappy creditors. It seems he's gone after the Chemay legacy just in time."

The First Officer came up to Drake. "Excuse me, Captain, we're ready to embark."

"Thank you." Drake turned to William. "Looks like it's time for you to go ashore."

"Will you really be back in six weeks?"

"That's what we think. Steam engines are much faster than sail and capable of going faster all the time. One of these days we'll be traveling to the States in a week."

"Doesn't seem possible to travel so fast. The speed takes all the romance out of the voyage."

Drake shook his hand and clapped him on the back. "You're one amusing fellow. You've never traveled by sea in your life."

"It always seemed to be such a long trip, but now I may consider traveling across the Atlantic."

"I know Mimi and Elijah would be glad to see you. Despite all of their children, they still have ample room for visitors in their big house."

William's expression grew sheepish. "I was thinking of making a trip to Pennsylvania."

"Why would you . . . aha! Lisette is right. You've developed a *tendré* for Caroline Burgess."

"We're only friends right now. It would be premature to call our relationship more than that."

Drake prodded him toward the gangplank. "Be off with you. Take care of Lisette when you can." He watched William stride onto the dock. "And give Miss Burgess my regards."

Mrs. Arnold entered the sitting room, her face pinched in a thunderous frown. "That man is here again, Miss Burgess. He says he wants to talk to you."

Caroline sighed and put down the book she was reading. "Did he say what he wants to talk to me about?"

"No, Miss, you know him. He thinks he's too lofty for the likes of me."

"He's nowhere near your equal." She stood and patted the arm of her lifelong companion. "Send him in, I'll see him and send him on his way."

Mrs. Arnold nodded and turned with a wry smile. "I'll bring him in."

Caroline stood in front of the empty fireplace and faced the door.

"Ah here you are at last." He moved to her with a flourish and a courtier's bow from another era. "How are you today, my sweet?" He moved to her and kissed her cheek.

"I am much better since the play closed." She indicated a chair for him. "Please sit down. Would you like refreshment, some tea, perhaps and some cakes?"

"I do not want anything, thank you." He carried a portfolio, which he opened on his lap. "I've got some sketches to show you." He paged through the drawings until he found the one he sought. "Here we are." He held up a drawing with bravado. "What do you think of this?"

What is he doing? She looked at the picture of a blonde woman wearing sheer fabric draped over her body and a wreath of wildflowers in her hair. "This better not be me depicted in the sketch."

His smile ingratiating, "Come now, Kitten, of course it's you. Who else would I allow to play Titania?"

"I don't know, but it will be someone else. I have not changed my mind. My acting days are over, period. Now what can't you understand? Is the concept of a woman immune to your charm inconceivable to you?"

"I know you only seek to make me beg you to take this role."

"The only thing I want from you is to be left alone. Why can't you stop pestering me? I will not act again. Those are my final words on the subject. If that's all you came for this afternoon, you can leave now."

He appeared to be considering. "Let me offer another proposition to you. Suppose I do not cast you? Would you be willing to put up the money to stage the production?"

"How much would you need to stage the play?"

He pondered for a moment and then named his price.

"You ask a great deal of me when I'm not even going to appear in the production."

"I only want to mount a production in which you'd wish to appear."

She dismissed him with a flick of her wrist as she perused the other sketches he brought. "The costume drawings are lovely. Will the entire cast be garbed in this style?"

"Of course," said Gareth with a smile. "Only the best is good enough for our star."

He will never stop this insanity. She sighed. "I'll counter your proposal. Come back to me with the finished cast list and I will consider investing in the production."

For only a moment he gazed at her, his eyes the tilted slits of a predator about to devour his next meal. "You make a reasonable request. I will return when the roles are assigned and we will talk again." He packed up his portfolio and rose to go.

Standing to escort him out of her sanctuary, she turned to him. "When

I said to bring the finished cast list, I mean all of the roles must be cast, including Titania. My name is not to appear on that list or our negotiations will be over."

He lifted her hand to his lips. "Of course, whatever my lady wishes." He kissed her hand with grace.

She led him to the doorway. "Mrs. Arnold will escort you the rest of the way."

He turned and smiled at her, "Farewell until we meet once more."

She nodded to him, sighing when he disappeared around the corner of the hallway.

Jayne entered the room, careful to avoid the impresario. "I didn't think he would let you go easily. Jack says he talks about you all the time."

"I can only imagine what he says. He is trying to get me back onstage. I must be better at manipulation than he is."

"Are you up for it? Jack says he can be a formidable enemy."

She grinned at her friend. "Oh he does, does he?"

"I'm just passing on what he tells me." She looked down.

Caroline took her hand. "I don't mean to upset you. I'm glad we've got a spy in his group so we know what his next move will be. Hopefully I can outwit him."

"You can win this battle. I know you can." Jayne squeezed her hand. "You're the strongest woman I've ever met."

"Thank you for the praise. He's wily, clever, I hope he won't try to trick me." She slapped her forehead as she moved back to her favorite chair. "Certainly, he will try to trick me. He's still breathing, isn't he?"

Chapter Twenty-One
Brenham House

"Have you received any more news from the Emperor?" William looked down at the brandy snifter in his hand as he swirled the liquid.

"I met with their ambassador yesterday and confirmed they were free to give the inheritance to Afton, as Lisette's husband." Sheridan gazed out the window at the clear night.

"Why did they need more verification of Lisette's right to inherit and Afton's status? You already confirmed both with their emissary."

"I suspect the Emperor met Afton and became suspicious of his attitude."

"Well Afton is such a cocky bastard anyone would suspect his motives." William looked down once more. "I imagine the sight of Lisette's injuries played into the Emperor's suspicions as well."

"I wish we could take her away from him. Are you certain there is no way?"

William shook his head. "If we try to take her by force, she's likely to return to him. Caroline said she must be willing to leave him."

"The hardest part of all this is seeing my daughter in the hands of a cruel bully. I want to cut him down with my saber. I cannot save her or even help her if she chooses to stay."

"Perhaps he'll leave her alone when he has the money."

"He might kill her. He could arrange an accident, a fall down the stairs or something similar. Given his history, he will no longer be interested in her when he receives her inheritance." Sheridan's mouth tightened.

"It is a possibility, but he could also use her as a shield from any other young women foolishly wanting to marry him. As long as Lisette's alive, he can play as he likes with no consequence of being forced into marriage."

Horace wiped his mouth with the linen napkin and smiled at his daughter. "A wonderful dinner, wasn't it? Our cook outdid herself this evening." He rubbed his burgeoning belly in contentment.

Caroline pushed her plate aside with most of her meal left untasted. "Yes it was a fine meal."

"Are you coming down with an ague? I'm not used to you being such a picky eater."

She shrugged. "I wasn't hungry. It's nothing dire."

"I should hope not. Aren't you enjoying our time here?"

"Not really, with so few friends, there's little for me to do these days."

He pursed his lips as he looked at her. "Why don't you get back into the social whirl? You'd be around some of your friends once more."

She touched his hand across the table. "Father, you're so kind to worry about me. Since my interlude on stage I am no longer invited to the balls and parties."

"Those damned hypocrites! They loved you in the play. I watched them giving you standing ovations at every performance. Now you're not good enough to socialize with them? I've half a mind to call in several loans I've made to members of the gentry. They'd be falling all over each other to see who could invite you first if I threatened them."

"Please don't do anything. It's not important."

"I've got an idea. Let's throw a whopper of a ball here. I bet those society fools will all accept my invitations. They wouldn't dare offend me if I hold their markers, and I hold several."

"Father, I don't think . . . ."

"Nonsense, my girl, let your old papa handle things. We'll give a grand shindig. The snooty ones will be talking of nothing else for months."

I can imagine what they'll say. She sighed and folded her napkin with care placing it beside her china plate.

"I heard Grayson came to call today. What did he want?"

"He's still determined to lure me into playing Titania."

"I understand your reluctance to go back onstage, but you know you'd be a great Fairy Queen. I think you should consider it."

She shook her head. "I made up my mind. I don't want to work with Gareth any more. He wants more of me than I am willing to give."

"Is there any other reason why you don't want to go back to the theater?"

"I don't want to portray someone else's life. I want to live my own."

Horace looked at her, his eyebrow raised. "Have you seen Baron Hargreaves lately?"

"We've met a few times in the park during the day."

"For all his posturing when we first met I like him. There's more to him than the fops who call themselves gentlemen."

"Father, we're just friends."

He stood and moved to her chair, helping her to her feet. "Why don't you sail back home then? I understand more of the new steamers are making the voyage every few weeks. You could be back in Pennsylvania before the winter."

She walked with him out of the dining salon. "I'm not ready to go home yet. William may need my help with his poor sister."

Horace laughed a deep rich sound and patted her hand as they walked toward his study. "That's my girl, always wanting to help. Very well, we'll stay for a while." He peered down into her eyes. "I'm still going to hold a ball. It will be good for all of us."

Chapter Twenty-Two
Vienna

Will this hell never end? Lisette trudged along behind her ebullient husband. *He's been everybody's friend since he received my inheritance.*

Afton stopped here and there in the crowds to kiss a pretty girl or pat a buxom woman.

Quite pleased with yourself, aren't you?

Forgetting his wife, Everett all but waltzed through the throng of people. Each night he sought excitement and left her behind.

I suppose it's preferable to him carrying through with his threat to kill me.

Ahead of her, a prostitute squealed as Everett grabbed her breast and yanked it free of her low bodice.

"Ya like that, don't ya?" His drunken leer roamed over the woman's body. "What say ya to a tumble?"

"Anything for you, *Mein Herr.*" The woman rubbed her dirt-soiled gown against his fine coat.

Dropping the wine bottle he held to the cobblestones, his hoarse laughter bounced off the surrounding buildings. Lisette shivered as the sounds surrounded her.

That's it. I don't have to take this. I'll go back to London without him. I'm certain he won't even know I am gone. She slipped through the crowd and walked in the direction of their hotel.

I can sell my jewels to pay for my passage home. She pulled a letter out of her pocket sniffing it with a sad smile. *It smells like Maman.* She read the single page.

"Come home to us," her mother wrote. "You are always welcome. We love you."

She doesn't even sound angry at what I did. I thought they would chastise me for eloping. But even when Father came to see me all he did was ask me to come home. I should have listened to Uncle William and never married Afton.

Wiping her eyes, she put the letter back into her pocket. The next morning she left the hotel room with her trunk and valise. Everett didn't return from his night of debauchery. *His absence is all the better for me. I hope I never see him again.*

After stopping at an expensive jeweler's shop, her reticule bulged with cash. Within the hour, she was off on the first leg of her journey back to London.

"I wonder if he'll even notice I am gone." She rubbed her bruised and swollen wrist her husband twisted in the final effort to gain her compliance.

"Darling," cried Gareth as he approached her with his arms extended. "Come to me and give me the kiss I deserve."

Caroline stood still and looked at him with a lifted eyebrow. "I take it you bring good news?"

"Now don't be that way, can't we celebrate our good fortune?"

She turned away from him and moved to a chair. As she sat, she glanced at him. "I want to be clear with you. We are not involved in any relationship beyond one of business."

"But Dearest, surely we . . . ."

She raised her palm to stop him. "If you want my backing you will agree to my stipulations. Otherwise you may seek your funding elsewhere."

He took a deep breath as an ugly expression flickered over his features. He looked at her as if weighing the strength of her determination.

Finally, he sighed and sat in a chair opposite hers. "Are you certain you don't want to play Titania?"

"I'm resolved never to set foot on stage again. Now do you have an actress cast in the role or not?"

"Yes, I do." His voice became neutral with an impersonal tone.

"Madeleine Lefebvre has agreed to take the part."

"She is quite famous. I heard of her back in Pennsylvania. Father followed her career, as an ardent fan. I'm sure he'll be pleased with the news."

"As long as we please Father," he mumbled in sarcasm.

"Don't act so put upon. I told you how it would be. If you don't like my terms, surely you can find other backers for your production."

"No, no, there is no need to search elsewhere. I am satisfied with your terms. There is only one problem."

I want him gone. "And what problem might it be?"

"We need an understudy for Titania. I was wondering if you would consider . . . ."

"No, I will not. Is my intention plain enough for you to understand?"

His mouth turned down in an ugly sneer but faded quickly. "I see you are obstinate in your refusal ever to act again."

"Yes, I am. If you need an understudy I suggest you promote one of the younger actresses to the position and perhaps the costumer's daughter to understudy the lesser role."

He raised his head in pride and stood before her. "I see you have thought of everything. If you will excuse me, I will return to the theater. I must set the rehearsal schedule." He bowed to her.

"I look forward to seeing the play on opening night."

"Pardon me, Miss, the caterer is here to meet with you." Mrs. Arnold stood in the doorway.

"Very well. Thank you for coming, Gareth. I am wanted elsewhere." She rose and gestured for him to leave.

"Are you planning something for which you need the services of a caterer?"

"Father sent invitations for a ball we are giving. There's always so much to do to prepare for large gatherings.

"Indeed." His eyes raked over her. "So they welcomed you back to the fold?"

"It would appear they did, at least the gentry who accepted our invitation."

His lips pursed, he bowed to her once more. "Good day, Miss Burgess, I will be in touch." He turned and hurried down the corridor, his greatcoat flowing behind him.

She waited until he left. Taking a deep breath, she started for the kitchen.

Jayne met her in the hallway. "Are you all right? He didn't say or do anything to upset you, did he?"

"No, he didn't do anything, although he was not happy when I dismissed him in favor of the caterer."

"I don't imagine he was, serves him right, though. He's much too puffed up with his own importance. Why Jack says . . . ." She stopped, her face pink as if she realized she said too much.

"What does Jack say? It's all right. You can tell me."

Jayne looked around to see if they were alone. "Jack says Grayson brags he will have you back in his bed as well as the show."

Caroline pursed her lips tight and shook her head. "*Back* in his bed? I should have known. That does it. I will be on guard from now on." She looked at her friend. "I never took him for a lover, though he made his intentions clear."

"I knew you wouldn't do such a thing. I told Jack the impresario was lying."

"You're a good friend. I'm glad we met." Caroline hugged her and led her toward the kitchen. "Let's go see what trouble we can get into with the caterer."

Chapter Twenty-Three
Hyde Park

"Our meeting this way is becoming a habit." William led his horse to a tree and tied him there.

Caroline smiled as he approached her. "If I didn't know better, I'd say you planned this."

"Let's just say I hoped to run into you." He hugged her in greeting.

She pulled back from him and grinned. "I hope you don't mean that literally."

Laughing, he looked into her eyes. "You should know me better than to have such thoughts. I thought our difficulties are behind us."

"They are." She took his arm and walked with him to the water's edge.

"How are the preparations for the ball progressing?"

Stooping, she picked up some stones and handed him a few. "Shall we relax a bit?"

"I'm always up for a competition. What is wrong with you? Is Grayson troubling you once more?"

"No, since I gave him an emphatic refusal on his plans to cast me I've heard nothing more from him."

He took her free hand. "What troubles you?"

"I'm worried about the upcoming ball."

"Don't tell me the acceptance is minimal. I will spread the word. Your *soiree* will be a social must."

Her expression grew tender as she smiled at him. "You are very kind to think of it. The problem is I have so much to do. I never planned such a big event before. Our gatherings back home tend to be smaller and simpler. I'm afraid I'm at a loss here in London."

"I know a solution to your predicament. I will ask my sister Celeste to help you. She is an experienced Lady of the *Beau Monde*."

95

"It is sweet of you to offer, but doesn't she have other concerns for the time being?"

He nodded. "Lisette's situation preys on all our minds. I think it will help her mother to have a bit of distraction, something else to focus on for a week or two."

"Have any of you heard from her?"

He sighed. "Sheridan received a dispatch from the Emperor's emissary. Afton got the money. None of us have heard anything else."

"I know how difficult it must be for your family. Not knowing is the worst situation."

"I think Celeste needs to keep occupied. Please let me ask her to help you."

She pulled her hand out of his and patted his face. "I would be most grateful for her assistance."

He smiled at her, their faces moving toward each other. "Caroline, I . . . ."

With a wink, she turned and tossed a rock into the water, cheering as it skipped six times. "Beat that, why don't you?"

"Oh, so this was all a tactic, was it? You're on, my lady. The loser will take the winner for ices."

"I accept your challenge." She laughed.

He tossed a stone and watched it skip six times. "The race is on," he cried.

She grinned at him. *Celeste isn't the only one who needs to be distracted.*

Lisette stepped aboard the steamship in Calais preparing to embark for London. She gathered her black dress and walked up the gangplank.

Bless Aunt Mimi for wearing her widow's weeds so long. They do make an effective disguise and a deterrent from unwanted attention. I must remember to thank her for the inspiration.

The steward led her to the small cabin she reserved for the two-day journey.

"I 'ope you will be *com-fort-able*, Madame." He bowed as he shut the door behind him.

Alone and safe after she locked the cabin door, Lisette tossed off her bonnet with the long black veil and breathed. Spying the porthole, she moved to it and opened it, looking out to the harbor and the open sea beyond. *It smells clean.*

Her heart sped as she looked toward England and home. *I wonder what* Maman *and Father will say when I arrive back home?*

Once she decided to leave Everett, cold logic replaced her tortured emotions. She had plotted her route, secured funding, and booked passage taking her northwest to France and then to Calais.

Along the way, she attracted unwanted attention from some of her fellow travelers. When they stopped in Strasbourg, she found a dressmaker's shop and purchased the black dress and veil. The woman was compassionate when Lisette spun her tale of being widowed so young.

"*Ach, mein Kind*, it is so hard to lose one's love." The older woman smiled in tender sympathy.

I wonder what she would say if she knew the truth?

On the rest of the journey to Paris and then to Calais, Lisette was left alone by the other passengers. She said nothing to anyone. *I suppose they all thought I was in mourning. In a way, I guess I was.*

She sighed as she watched the seabirds dive for fish. *I lost my innocence and my notion of a loving marriage.*

Shivering, she wrapped her arms around her body. "How could I be so stupid?" Her whispers hid beneath the sounds of the water and the wheeling gulls.

"Why was I so sure he loved me? Why was I naive? There must be something missing in me."

She sat on the bunk and remembered. "Everett is a monster, the things he did to me . . . ." She shook her head. "I grew up watching my parents. They are so much in love to this day. I thought my marriage would be like theirs."

Engulfed in sudden anguished sobs, she collapsed on the bed. "I can never tell anyone what he did to me. They must never know how bad it was."

As her breathing slowed, she wiped her face with her fists. "From now on, I will lock my heart and never love again. I will never go back with Everett. I will never allow another man close to me."

Chapter Twenty-Four
Burgess House

"How did you learn to do all this?" Caroline stared open mouthed at the orderly stacks Celeste made from the messy piles she found.

"It's simple. You'll learn, once you've done it a time or two, you can do it without thinking."

"I don't know if I can ever learn these things." She shook her head.

Celeste touched the younger woman's shoulder. "First, you're looking at these tasks as something beyond your capabilities. You can manage this with a bit of practice."

"But . . . ."

"No, stop telling yourself you cannot. If you could memorize the lines in *Romeo and Juliet*, as well as the necessary movement onstage, organizing a party is a simple matter."

Caroline smiled at her. "I'm being silly. Of course I can manage this. I guess I'm distracted."

Celeste stacked one pile of notes on top of another. "I understand. I'm diverted by other matters these days."

How could I be so thoughtless? Of course she's thinking of Lisette.

"Have you heard from your daughter?"

"Not since she left with her husband for Vienna." Celeste looked down. "I fear what may happen when he realizes he doesn't need her any longer. I remember my own experience with the Duc d'Alençon. He told me if I died after he got the money, it wouldn't bother him. I keep hearing his voice." She shivered at the memory.

Caroline hugged her. "I know Everett Afton from my own encounters with him. I think he will be far too preoccupied with his pleasures after he receives the inheritance. If Lisette is strong enough to stay out of his way, her life could get better."

"I hope you're right." Celeste sniffed.

"Come let's sit down for a moment." Caroline led the way to a pair of matching chairs. "Would you like some tea or lemonade?"

"No, thank you, I don't want anything."

"All right, if you don't mind, I'd like to tell you what my experience taught me about women who are abused. Do you think Lisette is a strong woman?"

"Yes, she always seemed to be. Afton swept her up with his talk of love. She enjoys reading novels about love. I suppose she thought he was her destiny."

"I can understand how she could believe he was her prince. He played whatever role he needed to win her. I became concerned when he began paying such attention to your daughter."

"I'm glad you shared your observations with my brother. He convinced Sheridan we faced a problem. If only we acted sooner."

"She was determined to see Afton, thinking he loved her. You could not stop her from seeing him when they were invited to the same events."

"But if we had, she wouldn't be in danger now."

"You can't be certain. He was determined to marry her for her money. He would do whatever he must to accomplish his goals." She looked directly into Celeste's eyes. "This will be resolved, sooner than you think."

"How? Do you know something?"

"From my own observation of your daughter, I think she will find a way to escape her current situation and come back to her family."

"I hope you're right, I truly do."

Everett stumbled into the silent hotel suite. "Lisette, where in hell are you, woman?"

Hearing nothing but silence, he tripped and landed in a chair.

"Where is she? Why isn't she here to greet her lord and master? Ha, that's a good one! I'll make sure she calls me that from now on." Wiping his nose on the back of his sleeve, he looked down at his filthy clothes. "This will never do for the wealthy Lord Afton."

Staggering up to the bell pull, he summoned his valet. "A bath and a change of clothes will rouse me. I must be at my best for the tables tonight. I feel a streak of luck coming to me. I'll be so rich, no one, not my mother or my puling wife will ever dare gainsay me again." He whirled at the sound of discreet knocking from the door. "It's about damned time, Herbert. Why . . . ."

He pulled open the door and found a stranger standing there. "Who are you and why do you dare to disturb me?"

The man sauntered into the suite, his eyes looking at the disheveled splendor.

"I always wondered what these accommodations were like." He turned back to Everett. "Forgive me, I am Eduard Hollenbach."

Afton looked at his outstretched hand and back up to the stranger's face. "What are you doing here? What do you want?"

Hollenbach circled Afton as if sizing up his prey. "I came to settle accounts with you."

"Accounts, what accounts do you mean? I never did any business with the likes of you."

"Perhaps Lord Afton's memory is faulty from his nights spent in pleasure. I doubt you forgot the lovely Hilda who pleasured you these two nights past."

"Of course I didn't forget her. What man could forget nights spent in such bawdy play?"

Hollenbach smiled with his grin stretched like Satan himself. "It is time for me to collect payment. Let me tally up your bill . . . ."

With a flick of his wrist, Afton dismissed Hollenbach. "You needn't worry. Whatever I owe you is but a trifling sum to me. You will receive your money."

"I'm glad to hear you say it. Perhaps you would care to let me organize your evening's activities for tonight as well? If you tire of the ladies, how would you like to visit the gaming tables?"

Afton snickered as his valet entered the room. "Why can't I do both? Lord knows I'm wealthy enough. Herbert, draw me a bath and lay out fresh clothes for the evening."

The valet bowed. "Very well, my lord." He hurried off to complete his task.

Stripping off his soiled clothes, Afton dropped them to the floor. Looking up to find Hollenbach still in the room, he ordered, "go ahead and have a seat. I'll be ready to deal with you in a short time."

The procurer sat with ease on the brocaded chair. "Where is Lady Afton?"

"My mother is back in London."

"No, I meant your wife. Did she return to London?"

Afton looked around the room and shrugged. "I dunno where she went. Doesn't matter, I have more fun without her frowning at me like she does."

He scratched his naked posterior with apparent lack of concern.

Hollenbach nodded, "Yes, I expect you do. Tonight I will show you the time of your life. An evening you will never forget." *You don't even know your wife left you. I almost feel sorry for you. Almost. Oh, you're ripe. I will enjoy taking everything you own.*

Afton giggled like a manic cherub as Herbert directed the hotel servants bringing in the tub.

Chapter Twenty-five
Brenham House

"Miss, uh your pardon, Lady Afton, please come in." The unflappable Weston appeared to be flustered at her sudden appearance in widow's weeds.

"I heard you were abroad." He smiled and bowed as she walked into her family's home.

"I was in Vienna for a time. Are my parents here?"

"Yes, I will announce you immediately." He hurried off down the long corridor.

Taking off the hat with the stifling veil, she followed him.

"Your pardon, my lord." Weston interrupted Sheridan in his study. "Lady Afton is here."

"Lady Afton, what the deuce does she want?" He started to rise from his chair but sat with an abrupt thud, his mouth gaping as he saw Lisette.

"I'm also Lady Afton," she whispered, standing back a bit. *Please welcome me back home.*

Sheridan moved fast for an aging wounded veteran. He embraced Lisette, almost crushing her.

"Dear girl, I am so glad to see you. When did you get back? Are you here to stay? Have you come home?"

"Oh, yes, Papa, if you will allow me to stay." She gazed up at him, shaking at the thought of him refusing.

"Of course you'll stay. This is your home." He smiled down at her. "You haven't called me Papa since you were twelve years old."

She put her head on his chest. *I feel so loved with him.* She blinked as the tears began to flow.

Sheridan held her tighter still. "No one will ever hurt you again. If that evil self-centered devil tries to take you out of our house I will kill

103

him."

"Oh, Papa, he might hurt you." Her sobs ruined the impact of her words.

"Nonsense, he likes to intimidate women and fears other men. He's never faced an old soldier. I'm still capable of wielding my cavalry sword."

She laughed and sniffled when her mother ran into the study.

"Lisette, I'm so happy you are here." Celeste took her daughter and wrapped her arms around her while Sheridan looked on with love for them both in his eyes.

Her *maman* pulled back from Lisette and looked her over. "Why are you dressed as a widow? Never tell me the brigand is dead."

"No, not that I know of. At any rate, these clothes made my journey easier. Men did not view me as a female to approach."

"You're clever to think of such a thing." Celeste stroked her daughter's cheek, frowning at the fading bruise.

"I remembered Aunt Mimi and the trouble she had when she came out of her mourning clothes. Of course, the black veil didn't stop Elijah for long."

"If only you could meet a man like Elijah, your troubles would be over."

Lisette pulled away from her mother. "I am through with men. Afton ruined me. I shall live my life a happy aunt to Drake's children, if he ever sires any."

"You may wait a while for him to win his Bridget." Celeste took her daughter's arm. "Come along, your room is ready for you."

"How could you know I'd come back?"

"Let's say I hoped you would. I expect you'd like to bathe and rest for a while." They walked out into the corridor. "Don't worry, *Cherie*, your old wardrobe awaits you."

Their voices faded as they moved toward the stairs. Sheridan stood watching them go.

"Did I hear Lisette?" William came from the direction of the front door.

"Yes, she arrived a few moments ago."

"Is she alone?"

Sheridan nodded. "She left him in Vienna but said no more about it." He grinned, his expression relieved. "Caroline was right in her assessment of Lisette's character."

"She's been right about a lot of things." William gazed out the window.

"I think you are changing your opinion of Miss Burgess."

"Yes, I believe I am."

Upstairs, Lisette, dressed in a wrapper, sat as a young maid brushed her hair. *Oh, that feels good. I feel so safe here in this house. I never appreciated being safe, protected. I won't make such a mistake again.* The brush snagged a snarl, bringing her out of her reverie.

"Oh, my lady, 'tis sorry I am. Did I hurt you?" The maid trembled in anxiety.

Lisette touched the girl's hand. "Don't worry about it. I'm fine. Please continue brushing my hair, it's soothing."

"Yes, ma'am, thank you."

She sighed as the rhythmic strokes continued. *As if she could harm me after the hell my husband visited upon me.* A quiet knock sounded on her door.

"Come in."

Celeste appeared in the open doorway.

"How are you? Did you find everything you need?"

"I'm fine, *Maman.* I'm so glad to be home where I belong."

Celeste took her hand. "We're all very glad you are back with us." Tears appeared in her eyes. "We all want you to be happy and safe."

"Everything is all right. I don't care what Afton says, I won't live with him again. He's got the money he wanted and he's welcome to it. I doubt he'll want me."

"You've learned a bitter lesson. I wish you never were put in such a

105

position."

Lisette shrugged. "It's my own fault. I should have listened to Miss Burgess, but my mind was closed to her. I thought I knew him better than she did. But it turns out she was truthful with me, only trying to spare me from what I could not envision."

"Caroline will be here for dinner this evening with the family. If you would be uncomfortable, I can send her a message with our regrets."

"No *Maman*, don't do it. I've got a lot to say to her, a lot for which to apologize. I look forward to seeing her."

"She's been wonderful to us while you've been gone."

Lisette nodded. "Let me guess, Uncle William invited her."

"No, Miss, I invited her. I am helping her prepare for the grand ball she and her father are giving next week."

"I didn't know you two were so close."

"We've grown closer in recent weeks."

Lisette grinned. "I knew Uncle William was smitten with her. Do you think they will marry?"

"They're both still feeling their way around each other. Who knows what may happen. Now don't you tease him." She laughed as she chucked her daughter under her chin.

"I don't think I will ever be so cruel to make a jest of someone's true love again in my life."

"Oh, *Cherie*." Celeste enveloped her daughter in an embrace.

The goggle-eyed maid quietly slipped out of the room.

Chapter Twenty-Six
Vienna

"Afton is a drunken fool," Hollenbach whispered to the lovely brunette at his side. "Keep him happy. We can relieve him of his considerable fortune in a week if we're careful."

"Don't worry, *mein Herr*, I know what to do." She rubbed her impressive, satin-covered breasts against his arm.

"Eva, come blow on the dice, you're my talisman. Or is it taliswoman?" Afton, drunk and leering, giggled like a young girl, high-pitched and silly. "I want to keep my winning streak."

She swayed over to him, her topaz eyes glittering with feline glee in the smoke-filled room. Her prey made his downfall easy to accomplish. "*Glückshaus* is a lucky game for you."

"Ah, here you are in your red dress, come to assist me. Hurry now, bless the dice." He held up his open hand.

With a seductive smile, she purred. "Whatever you want, *mein Liebling.*" Conscious of her display, she bent over and gave him a look at her bosom. While he stood and stared, she took the dice from him, made a show of pursing her lips, and puffed on them. Mesmerized by the view, he never saw her switch the dice with a pair in her other hand.

"Now you are ready for your next throw." She nibbled his ear as she gave him the ivory cubes.

"I am." He swung lopsided back to the table and tossed the dice.

"Oh, such a shame, *Liebling*, you threw a four and must pay."

A general groan sounded from the crowd surrounding the table.

Eva leaned over to him and whispered, "Why don't you put down a handful of coins? I know you will roll a twelve next and win all the coins on the board."

He snorted, threw a handful of gold coins on the table and rolled once more. Again he rolled a four.

The croupier scooped up the dice and proclaimed, "You have lost, *mein Herr.* You must put more coins on the board or quit the game."

"What do you mean? I din' lose. Why I ought to . . . ." He lurched toward the man, fists raised.

"*Liebling,* why don't we enjoy some champagne? You can return to the tables later."

Afton bobbled his head. "Good idea."

She led him to the back room. "Come along, with a bit of rest you will feel much better."

"I'll feel better," he parroted, following her in docile acceptance.

Hollenbach watched them and grinned as Eva's talented fingers relieved Afton of his purse. *You will be much lighter as we relieve you bit by bit of all your gold.*

Lisette wore a simple gown of pale blue and smiled with apparent ease.

Caroline watched her. *Her lips smile but her eyes do not. She has a journey of healing before her, but she is well on her way.*

"I am glad you could join us tonight." Celeste touched Caroline's hand. "We are all grateful to you."

"I didn't do much."

"Yes, you did, you gave us hope our daughter would return to us."

"From the time I met her, your daughter showed me her strength."

"I did, didn't I? But not in a good way, I'm afraid." Lisette frowned at the memory of the gossip she led about their guest.

Caroline looked into her eyes. "We all make mistakes when we are young and sheltered from life's realities."

"You are more generous than I would be in your place. I am sorry for all the unkind things I said, some of which you never heard."

"Oh I heard your conversations, you may be sure. The remarks made their way around the elite, inevitably reaching me."

Lisette sighed. "I wish I'd never met Everett Afton. I acted such a fool for him and his ridiculous lies."

"This part of your life is over if you choose." Caroline reached out to touch the younger woman's shoulder. "You can decide what you want to do. You are free now."

"I would like to dissolve the marriage, but I'm not certain I would be allowed to do so."

"You needn't worry about the marriage. I instructed my solicitor to determine the best way to do it." Sheridan nodded at his daughter.

"We hoped you would never want to return to him." Celeste smiled at her daughter.

"If you wish, when it is over, you could come with me back to my home in America. You could spend time with me and see your aunt and her family in Norfolk."

"It's most kind of you to bother, Miss Burgess, but . . . ."

"Please call me Caroline. It isn't a bother. I would enjoy your company unless you don't want to be seen with a notorious actress."

"You aren't notorious. You are a sensation. I don't know why you don't want to appear again."

She shrugged. "We all do things we regret later. I loved being onstage. I didn't like the backstage drama."

"What do you mean?" William's eyes blazed fury. "What did Grayson do?"

"It's nothing to worry about. It's over now and not important."

"If he upset you he needs to be taken down."

She shook her head. "It is finished. There's no need to stir things now when I will leave in a few weeks. I assure you, I made my feelings known."

Across town, the theatrical company rehearsed their upcoming production. Gareth strode about the stage, his expression furious. "What is wrong with you lot? None of you know your lines. We open in three weeks. If you don't improve, I must cancel the run of the play. I will not allow my name to be associated with such shoddy performances. This is a light, witty play, not some heavy-handed music hall parody."

"Pardon me, Mr. Grayson, but I wonder . . . ." began George Harrington, stuttering in evident fear.

"You have me wondering, too, Mr. Harrington." Gareth's voice rang over the audience seats.

The unfortunate subject of the tirade in progress slumped down in his chair, as if to make himself a smaller target.

"What about, Sir?" His insubstantial voice grew weaker.

"I wonder how an actor with a reputation such as yours cannot play Oberon with any strength. You make the King of the Fairies seem a lily-livered coward who jumps at shadows. He could never match wits with Titania."

Harrington sniffed. "I could play better with someone other than Madame Lefebvre. She elicits all the passion of a toothache."

"How dare you, you insignificant worm, I am known throughout Europe for my portrayal of Titania and Lady Macbeth. I am a strong actress. The audiences love me."

"If they knew you they'd hate you as much as I do, you old cow."

"Enough." She rose from her chair, wrapping her cloak around her with shaking, wrinkled hands. "I am able to play a woman of any age. I will not stay in this vile city that smells of coal fires and refuse. I will go home to Paris where I am respected and adored."

"Yes, go back, why don't you?" Harrington sneered and gained strength from his perceived victory. "You seem to have a faulty memory in your dotage. Paris smells like its sewers, always has as far as I can tell."

"You are nothing but an ill-bred fool. I will not tarnish my reputation appearing opposite a low class mongrel such as you."

Gareth watched the fray and said nothing. He pursed his lips as Madame Lefebvre stalked offstage and disappeared.

Excellent, I couldn't plan her exit better.

Chapter Twenty-Seven
Brenham House

"Really, Father, I've told you all I can remember." Lisette wiped her eyes with a lace handkerchief. "I don't see why we must go over all of this again. What good does it do?"

Sheridan hovered over his daughter, a concerned expression in his eyes. "We must disclose everything to Mr. Barrows-Smythe if he is to convince Parliament your marriage should be dissolved."

Her face heated. "I will not discuss certain details of an intimate nature. It will serve no purpose other than to upset me."

"You must be returned to your rightful place in society. You may meet someone in the future and wish to marry. Unless Parliament declares your first marriage over, you will not be able to marry someone else. You'll be trapped with Afton in your life until one of you dies."

I am so tired of this. "I appreciate what you're trying to do, but I cannot imagine a time when I'll ever be interested in marrying anyone. Can't we let this alone for now?"

Sheridan sighed as he looked at her. "I only want to protect you, keep the blackguard away from you, remove his rights to you."

She rubbed her hands over her eyes. "The last thing Everett wants is me. Now he has the Chemay inheritance. The last time I saw him in Vienna he grabbed a streetwalker and propositioned her in front of me while he groped her. He didn't come back to the hotel that night, which gave me the opportunity to slip away from him. I doubt he'll ever want me again."

"What if he spends the entire fortune? He will come back to you demanding the rest of your money. I can prevent him from receiving it as long as I'm alive, but when I die your family inheritance will go to him if he is still your husband."

111

"I won't give it to him. He doesn't deserve anything else from me." *If that arrogant twit comes back to me demanding anything else, he won't get it.*

Mr. Barrows-Smythe cleared his throat. "Your pardon for the intrusion, but you will have no control over your own money. Technically it all belongs to your husband as long as you are still married."

"That isn't fair. He tricked me into the marriage." *There must be some way to stop him.*

"I'm sorry, Lady Afton, it is the law. Married women cannot own property or retain their inheritance. It all belongs to their husbands. Any magistrate or justice in this land will give him what he wants with no thought to you."

Sheridan put his arm around her. "You must have the marriage dissolved or he'll take everything else from you."

"Oh very well, if it's the only thing I can do." She shook her head while her tears fell as she stared at the floor. *I made a fool of myself, manipulated by Everett. I never saw the abyss into which I fell.*

Ah, here they are at last. Caroline hurried to Lisette's side. "I didn't think you were coming. What happened? Are you all right?"

Lisette stepped out of the carriage. "I had to meet with Father and his solicitor. It was not a pleasant experience."

William stepped down to the ground. "Wells," he called to the driver, "why don't you give the horses a rest? We won't need you for a while."

"Of course, my lord." The driver saluted with the whip and urged the team toward the lake.

"Caroline." Lisette took her hand. "There's so little I can do. Everett can claim all my money as his so long as we are still married. I don't know what to do. We'll have to get Parliament to dissolve the marriage. It's the only way to do it."

"Try not to panic, you can do it. If it's the only way, you must do it."

"I don't know if I have the strength."

"Of course you do," William huffed. "You are a strong woman."

Lisette fell sobbing into Caroline's arms.

"What did I do?" William seemed bewildered. "I didn't mean to upset her."

"Perhaps it would be best if Lisette and I spoke alone for a bit. Do you mind?"

He shook his head. "Not if you think it's best."

"I do." Caroline smiled at him above Lisette's head. "Go on, sit over there, just out of earshot. You can keep an eye on us from there."

He nodded and moved away to sit beneath a spreading tree, his expression hurt at their rejection.

"Come along," Caroline whispered to the younger woman. "Let's sit on the flat stones at this side of the lake."

When they were perched side by side on the large rocks, she turned to Lisette. "What is it that bothers you the most, Afton taking everything you own? Or do you doubt your ability to defeat his plans?"

"I'm not sure, perhaps a bit of both."

Caroline nodded. "Your answer is honest, one I've heard before."

"He already took so much from me. My innocence, my love, my family inheritance. I don't want to give him anything else to squander. He never loved me at all. He couldn't, and do what he has."

"Your husband is not a man of good character. I don't know what made him the way he is, but I've seen his type before. He is sure to try to come after the rest of your money unless you stop him legally. Are you up for it?"

"I . . . don't know. I worry about the story of my awful marriage becoming common knowledge." Lisette looked up at her mentor. "What will people say about me?"

"The men will likely express their outrage at a woman having the gall to challenge her lawful husband." Caroline shrugged. "The ones who do are beneath your notice. You shouldn't care what they think or say."

"They will say I'm a failure at marriage, an unnatural woman. They will blame me."

"Yes, they might, but it comes from their own insecurities, their secret

113

fears of their own wives speaking out against ill treatment."

"The ladies of the *Ton* will call me a pariah, a loose woman if I succeed in ending my marriage."

"Think about the august personages of the *Ton*. They comprise only a small portion of your country's population, yet they possess most of the power. In my country no one cares what they think at all."

"How is that possible?"

"There is no royal family with a coterie of loyal aristocrats in America. It is an outdated concept our country has rejected. We rebelled, remember?"

"Yes, but here they have all the power."

Caroline smiled at her. "They are allowed the power only so long as the rest of the population agrees."

"Are you saying we aristocrats should be rounded up like they did in France and . . . ?" Lisette's voice rose in astonishment.

"Heavens, no, I would never suggest such a thing. What I mean is you are not bound by the dictates of others in the way you choose to live, if you possess the strength to break free."

Lisette cocked her head and appeared to think of her friend's words. "You're talking about not following tradition, the way you did when you appeared onstage."

"Now you've got it. Think about what you want in life. Do you want to remain shackled to a villain who will use you in any way he chooses and be sanctioned by your society? Or do you want to gain your freedom and live your own life?"

"When you offer me those paths, my choice is obvious. I choose freedom."

"Even though it isn't what many others would choose?"

Lisette took a deep breath. "This is my life and I will do what I want." She turned with uncertainty in her eyes, "If I have the strength to do so."

Caroline hugged her. "Your family will support your decision and so will I. Your true friends will rally behind you. The rest of them don't matter."

"But do I have the power within me to succeed?"

"Yes, you do. When it's all over, you will be free and Afton will be standing on the sidelines wondering what happened."

"I hope you're right. How did you get to be so knowledgeable in such matters?"

Caroline waved to William, gesturing for him to come back. "I lost my mother when I was a young girl. My father raised me like a son, never mincing words with me. I've also worked with many women who were beaten or abused in other ways. We've helped most of them start new lives."

"I'm glad to have you here with us."

"I'm glad to be here, too. Remember when it is time for me to return home, you are welcome to come with me. You might like meeting the other independent women of my acquaintance."

"I just may take you up on your invitation."

Chapter Twenty-Eight

"Caroline." Jayne motioned to her from the door. "Jack is here. May I bring him in to speak to you?"

"Of course, I'm glad to see him."

Jayne brought a tall, gangling young man with her. "Doff your cap." She poked him with her elbow.

He grabbed the cap off his unruly black curls. "Oh, sorry, mum, it's good of you to see me." He managed a lopsided bow.

"Please sit down. I'm happy to have you here."

He ducked his head and glanced back at her, his blue eyes shining. "I came to tell Jayne what's happened and she thought I needed to tell you."

"What's wrong at the theater?"

He sighed in apparent relief. "The old French actress walked off, she did. Says she's not coming back. Mr. Grayson acted like it was the best news ever."

"I can well imagine he did."

Mrs. Arnold appeared in the doorway. "That evil nincompoop from the theater is here, insisting to see you." She stared at Jayne and then Jack. "I thought you two would want to make yourselves scarce before I show him in."

"Good idea." Jayne grabbed Jack's hand. "Come on, I'll get you something in the kitchen." She looked at Caroline. "Will you be all right?"

"I can handle him, don't worry."

"All right, if you're sure." Jayne led Jack out of sight.

"Please show in the impresario, Mrs. Arnold."

"I will, but I will stay in earshot, in case you need me."

"Thank you." Caroline arranged her skirts and folded her hands in her lap. Footsteps sounded in the hallway coming toward here. *Here we go. I hope he's not here to try to lure me onstage again. Who am I kidding? Of course he will.*

"Hello, Gareth, what a surprise to see you today. I thought you'd be in rehearsal for your opening next week."

"I've come to see you about that very thing, how clever of you to deduce the reason for my visit."

"Please sit and tell me all about it." *I won't offer him tea, perhaps my rudeness will speed his exit.*

He sat and arranged his frock coat before smiling at her. "Perhaps you've heard we lost Madame Lefebvre."

"No, I hadn't heard, was it a sudden illness?"

He frowned, a glimmer of his exasperation showing in his eyes. "You misunderstand me, she did not die. She left the company to return to France."

"Why would she do such a thing? I read she is a disciplined as well as talented performer."

He shrugged, unable to hide his anger at her response. "In the past perhaps, but now she is but a shadow of a once great actress."

"It is a shame to lose such a pivotal character so soon to your opening. What will you do?" *I know what you're going to say. You will not like my response.*

Leaning toward her, he smiled. "I'm so glad you asked. We have no one to fill the role of Titania. The other women in the company are all too weak on stage. None of them would make a convincing Fairy Queen."

"Indeed." Her tone was bored as she studied her fingernails. "Well, I will expect a refund of whatever remains of my investment after completing an audit of your books."

"No, no, no . . . ." His hands fluttered toward her palms out and agitated. "I hoped you would agree to save the production."

Here it comes. "How could I do that?"

His sigh was audible, his expression exasperated. "By taking the role of Titania so the show will go on as planned."

"No." She stood, forcing him to do the same. "If that's all, you may leave now."

"Dear Caroline, surely you won't put the cast members out of work.

They need the salaries they will earn." He moved toward her his hands outstretched.

"You paid them up to this point, did you not?"

"Yes, but what . . . ?" He reached out and touched her shoulder.

She shrugged his hand away. "No, I won't listen to any more of your pleading. They are now free to pursue other work. Tell them that for me."

"You cannot be so cruel. Think of their children."

"Ha, that's a good one. You and I both know none of the cast members have children. Quit trying to play on my sympathy. I'm on to you. It won't work. I told you in the beginning my conditions for backing the show. You violated our contract. I expect the remainder of my money back. Now please leave my house."

He looked at her with his head cocked to one side. When he spoke next his voice cajoled. "You seem upset, my dear. Let me relax you in our special way. Come put yourself in my hands."

Laughter burst from her throat, rippling merrily against his shocked silence.

"What's so funny? Let me in on the joke."

Mrs. Arnold rushed into the room behind William. "I'm sorry Ma'am, he wouldn't wait."

Still giggling, Caroline smiled at her new guest. "It's all right. Please show the impresario to the door, Mrs. Arnold. He is ready to leave." She wiped the tears of mirth from her eyes and tried to stifle the laughter. "Baron Hargreaves, what a pleasure to see you."

"Miss Burgess." William acknowledged her, his eyebrow lifted as he looked from her to Grayson.

"I will be back," declared Grayson as he turned to go.

"You'd best bring my money when you come back. If you don't I shall take sterner measures." She stood straight and faced him.

"You'll never get your money. I'll take it in penalty."

"Now see here . . . ." William stepped toward him.

She put her hand on his arm. "It's all right. I can handle him. Hear me well, Gareth, if you don't return my money, I will impose a penalty on you."

"What could you possibly do to me?" He sneered as he looked in her eyes.

She smiled and winked at William. "It isn't common knowledge over here, but back home I'm known for always carrying a brace of pistols. I'd hate to have to hurt you."

"You couldn't hurt me." Grayson laughed. "You're like every other weak-willed woman. Besides you'd be ruined."

"I let you intimidate me in the past, but no more. In helping a friend find her strength, I remembered my own." Her eyes focused on his in an overt threat. "I suggest you bring me the rest of my money or I will take the necessary action against you."

"You wouldn't dare."

William moved close to him. "I don't think I'd test her, if I were you, my friend."

"What do you know, you useless aristocrat?"

"I know enough to heed a warning."

Grayson sneered at him. "So you've staked your claim, is that it? Is she under your protection now?"

"Miss Burgess is an independent woman, capable of dealing with hazards on her own. She doesn't need my help."

"You do not know her as I do. I found her to be easily influenced."

William grinned at the angry man. "You're right. We did not experience Miss Burgess in the same way. I'd suggest you back down. You will not win this battle."

"Hah, there is no battle. I can change her mind with ease."

Caroline moved between the men. "Oh, is that so? I asked you with common courtesy to leave now I order you to do so."

"Very well, but I shall return. You have not seen the last of me."

William stood beside her as Grayson stomped out of the room. "I almost pity him." He grinned at her.

"You're right, you should pity him." She poked a finger at his chest. "And you better not anger me, either." Her smile belied her tone.

He threw his hands up in surrender. "You have my word." He winked at her.

Chapter Twenty-Nine
Vienna

"You thieving witch!" Afton's face flushed deep red as he scowled at Eva. "I know better than to trust any female. You think you're clever. I know you stole my gold. What did you do with it?" He staggered toward her in the dim alleyway his hands outstretched to grab her by the throat.

"Now, *Liebling.*" She backed easily out of his reach. "You know I would never steal from you. I love you. Don't you remember our bed sport? Could I do what I did with someone I didn't love? How could you distrust me so?" She glanced over his head as Eduard crept up behind him, a cudgel in his hand.

"Where's my gold? Give it to me." He stomped his foot like a child. "I want my gold." He slurred his words and wobbled.

Moving closer to Afton, she stretched her hand and ruffled his tumbled curls. "Come now." Purring, she drew him to her breasts. "This is better, is it not? Tell me what troubles you. Tell me how I can help you."

He sniffed and drew the back of his fist across his nose as he cuddled against the lovely cushions. "You really didn't steal my gold?"

"I would never steal from my only love. Surely, you know that. I've proved my love to you over and over."

He sighed and nuzzled her breasts.

"If you're worried, why don't we go look for your gold? Where did you last see it?"

"In the hotel room, before my wife left, I hid the gold inside the wardrobe." He looked up at her with adoration in her eyes. "Nobody would ever look there."

"Are you certain it was there when last you saw it?"

He nodded.

"Well, then." She glanced at Eduard, "Perhaps you should rest now."

"I'm tired . . . ." His voice faded as he burrowed deeper into her chest. She held him out at arms' length. "Very well, *Liebling.* Go to sleep."

Unseen by their victim, Eduard swung the cudgel and bashed in the side of Afton's head. The English lord crumpled to the cobblestones.

"Is he dead?" Eva looked down at him. "We mustn't leave him alive to testify against us."

"If he's not dead now, he soon will be." He knelt down beside Afton. "Help me strip him. We mustn't leave any trace of who he was for someone to find. With any luck, he'll be another faceless fatality who met up with the wrong man."

"Once we're done . . . ." she emptied Afton's pockets." Why don't we toss him in the river? By the time they find him, even his own mother won't recognize him."

Smiling over their grisly task, he reached out and touched her chin. "There's my girl, always thinking ahead."

"Do you have a plan for getting the gold from his suite?"

Grunting as he pulled the pants off the corpse, he grinned. "I've got a foolproof plan. When we're done, they will all be certain Lord and Lady Afton took their baggage and checked out."

"But what about his manservant, won't he know the truth?"

"We'll take care of him when we get to the hotel. Have faith in me. We'll come out with the rest of the fortune and no one the wiser."

Lisette sat in the salon staring off in the distance, an unread book open in her lap. *Even the work of Miss Austen does not catch my interest these days."*

Sighing, she closed the book and put it on the table beside her chair. *I don't think I'll ever be interested in love stories again. They're frivolous drivel meant to entertain weak females.*

"Hello, Lissi," spoke a deep voice from the doorway.

"Drake, what are you doing here?" She ran to his open arms. "I thought you sailed to America?"

He hugged her and looked down at her face. "I'm already back. We docked this afternoon."

She hung her head, "I've got something to tell you, but . . . ."

He took her hand and led her back to her chair. "I already know. I stopped by the shipping office. They told me you were home."

"So soon, how is that possible?"

He sat beside her. "It's the miracle of modern steamships. We don't need to rely on a good wind and well-rigged sails." He paused for a moment. "Are you all right? Did that monster hurt you again?"

You do not want to know. "He was a miserable husband and worse after we got the Chemay inheritance." She shrugged. "I finally left him. He didn't even notice I was gone. At least he hasn't tried to contact me. So much for the love of my life," her eyes filled with tears.

He put his arm around her and drew her head on his shoulder. "I could thrash him, if you like."

She shook her head against him. "Do not bother. I'm through with him. Father's solicitor is preparing a case to be heard in Parliament."

"Sounds like the right thing to do, dissolve the marriage and be done with the blighter."

"I think so, too." She sniffled and looked up at him, unwilling to continue the topic of conversation. "Have you heard any word from Bridgett?"

"I was at sea, how would I hear from her?"

"I bet you asked if you had any letters when you stopped at the office."

He stiffened against her. "It was only prudent. I might have received a letter."

"You will I'm sure of it. She won't be separated from you forever."

"Where is the rest of the family tonight?"

She snuggled against her big brother. "They are all attending Caroline's ball."

"Why aren't you with them?"

"Now, that's a silly question, if I ever heard one."

"What do you mean? It's a legitimate question. You haven't done anything wrong."

She rose and walked to the window. "I don't want to see people yet. I don't want to deal with their questions, their curiosity."

"I never knew you to be afraid to voice your opinion."

She turned back to him. "I never made such a big mistake before, either. Can't you understand why I'm not ready to face those people?"

"But . . . ."

"No, let's not talk about this any longer. I need time to heal. I don't want to see the girls who will laugh behind their fans at my failed marriage."

"If you wish, but if it were me, I would face my detractors down."

"Men and women are not the same."

"As if I needed reminding . . . ."

Chapter Thirty
Burgess House

"I cannot believe I let you talk me into this." Jayne hurried to keep up with Caroline's longer stride.

"Relax. You look lovely in your rose gown. No one will recognize you from your former position as the chambermaid at Afton House. Besides, I need my friends around me tonight."

"Viscount Brenham is here with his wife. Her brother came with them. You and Baron Hargreaves seem much closer in the last few weeks."

Caroline nodded to a group of gossiping dowagers as she passed them, her skirts of azure silk sweeping the floor in an opulent display. "Celeste is wonderful and helped me pull this affair together. But she has enough about which to worry. She doesn't need my worries on top of hers."

"You don't have any worries." Jayne ran into her suddenly frozen employer.

"Oh no, isn't that Gareth Grayson walking this way?"

"Did you invite him?"

"Of course, I didn't. I feared he might do something like this. Well, there's no time like the present, I suppose." Caroline straightened her spine as her nemesis approached.

"Good evening, darling." He moved to her and kissed her cheek.

"Gareth, what a surprise to see you here this evening." She did not respond to his kiss, she did not cower, but faced him as an equal.

"Yes, it seems my invitation was lost. I never received one."

She said nothing. *Get on with what you want to say, you manipulative fiend.*

125

Eduard led Eva up the grand staircase at the hotel.

"Do you think anyone recognized us?" She leaned to whisper to him, the picture of a dutiful wife.

"Trust me, people see what they want to see. We will be fine." He unlocked the door to Afton's suite, stopping to peer inside. "No one seems to be here." He entered the room and pulled her behind him.

"I'll search the wardrobe, shall I?"

He nodded. "I will write a note for his valet."

"I'm so glad you asked at the desk about him."

"I wanted to be sure he was still out for the evening. I hope he enjoys his outing. It may save his life." He grinned down at her. "He will make a good witness when he tells the authorities Lady Afton returned from her journey in time to travel home with her husband."

Her brow wrinkled, "I thought you said his wife returned to England? His family will know the woman in Vienna was an impostor."

He took her chin in his hand. "They will think he went off with a beautiful mistress and disappeared."

"Ah, *Liebling,* you are a clever fellow."

He kissed her forehead. "Be about your business. Let's be certain to get everything of value before we pack the luggage."

She patted her blond wig back into place and turned to do his bidding.

Gareth reached beneath his cloak. "I've brought something for you, my sweet."

Caroline frowned at the garment he held. "What on earth is that?"

"This is your costume for the play, darling. I thought it best for you to try it on so the seamstress can alter it to fit you." He held the transparent garment up for all to see, waving it in his hands. "You'll be more beautiful than ever as Titania."

"It won't work." Her response was low-pitched, intimate. "I never agreed to appear in your production. I made my decision clear to you."

"Yes, but when you came to me in the night, we worked it all out after our passionate interlude. You know you promised me, my love."

She inhaled a sharp breath. "You are delusional if you think anyone would believe such a story. I told you no. I mean no. The subject is closed."

"You changed your story since last night when you were in my arms." His voice rose as though he was playing to the back row of the theater balcony.

"What are you going on about? I wasn't anywhere near you last night."

"That's right." Jayne stood beside her friend. "She was here at home all night. We prepared for the ball."

"Of course you would lie for her, my poor child, after the hell from which she rescued you."

"I've heard quite enough of this drivel." William moved between Grayson and Caroline.

Grayson looked at him with pity in his expression. "Isn't it a shame she couldn't rescue your niece from Afton's clutches like she did her servant? And by the way, what is her servant doing dressed in a lady's finery, attending the ball?" He shook his head and gazed at the guests crowding ever closer to the scene.

As he spoke, the eyes of the guests looked at Jayne with derision and scorn.

"*Doesn't do to allow them to step out of their station,*" one matron whispered loud enough for all to hear.

"*Can you imagine the gall?*"

"*That's an American for you, no sense of propriety.*"

"*Well, I always said class will tell, no matter how much money her father amassed. She's still nothing but the daughter of a coal miner.*"

"*My dear you are correct in your beliefs. We should never have attended this farce. Did you see the wicked gown the actress is to wear in her next role? Why you could see right through it. The lowest whore in East End would never be so obvious, so free with her charms.*"

"*My daughter should not be privy to such ribaldry. We're leaving.*"

Soon the crowd jostled and pressed each other in their efforts to leave.

Caroline looked at Grayson. His expression was triumphant.

"You will pay for this. The magistrate will close your production tomorrow for unpaid debt."

"It's worth it," he sneered. "You are ruined in London society now. It has been my pleasure to bring you down."

Horace Burgess stood in the doorway, his voice booming out over the churning mass of people. "Anyone who leaves will have their notes called tomorrow morning. I expect full repayment of all outstanding debts. If you do not comply, I don't care what your family name or title is, after the liquidation of all your assets, you will go to debtor's prison."

The women hurried forward, determined to leave. Several of their husbands stopped in their tracks.

"That's right, gents, think about your situation. I am not playing. I will brook no insults to my daughter, now or in the future."

The men cleared throats or murmured and looked at their wives. Only one man, a Marquise, met Burgess' gaze and escorted his wife and two daughters from the ballroom.

"Anyone else dare to do the same?" Burgess surveyed his guests.

Caroline watched as no one else met his glance. She shook her head. *At least I am right in their assessment of me. Ah well, I never cared for their good opinions.*

Horace nodded to the orchestra and the music began once more. "Come along, everyone, we're here for a ball. There's music and food and good wine, enjoy your evening."

The rapt attention of those in the room dissolved with audible sighs. The guests moved to the dance floor or the food-laden tables as their murmurs resumed.

Celeste touched Caroline's hand. "My dear, are you all right?"

"I'm fine, thank you. I'm sorry you witnessed Grayson's tirade."

"It doesn't matter. We expect there will be gossip, it cannot be helped." She tipped her head at her hostess. "He seems quite taken with you."

Caroline snorted. "He's quite taken with my money and its ability to make him the most noted director in London. I didn't think he would go so far."

"It appears he is going farther." Celeste gestured toward a scowling Horace as he dragged Grayson out of the room by his coat collar with William following, his face filled with fury.

"If you ever darken my doorstep again, I will hire a gang of roughnecks to mark up your pretty face." Horace tossed Grayson out the door followed by a swift kick to spur him on his way. "You'll be finished on the London stage and unable to cajole other wealthy young ladies of their fortune."

Chapter Thirty-One
Vienna

"I found it," Eva screamed in triumph. "Oh, Eduard, this chest is so heavy I cannot lift it."

"Here, let me try." He elbowed her aside and reached into the ornate wardrobe. "*Gott im Himmel*, it is heavy." He grinned at her. "We're rich beyond our imagining." He paused to kiss her with fervor and ran to the window facing the street.

"What are you going to do?"

"You'll see how clever I am." He pushed aside the heavy drapes and leaned out to whistle. Eduard nodded to someone in the street and closed the window. "They're coming up."

"Who is?"

"Rolf and Manny. Hurry, they'll be here in a moment. Help me with this trunk." She helped him drag the big trunk to the middle of the room. He opened the lid and began tossing out the garments packed inside. "There. The chest should fit."

A knock on the door sounded. "Remember," Eduard said as he moved to the door, "if it's anyone else, we're Lord and Lady Afton returning to England. Right-o, old thing?"

"Whatevah you say, milord."

"Your accent needs work."

"If I lean over to welcome whoever it is, he will focus on my bodice and forget about my accent."

"Good point." He opened the door, standing stiff and proper. "Ah here you are at last. Lady Afton and I need some assistance with our trunk."

"As you vish, my lord." Rolf bowed and entered the room.

After Eduard shut the door behind them, the men burst into laughter. "You did it, you got rid of him?"

Eduard nodded in acknowledgement. "If you'll carry the trunk down to the wagon, we'll follow and take our leave as the Aftons."

The two men lifted the trunk in their brawny arms. Edward hovered.

"Remember, if you try to cheat me, I know where you and your families live. Do as we agreed and there's ample coin for all of us."

They nodded and toted their burden out into the corridor, their footsteps heavy on the carpeted staircase.

"Well, Lady Afton, at last we leave the scene of so much merriment. Are you ready to play your role?"

"Of course, milord." She fastened her cloak and drew on her long, elegant gloves. "What will we say about these garments we're leaving?"

"We'll tell them our shopping spree left us without enough room for these things. We'll instruct the concierge to give them to the poor."

She took his arm and smiled up at him. "Aren't we kind, my dear?"

At the front desk, Eduard paid the bill for Lord Afton and gave the manager a more than generous gratuity. He then gave him an envelope. "Please see that my valet Herbert receives this. I will no longer need his services. He is free to seek employment elsewhere."

The manager bowed. "Of a certainty, my lord. I shall speak to him personally."

Eduard led Eva through the opulent entry and out to the waiting coach. "I'd say we succeeded very well." He murmured to her as he handed her into the hired vehicle.

"I'm proud of you, *mein Liebling*. No one will ever know the elegant Aftons were impostors."

"It's a wonder what a bit of greasepaint and a well-chosen wig will do, isn't it?" He winked as he reached into her bodice and palmed her breast.

"Ooh, your fingers are so talented, Lord Afton." She giggled in pleasure.

With aristocratic hauteur, he banged his walking stick on the ceiling and signaled the coachman to move forward.

The coach lurched as the horses pulled it forward.

"I may have to increase Rolf's share," he whispered into her ear.

"Good servants are so hard to find." He took her earlobe between his teeth.

Eva snickered low in her throat as they drove off to their new life.

Father Johann held his lantern high and peered through the darkness of the waterfront.

Blessed Mother, please guide my steps this night.

He sighed as he limped along the cobbled streets by the Danube. *It's a cold, damp night for the poor souls with no home.*

A moan sounded out of the darkness. Using the noise as a beacon, he discovered a man, lying on the street.

"What happened to you, my son?" He bent down to the figure.

"Go 'way, let me sleep," the man mumbled, his breath fouled with the odor of schnapps.

"Let me help you." The priest reached down to offer a hand.

"Leave me alone." The drunk batted his hand away. "Don't need your help."

Father Johann straightened up with an effort. *The damp chill off the river does my old bones no good.* "Very well, my son, I will leave you to your rest."

Breathing deep of the biting air, he moved on past the warehouses. *No one else is out here, perhaps I should return to the church. I would like to be beside a good fire with a bit of tea to warm my bones.*

As he turned to go back, another sound caught his attention. Something bumped against the pilings in the river. Raising his lantern, he moved to the edge and discovered a body washing against the dock with the wake.

Another drunk, I suppose, why do so many men drink themselves numb? They must be in terrible pain. I'd best try to help him.

"My son, I am here to help you." Father Johann looked down at the form in the water. He bent. "Please let me assist you. I can take you to a warm place where you can pass the night. It's better than freezing in the water."

With great effort, he dragged the limp body up to lie on the ground.

Something ominous drew his attention. He moved the lantern to a hole in the back of the man's head.

Heilige Vater, is that dried blood?

When he drew nearer, the priest saw the young man had no need of a warm place to sleep. The eyes of the corpse stared off in the darkness with an expression of surprise forever etched on his face.

My son, I am sorry for what you endured. Robbed of all but your smallclothes, such a shame to leave a vigorous young man like this.

The priest touched the hands of the cadaver. *These are not the hands of a laborer. He must be a young gentleman of good family, poor boy. His mother may never learn of his murder. There is nothing to identify him. At least the Lord guided me to him.*

Shaking his head, Father Johann stood once more. "I will come back with the cart. It is a pity he was killed but he will rest well buried in the churchyard."

Chapter Thirty-Two
London

"Shall we take these as well, Miss Burgess?" The boss of the hired men held two flats painted with fantastic flowers, part of the scenery for Shakespeare's most beloved comedy.

"Yes, they are part of the scenery, bought with my money. Take everything you find, except the personal property of the cast and crew." She turned and scanned the stage. Stripped of the set pieces, it no longer seemed a magical place. It became an aged, faded theater, dusty and miserable under the harsh daylight streaming from the bare windows.

Shaking her head, she stepped over a pile of sections of the discarded curtain. *This will never rise again, at least not on a Grayson production.*

"You can't come in here. You were warned before." The Constable's deep voice came from backstage.

"How dare you? Do you know who I am?"

"I do and I know you're to be ejected if you come here."

"By whose orders?" Gareth's voice rose in indignation.

"Mine." Caroline walked to the stage entrance. "You know you are forbidden to interfere with this process."

"You are stealing my set pieces, costumes, the very essence of my production." He struggled against the Constable's confining arm.

"Well, you shouldn't have bought these things with my money when you broke the terms of our contract. You knew the consequences of doing so. I might not be so anxious to close your show, but no, you had to parade that disgusting bit of transparent netting before half of the members of the *Ton.*"

He sneered in smug satisfaction. "I got the result I wanted."

"And now you are paying for what you did. It's your fault you lost it all."

"I will find a way to get you for this." He lunged forward only to be pulled back by the officer.

Caroline sighed and reached into the deep pocket of her cape. She pulled out a long-barreled pistol.

"If you try to hurt me, I will shoot you."

"You don't have the courage." He spat at her.

With pursed lips, she aimed and fired without hesitation.

The Constable jumped back as Grayson screamed.

"Don't wail like an infant. I only grazed your arm."

She held the pistol pointed at the floor as she watched him writhe against his confinement.

"Nice performance, by the way. Someone who didn't know you might believe you are wounded."

He jerked back from his captor and rubbed his wounded arm. "I can see I must take a different tack with you."

"Do your worst, I am ready for you, however you come at me."

"I'll incite the cast members to decry your actions all over London. When we're through you'll be called the cruel Yankee who put all these people out of work."

"Jack," she called over her shoulder. "Perhaps you'd like to answer him?"

The lanky stage manager walked up beside her and peered at Grayson from the stage entrance.

"Thanks to Miss Burgess, most of the cast found work in other productions. Those who didn't are being paid a stipend until they are hired elsewhere. No one will go without."

"And I suppose she found you another job as well. Who are you working for, the Dillingham Company, or is it the Westwood Society?"

"Miss Burgess hired me to return to Pennsylvania with her and open a Shakespearean Company in Philadelphia, if it's any of your concern."

"Oh so that's the way of it, is it?" Grayson sneered and looked at her once more. "I see you've taken to dallying with your servants. What a delicious tale I will tell to the ladies of the *Ton*."

Jayne walked to Jack and took his arm. "Caroline is helping Jack so we can be together. Keep your filthy thoughts to yourself."

Grayson attempted to bow. "You are a paragon of virtue, Miss Caroline Burgess. Too bad you were not much of an actress. Certainly you bloomed to some extent under my tutelage. I hope they welcome you on the stage in Philadelphia. It is well known backward Americans have no grasp of the arts."

"I won't be acting any longer. I found once was enough to slake my desire for the notoriety."

"Pardon me, Miss Burgess, but we're finished removing the items." The supervisor leading the process doffed his hat as he spoke to her.

"Thank you. Constable, you needn't confine Mr. Grayson any longer. We are done here."

"As you wish, Ma'am."

"What did your slut of a daughter do to my son?" Lady Afton stood in the open door of Sheridan's study. "Where is he? I demand to know."

He looked up at her, never rising from his chair. *It may be proper etiquette to stand for a lady, but I'll be damned if I'll stand for her, especially with my leg aching.*

"I don't know what you're talking about. Lisette returned home to us weeks ago. I assure you, she wants nothing more to do with your son or your family."

"Where is Everett? I will not brook your nonsense."

He put down the quill and sanded his signature on the document before him. "I don't know where your whelp is. Frankly, it's best for him if I don't. If I see him again, I'll be forced to kill him. If I fail, my son Drake will take the responsibility. You bore a monster, madam. He will face divine justice one of these days should he escape ours."

"I don't care what you think of him. What did you do to him?"

Sheridan sighed, looking at the hysterical woman. "None of us have seen him since the day after he eloped with Lisette. When she returned to us, she was alone. We have begun proceedings to have the marriage dissolved by Parliament."

"By all means, break them apart, but the money remains in my family."

"You're welcome to your blood money." Celeste stepped around their visitor and moved to stand beside her husband. "It was the reason my father and grandfather died. We never wanted the inheritance." She looked at Sheridan. "We had no need of the cursed fortune."

Lady Afton waved an impatient hand and stepped toward the door. "I demand to speak to your daughter. Let her tell me what she knows."

Celeste blocked her way. "She knows nothing more than we told you. I won't let you upset her."

For a moment, Sheridan thought Lady Afton would strike his wife, but she appeared to think better of it, as she backed away.

"Why don't you tell me why you think your son is missing?"

Lady Afton wrung her hands and she paced in agitation. "I heard nothing more from him after he wrote me he received the full inheritance. I sent a communiqué via our Embassy last week to his hotel. The response came back saying they checked out days earlier and left no forwarding address." She stared at Sheridan, accusation in her eyes. "They reported Lady Afton returned in time to journey with him to his next destination."

"Whoever the woman was, she was not Lisette." Celeste's voice was quiet. "She rarely leaves the house these days and does not go out in society."

"What can I do?" Lady Afton wailed and crumpled into the nearest chair. "I don't possess the means to travel to Austria. We need the money to keep our home."

Celeste looked at Sheridan, her eyes beseeching.

He frowned and shook his head. *Surely, she cannot expect me to help this woman.*

"With the expected procedure before Parliament we might need to be able to contact Lord Afton. Isn't he allowed to testify?" Celeste stared at her husband.

He rose and leaned on his desk, sighing in the process. "Yes, it would be good for us to locate him in case we must contact him. I can ask the Austrian attaché to investigate for us."

Lady Afton raised her head. "You would do that for me?"

"Make no mistake; we will do it to help our daughter's case."

"Thank you, I know my son is troubled, but he is my only child. Please let me know what you find."

Sheridan nodded to her. "Weston." His voice echoed in the hall. "Please escort Lady Afton to her carriage."

"Of course, my lord." The butler entered and bowed before their visitor, "If you will please accompany me, my lady."

With a nod and a sniff, she left on his arm.

Celeste watched them disappear down the corridor and turned back to her husband. "What do you suppose really happened to him?"

"I think he left with his current mistress. They're probably in Paris or Rome living in opulence at the expense of our daughter."

Chapter Thirty-Three

"Here you are at last." William walked to greet Caroline as she stepped out of her carriage. "I worried he would cause problems for you."

"Grayson tried." She took his arm and they walked toward the water. "But he didn't do anything I could not handle."

"Did you take back everything as you planned?"

"Oh yes, and all I had to do was shoot him."

He dropped her arm. "You did what?"

She grinned as she picked up a stone.

"Don't worry, he was only grazed. He didn't even bleed, well not much anyway." She tossed the stone and watched it skip across the water.

He shook his head as he grinned. "You're a heartless woman, even for an American."

"Watch it." She handed a stone to him. "You know I go about armed now."

"I'm not afraid of rocks." He tossed it over the water and watched it skip seven times.

"How do you manage to make it skip so many times? You never miss."

"I tried to improve your technique."

She shrugged. "I suppose I am secure knowing my pistols are always with me."

His mouth dropped open. "Don't tell me you've got them with you now?"

Caroline withdrew matching pistols, one from each of her two pockets. "What do you think?" She pointed them into the air.

"I think Grayson is lucky you only grazed him."

"I'm too good a shot to make a mistake."

"Prove it." William smiled at her. "Show me how good you are."

"All right, toss another stone over the water on my count, one, two,

139

and three."

He threw the rock over the water.

With one fluid motion, she raised the pistol in her right hand and shot. The bullet struck the stone and split it into pieces.

His mouth hanging open in awe, he turned to look at her. "You are an amazing woman. I thought Mimi's sister-in-law was a prime example of a strong American woman, but you make her look like a fragile flower."

"I can take care of myself. You want to see me shoot with my left hand?"

Father Johann wiped his hands as he walked into the church.

I need to get one of the younger men in the congregation to help me with burials.

As he entered the sanctuary, he saw a police officer waiting. "May I help you?"

"Yes, are you Father Johann?" The young man's eyes swept over him as if looking for clues.

"I am. Is there something you need?"

"I am Officer Weiss. I'm investigating the whereabouts of a young English Lord."

"I know of no such person. Why did you come to me?"

"We were told you found a body in the Danube with no identification."

The priest nodded. "Yes, the poor soul was robbed and murdered."

"Why do you say that?"

"The young man wore only his smallclothes. And as to the murder, he had a hole in the back of his head where someone struck him."

"There was no identifying information, say, a ring or some article of clothing?"

"I told you, there was nothing."

The police officer peered at him once more. "Did you rob the corpse, Father?"

His mouth dropped open. "Of course not. I am a servant of God. How dare you suggest I would do something so unholy?"

The officer shrugged. "Sorry, we are required to ask such questions."

"He was dead when I found him. It did not seem he was in the water very long."

"How could you tell?"

Father Johann sighed and spoke with patience. "His body was not swollen from being in the water a long time. Nothing had interfered with the corpse."

"What do you mean by interfered?"

"Nothing had nibbled his fingers or toes or eaten his eyes. Fish are attracted to fresh meat in the water, birds as well."

The police officer looked down, his skin turning a pale green.

"Come." Father Johann guided him to a pew. "Sit and rest for a while."

After the younger man was seated, the priest sat in the pew in front of him. "I have patrolled the riverfront many times looking for the sick, the homeless, and the starving, people I can assist. It wasn't the first body I encountered. You soon learn the signs to tell if a body was in the water a while. I did not mean to upset you."

"Don't mind me, I never heard of such a thing before."

"You haven't been with the police very long, have you?"

He wiped his mouth and looked at the priest. "I joined six months ago. This is the first month I have been allowed to patrol the streets alone."

"Were you born in Vienna?"

"No, I came from Salzburg. My father has a shop there."

Father Johann touched his shoulder. "Come with me to my residence and I'll make us a cup of tea. Then you can tell me about the missing Englishman."

Caroline hovered at the open door. "After Lady Afton's sudden appearance, are you sure you feel up to a visitor?"

Lisette smiled at her. "I'm fine. Nothing Everett Afton does will ever surprise me again. Come in, please, and tell me what you've been doing."

"I took care of Gareth Grayson. He won't meddle with me now."

"How can you be so sure? What did you do?"

William found them giggling like schoolgirls an hour later.

"Whose reputation are you ruining now, ladies?"

"She was telling me about her encounter with the impresario today. I'm glad you took some of his self-importance from him. He deserves to be taken down a bit."

"I don't think he'll plague Caroline from now on." William grinned at his niece. "Did she tell you she shot him?"

"You did not!" She looked at her friend, her eyes astonished. "Don't tell me you fought a duel with him."

"Certainly not, I merely stopped his ranting."

William leaned in to whisper in Lisette's ear. "If she wanted to duel with him, he would flee from London in all haste, possibly never to return. I've seen her shoot. She's quite the champion shot."

Lisette laughed until the tears flowed down her cheeks. "I can see that odious man fleeing from Caroline. It's a long time since I enjoyed an afternoon so much."

"Glad we could be of service, Sprout." William sat beside her, his face solemn. "There is another matter we must discuss."

"I don't like your tone. You're going to speak about something serious now, aren't you?" Her expression, lately so happy, became grave as she watched her uncle in dread. "What did Everett do now?"

"Would you like me to leave you?" Caroline watched them from across the room.

"No, you already know what he is. Please stay. It will save me from repeating the story for you."

Caroline nodded.

"Afton left his hotel in Vienna with a woman pretending to be his wife. No one has heard from him since. I'm sorry, Lisette."

"There's no reason to be sorry. He sampled every tart he could find after he got the gold. I didn't mind. It kept him away from me. I slipped away when he didn't come back to our suite. He's likely taken his current ladylove on an expensive tour of Europe."

William nodded. "I agree with your assessment, as do your parents. It's unlikely he will return to challenge the motion in Parliament."

"Will his absence work for or against us?"

"In this case I don't think his presence is necessary. His mother was told he left with his *wife*. She is aware you haven't left London since you came back. It's obvious he's parading someone else as the wife."

"Whoever she may be, I pity her. He'll soon tire of her and use his fists on her." Lisette looked down at her hands folded in her lap, her voice choking. "Maybe she isn't a starry-eyed fool like I was . . . ."

"You weren't ever a fool." William put his arm around her. "He tricked you, the fault was his."

"I should have seen what he is." Gulping sobs interfered with her words.

William looked up at Caroline, his eyes pleading for her help.

"Here." She took his place. "Lisette, we all make mistakes when we are young. None of us know the dangers out there before us until we've experienced them." She hugged the younger woman. "You were fortunate to grow up in a loving family. Not everyone gets to experience a family's love."

"What do you mean?" She raised her tear-streaked face.

"With your background and your family's support, you are a strong woman. You can face anything and get past it. You are a survivor."

"Ha, some survivor. I can't even stop whimpering."

Caroline hugged her and then pulled back. "You were wounded in the worst way. You may not realize it, but you've already progressed well in your healing."

"If you say so." Lisette's tone plainly held her disbelief.

"I do say so. We need to get you out of this room, out of this house, and not just to the park. What do you say to a carriage ride tomorrow afternoon ending at one of the fashionable tea shops? It's a good outing to begin your return to public life."

Lisette squirmed a bit. "I don't know if I can. What shall I say to people?"

"Tell them the matter is being settled now if they're rude enough to ask."

"They'll ask, all right. You have no idea how cruel these people can be."

Caroline paused and looked her in the eye, "Don't I?"

Lisette's mouth dropped open. "I'm sorry I was awful to you. I was such a brat. How can you stand to be around me?"

"I was innocent once. My work at the settlement house gave me knowledge you didn't have. I know what the inner turmoil is like. When we grow, we can look back and see where our lack of experience caused problems. Come now, what say you? Shall we have an outing tomorrow?"

Lisette managed a weak smile. "Very well, with you beside me I can face anything."

"I shall accompany you both." William spoke in an unctuous manner. "With my escort, no one will dare say anything improper to you out of fear of my wrath."

Lisette cocked her head and looked at William. "They'll be much more frightened of Caroline if Grayson has told of her prowess with her guns."

Chapter Thirty-Four
Vienna

A crowd of police officers watched with interest as the coffin was raised from the grave.

"How will you be able to tell if he is Lord Afton?" Father Johann stood with them.

"His mother sent a miniature portrait of her son. We should be able to tell if it is or is not Lord Afton."

The men dragged the coffin to a patch of ground beside the open grave. Father Johann pried the lid off, grimacing at the smell of the stale air released.

"Let me see." Weiss pushed his way through the curious officers. "I've got the miniature, let me see."

"What do you think?" The priest looked at the face of the corpse. "Is he like the painting? Does he look like Lord Afton?"

The young officer held a handkerchief over his nose and glanced from the miniature to the body.

He nodded and gasped, "It's him. The hair matches, as does the mole on his left cheek. He looks like the portrait."

Father Johann shook his head. "What could such a fine young lord have done to deserve such treatment? Will you be able to find his killer?"

"We'll gather the clues but if it was a random killing of a wealthy man for his purse, we may never find the murderer." He sniffed and put away the handkerchief. "Let's get the lid back on the coffin. Lord Afton will be sent home to his family, at the request of his mother."

The priest made the sign of the cross. "He will rest better surrounded by his family."

Lisette relaxed and sipped her tea.

145

Caroline smiled at her. "Are you enjoying our outing today?"

"Yes, I am. I never realized how even a sanctuary could become so confining. It's wonderful to be here and enjoy a pleasant afternoon."

"Why Lisette Afton, I did not expect to see you here. Aren't you supposed to be in seclusion? And yet here you are." The dark-haired beauty smiled in a superior fashion. "Everyone is talking of little else since you and Afton eloped. Then of course, you came back without him. It's the biggest *on dit* of the year." She pulled out the vacant chair and sat with no invitation.

"Caroline." Lisette's voice was soft, "Have you met Lady Felicity Smythe?"

"Yes, I believe so. I hope you are well, Lady Felicity."

"Well, isn't this delicious? The two biggest scandals in London are here together in the Rose Tea Shop." She leaned forward, her eyes avid. "You must tell me everything. I want to get it all straight before I share your stories."

Lisette bit her lip and looked away.

Caroline faced their opponent. "Lady Felicity, I once believed the English aristocracy to be superior to the rest of us. Upon the acquaintance of people such as you, my opinion of the lot of you diminished . . . significantly."

"How dare you, a low foreign commoner, speak to me in such a manner? Lisette, you cannot countenance such behavior. It is not done."

She took a deep breath and faced their nemesis. "Felicity, I share Miss Burgess' opinion of people like you. Is your own life so empty you live vicariously through the troubled lives of others?"

The outraged aristocrat rose to her feet. "You made a serious mistake addressing me in such a manner. I shall see to it your reputation is lower than this daughter of a laborer, a woman turned actress. You'll never be received anywhere again when I'm through with you." She turned to walk away.

"You'd best include me in your discussions." William had entered the shop during her tirade. "I must apologize for being detained by business concerns." He nodded to Lisette and Caroline.

"Baron Hargreaves, surely you as an arbiter of taste and fashion, do not agree with your niece and this common actress?"

"You would be astonished how my tastes changed in the recent weeks. Please leave us now and return to your friends. There is nothing of interest for you at our table." He remained standing until the woman stalked away. Then he sat in the vacated chair.

"Uncle William, I am so proud of you. What made you change your mind?"

"I'm proud of you, too. You handled the virago well." He took Lisette's hand, giving it a gentle squeeze. "You were wonderful." He turned to Caroline. "You were excellent in the way you dealt with the lady."

She smiled and started to speak.

He stopped her with a teasing grin. "You're not carrying your pistols, are you? Can you imagine what she would have said if she knew?"

Excerpt from the *London Standard*—column of *Jolie Madame*:

My friends, I have news of a delicious scandal brewing. While taking tea in a certain floral-scented shop, who did I see? Only a pair of unlikely friends, each with tarnished reputations. I was amazed to see them out in public together. One is a wealthy heiress from across the sea, her bloodline tainted with coal dust and a penchant for the theater. And who is her bosom friend? Why none other than the Viscount's daughter, whose own grandfather was the biggest disgrace of his day. It seems the young matron of the Ton has abandoned the husband with whom she eloped last month. Why is she spending time in such unsavory company now? I am determined to learn the truth of this strange relationship and report it all to you, my faithful readers. Ever yours . . . .

"Caroline, may I speak to you for a moment?" Jayne stood in the doorway, her expression solemn.

"Of course, you don't need to ask, come in and sit down. I'm finishing the letter to the Dillingham Company, presenting the scenery pieces and props to them."

"I don't want to interrupt you, I could come back."

"Nonsense. Let me sign the letter and I'll be free. There, it's done." She folded the paper and affixed the wax seal. "Business concluded, now what I can I do for you?"

Jayne took a deep breath. "I brought something to show you." She held out a newspaper.

Caroline frowned and took the paper. "What is it? Why do you look so somber?"

"Read the article on top of the page."

After reading the short passage, she threw back her head and laughed in a delighted fashion. "Don't let this folderol upset you. I've seen worse written about me. My work in Philadelphia doesn't win me many friends."

"Will Miss Lisette laugh about it as well?"

"You're right, of course, she won't find this amusing. Bless her, I'd best call on her and hope she hasn't seen it. Thank you, Jayne. I'm glad you brought this to me. Do you think many people will read this?"

"Many of the servants and more of the aristocrats, I suppose. It is the most popular column in London."

"Then I'd better hurry."

Chapter Thirty-Five
Brenham House

"Are you sure it's Afton?" Sheridan stood supported by his cane, his face stern.

"Yes, Sir, we are." The Runner looked down. "I thought you should know when we caught wind of it, I came straight to you, seeing as how it concerns your daughter."

"Has his mother been informed?"

"From what I was told, yes, she knows. She expected the body to arrive. Arrangements have been made to bury him in Abney Park."

Sheridan sighed and shook his head. "Do you know anything about the way he died?"

"According to the Police in Vienna he was murdered."

"I cannot say I'm surprised with the life he led. Something was bound to happen to him."

William frowned as he looked at the messenger. "Why bury him in Abney Park, why not their estate in Devonshire?"

"I couldn't say, Sir. I've told you all I know."

"Thank you for coming." Sheridan nodded to him. "I appreciate hearing the news from you. Weston will see you to the door."

"Who do you suppose killed him? A robber, or a jealous husband?" William looked to his brother-in-law when they were alone.

"Who knows, it could have been either or someone else entirely."

"Drake threatened him. It's a good thing he's at sea or he might be suspected."

"I'm thankful my son has an alibi. He's in Norfolk by now, visiting his aunt and her family. Thank heavens for his travel manifest." Sheridan started forward. "Come along, we'd best find Celeste so we can tell Lisette together."

"I doubt she'll grieve over her husband." William followed him down the corridor. "At least she will be spared the ordeal of appearing before Parliament and discussing the details of her marriage."

They found Celeste sitting in her sunlit morning room, gazing at her gardens beyond the windows.

"What a welcome surprise." She smiled up at them from her wing chair, a piece of untouched embroidery in her lap. She reached up to caress her husband's cheek as he leaned over to kiss her. "To what do I owe the pleasure of this visit?"

"News has come of Afton."

"Has he married yet another young lady?"

"No, I'm afraid this is serious. He's dead. He was murdered in Vienna."

"Oh, no." She stood and moved to her husband. "How will we tell our daughter?"

"Tell me what?" Lisette's voice came from the open doorway.

At the same moment, Caroline stepped aside for the Runner leaving Brenham House. *I wonder what's happened.* She turned to see Weston standing in the doorway.

"Good afternoon, Miss Burgess, I trust you are well today."

"I am, Weston, thank you. Is Lady Afton at home?"

He glanced behind him, his teeth worrying his lip. "I do not know if she is receiving. Please step inside and I will inquire."

Something is wrong. I've never seen him so rattled. I hope Lisette is all right. Strong footsteps drew her attention to the corridor. William strode toward her, his face stoic.

"Caroline." He kissed her cheek, "We're in a bit of an uproar. We were just now informed Afton was murdered in Vienna. Lisette is quite undone." He looked at her for a moment. "You're precisely the person she needs to see. Are you up for it?"

"Of course. Take me to her, I'll talk to her."

As they neared the back of the house, the sound of sobbing echoed.

William opened the door to the morning room and allowed Caroline to precede him.

"He's dead and it's my fault." Lisette cried in her mother's arms. "He might still be alive if I hadn't left him."

"Nonsense." Caroline's voice was clear in the small room. "If you stayed, you might be dead now, too." She moved to Lisette and knelt beside her. "This has nothing to do with you. His lifestyle no doubt killed him. You said he was always drinking, tossing his coins about, dallying with women of the street." She hugged her friend. "What better way to attract attention to his wealth?"

Lisette sniffled and wiped her tears. "Do you really think he was killed for his money?"

"Yes, or else he met with the wrong woman. One way or the other, his behavior caused his ruin." She rose to her feet. "He put himself in danger by his rash actions."

"I don't know how you can still care about the blighter." William's face turned red as he shouted at his niece. "His death is convenient. Now you are widowed with no need to end your marriage."

Caroline put her palm up to him. "None of us control who we love. And when the relationship ends, we cannot turn off our feelings as it they never happened."

"I, uh, I didn't mean to say . . . ." William looked away.

She touched his hand. "Perhaps it would be best if I could speak to Lisette alone." She looked at Celeste and Sheridan, "Would it be acceptable to you?"

"Yes, please." Celeste nodded. "I trust your judgment."

"Shall we leave you two in here?" Sheridan spoke in a soft voice.

"I thought perhaps we could go out and sit in the rose garden. Is that all right, Lisette?"

She nodded as she twisted her handkerchief in her shaking hands.

"Come along, then, let's go out in the fresh air." Caroline took her hand and led her out of the room.

Sheridan watched them go. "I hope she can help our daughter."

"She will." Celeste stood beside him, her hand on his arm. "She's an intelligent young woman, surprising in her maturity."

"I think William makes sense. Afton's death is the best thing to happen to our daughter since she met him."

Chapter Thirty-Six
The Hag's Head

Grayson sighed and raised his empty tankard. "Give me another," he demanded, his words slurring.

"Look, friend, you don't need another one. How are you going to walk out of here? You can't even stand." The burly barkeep shook his head at his frequent customer. "Unless you want to sleep on the floor, I'll get someone to take you home."

The drunken impresario shook his head in sloppy motion. "Need another tankard, then I'll go after the bitch that ruined me."

"Look Mr. Grayson, you're in no position to get your revenge now. You'd best sleep it off tonight. Tomorrow you'll be better able to follow your plans."

"You don't understand. She stole everything from me and then she shot me. I need to take her down."

The pub owner looked at him, his brawny arms folded over his chest. "You don't look wounded to me."

"Well, I *am* wounded." He pushed up his sleeve. "Look at that and tell me I'm not wounded."

The big man peered closely at the elbow before him. "I don't see anything. If she shot at you, she must have missed."

"She did not miss. I got the wound to prove it."

"Where is it then?"

Grayson sat with his brow furrowed. He looked at the man behind the bar. "It's on my other arm." He pushed up the other sleeve and held out the arm for inspection.

"Well, now that you mention it, I do see a mark there, more like a burn than a bullet hole, though."

"I tell you she shot me, stupid American witch. She scarred me for life."

"A pity she shot you and left the mark." He winked at the other patrons. "Now I suppose you'll never bare your elbows in public." His laugh rumbled deep from his massive chest.

"Maybe you could put some greasepaint on your *e-nor-mous* scar when you have to wear one of those bed sheets to play that old Roman king, Julius somebody-or-other."

Merry laughter sounded from the bar and then the tables.

Grayson put his hands over his ears. "Stop it. I can't think."

His words were drowned in the comments and laughter still bounding around the establishment. "Stop it!"

His comment caused more merriment.

"To hell with the lot of you. Peasants never understand the workings of the artistic temperament." He rolled off the stool and lurched while attempting to toss his cape around his shoulders. The impresario grimaced when the ends of the cape slapped his face. "I'll get my revenge, see if I don't."

"Sure ya will, ya lily-livered twit!"

He lumbered out the door as the sounds of hilarity followed him down the street.

"Are you sure you want to do this?" Celeste held her daughter's hand.

"He was my husband. It doesn't matter that he was cruel to me. I need to attend his funeral."

Sheridan looked out the window of the barouche. "Quite a crowd is gathered."

"Most people only saw his charming side, a true *bon vivant* of the *Ton.*" Lisette's tone was bitter. "Very few people knew him for what he really was."

William fidgeted on the seat. "Was Caroline occupied this morning?"

"No, she wanted to come, but I told her not to. She is one of the few people who saw Everett's actual character." Lisette daubed her eyes with a lace-trimmed handkerchief. *I see no reason for my friend to suffer through this charade.* She smoothed her dark blue dress with her gloved hands.

"People will wonder why you're not dressed in mourning."

"Let them wonder, Uncle William. You are the authority on proper behavior, the worst critic of all. Do you think I should pretend to be a grieving widow?"

"Absolutely not, after what he did to you, but other people will talk."

"I don't care what people say. This is my final duty to my late husband. I will perform it and never speak of him again. What others think or say is up to them." She put her hand on the door just as the footman opened it. "They appear to be starting the rite."

Sheridan stopped her with his hand on her arm. "Let me alight first and then your mother. We can shield you."

"And it will look like you're trying to do exactly that. It will make me look guilty." She shook off his hand and took the offered hand of the footman as she emerged from the vehicle.

She stood aside and waited for the rest of her family. People were making their way to the gravesite. Several saw her standing beside the barouche. Instead of waving to her or acknowledging her presence, they began talking to each other. A constant murmuring wafted back to her on the breeze. Heads turned around to look at the object of their gossip.

Sheridan took Celeste's arm and followed the crowd. William offered his arm to Lisette. They reached the grave just as the vicar began to speak. She sighed and shut out his droning voice.

This is my last duty to you, Everett. I wish you peace, though I doubt you will know any.

As the coffin was lowered into the ground, Lady Afton began to scream. "They took my son. How could they take my only son?" She turned to look at her daughter-in-law. "I know you arranged for his murder. You were very clever, or so you thought. You hired someone to do it, didn't you? Then you hurried back to London to have an alibi."

Her voice grew in strength and volume. "You killed my Everett, even if you didn't do the deed yourself. Who did you hire? Who killed my boy?"

155

Sheridan shielded his daughter from the crazed woman. "Lady Afton you are in mourning. Now is not the time to . . . ."

"Oh shut up, can't you? Nobody cares what you think." She broke away when the vicar tried to take her arm. "I don't care if you are a Viscount. You're upset because my boy was smart enough to grab the inheritance you were too stupid or lazy to take."

"Enough!" Lisette's voice rang out. "You are the money-grubbing one, desperate to keep your estates from failing. You told me as much yourself."

"How dare you?" She rushed her daughter-in-law with her claws extended.

Celeste jumped in front of her daughter. "Lady Afton, you will regret this scene later. Please stop."

The crowd encircled them like an avid horde watching gladiators battle to the death in ancient Rome. They pressed in until there was little room for the combatants to maintain distance from each other.

"The only thing I regret is encouraging my son to marry your daughter. If I had not he would still be here with us."

"Lady Afton." Celeste's voice held a soothing tone. "Please come back with us to our home where we can speak in private."

"There is nothing to discuss. I know your daughter is responsible for my son's death. I will shout it to the skies until she is arrested and executed for her perfidy."

Celeste's face paled at the thought of her daughter's execution. William reached for her and steadied her with his arm.

"It's all right, CeCe." His whisper went unheard by the others. "Your daughter will never die like Papa did. There is no evidence to support this woman's claims."

Lisette stepped forward to Lady Afton. "I'm sorry your son died, even though he was a monster. I did not arrange for anything to happen to him. Instead, I fled from him for my own safety. You know well what he did to me in your own home."

The older woman swung and slapped Lisette with a vicious hand.

"He did nothing unwarranted to you. You were a miserable bride. I heard you complaining to him on your wedding night. No wonder he was forced to discipline you."

"You call it discipline, I call it cruelty. You know he beat me."

"You deserved it, every blow. What kind of wife were you? Look at you appearing at your own husband's funeral in a blue dress. Where are your mourning garments? Where is your veil? You heartless jade, you never cared for my son."

It's no use. She will never accept her son's true nature. Lisette looked at the faces in the surrounding mob. Many of the women whispered and watched her, while the men stared at her with no sympathy in their expressions.

At last, the vicar elbowed his way through the throng.

"Lady Afton, it is time for you to rest. This experience is too much for you, beset as you are by your grief. Come along with me." He called back over his shoulder as he gently led her away. "The rest of you disperse. There is nothing else to be seen here. Give the deceased's family some respect."

The people went toward their carriages. Occasional comments stirred throughout the exodus.

"I always said Lisette St John is a proud one who will come to no good."

"Did you see her when Lady Afton questioned the dress she wore? And it was most inappropriate. She is the most uncaring female I ever met."

"No one will associate with her now. She is utterly ruined."

The tears trickled down Lisette's cheeks as she stood in stunned silence. *None of this is my fault. I am the victim, aren't I? Why don't they see it?*

"Come along." Sheridan's strong arm enfolded her waist. "Let's go home now." He leaned down to kiss her cheek as they walked. "This talk will fade away when the next person is targeted."

"I love you, Papa." She sniffled as they neared the barouche.

Excerpt from the *London Standard*—column of *Jolie Madame*:

More delectable news for you, my dears. A certain recently widowed lady appeared at her husband's funeral in a gown of blue. It seems the Viscount's daughter held her late husband in little regard despite his good nature and many friends among the Ton. Rumors are flying in which she is said to be responsible for Lord A's unfortunate murder. She says she was in London when he was killed in Vienna. But could the Scheming Widow have hired someone to do it and never soil her dainty hands? So much easier than a dissolution of the marriage! One quick blow and you are free, no muss, no fuss, and no witnesses . . . .

Chapter Thirty-Seven
Foster Shipping

"As it happens, Miss Burgess, the *American Eagle* is due back in three weeks. Captain St John will be sailing for the United States two weeks after he arrives."

"Will he sail to Philadelphia?" Caroline drummed her fingers on the man's desk. *I am more than ready to go home.*

"Yes, it is on the schedule. He's due to dock in Philadelphia and then sail on to Norfolk, our home office."

She nodded. "Good, my plans will fit with the schedule. I'd like to reserve accommodations for three, separate cabins if you have them."

"I am certain we can fit your needs. The *American Eagle* as a steamship carries more passengers than the old sailing ships ever could."

"Excellent, when the ship returns and you have the exact date of departure, please send our tickets to my residence."

He bowed to her as she stood. "We will be pleased to be of service, Miss Burgess."

She smiled and began to walk toward the door but slowed as the man spoke again.

"May I say, Miss Burgess, how very much I enjoyed your performance in *Romeo & Juliet*?"

"Thank you for your kindness." She smiled at him once more and hastened out into the street. *At least at home, no one has seen the dratted play.*

She approached her coach, shaking her head.

"Hello, Caroline." The voice was familiar and unwelcome.

She turned to see Grayson, who looked the part of the *Impresario,* walking up behind her. "Gareth, I didn't expect to see you."

He looked down for a moment and fiddled with his lace cuffs, as if ashamed. "I was pretty upset with you, wasn't I? I should never expect you to fall to my tricks. You're too intelligent for such tomfoolery."

Her brows drew together. *What does he want now? Surely he's not trying to trick me once more.*

Grayson sidled closer to her. "There's no need to look like a thundercloud. I won't bite, you know."

She stood and looked at him, one eyebrow raised. "Won't you?"

"You made your point to me when you shot me. By the way, you don't have your gun with you now, do you?"

"No, I don't have my gun." *I have my matched set of pistols, you dolt. Do you think I'd walk around unarmed as long as I am within your reach?"*

"I'm relieved." His smile was charming as he linked his arm with hers and led them down the road away from her coach.

"What do you think you are doing?" She stopped and refused to budge.

"Come now." His ingratiating smile made her cringe. "Don't act that way. I only want to talk to you, to apologize."

"You can tell me you're sorry right here. I don't want to go anywhere with you."

"Caroline, I'm wounded once more if you won't accept my word not to harm you." His unctuous tone slithered over her skin. "It's not my intention to hurt you."

"Good, then a nice cup of tea will do the trick."

He pointed down the street. "We will go to the tea shop on the corner. It's within sight of your coach."

I shouldn't trust him, but I'd like a cup of tea. "Very well, I'll instruct my driver to move down to the tea shop."

Soon they settled at a table by the window in the posh little shop.

"I've never been here before." She looked around at the elegant décor.

"It is one of my favorites. All the best people come here." He turned to order for them both.

I wonder they let you in. And who told you to order for me? She sighed. It wasn't important enough to make a fuss about. *Besides, if we argue I'll be delayed here longer with him.*

The waitress poured two steaming cups of tea and brought slices of rich cake, plump with currents. The tantalizing aromas surrounded them.

"Everything smells wonderful." Caroline sniffed her tea in appreciation.

"So are you planning your trip back to America?"

"How did you know?"

He shrugged. "It was simple to deduce when I found you outside the shipping office.

She sipped her tea. *Be careful how you speak to him. He looks nervous, edgy. You don't want to set him off on a tirade.* "I need to return to my responsibilities at home."

"Ah yes, your work at the settlement house, isn't it? You must save all those poor weak females from vicious men."

Something dark overtook his expression.

I'm not touching that statement. He'll ignite for sure. She nibbled her piece of cake. *He's trying to goad me into a fight in public. I wonder why? What will he gain?*

"Do you like the cake?" His voice was soft as he focused on her.

"Yes." She smiled. "It's excellent. Thank you for ordering it." *His eyes look feverish. I best be on my guard.*

She slipped her hand into her right pocket, reassured to feel her pistol.

"So you keep your gun in your right pocket. I wondered where it was." He wore a triumphant smile.

"Don't worry about my gun. You won't see it today." She tossed down her napkin and rose to leave. "Thank you for the tea. I must be going."

He looked down as if embarrassed and back up to her with a sly expression. "I'm afraid I am without funds at the moment."

"No matter." She opened her reticule. "I don't mind paying." She dropped the money on the table.

"Don't you? Isn't it admirable of the wealthiest woman in London to spread her largesse to include a poor theater director?" His voice ringing through the shop, he stood and bowed with a flourish. "I thank you for the tea and cake."

The other patrons stopped their own conversations to observe the display.

He's planning something. I remember this expression. He looks insane. It's time for me to leave.

"Yes, we enjoyed an interesting afternoon. If I don't see you again before I leave, I wish you well." She nodded to him and hurried out the door.

"Not so fast, you scheming hussy, I want a word with you." He stood in the doorway, his voice echoing in the street.

Oh good, now he's playing to the balcony. Couldn't you speak any louder? I doubt they can hear you in Buckingham Palace.

"There is nothing left for me to say." She turned to walk to her coach.

"Well, I'm not done yet, and you will listen." Without warning, he rushed to her, grabbed her and pulled her gun from her right pocket.

"Ha! Now I've got you where I want you."

He pushed her away as hard as he could and brandished her pistol.

She stumbled but regained her balance. "Is this how you treat a lady on the street?"

"You are no lady. You are lower than the worst harlot walking the docks. It's time the good people of London know you as you are."

She glanced behind him to see the patrons of the teashop lining the windows staring in open-mouthed attention at the scene before them.

"Gareth, is this necessary? I know you're angry but you signed a contract. I was well within my right to take back everything you purchased with my money. It's a matter of business, nothing else."

"You call our nights together a matter of 'business'? How could you feel nothing? You acted like you enjoyed our nights." He screamed the words at her, the pistol shaking in his unsteady hand.

"We had no nights together, at least not in the way you imply. Our time was spent rehearsing or performing, nothing more."

"You performed all right, after I taught you to please me. Deny it, if you can."

He's drooling and red-faced. I must tread carefully. "We performed a play, and not in the manner you suggest." She kept her voice low.

"You denied me everything, ruined me, and now you refuse to acknowledge our love?" He screeched to the skies.

"Gareth," she began, "please calm down."

"I won't calm down. You have destroyed all that I am. You deserve to die for my pain."

He pointed the gun at her.

She slipped her hand into her left pocket and withdrew her other pistol, holding it at her side. "I didn't lie when I said I didn't have my gun. I carry both my guns. Now lower your weapon. I don't want to hurt you."

"You're through hurting me."

"I'm a champion shot. I won't miss if I fire at you."

She slid her finger on the trigger. *I don't want to shoot him, but I will if I must.*

"Then we'll die together, like Romeo and Juliet in view of our enthralled audience."

With a triumphant laugh steeped in madness, he raised the gun and blew her a kiss. "Thus with a kiss YOU die!" He fired the pistol.

Caroline returned his fire as soon as he shot. A burning force knocked her backward to the ground. Scalding pain filled her right shoulder. Time stopped and the world tilted. She opened her eyes to the worried face of her driver.

"Miss Burgess, you're injured." He picked her up in his arms. "Let's get you in the coach. You need a doctor."

Shaking her head, she heard screams. *Why are those women screaming?*

"What happened to Gareth?" She turned to look.

Grayson lay unmoving on the street. A crowd of people stared down at him.

"I think he's dead, Ma'am." He put her into the vehicle. "Here take my coat. You're bleeding. Hold it on the wound."

A man knelt down to Grayson. "He's dead, all right. Whatever possessed him to shoot at a woman?"

"He acted crazy, screaming at her like he did."

"Poor thing." One woman shook her head. "Even if she is an actress, she doesn't deserve to be shot at by a maniac."

"Indeed no," replied her companion. "She said she was a champion shot. She was correct, unlucky for him. He caused his own death by firing first."

"He shot first. I saw it clearly."

A constable walked up to the group. "Are you certain?"

"Yes." The workman nodded. "He shot at her and she returned the fire."

"What about the rest of you? Is that what you saw?"

"Oh yes . . . ."

The voices became muffled in the darkness as it smothered her.

I didn't want to kill him . . . I didn't want . . . .

The black cloud engulfed her, snuffing out everything, her thoughts, the sounds, and her remaining sensibility.

Chapter Thirty-Eight
Brenham House

"What the devil is that pounding?" Sheridan tossed down his spectacles and looked up from his paper-strewn desk. "Why doesn't Weston answer the door?"

The pounding stopped. He sighed and picked up his spectacles to return to his reading.

Footsteps ran down the corridor, followed by Weston's harried face peering around his open door. "I'm sorry, my lord. There is a messenger here for Miss Lisette and Baron Hargreaves. He brings grave news for them."

"Bring the messenger to me and find them." *Good Lord, I hope it's nothing else about Afton.*

"You may come in." Weston nodded to his employer and hurried out of sight.

The lanky man stood, hat in hand, panting with exertion.

"Come in, it is all right."

He ducked his head. "Thank you, milord," he gasped.

"Sit down, man, before you fall down. Now, what's this all about?"

He gulped. "Miss Burgess was shot."

"Is she alive?" William's voice choked as he rushed into the study, Lisette close behind him.

"What do you mean, who shot her?" Lisette's face lost all its color.

"Yes, she's wounded but alive. The physician was there when I left. Grayson shot her."

"Is he in custody?" William's tone surged with menace. *How dare he hurt her? I will see him punished for this. If I lose her, I will see him hang.*

"No, milord, he's dead."

Don't tell me . . . .

"He shot Miss Burgess and she shot back, killing him on the spot."

Lisette dropped into a chair, her mouth open in shock. "How serious is her wound? Will she recover?"

Jack turned his hat in his hands. "He shot her in the shoulder. She's lost a lot of blood. I'm not sure of her chances."

"Sheridan, you've been in battle, could a wound like that threaten her life?"

He looked at William. "It's hard to say. If she got medical attention soon enough, I'd say she has a good chance."

Lisette jumped up. "I'm going to her. Where is she?"

"They took her home, Ma'am."

"Good." She started to leave.

"Do you think it's a good idea for you to go see her now? Perhaps it would be better to wait."

"Father, she's my friend. She's helped me through hell. It is my job to guide her through it now."

"I'll take her." William led her out of the room.

Sheridan looked at the messenger. "Please tell Mr. Burgess if he needs anything I am ready to oblige him."

Jack nodded. "Thank you, milord." He followed the others out of the study.

At Burgess House, Horace stood in the hallway with Dr. Matthews. "Is her condition dangerous?"

The physician cleaned his pince-nez and replaced them on the bridge of his nose before speaking. "If she does not develop a fever within the next twenty-four hours she should heal in a matter of weeks."

Horace nodded. "She is planning to return to America later next month. Is there any reason to delay her voyage?"

"No, as long as there are no complications." He looked at the father, his brow drawn down in confusion. "I say, is your daughter prone to such dangerous folly as shooting men in the streets?"

"If you're asking if she's ever killed anyone before, she has not. I'm proud to say my daughter is a strong, independent woman quite capable of facing any trouble to come her way."

The doctor gazed at the huge man before him. "If that is something you value, you seem to have the daughter you wish. You should know, however, she has gone well beyond the boundaries of proper behavior here in England. First there was the unfortunate escapade onstage and now she has murdered a man in daylight on the street for all to see." He adjusted his coat and put on his stovepipe hat. "She won't be received by the aristocrats now, even with her fortune. Pity, really, for her to be ruined in such a way. She's gone well beyond high spirited pranks and become notorious. She'll never find a decent husband." He sniffed and wiped imaginary lint from his coat. "Good day to you."

"If the sons of the aristocrats here are too weak and foolish to appreciate my Caroline, it's fine with me. I'd never give my permission for such a marriage, anyway. They are not good enough for my girl." Horace narrowed his eyes and raised his voice. "Keep your petty judgments to yourself. Send me your bill like the common tradesman you are. Good day to you, little pipsqueak. Get out of my house."

He kicked in the direction of the frightened man, encouraging him to leave.

The doctor ran out the front door and down the steps, missing a collision with Baron Hargreaves in his haste.

"Your pardon, Sir, Madame." He never faltered in his pace, yet managed to tip his hat.

"What was wrong with him?" Lisette watched him scurry away.

"I told him what I thought of his prognosis." Horace stood at the front door. "Please, come in."

"That was the doctor? What did he say? Is Caroline in danger?" Lisette ran up the steps.

Standing aside to allow them to enter, Horace's voice quieted. "She's in greatest danger of being judged by your peers and found wanting." He extended his hand, "She's awake. I'm sure she'd like to see you. As members of the *Ton*, are you certain you won't risk your own reputation by meeting with the notorious murderer?" His lopsided smile belied his words.

Lisette laughed. "Haven't you heard? I'm known as the *Scheming Widow*. My reputation is already shattered. Who cares what anybody else thinks?" She moved to follow him. As she walked down the corridor, she turned back.

"Uncle William, aren't you coming?"

Startled as if deep in thought, he glanced at her, "Yes, of course, I'm right behind you."

Excerpt from the *London Standard*—column of *Jolie Madame*:

My dears, while everyone agrees, the Impresario was a mad dog who certainly overstayed his welcome in our midst, the cruel manner of his execution was not deserved. Some say the notorious American engineered the circumstance so she could kill him. What kind of woman, much less lady, would do such a thing? This brazen daughter of a coal miner is said to be recuperating at the elegant home purchased by her father. Rumor has it she returns to America soon. I say well done, Miss B. We do not need the likes of you in our exalted company. You're liable to give our young ladies the idea any behavior is acceptable, when all arbiters of taste firmly tell us it is not. So this is farewell to the rude incorrigible Yankee. You will not be welcome in stately England again. Go back to the city of Philadelphia where a group of filthy revolutionaries created the most grievous act of sedition against their betters—the revolution against their Sovereign.

Oh, and in my estimation, Miss B was, at best, mediocre in the role of Juliet . . . .

Chapter Thirty-Nine

"Didn't William come with you?" Caroline looked beyond Lisette as she approached, walking her mare.

"He left earlier. I asked him if he remembered our plans to meet. He never answered, just hurried out the door. I'm sorry. Caroline. I don't know what's wrong with him these days. He always seems lost in thought."

"It doesn't matter, I just . . . I was hoping to challenge him with some stone tossing. Guess I won't need these." She dropped the stones in her hands. Turning to Lisette, her smile too bright, "I'm always glad to see you, at any rate."

"You know Uncle William, he'll come around. He's always stiff and stodgy as if he's afraid to let go. I hoped with you he would learn to stop caring about the good opinion of the aristocracy."

It's probably for the best. I'm sailing next week." Caroline walked away, her head down, tears flowing down her cheeks.

Why should I cry over the pig-headed fool? If he cared about me at all, he wouldn't listen to the opinion of the other aristocrats.

"I'm sorry I didn't mean to make you cry." Lisette touched her friend's shoulder.

"No, you didn't do anything. You certainly did not make me cry. I hoped your uncle was . . . never mind. Obviously I was wrong about him. We seemed to have a growing friendship. But thanks to *Jolie Madame* and her snide innuendoes, he's reserved, distant once more." She shook her head.

"Don't let that cruel woman upset you. Nobody cares what she writes."

"Apparently your uncle does." Caroline wiped her eyes with a dainty handkerchief.

"It's nearly tea time. Why don't you come home with me? I'm sure *Maman* would love to see you."

169

"Won't William be there?"

"I doubt it. He doesn't stay at the house very much these days. Who knows where he is? Besides if he comes home I promise to act as referee. What do you say? We won't have too many opportunities to see each other before you leave."

"If you're certain . . . ."

"It's settled." Lisette walked to her horse. "Let's have your driver tie Genevieve to the back of your carriage and I'll ride home with you."

"Genevieve, what kind of name is that for a mare?"

"A very good French one." Lisette grinned. "Come along, I'm hungry."

Caroline and Lisette were soon seated in the open carriage.

"Look over there, beyond the trees. Are those people watching us?"

"I think so. I wonder why they're so interested." She shrugged. "Hilton, please drive us to Brenham House."

Lisette leaned to whisper to Caroline on the opposite seat. "What kind of name is Hilton for a driver?"

Excerpt from the *London Standard*—column of *Jolie Madame*:

My dears, such scrumptious scandal is brewing. The pistol-packing Wicked Lady met the Scheming Widow privately in Hyde Park. Not knowing they were observed they seemed to be in the middle of a serious conversation. One can only imagine what they discussed . . . .

Rumors are darting about the Ton. *Speculation says the Scheming Widow asked the Wicked Lady for advice in offing Lord A. Can you imagine? Though both were in London at the time he was killed, it is said the Wicked Lady has criminal connections on the continent. We have ample evidence she is willing and eager to kill.*

Suppose they plotted to rid the Scheming Widow of her bothersome husband? Even though the Widow is the daughter of a well-known Viscount, she could be prosecuted for a criminal conspiracy.

Imagine the Widow could be hanged for her part in her poor husband's murder. Her own grandfather was executed as a traitor. It is as

I've always said, blood will tell.

I'll keep delving into the story and share it with you, my loyal readers, in upcoming columns.

The sound of the front door crashing open startled Celeste as she walked to the staircase. Hurrying forward, she found Lady Afton with a tall, dour man.

"What is the meaning of this? How dare you enter our home in such a manner?" Celeste's violet eyes blazed as she faced the older woman.

Lady Afton turned to the man beside her. "Go ahead, do your duty."

The man hesitated. "I'm sorry, is Viscount Brenham at home?"

"No, the Privy Council is meeting."

"Then I must ask you to produce your daughter, Lisette Afton née St John for questioning."

"I will not." Celeste stood as if to block their entrance farther into her home.

"I'm afraid you don't have a choice." He loomed over her.

"*Maman*," cried Lisette running down the stairs. "What's happening? Are you all right?"

"That's her," cried Lady Afton, "She's the bitch who murdered my son."

Jayne sat beside her friend and employer. "What's wrong? Aren't you glad to be going home?"

"I am anxious to leave this city. Everywhere I go people whisper and point. I'm tired of being the object of gossip." Caroline slumped on the window seat, looking out at the twilight.

"It looks to me as if you will miss the arrogant baron." Jayne put her arm around Caroline. "If you ask me none of those people are good enough for you. Why let him hurt you this way? Forget about him."

"If only I could." She sighed and stood. "I'd better finish packing my trunk."

"Isn't it the job of your companion?"

"You're far more than my companion. You're my friend. Mrs. Arnold gave you enough to do today. Stay there. I can fold a few clothes." She moved to the open trunk and grabbed the first garment in the pile on the bed.

"Well, I'll take advantage of my chance to be a lady of leisure." Jayne smiled as she curled up on the plush cushion.

"Yes, we'll both be busy when we dock. I wonder what . . . ."

Caroline didn't hear the rest of the sentence. She held the ball gown she wore to the musicale where she warned William about Afton. *That was the first night we ever conversed without rancor.*

She stared at nothing, remembering his expression when he beheld her that night. *Though he was wary I could swear he looked at me with some admiration. I thought we might become friends.*

While Jayne spoke in the background, Caroline folded the dress and picked up the next garment. It was the dress she wore to the park the day William saw her tossing the stones. She smiled as she saw the grass stains on the skirt.

We sat there and talked with few barriers between us. She sighed and put the folded dress into the trunk with the others.

"Don't you think it's a splendid idea?" Jayne's voice sounded happy.

"Oh, yes, of course . . . ." She turned and picked up the next garment from the bed. Folding it without seeing it, she stopped when Jayne spoke once more.

"Will you do it? Will you stand up for me at our wedding? Jack said you wouldn't but I told him you would—"

Caroline froze as she realized when she last wore the walking ensemble in her hands. Though it had been cleaned, faint traces of the blood from her shoulder wound were still visible. She dropped it to the floor and jumped back. *I can hear the shot fired at me and feel the pain in my shoulder.*

She began to pant, her breath coming in uneven rasps. *Gareth's lying on the street, dark red pooling around his body. I didn't mean to kill him. I didn't mean it . . . .*

"What is it, what's wrong?" Jayne looked at the garment on the floor. "Oh dear, we meant to dispose of it. I don't know why someone put it with your other clothes."

"Take it away, out of this room, now." Caroline trembled and turned her back to the evidence of her crime.

Jayne picked up the garment and left the room.

Caroline sat down once more. *You killed a man. You took his life and you did it with as little thought as you'd give to choosing what to eat for breakfast. How can you be so callous?*

She stood and began to pace, her eyes looking at the floor, seeing nothing. *You've slipped through the last two weeks never thinking about the shooting.*

The door opened and Jayne spoke in a soft voice. "Mrs. Arnold will give the dress to the poor. You won't see it again."

Caroline cleared her throat and waved her hand at her companion. "It doesn't matter. I'm over my little snit now."

"It wasn't a snit. You just now faced the incident. It's like you always told me. We begin to heal when we're ready to face our pain."

"What an absurd thing to say. I sound pompous, don't I?" She managed a weak grin at her friend.

"Don't call my best friend *pompous*." Jayne smiled back as she hugged her. "It's because of your help I accepted Jack's marriage proposal. I never thought I'd ever want anything to do with men."

"Jack isn't the same sort of man Afton was."

"No, he isn't." Jayne moved to the clothing on the bed and folded the top garment to put in the trunk. "If he acted like that monster, I wouldn't have anything to do with him."

"So, tell me about the wedding plans." Caroline worked in tandem with Jayne, packing the clothes.

"We want to get married here before we leave. Then we could share a cabin and spare you the expense of paying for three."

"I don't mind the expense, you know that." She put the last piece of clothing into the trunk and shut the lid.

"We'd like to get married at St. Thomas' Church. The vicar is one of Jack's friends. They've known each other since they were lads. We've already spoken to him. He's agreed to perform the ceremony. Will you stand up with us?"

"You know I will, try and stop me." Caroline hugged Jayne and pulled back. "We've got to get you something nice to wear."

"Oh no, don't bother about it. I can wear my Sunday dress."

"No bride in this family is going to be married without a proper dress."

Jayne shook her head. "You've done so much. You don't have to buy my wedding dress."

"No, I don't, but I want to do it. Please let me, it will help me get my mind off Grayson."

"Why don't you invite Baron Hargreaves? It should be a merry day."

Caroline looked down. "He is no longer a close acquaintance. It seems my latest escapade went too far beyond propriety for his taste."

"You don't know for sure."

"Don't I? Has he come to see me since the day it happened?"

"Well, maybe he's been too busy."

"Right, he's too busy putting distance between the two of us. Even Lisette admits it now."

"Caroline, I'm so sorry."

She shook her head. "Don't be, I'm not. I knew it would end when I went home. I'll think of it as an interesting interlude in my life and move forward." *I don't think I'll ever forget him.*

She dabbed her face with her handkerchief. "Goodness, it's warm in here." She wiped the tears off her cheeks and smiled by forcing her lips into a stretch.

Chapter Forty

"You killed him, I know you did." Lady Afton snarled in Lisette's face.

"Don't be daft, I left him. He got his money, which is what you both wanted. He was carousing with all sorts of other women. I said *good riddance* and came home."

Celeste put her around her daughter's shoulders. "My husband was preparing the case to dissolve the marriage before Parliament. Why would he do such a thing if Lisette already knew her husband was dead?"

"To cover her crime. She is a devious witch, always was."

The constable seemed uncomfortable. He worked his finger around the inside of his collar as if to loosen it.

"You say Viscount Brenham was going to Parliament with the matter?"

"Indeed he was. You may ask him yourself. He received the Queen's permission to do so."

"Her Majesty supported the action?"

"Yes, when she heard my husband describe Lisette's injuries the day after her wedding—injuries he saw for himself."

"Viscount Brenham will verify this to be the case?"

"Yes, I will." Sheridan stood behind the startled constable. "I will also suggest to the magistrate he contact my solicitor should you want additional questions answered."

"Yes, milord." The man all but saluted. "Come along, Lady Afton, our business here is done."

"You weak-livered fool, are you giving up simply because he mentioned the Queen? His daughter killed my son, I know it."

Sheridan towered over their nemesis. "If you persist in your accusation, I will escort you to Her Majesty to explain your part in your son's perfidy."

175

She looked at him and his wife. Her expression changed as she tried another bit of manipulation. "I am only a poor widow. The lax Viennese police did not find any trace of my son's money. How am I going to run my household in the manner to which I am accustomed?" She whined the words, playing for sympathy.

"Don't play the innocent, Lady Afton. We have a witness who overheard your son discussing Caroline Burgess' fortune and the need to secure her for his bride."

"That's preposterous, such a conversation never occurred. Who dared make such a claim against me?"

"Furthermore, my man in Vienna spoke to the lawyer who investigated my wife's unclaimed inheritance and reported to you it was available to Lisette as well. You knew about the blasted fortune and prodded your dullard son to marry my daughter for that reason only, not caring what happened to her in the process."

"But I won't survive without money. What am I to do?"

Sheridan's eyes grew icy. "I suggest you sell your country estate and your town house. The proceeds from the sales should allow you to retire to a sensible cottage in the country."

"But I won't be a part of the *Ton* any longer, how shall I fill my days?"

"Try knitting for those worse off than you are or working with the vicar of the church wherever you settle. Many people need help. You could benefit from the lessons you would learn." He nodded to the constable.

"Yes, milord, thank you." The young man took Lady Afton's arm and escorted her out the door.

"I am ruined—" Her whining voice faded as they left the house.

"Papa, you came back just in time." Lisette hugged him. "I was afraid she would succeed in her accusations."

He smiled down at his youngest child. "I would never let that happen."

Celeste looked on. "Lady Afton is a grieving mother, no matter what a villain her son was. I pity her."

"I would never belittle a mother's grief." Sheridan winked at Lisette.

"I think Lady Afton grieves the loss of the fortune as much as she does her son."

"Papa, something you said made me think. I've never been of use to anyone. I'd like to change my life."

Sheridan looked down at Lisette. "How would you change?"

She took a deep breath and looked from her father to her mother. "Caroline once asked me if I'd like to go back to America with her. She works at a settlement house with women and children who have been victims of abuse. I'd like to go with her. She's sailing with Drake in two days."

Celeste frowned, "Why would you relive your own abuse like that? Won't dealing with someone else's pain bring yours back?"

"No *Maman*, sharing our stories will let me know it could have been worse for me. Helping other women work through their experience and heal will help me heal as well. Please let me go. I'm through with the *Ton*. I don't want this life any longer."

"What will I do with both my children grown and gone?" Celeste hugged her daughter.

"You can make Papa bring you to see me. You could even sail with Drake and visit with Aunt Mimi as well. Please, *Maman*?"

"I agree if your father does."

Sheridan grinned, his eyes shining. "I'm proud of you, my little one. You're growing into a fine young woman. I will miss you as much as your mother will, but I will not stop you from stepping into your life."

Caroline stood on the polished deck of the *American Eagle,* watching the final activity on the dock. *I'm glad Papa went back to his offices. There was no need to make him wait until we sailed.*

She smiled and waved back at Celeste and Sheridan, taking one last moment with their daughter.

William looked up and nodded at her before he turned away. Her face heated when he cut her as if she was a mere acquaintance. *I know it's my own fault. Trust me to alienate the one man I ever loved.* She sighed and swallowed a sob. *I've never been so alone in my life.*

Jayne and Jack disappeared into their cabin with all the zeal of the newly wed.

I'm happy for them both. They deserve the best in life. I only wish I had . . . oh never mind. You lost the one companion you wanted. Grow up and get over it. The door is closed. He's lost to you forever.

The ship's bell rang, startling her from her reverie.

Lisette kissed her mother and father once more. She hugged her uncle and held him at arms' length, her expression scolding him. His face looked carved from stone, his eyebrow lifted.

He's back to being the arrogant aristocrat I first met when I arrived. Caroline sniffled and held her handkerchief to her nose. *I couldn't bungle our relationship worse if I tried.*

Below on the dock Lisette sped to the gangplank, turning to wave before running to board the ship. She raced to Caroline's side.

"At last, we're on our way." She smiled and waved at her family, blowing kisses. She glanced at her friend. "Isn't this wonderful? I'm so excited to be on this journey with you. We shall have a splendid voyage."

Caroline nodded but said nothing.

William stared up at her as the moorings were dropped. His blue eyes glinted like an ice-encrusted pond, devoid of feeling, of life.

That's it. I won't take any more of this pain.

Caroline turned to Lisette. "I will leave you to your farewells as we depart. I'm tired from all the excitement of the last two days with the packing and Jayne's wedding. I'll see you later."

"All right." She watched her friend enter the corridor going toward her stateroom.

Watching the ship's slow move away from the dock, Celeste touched her brother's arm. "William, I am surprised you did not say goodbye to

Caroline."

He turned to look at her, his supercilious mask in place.

"I waved to her. It was sufficient leave-taking for such a casual acquaintance."

"For a time I thought you were much more than acquaintances." Her voice chided him.

"I could ill afford to be seen in league with a murderess. How could I? It would be improper to say the least. I have our family heritage and my reputation to maintain."

She sighed. "I see you're back to being the haughty baron. You will never be happy behaving in such a manner."

He grasped his lapels as he stood before her and Sheridan. "It is not my lot in life to be happy. I must assume my responsibilities for our legacy. I must manage my estates and find a suitable wife to give me an heir. Our family must continue to thrive with honor. I owe it to our mother and father." He turned back to watch the progress of the ship in the harbor.

I will forget Caroline. I must. I am not free to love where I would. My legacy demands a different course. She would never be accepted in my world after her notorious escapades.

He sniffed as his eyes filled. *Blasted salt air.*

Part II

Yankee Doodle Dandy

Chapter One
Sisters of Mercy Settlement House

"Jayne," called Caroline. "Could you take Mrs. Meacham and her daughter Josie to their quarters?"

"Of course I can." Jayne smiled at the newcomers. "If you'll come with me, Ma'am, we'll get you settled in your new room." She took the woman's hand and led her up the stairs, talking as they went.

"Bless you, lady, we didn't have nowhere else to go."

"I'm nobody's 'lady'. Please call me Jayne. We're all friends here."

Lisette watched their progress from the foot of the stairs. "Poor things," she whispered to Caroline. "Both of them are bruised, I'm guessing from a large fist. Who would strike a six-year-old child?"

"Someone who I hope will never get the opportunity to do it again."

"You don't think she'd go back to the brute, do you?"

She cocked her head. "You'd be surprised how many of them do. They've been dependent on men their entire lives. When things get tough, they run back to the only safety they know.

"They go back even if the man abuses them and their children?"

"The ones who don't think they can make it alone go back. They're too afraid to face the world without help."

"What a shame," sighed Lisette, resting her chin in her hand as she leaned against the high desk at the entrance.

"Most of the women who come here have little or no means to support themselves much less their children. They are not trained to do anything beyond keep house, cook meals, and sew."

"You'd think their families would take care of them."

"They either come from poor people glad to be relieved of the burden of another mouth or two to feed, or they are alone. These are not young ladies of the *Ton*."

Lisette blushed deep pink. "I'm sorry. Sometimes I still think like a viscount's daughter."

"Don't worry. We'll cure you of the tendency in no time." Caroline grinned at her. "Oh, look, I think someone's here to see you."

Drake St John, his hat under his arm, entered through the front entrance, resplendent in his immaculate captain's uniform. "Good afternoon, Ladies. I've come to bid you farewell."

Lisette rushed to her brother.

"I've got a letter or two for *Maman* and Papa. Will you deliver them for me?"

He returned her hug. "That's one of the reasons I stopped by."

"What's the other reason? Did *Maman* ask you to report on my well-being?"

He didn't answer immediately.

"That's it, isn't it? You're spying for her." She slapped his arm. "Shame on you." She laughed.

"You caught me." He rubbed his arm. "I forgot how much your slaps hurt."

"Don't forget it next time." She flounced away. "I'll get the letters."

He stood and watched her run up the stairs. "How is she really?"

Caroline sighed. "She's mostly all right. Some of the women here have survived terrible beatings and abuse, along with their children in many cases. Lisette was overwhelmed at first. But now her first week is behind her, she's coping much better."

He nodded, then appeared to search her eyes with his own.

"How are you doing? Are you coping with the trauma you suffered?"

She looked away. "If you're talking about Gareth, I'll always regret I took his life. But being here gives me a different perspective. Many people on this side of the ocean would have shot him long before I did. That doesn't make it right, but it helps me cope more with the guilt."

He took a deep breath. "Do you want me to convey messages to my family? Or take a letter to your father?"

"Give your parents my love. You needn't worry about taking a letter to my father. He's due to sail back in a few weeks."

"What message would you like me to give William?"

Startled by the question, she frowned as she looked at him. *Just let it go.* "I can't think of anything I need to say to him. Thank you." She turned to shuffle the stack of papers on the reception desk in front of her. "Oh, and thank you for having the scenery we shipped carted to the warehouse."

"You're quite welcome. Are you going to open a Shakespearean theater here in Philadelphia?"

"Don't sound so surprised. People here are very well read. I think we'll be successful. With Jack to stage and me to lead the interpretation, we will be able to put on excellent plays."

"I'm certain you will." He leaned toward her, pausing before speaking. "Aren't you worried your reputation as an actress . . . ." he stopped in a comic pose and pretended to shudder. ". . . will follow you here?"

"No." She grinned at him. "The people who truly care about me won't listen. Besides, my biggest critic is at home in London, where he belongs."

He looked around and spoke in a soft tone of voice. "If it helps, I think he's just as miserable as you are."

I doubt it. She smiled at him. "So when will you be sailing back this way?"

William stifled a sigh as he glanced around the crowded ballroom. *Another ball, another tedious evening spent in boring company. I haven't experienced an enjoyable evening since . . . since Caroline murdered Grayson.*

Lady Morehouse continued to prattle on, talking about the virtues of her plain daughter, Annaliese. "And furthermore, she is a most accomplished singer, paints excellent watercolors, and knows how to run a proper household in town or on a country estate. She's an absolute gem." She pulled her silent daughter forward.

With a nudge from her mother's elbow, the girl forced a wooden smile.

"So nice to see you once more, Baron Hargreaves." She stared at his cheekbone, avoiding his eyes.

"A pleasure to see you." He inclined his head.

Gad, she's as ugly as they come, dark as a gypsy with crooked teeth reminiscent of a rawboned nag.

"Are you engaged for the next set?"

"No," she mumbled, never looking up at him.

"Then I beg the pleasure of taking you as my partner."

She curtsied and said nothing.

He extended his arm and escorted her to the dance floor. They took their positions, bowed and curtsied as good manners required. When the music began to play, they performed the steps.

She's surprisingly good at this. She must have an excellent dancing master.

Never speaking, they completed the dance. He led her back to her mother.

"Lady Morehouse, here is your daughter. Thank you, Miss Annaliese, for the dance." He bowed and walked away.

Behind him, he heard Lady Morehouse scold her daughter. "What did you do now? Did you offend Baron Hargreaves in some manner? You are a fool, he's an excellent prospect. What are you aiming for, a duke? Don't be ridiculous." The voice faded into the background.

Though the dancing resumed, he did not stop to speak to any other young ladies. He kept going, leaving the ballroom far behind him. *I cannot stay in this crowded house.*

William walked outside to the balcony that overlooked the garden. The night was chilled as frost twinkled on the plants in the moonlight. Hands deep in his waistcoat pockets he stood and stared out over the grounds. *Caroline, I wonder what you're doing at this moment.*

He pictured her face, so pleasing in symmetry, wearing an open expression. He shook his head and smiled.

No one could ever doubt your opinion of anyone. It is always written in your eyes.

"How can you stand out here in the cold?" Sheridan's deep voice startled him.

"I'm more comfortable out here than in the crowds of people inside."

"I can understand. Would you like a cigar? We might as well take the opportunity to smoke if we're going to stand out here."

"Yes, thank you." William took the offered cigar and waited until Sheridan lit it with his own. "Did Celeste send you out here after me?"

The Viscount chuckled. "I should know by now how well you can read your sister's motives. She's worried about you, says you've withdrawn from all company."

William puffed on the cigar for a moment. "I'm bored by all these people. It's always the same guests, the same anxious mamas with their nervous daughters trying to win my favor."

He sighed and shook his head. "Who wouldn't be bored?"

"I remember those days well from my youth. Of course, my mind was set on Celeste, even when she hated me. I was determined to win her back."

"Oh yes, I recall those days well. I remember greeting you with a hail of stones. Even my actions did not deter you in your pursuit."

"I knew she was the only one for me. As I said, I was determined to do whatever it took to win her."

"I envy you the certainty she was to be yours. I wish . . . ."

Sheridan looked down for a moment, tossing his spent cigar and grinding it beneath his heel. "I thought you found the one for you."

William remained silent though his body tensed.

"Have you heard from Caroline since she left?"

Chapter Two
The Burgess Shakespearean Theatre

"Caroline, I was beginning to worry you wouldn't come." Jayne hugged her with enthusiasm. "Look at all Jack and his crew accomplished."

"Don't let me take all the credit." Jack walked to his wife and hugged her. "You've been a great help."

"Who built the stage?" she asked.

"I did, with the help of the crew."

"And who built the risers on which the seats will be placed?"

Jack looked down at her, his grin wide.

"And who is working on the balcony today?"

"I am, but you are helping me."

Jayne put her arms around his waist. "And how am I helping?"

His facial expression was one of merry confusion, "By providing moral support?"

Caroline watched as the happy couple laughed and kissed each other. *What must it be like to be so happy? I will probably never know.*

She shook away her wayward thoughts.

"It's amazing how fast you built all of this. We're almost ready to begin working on the first play."

"What will our first production be?"

"*Two Gentlemen of Verona.*" Caroline spoke with assurance.

"But why—" began Jack.

"Because it has the smallest cast of any of his plays, that's why. We don't want to get mired in a huge production in the beginning. We must build our reputation to attract audiences."

"I don't suppose we'll be staging *A Midsummer's Night Dream* any time soon."

Caroline froze, her mouth open. A vision of Gareth wheedling and trying to make her take the blasted part invaded her thoughts. She shut her eyes and shook her head.

Go away, can't you? Stop haunting my waking hours as well as my dreams. It's because of you I lost the man I love.

"Jack." Jayne touched his arm. "How could you bring up that subject?"

His expression grew chagrined, as he put his hand out toward his employer in supplication.

"I'm sorry. I didn't mean to upset you, Ma'am."

She looked at him, recognition returning. She shook her head. "You didn't do anything wrong. I was just remembering."

Oh William, I wish I could forget you.

"I'm sorry for his mistake, Caroline, neither one of us would hurt you on purpose."

"I'm sure you wouldn't, Jayne. Please think nothing more about it." Caroline turned around. "This is all excellent. You progressed so far in a few days. I'm quite pleased. If you will excuse me, I must go to another appointment." She walked toward the door. "Oh, and I've decided this theater will be a good place to provide some of the women at *Sisters of Mercy* a chance for employment."

"Why it's a lovely idea, when did you—"

"I can't stay and chat or I'll be late. I'll see you later at home." She hurried out the door into the cold, gray afternoon. Caroline leaned against the building, taking deep breaths. *I must get over this. I can't allow him to continue to hurt me. I cannot think of him as I'm certain he no longer thinks of me.*

Pushing away from the brick wall, she hastened her steps and strode to her coach.

"Your pardon, Baron Hargreaves, but a lady is here to see you."

"What lady?" William looked up at Weston. "I'm not expecting visitors."

Weston fidgeted in discomfort. "She gave me her card for you." He handed the card to the baron.

He looked at the card. "Lady Susanna Aimsley, what the devil can she want?"

"She would not say. If I may, my lord, she is most insistent on seeing you."

William sighed. "I suppose I should see her. It shouldn't take too long. Bring her in, Weston."

"As you wish, my lord." He bowed and walked out the door.

I don't have the first clue why she would come here. We were never great friends, only acquaintances. What ever could it be about?

"Lady Susanna Aimsley, my lord." Weston stood aside to allow the lady to enter.

She walked into the room, her posture correct, her ensemble the height of fashion.

"William, it is good to see you once more. It's been ages."

"Yes it has. Please sit down Susanna. Weston, tell Cook we would like some tea."

His guest put up her hand. "Please, it isn't necessary to entertain me. If I may speak to you alone, it won't take too much of your time."

"Very well, Weston you may go."

Waiting until the butler left, William looked at his guest. "Susanna, I cannot think why you would want to talk to me after the way we parted."

She put aside her fur muff and shrugged her cape off her shoulders.

"You were never one to chitchat, were you? Your manner suits my purpose. I will be most direct with you."

"Please do." He leaned back in the chair and watched her.

"I'm in a bit of a bind. My father decreed it is time I marry, in fact, he will force me to marry Eldred Winslow unless I present him with a suitable alternative."

"Eldred Winslow must be close in age to your father."

"He is, and I find him disgusting. So I am here to plead my case with you."

With suspicion overtaking him, he frowned at his visitor. "What can I possibly do in this situation?"

She smiled in calculation and smoothed her black curls beneath the fashionable red hat she wore. "You can make an honest woman of me."

"I hope you don't expect me to marry you, because I will not."

She sighed, her smile still in place. "Pity, because you will leave your son without his father, a bastard alone in an uncaring world."

"Are you daft? I do not have a son. You and I never . . . ." *Does she mean she conceived after our drunken tumble? She could not. She would have come to me if she was to give birth. Wouldn't she?*

Susanna's dark eyes sparkled. "You remembered the night after Lady Metcalf's garden party eight years ago, didn't you? I can read you, I always could."

"If this is true why did you not tell me at the time?"

She shrugged. "I didn't want to be forced into a marriage. I still don't, but you are a much better option than Lord Winslow."

"How do I know you're telling me the truth? How can I be certain the child is mine?"

Her laugh raked along his spine. "All you need to do is meet him. You'll see he is the image of his father, red hair and all."

She's lying, this cannot be true.

"You look like a fox after a hound has gotten it. I never saw you look so shocked. This isn't so bad. He's your son and heir, the next generation of your exalted family."

"I . . . ."

"Left you speechless, didn't I? Accept it, Will, I brought an acceptable solution to a difficult problem. We marry and become a family united with our boy. You can raise him, train him to succeed you. We can go our separate ways. We needn't see much of each other at all. It will be a typical *Ton* marriage."

"There will be talk. This will be a well-discussed scandal. I cannot do such a thing to my family."

She reached across the table and patted his knee.

"Face it, Will, you shall make a greater scandal if we don't marry, especially after I introduce our son to the *Ton*. All it should take is a whisper into the ear of one of the dowagers. Lady Morehouse, perhaps. Imagine it, the talk leaping from family to family within the space of a day or two. Everyone will be in alt over the scandal of the much-touted St John family."

"You wouldn't dare."

"You know me better than that." She grinned at him. "So do we have an agreement?"

He stood and ran his fingers through his hair. "I want to meet the boy first."

"It's easily arranged. He's been living with a family in the country in Essex near London."

She better not be lying. I hope I can tell when I see the boy.

He held out his hand. "Come along, let's go find him now."

"Why are you in such a hurry?" She smiled as she retrieved her muff. "The urchin isn't going anywhere."

He turned to her. "Madame if this lad is my son, you won't speak of him in such a way. He is your child? Or are you lying about him? Where is your maternal instinct?"

"Right beside your paternal one." She laughed as she followed him down the corridor.

Chapter Three

"Where in hell is my wife?" The huge man stood in the entry of *Sisters of Mercy*, his bellowing echoed through the building.

"What is this about?" Lisette strode in, stopping behind the reception desk when she saw the size of the man.

"M'wife is in here. I come to take her home where she belongs."

"What is her name?" She held her clasped hands on the desk. *He mustn't see me shaking.*

"Same as mine, ya little tart. Meacham. Bring her out here. She's going home with me."

Caroline came down the stairs at a normal pace. "She may not wish to go with you."

He charged at her like a drunken bull. "Ya think I'll let the likes of you keep her from me?"

"Now, Mr. Meacham, why don't you calm down? Let's discuss this matter."

"Get outta my way." He knocked Caroline aside, intent on racing up the stairs.

"Donald, what are you doing?" Mrs. Meacham stood at the head of the stairs, Josie peeking out from behind her skirt.

"I'm takin' ya home, get down here."

She edged her way down the staircase. "I'm coming, don't get mad."

"Hurry up, I want my supper, dadblast it." When she got within reach, he grabbed her, knocking her to her knees as he dragged her down the stairs.

Lisette looked at Caroline with a question in her eyes. Caroline shook her head.

"Mama!" screamed Josie. "Mama, come back here, don't let him take us."

"Ya little brat, ya can stay right here and rot for all I care." He did not

193

slow his pace as he dragged his wife to the door.

"Mama! Mama!" Josie tried to run but Caroline caught and held her.

"Mr. Meacham, how can you treat your daughter like this, much less your wife?"

"Listen to me, Missus, I'll treat my wife anyway I see fit. Not you or anybody else can stop me. Keep the brat, she's not even mine."

"I'll come back, Josie," Mrs. Meacham called as he pulled her out the door.

"The hell you will." His voice came from the porch, accompanied by the sound of his meaty fist hitting her face.

Caroline lifted the crying child in her arms and carried her down the stairs. "It's all right, Josie, you can stay with me in my house." She stroked the child's back.

"How could you let that ruffian take his wife out of here?" Lisette's expression was outraged. "Why didn't you try to stop him?"

Caroline shifted Josie to her other shoulder. "I couldn't stop him. Besides, she came downstairs on her own. She decided to obey him."

"But—"

"No, we must think of what's best for Josie. Not to mention the other women and children residing here. According to the law, his wife is his property. We would only interfere if she wanted us to do so."

"How horrible, you mean we cannot help them?"

"We offer the women and their children a safe place to stay and the means to make a new life. If one of them decides to return to her husband, we cannot stop her. We must concentrate on the ones who want our help. It's all we can do."

"It isn't fair, we should help her."

"We have no standing to help her. She knows what she is returning to. We have to think of Josie now, give her the very best in life as long as we have her."

"But I—"

Caroline handed the exhausted child to Jayne. "Take her and give her something to eat or some milk. I'm taking her home with me this evening."

Jayne nodded and led Josie in the direction of the kitchen.

"Now Lisette, let me ask you something. Why didn't you go with your father when he came to get you the day after your wedding? You stood there making excuses for Afton, claimed you were clumsy and caused your own injuries."

Lisette looked down at her feet. "I was ashamed." Her voice was almost a whisper.

"And you thought you must have done something to cause the fight, didn't you?"

"How did you know?"

"Remember, every abused woman believes it's her fault. Many of them never find the strength to leave the husband or lover who beats them. You did because inside you are strong, determined."

"I don't feel very strong."

"You will. We must overturn an attitude that prevailed for centuries. To do that we must help the stronger women find their means to be independent. Do you understand?"

"I think so, but I still don't like the way he dragged her out of here."

"I don't, either. It happens around here sometimes. We do the best we can."

"Why didn't you get your gun?"

"I hope you're not serious. I would never endanger the other residents here for the sake of a woman willing to go home with her husband."

William stared at the lackluster cottage on bare ground surrounded by winter-dead trees. *Even Tideswell was better than this.*

Susanna spoke to the grimy woman who appeared in the doorway wiping her hands on her dingy apron at the sound of the coach. "Bring him out here. His father wants to meet him."

The woman grinned at William. "Coo, there's no denying they're father and son."

"No there is not."

"Hey, Frankie, get out 'ere. Yer lady mother wants to see ye."

195

William watched in growing horror as a filthy boy edged his way out the door. Barefoot on the frozen ground with no coat, the urchin stood in defiance, his head held high. "Yeah, what d'ye want?"

The woman cuffed him on the side of his head. "Watch 'ow ye speak to yer betters, ye hellion."

"Ow!"

Dear Lord, they're right. He is my son. He looks exactly like me. Something that felt strangely like rage sparked inside him at the woman's treatment of the boy.

"Here now, none of that. You will not hit my son again." William's voice was tight.

"Ye got nerve, ye do. Sashaying in here as proud as ye please snapping orders to the only mum this poor lad's ever known." The woman tried to pat the boy but he shrugged off her hand.

William took a deep breath. *I must be insane to believe this with no proof, but I know he's mine.* "Come along with me, we're going home."

"What if I don' wanna?" Frankie stood with his arms folded, defiant in his dirty clothes, shivering in the cold.

"You don't have a choice."

"And why in 'ell not?"

"Because I'm your father and you will do as I tell you." William grabbed his arm. "Come along, now."

Frankie dug his bare feet into the ground. "I've 'eard about men the likes of you. I ain't going anywhere with a bad 'un."

Susanna grinned at the picture and she stifled her laughter. "I never thought I'd see the day, Baron Hargreaves accused of such a crime."

"Madame—" William clenched his teeth, determined to hold on to his manners.

"Oh, very well. Franklin, this man is your father. He is Baron William Hargreaves."

"Well. Whoever thought my pa would be a toff?" Frankie expanded his skinny chest and strutted toward the coach. "Well, what are ye waitin' for?"

Susanna tossed a handful of coins at Frankie's former guardian. "That should suffice, and thank you. Mrs. Garner. Your services are no longer needed."

As William stood aside to let Frankie step up into the coach, the boy reached down and scooped up a handful of stones. "Ye never know when these'll come in 'andy." He scrambled up into the plush vehicle, his dirty feet leaving tracks on the pale carpet.

Susanna turned up her nose in disgust at the smudged footprints. Holding her skirts away from the smudges, she took a seat on the opposite side of the coach. She did not look at her child throughout the entire journey back to London.

William stared at the boy in wonder. *He couldn't be more like me if I had him since his infancy. Celeste will laugh over the son who is going to run me a merry chase. She'll say it is divine retribution for all the trouble I caused her.*

I wonder what Caroline would think?

"Jack, you're a wonder. You and the crew are almost finished. This is amazing." Caroline twirled around looking at the stage, the seats, the curtains hanging from the proscenium arch, and drapes over the high windows. "You've turned the warehouse into a proper theater."

"We hoped you'd be pleased." He hugged a beaming Jayne to his side. "He worked so hard."

Caroline nodded. "I can see he did."

"Miss?" Little fingers tugged at her skirt.

"Josie, what do you think of this place?" Caroline reached down and took the girl's hand.

"I never seen nothing like it. What's it for?"

"We will stage plays in here to entertain people."

Josie frowned, "What's a play?"

"People tell a story by acting it out in front of an audience."

The little girl looked up at Caroline. "Do they make people cry?"

"Sometimes, but they make people laugh, too."

With the wisdom of a six-year-old, Josie considered what she heard. "I'd like the funny ones best. I don't like to see people cry." She yawned, her eyes drooping.

Caroline picked her up. "Jack, I'll send you a copy of the play. We'll read it together day after tomorrow, all right?"

"Sounds fine, enjoy your evening." He glanced at Josie and grinned.

"Do you need anything right now?" Jayne stood with her arm linked with her husband's.

"No, you two are on your own tonight. I'll see you later at home."

As Caroline walked out, she glanced at the couple. *They're so much in love. I'm happy for them both.*

With the coachman's help, she put Josie on the seat and wrapped her in a blanket. Taking the seat opposite, she stared out the window on the drive home.

I miss William, or at least the man who was my friend. I hoped for so much more with him at the beginning.

She shook her head.

Talk about a wasted hope, he's too hide-bound in his own traditions to accept an American actress like me.

Josie stirred on the seat, mumbling in her sleep.

Who would think I would end up back home with the responsibility for this little girl? I guess there is a reason for everything. I couldn't take care of Josie if I was still in England. I never would have met her.

She watched out the window as a dusting of snow began to fall.

Enough of this drivel. It's time to stop looking back and face the future. Josie needs me. I will see to it she has the best life I can give her. It will be the atonement for my sins.

Chapter Four
Brenham House

"Weston, is my sister at home?" William led Susanna and Frankie into the house.

The startled butler stared open-mouthed at the grubby, barefoot boy striding into the marble entry with the self-assurance of absolute ownership.

Apparently realizing the Baron was speaking, Weston looked at him. "Your pardon, milord, what did you ask?"

"Is the Viscountess at home?"

"She . . . she's in the small salon." He shook his head as if to clear it. "Shall I announce you and your—party?"

"Never mind, I think I'll surprise her. Come along, my dear." He held out his elbow for Lady Susanna and glared at the boy. "Don't touch anything until you are clean."

"Here, here," whispered Weston, watching them walk down the hallway.

The sound of voices greeted William as they neared the salon. "Oh good, Sheridan and Drake are with her." He smiled at Susanna. "We can tell them all at once."

She nodded, her sly smile in place.

Frankie looked from his mother to his father. "Tell who what?"

William glanced down at the boy. "You'll see." He stepped into the open doorway.

Celeste, Sheridan, and Drake were seated, chatting with each other. They looked up as he entered. The room grew silent.

"We've got some news for you." William tried to smile, but his lips refused to cooperate.

Celeste furrowed her brow as she glanced from her brother to the woman at his side. "Hello, Lady Susanna, I hope you are well."

"Very well, thank you."

Celeste looked at the boy. "And who is this young man?"

William hesitated then put his hand on Frankie's shoulder. "I'd like you all to meet my son, Franklin Henry Hargreaves."

"Oy, my name's not 'Enery."

"It is now, I'll explain later." William spoke in a low tone out of the side of his mouth.

"I don't care what ye want, ye can't call me by that stupid name." Frankie writhed to remove his father's hand.

"Behave, can't you?" William tightened his grip.

Celeste's eyes danced as she attempted to control her smile. "It seems you do have news for us."

William stared at his older sister, his mouth dropping in disbelief. *I thought you'd demand to know about my son, yell at me for my carelessness, yet you react like this?*

"Come, all of you, please sit down. Let's discuss this in comfort."

She smiled at Frankie. "Why don't you sit next to me, young man? I'm your aunt."

'The devil ye say." He plopped down on the silk-covered chair beside hers.

"How can you bear to let the little waif dirty your furniture?" Lady Susanna sniffed and looked away.

Celeste frowned. "The chair can be cleaned and so can the child. I want to know more about my nephew from William. This is my only nephew, is he not?"

William nodded quickly.

"Why don't you and William tell us how Frankie came to be, Lady Susanna?"

Frankie looked at his aunt. "Don't ye know? I thought a skirt as old as—"

Stifling a laugh, she smiled at the boy. "Of course I know, but I wanted to learn how your mother and father, um, got together."

In a rush, using indistinct words, William explained their reunion at Lady Metcalf's garden party and how it led to the activities that produced Frankie.

"It's quite a story." Sheridan looked at William. "How is it you never mentioned your son to us before?"

Celeste looked at the boy. "Frankie, would you like something to eat? I imagine you're hungry. Your father always was when he was your age."

"Yes'm." He smiled at her, his eyes shining through the dirt on his face. "I could sure use somethin' flavorsome. It's been a time since I ate."

She rose and took his hand. "Come along with me to the kitchen. I'll introduce you to our cook. She's always loved young lads she could spoil."

As she led him out of the room, she glanced back at her brother. "Wait for me before you tell your tale."

Later, after she left Frankie stuffing his face with Cook's gingerbread, Celeste settled into her favorite chair.

"All right, William, what have you to say for your behavior?"

"I did not know of my son's existence until today." He looked to Susanna, his eyes pleading her assistance.

In a bored voice, she began, "He didn't know about his son because I never told him."

"Why would you keep such a thing from a man? He has a right to know he is a father." Sheridan's expression was outraged as he looked at her.

"He knows now, doesn't he?" She shrugged. "Earlier there was no need to bother Will about the boy. I found a family to take care of him and forgot about him."

She glanced around at the astonished faces.

"Oh, don't look so shocked. I remembered to pay the people for his care, that's all that matters."

"Madame, you are either the most unnatural woman I have ever met or an uncaring monster. Now you've disclosed to William his son's existence, what do you propose to do? And why tell him now?"

"Calm down, Brenham, you'll bring on a fit of apoplexy. I need to get married, and soon, or my father will disinherit me. Since I prefer Will as a husband to the old man my father suggested, it was time to reveal the truth about Frankie." She grinned at Celeste. "I'm sure you realize it's best for our son if we marry, and the quicker the better. After all, people will talk. Now is the time for the scandal to brew and boil down before he's an adult."

"And what about you, William? Do you agree with Lady Susanna's plan?"

"Yes, I do. I will bring up my son as is proper. He will be given the best education and be prepared to take my place as the baron when it is time."

Drake had remained silent throughout the introduction and subsequent discussion. "What about Caroline? Did you give no thought to her when you made this decision?"

"She is no longer a part of my life. She chose to return to Philadelphia. We could not maintain a courtship across the sea even if she was a proper bride for me."

Susanna's laugh sounded callous as it scraped over the quiet room. "As far as I'm concerned, the Baron and Baroness Hargreaves will lead separate lives. I will still see my lovers and you can see yours." She turned with a sly smile to face William. "I'd be careful, my dear, of your American slut. Remember poor Grayson. Her aim is most deadly."

Your jibes hurt more than any bullets of hers ever could. "Very well, I accept your terms and I will not importune you with unwanted affections. We shall marry as soon as I can procure a special license. Is the plan agreeable to you?"

"Very much so." Her grin grew broad. "I don't plan to invite a guest list. Do you?"

"No. In this situation a small wedding for family only is appropriate." He glared at his bride-to-be.

"Excellent." She rose and retrieved her cape and muff. "I shall be off. Please have your man send for a hackney. I'll wait in the vestibule. Ta, I trust you will contact me in time for the ceremony.

"Yes, I will." He watched her, his fists clenched in fury.

"I'll go tell Father the happy news." Susanna shrugged into her cape.

"Don't you want to take Frankie with you to meet his grandfather?"

"Good lord, no. I can just imagine Father's face. He'd suffer an attack." She laughed once more. "No, you keep our whelp. Make a gentleman of him. It's what you want to do, isn't it?"

"Indeed, it is."

"Then I wish you luck. You've got quite a battle before you."

The rest of the room's occupants watched her disappear down the corridor in silence. Celeste turned to her brother and put her hand on his arm.

"Are you certain you want to marry that creature? She will bring you nothing but unhappiness."

"I couldn't care less if we never see each other again. I will marry her for the sake of our son."

"I understand, but I wish you could be happy with her."

He shook his head, a rueful grin on his face. "That, my dear CeCe, is impossible. I'm glad she doesn't want to live with me and our son. Frankie and I will be happier without her."

She nodded. "Let's get Frankie bathed and his hair cut. There are some of your childhood clothes in the attic. I'll send one of the footmen to bring them down. I'm sure some of them will do until we can have new ones made."

"He's lucky to have you for his aunt."

"Nonsense, he's more fortunate to have you for a father."

William scratched his head. "I've come rather late in his life. I doubt he will agree with you."

"But you're with him now. You'll see. The two of you will bond and grow to love each other." She turned and started out of the room. "I'd better send the footman for the large bathtub and then the clothes. I fear washing Frankie will take an effort."

He watched her hurry off to see to the task.

Sheridan rose. "I need to prepare for the meeting of the Privy Council."

He touched William's shoulder. "No matter how he came into being, treasure your son. You are both fortunate in your new relationship."

Drake stood. "I have something to do as well." He looked at his uncle. "I'm truly sorry this happened for you and Caroline."

"Thank you, but our parting was for the best, given the current situation."

"I'll see you later." Drake strode out of the room.

William sighed. *What a day this has been.*

He moved to the window and watched the darkness gather. *I've been so arrogant, judging everyone as if I am better than all of them. What a laugh. I'm still that frightened boy who had to take over for his executed father, the man I worshipped. I watched him kicking and gasping, suspended on the gallows until he breathed no more.*

The sound of a gale beginning to blow outside the window drew his notice. He touched the frosted pane and looked toward the west. *Somewhere out there over the wide expanse of ocean is the only woman I ever loved.*

Caroline, my greatest regret is the way I judged you. Who am I to be so critical? Here I carelessly fathered a son and never even knew about him. You are without doubt a much finer person than I will ever be.

I hope your life will be filled with all the happiness and love you deserve.

Chapter Five
Philadelphia - Home of Horace Burgess

"The little lamb never woke up when I put on her nightdress. She was worn out." Mrs. Arnold smiled at the memory.

Caroline put down the quill and rubbed her eyes. "Thank you for helping me with her. Josie may need some coddling, after what she's seen. I don't know if her mother will come back for her."

"From what you said about the man her poor mother married, I'd say Josie will not see her again."

"I expect you're right."

"You seem so tired. Can I get you something to eat? You weren't here for dinner. Did you eat anything?" Mrs. Arnold stood over her and rubbed the back of her neck.

Caroline melted into the neck rub. "That's so nice. It helps."

"Would you like me to bring your dinner in here?"

She shook her head. "I'm not hungry."

The massage stopped. "Now don't you go telling me that, young lady. You need to eat something. You're wasting away these days."

Caroline managed a weak smile. "Some people would say it's a good thing for me to lose some weight."

"Nonsense, you're not meant to be like those English ladies, frail and thin as a slat."

"Nobody could accuse me of being too thin." She looked up at her former nurse. "All right. Could you bring me some tea and toast, please?"

"Now you're making sense. I'll bring you a plate and you'll eat every bite." She bustled off toward the kitchen.

Caroline sighed. *I don't think I've ever won an argument with her. But she's right in this case. Maybe some food will make me feel better.*

She shuffled the paperwork on the desk. Sketches of designs for the

205

production were stacked next to bills for lumber and seats. *This is a big undertaking, though the result will be worth it.*

A drawing on top of one of the piles attracted her attention. She picked it up and looked at the sketch. It was a design for a costume for one of the women.

This is quite good. It would be lovely in the play. She turned the paper to the back and saw Jayne's signature. *I didn't know she was so talented.*

"Here you are." Mrs. Arnold bustled in, carrying a laden tray of food with a tantalizing combination of aromas. She pushed aside the papers and set the tray on the desk.

"You brought much more than tea and toast."

"You need much more than tea and toast. You're running yourself into the ground these days. There's the settlement house, the theater, and now you've taken on the child. Eat all of this. You need your strength." She stood over Caroline with a baleful expression of a prison matron.

"Yes, Ma'am." Picking up the fork, she tasted the slice of baked chicken.

"What's going on? You gave in too soon."

Caroline shrugged. "I don't have the energy to fight you. It takes less effort to agree." She buttered a flaky roll. "I'm hungrier than I thought."

"Humph, it's about time you listened to me." Mrs. Arnold reached into her apron pocket. "I almost forgot. A visitor came by to see you this afternoon. He left his card." She held out the card. "He's a good-looking man, too."

Caroline wiped her mouth with the linen napkin and took the offering.

"*Aidan Cavanaugh.* I don't think we've met. Did he say what he wanted?"

"He's anxious to see you."

Caroline frowned and looked at the card once more. "This is a calling card. There is nothing on it to indicate his business. I wonder why he would want to meet me."

"The man must have seen you somewhere and wants an introduction."

"If he does, he's wasting his time. I'm not interested." Caroline turned back to her meal.

"Darlin', you can't step off the world because of what happened in England. You've got a long life ahead of you. Don't you want to get married and have a family?"

The fork faltered in Caroline's hand. "I can't envision such a future for me at the moment."

"Don't tell me you're pining after that prissy baron."

"He isn't prissy, just dignified."

"He's so dignified he's a cold customer without an ounce of gumption. I thought you'd gotten over him. Lord knows, he's never going to get over himself. You're wasting your time with him, don't you know it?"

Caroline put the fork back on the plate and tossed down the napkin. "I've lost my appetite. Please take this away."

"You didn't eat much."

"I don't want anything else."

Mrs. Arnold leaned toward her with a coaxing tone.

"Now, Darlin'—"

I can't take any more of this tonight. "Take it away, now, Mrs. Arnold. You are excused from the rest of your duties tonight. I won't need you." She turned away and picked up the stack of papers from the desk.

"You can't hide forever, Caro. I hope you'll come back to your senses soon or I'll be too old by the time you start having babies of your own."

"I now pronounce you man and wife." The vicar droned on in a lackluster monotone.

William turned, resolute, but reluctant to seal the union with his new bride. He moved to kiss her. With a smug smile, she turned at the last moment, allowing him to graze her cheek.

"Well now." She spoke brightly to the four people present. "It is official. We are married."

"Didn't take long." Frankie, scrubbed clean and wearing his new clothes, scowled at his mother.

"There is no need to prolong this farce." She started up the aisle. "It was lovely to see all of you. We must get together soon." Hurrying out of the church, her laughter chimed on the breeze.

Celeste watched her go, an expression of shock on her face. "Where is she going?"

William shrugged as he walked to the pew his family occupied. "She does not plan to live with us. I suppose she sees no need to maintain the pretense of a marriage. She's probably late for an assignation."

"But I planned a wedding breakfast." Celeste stood with Sheridan as both of them stared in the direction the Baroness Hargreaves disappeared.

A sardonic smile on his face, Drake shook his head. "I'd say she isn't hungry."

"Well I am," piped Frankie. "Come on, let's get outta here and eat. Who cares what that snooty woman wants?"

William took his son by the arm. "Your first lesson, Franklin, is this: your mother is not a caring warm person, but she is still your mother. You will treat her with the respect she is due."

"And what if I don't wanna give her no respect?"

"Then you and I will have a longer conversation which you will not like." He pulled his son up the aisle toward the door.

I can't blame him. She does not deserve anyone's respect and neither do I.

Excerpt from the *London Standard*—column of *Jolie Madame*:

My dears, such scrumptious news! It seems the well-respected authority of all things of fashion, Baron H, kept a naughty little secret. He and Lady A produced a love child years ago. No one knew. Rumor has it Baron H did not know until Lady A dropped the seven-year-old lad in his lap. They had a shamefully brief wedding ceremony at St. B's followed by the new bride running out of the church at the end. Seems she was late meeting one of her numerous lovers. Are you certain the lad is yours, Baron? We're told he is the image of you, but you never know. Lady M, intent on securing the baron for her horse-faced daughter, is furious. To think she wasted all that money on gowns to attract a man with a by-blow son. What a shame the wicked American actress folded her curtains and departed for home. She would be more than happy to warm Baron H's lonely bed. C'est la Vie . . . .

"William." Celeste approached him in the dining salon. "Did you see the *London Standard*?"

He looked at her, his teacup midway to his lips. "No, is there something important in it?"

She glanced at Frankie, busy gobbling a large plate of food. "I think you will find *Jolie Madame's* column of interest to you."

She handed the broadside to him and watched his face grow red as he scanned the column.

He threw down his napkin. "I was afraid of something like this. I think Franklin and I will depart for Parkfield today."

She nodded, "It's a good idea. He shouldn't be distracted by the furor this column will cause."

Drake picked up the paper, frowning as he read the article. "Sounds like a good time to return to the country. You know how the gossips are. They're going to be talking about this for a while. It will be good for both you and Frankie to be out of reach."

"I agree. The talk will die down when some new scandal occurs. Come along, Son, we're going to travel to our estate in the country."

"What's an estate?" Frankie stuffed the last of the biscuits in his coat pocket.

"It's a big house sitting on one hundred acres. We breed horses there. It's time you learned to ride like a gentleman."

Frankie sauntered after his father. "I kin already ride a horse. Done it lots of times."

"I'm talking about the proper way to ride, not jumping up on a horse's back with your bare feet kicking him to make him go."

"What other way is there?" The voices faded down the corridor.

Celeste looked at her son. "I was afraid of this. We are embroiled in another scandal."

Drake grinned at her. "You should be used to it by now, *Maman*." He cocked his head for a moment. "Now might be a good time to visit Lisette and Aunt Mimi. What do you say? We've booked a full cargo and we sail back to Virginia next week. Would you and Father care to travel with us? We can sail up the coast to Philadelphia and see Lisette as well."

"I would love to do it, but I'll see if your father can get away now."

Weston entered the room. "Your pardon, my lady, here is the post."

"Thank you." She looked at the letters. "Drake, here's one for you."

He took it with an eager expression. As she watched, he sighed, his expression falling.

"What is it?"

"Bridget's father returned my letter to her. He's written on the outside *'Make no attempt to contact my daughter again.'* I can't even reach her."

Celeste's heart ached for her son. "I have faith it will work out for you. I feel it."

"Hold on to your faith, *Maman*."

Chapter Six

"Jayne, these designs are perfect for the women in the cast." Caroline smiled at her friend. "I didn't know you were so talented."

"It's not so much. I like to draw and sometimes I like to design clothes."

"Don't belittle your gift. Not everyone can create such lovely gowns. Our next step is to see which of the women at the settlement house can sew well enough to make these." She held the drawings out at arm's length. "These are beautiful."

"I think Pearl Loring could make the dresses. She had a seamstress shop until, well until her husband, you know."

Caroline nodded. "Yes, hers is a sad case, losing her only child and her husband at the same time. Ask her if she would like to take the job of sewing costumes for the theater company. Is there anyone else who might want to work as her assistant?"

"I'm not sure. I'll ask some of them."

A tall, well-groomed man entered the building headed for the two women. "Excuse me. I'm looking for Miss Burgess."

"I'm Miss Burgess. And you are?"

He grinned. "I'm sorry. I was so anxious I didn't think to introduce myself." He held out his hand. "I'm Aidan Cavanaugh."

She took his hand. "Oh yes, you stopped by my home two days ago and left your card." She looked at Jayne. "Run along to the settlement house, I can handle this."

"Are you sure?"

"Yes, don't worry about me."

Jayne nodded, gathered the drawings and left.

Aidan's brilliant blue eyes reflected the sunlight spilling in through the windows. "I don't mean to interrupt your meeting, but I need to speak to you about my daughter. I'm told she's staying with you."

She removed her hand from his. "Mr. Cavanaugh, there is a little girl staying with me. What proof do you have she is your daughter?"

He cocked his head to one side. "She is six years old now and inherited my dark hair and blue eyes."

So far, he's got everything right. But I won't trust a strange man with any child until I can verify their kinship. "How did you lose touch with each other?"

He sighed and looked down. "Her mother and I fought one night, a loud, long disagreement. It was silly, nothing for either of us to argue about. I went to work the next morning and came home to an empty house. She took Josie and disappeared. I've been searching ever since."

"When did you last see your daughter?"

"Almost a year ago." He looked at her. "I'd be very grateful if you know where she is."

"What did you argue about?"

He sighed. "She wanted me to quit clerking in the bank and take a job in the mills supervising the women working there. It paid much more and would bring more security to our family."

"Why didn't you want to take the job?"

"Have you ever seen those factories, Miss Burgess? Women and children work long hours for a pittance. They are encouraged to turn out garments as fast as possible, no matter the consequences. Some of the children have died, caught in the machinery. Some of the women have lost limbs."

"Sounds like an unpleasant place to work, indeed. But if you need the salary why not take the job?"

"I don't care about the money. It's not enough to make up for pushing people to work in such conditions."

She folded her arms and stood looking at Mr. Cavanaugh. *Are you telling me the truth, or is this some ruse? His expression is sincere, as if he believes what he says.*

"Very well, you may come to my home this evening and meet Josie. She'll tell me if you're her father."

He appeared to relax. "Thank you, Miss Burgess. I can't wait to see her."

"If you will come at six o'clock, you may see Josie." She turned away. "Now if you'll excuse me, I need to return to my own work."

He held his hat in his hand and inclined his head toward her. "I'll be there, thank you." He walked to the door and left the building.

I hope I'm not making a mistake. I'm so muddled lately I wouldn't know a good man if one appeared before me.

"What'd we come out here for?" Frankie looked at the brown foliage surrounding a running stream. "It's cold out here. Let's go back to the warm house."

"You've impressed me with your progress. I thought you deserved some time in the fresh air. You've been confined to the house for two weeks. Don't you like being outside for a change?"

The boy scuffed his shiny shoes in the bare patches of dirt. "I finally get warm after being cold all my life and the first thing ye want to do is take me out in the cold again. Make up yer mind."

William smiled for the first time in weeks. "You don't fool me, you know."

Frankie frowned. "What d'ye mean?"

"I'm on to you. I was just like you once." He reached down and scooped up a handful of stones by the water's edge. "Come here and show me how well you throw."

Frankie hung back, suspicion in his eyes. "I thought ye're all about me studyin' history, boring stuff about grand high poobahs and such."

"I expect you to learn all you can, it's important for your future. But for now, let's concentrate on tossing stones."

"Is this a trick?"

William laughed, at ease with his son. "I promise this is no trick. Show me how good you are." He held out the stones.

"What'll ye give me when I win?"

"My respect." William looked at him. "I bet I can make the stones skip more times than you can."

"Ha, that's a laugh! Nobody can beat me." Frankie took the stones. "I'll show ye what I can do."

He tossed the first stone and watched it skip twice. "There ye go. I bet ye can't beat me."

"Don't put down any money." William chose a stone, winked at Frankie, and tossed it. The stone skipped five times over the water.

The boy watched, his mouth open in awe. "Cor blimey, I never saw no one skip it so many times." He grinned at his father.

"I'll teach you how to do it."

"Can ye really teach me to do it?"

"I taught a lady friend of mine. When I was through teaching she could make the stones skip six times."

"A lady, I don't believe it. Ones I know don't want to get their clothes dirty. Yer lady must be dif'ernt."

William smiled. "Yes, she is."

Frankie scooped his own stones. "When kin I meet yer lady?"

"I'm afraid she's gone back to America now. It isn't likely you'll ever meet her."

"That's too bad. I bet she's a lollapalooza." Frankie moved to the waters' edge.

She is a wonder. My greatest regret will always be I didn't realize how special she is before I lost her.

"Are ye comin' or not?"

"Yes, let's start with the position of your arm and wrist. It's the secret of stone skipping."

Later in the evening while Frankie slept, William stood and watched his son.

I never knew what I missed until you came into my life. I'm so sorry your early life was hard, but it made you a fighter.

He shook his head.

You are so much like me you make me remember what it was like to be myself, not some cold, judgmental aristocrat, making malicious jest of others. I don't really like the man I've become pandering to the members of the Ton in an attempt to belong. It's time to return to my true character.

He reached down and gently swept Frankie's hair out of his eyes.

The boy stirred, murmuring in his sleep.

"Goodnight, Son." William slipped out of the room and closed the door.

Chapter Seven

"Daddy!" Josie ran shrieking down the stairs and into Aidan's arms. "I thought you left us. Where did you go? Mama said you didn't want us anymore."

His eyes filled with tears as he hugged his daughter. "I've looked for you over a year. Of course I want my little girl."

"But Mama said . . . ." she pulled back to look into his eyes.

"Mama was wrong. We had a fight and said bad things to each other." He looked at her, his eyes narrowed. Gently touching the fading yellow bruise on her cheek, he frowned. "Who did this to you?"

She shrugged and looked down. "He's a mean man. I don't have to live with him anymore. He said I couldn't."

"Where's your mama? Is she with him?"

Josie nodded. "He said I wasn't his and Mama made me stay with Miss Caroline." She glanced back at her. "She's nice. I like her."

"Thank you, Miss Burgess. Are you satisfied I am Josie's father?"

"No question she is yours, Mr. Cavanaugh." She smiled at him. "Do you have a place to live?"

He shifted his daughter to his other hip. "Not anymore, I've been traveling through the northeast looking for this one and her mother."

"You don't have a job either, I take it?"

"No, I don't. Why do you ask?"

She looked at him, appraising him before she responded. "As a bank clerk, you had experience with the books, didn't you?"

"Yes, I did. I kept the books for the bank manager. I also worked with customers."

Smiling, Caroline moved toward him. "One last question, Mr. Cavanaugh, do you have any objections, moral or otherwise, to the theater?"

He put Josie down and took her hand in his. "That depends on what

216

kind of theater you mean." His voice dropped to a low tone.

"Not that kind." She chuckled. "We're opening a Shakespearean theater and need a business manager. It will pay better than a bank clerk's position."

"What would I have to do? I don't think I'd want to appear on the stage."

"Don't worry. We use professional actors for the onstage work. You would keep the books, pay the bills, and distribute the salaries. Would you be interested?"

"The position is located here in Philadelphia?"

"Yes, we're opening the theater downtown."

"I'd have to find a place to live for Josie and me."

"That's no problem. My father owns several nice houses in the area, which he rents to good tenants. I'm sure he would be happy to rent to you." She smiled at him. "Wouldn't you like to settle and create a stable home for your daughter?"

"Please, Daddy, I want to stay near Miss Caroline." Josie tugged on his trouser leg.

He looked down at his little girl and grinned. "In that case, how can I say no?"

"Wonderful." Caroline shook his hand. "We are about to sit down to dinner, please join us. You and Father can discuss the available houses. You can stay with us until you're settled so Josie won't sleep in a hotel."

"Thank you." His voice dropped to a whisper. "I'd like you to tell me what happened to my wife, after Josie goes to sleep."

She nodded her face solemn. "I'll tell you what I know but it isn't much."

Celeste stood at the rail of the *American Eagle,* watching the coastline slide by. Sheridan came up behind her and put his arm around her shoulders.

She shot him a sidelong glance. "You'd better watch out. My husband is aboard. He may be silver-haired but he's still a fighter."

His deep chuckle sounded near her ear. "Very funny, CeCe, don't let either of our children hear you say that. I'd never survive all the teasing."

She leaned back against him. "Wasn't it wonderful to visit with Mimi and Elijah? I cannot believe she's got three sons now and is pregnant again."

"She'll have her hands full, but it's Elijah I pity."

Celeste turned and looked at him. "Oh, you're teasing, I should know you by now."

"Yes you should, but I am not teasing."

"Why would you pity Elijah? He's very happy from all I saw."

He leaned down to murmur into her ear. "The more children they have, the less time they have for each other."

"I didn't hear either one of them complaining." She turned back to watch the coastline as the sun disappeared beneath the horizon. "I wonder how Lisette is doing these days."

"From her letters, I'd say she is getting along well. She seems to like her work with Caroline."

"That woman is a godsend for our daughter. Lisette sounds more like the young lady we raised."

"Drake said she was in good spirits the last time he saw her."

"I hope she doesn't mind our surprising her."

"She'll be glad to see us."

Celeste settled once more in her husband's arms. "What about Caroline?"

"What about her?"

She sighed before she spoke. "Someone has to tell her William is married and has a son. I suppose the duty will fall to me. I don't look forward to it."

"She should not mind. They didn't part on good terms."

"Oh sometimes you men are all alike. They loved each other. He hurt her with his rejection after the shooting. Didn't you notice how he cut her at the dock when she left?"

"No I noticed they were not as friendly as they had been, but I focused on our daughter."

"William isn't happy with his so-called wife. It's such a shame the way things worked out for him and Caroline." She sighed. "I hate to be the one to tell her."

Frankie looked down and scuffed the toe of his boot in the dirt.

William saw him as he walked around the corner of the stable. "Come along, son, it's time for your riding lesson."

The boy did not answer. He sniffed and dragged a grubby fist across his eyes.

William knelt before him and touched his shoulders. "What's wrong? Did someone hurt you?"

"It ain't nothin'." Frankie refused to look at his father.

"Well, it's something to me to find you this upset. I've never seen you like this. What's happened?"

Frankie twisted away. "It's no use tryin' to teach the likes of me to ride like a baron. I ain't one and ain't never gonna be."

"Who told you such a thing? You're my son and my successor by right and law."

"They ain't never gonna allow a by-blow to inherit this place nor the title, neither. I ain't good enough. Just ask anybody."

William pulled his son into an embrace. "Who told you such rubbish? Tell me, I want to know."

"Mrs. Adams was talkin' to the maids down in the kitchen. I heard what they said."

"Oh they said that, did they?" He rose and took his son's hand. "Let's go, I'm about to give you your first lesson in how to be a baron and a father." He pulled the boy all the way back to the house where they entered by the kitchen door.

The housekeeper jumped when he burst through the entryway. "Oh my goodness, my lord." She held a hand to her chest as she curtsied. "You gave me such a fright."

"Mrs. Adams, you are dismissed as of this moment. Please pack your things and leave my property."

The woman gawked at him. "Why, what have I done?"

"You hurt my son." William scowled as he looked at the woman his father originally hired.

"You cannot be serious. I worked for this family for years. After your poor father and mother died was the only time I worked for anyone else. I came here to keep house for you when you were twelve. The Duke of Richmond found me to resume working for your family. I was glad to do it. You cannot dismiss me now after all these years, please, sir." She held her hands up in supplication.

"In recognition of your long service to the Hargreaves, I will give you adequate funds to establish yourself in a small cottage elsewhere. You needn't work again."

"But sir—"

"Enough." William's voice echoed around the kitchen, causing the maids and scullery to jump. "No one will denigrate my son and continue to work for me." He looked around the room at the servants present. "Are we clear?"

The women nodded and curtsied, none of them meeting his stony eyes.

Mrs. Adams sneered at him. "Your *son*! Are you even certain he is yours? Besides, he's a little bastard and should be begging on the street, not being trained to be better than he is."

William gripped Frankie's hand tighter, and glared at the woman until she looked away. "You have just lost half of the pension I planned to give you. One more cruel word about my son and I won't give you a farthing."

"I don't have anything else to say about him. Instead, I'll say you are not half the man your late father was. He was a true gentleman, a perfect baron in every way. Your mother was a beautiful aristocratic lady, for all she was French. It was an honor to work for them. Your wife is an immoral harlot with no concern for anyone else." She folded her arms and looked at him in defiance. "Now do your worst."

He inclined his head. "I will not punish you for speaking the truth. Be off my property by sundown." He led his son out the door. "We'll go back to our riding lesson."

Frankie followed him in silence until they were in sight of the stables. He stopped and his father looked back at him.

"Why'd ye let the ole witch talk to ye like that?"

William hesitated before answering. "I suppose this is your day for lessons. No one is a perfect man, least of all me. I've been proud and arrogant. Recent events taught me to recognize the truth of my actions and to regret many of them."

"But she . . . ."

"Mrs. Adams spoke her honest opinion of me. I agree with many of the things she said." He smiled at his son. "I've spent years trying to be the perfect baron and falling short. Do you want to know why?

Frankie nodded.

"To be the perfect baron you first need to be a good man, one who cares about people and takes their welfare to heart. All the glitter and polish means nothing if the man inside is cold and unfeeling. You have been part of the lesson for me. I'm not the frightened lad beneath the façade any longer. You taught me what it means to be a father."

"But, I didn't do nothin'."

"Yes you did, Frankie, you broke through my barriers and made me care." William used his handkerchief to wipe his son's damp eyes. Hugging him, he smiled. "Are you ready for your riding lesson?"

Chapter Eight

Lisette stood at the reception desk. "You're welcome, Mrs. Hoffman, I hope you are successful in your position at the new bakery. Your wonderful pretzels should be very popular."

"Thank you, Missus, I vill brink you some."

The two women hugged. "Take care." Lisette pulled back and smiled as she watched the older woman walk out to the street.

"She seemed happy." Drake entered the building and grinned at his sister.

"What are you doing here? You didn't tell me you were coming to Philadelphia when you took the cargo to Norfolk." She ran to hug him.

"I don't tell you everything. Sometimes I like to surprise you." He touched her face. "You look good, better than I've seen you in a long time."

She touched his hand with her own. "I am happy, more so than I ever dreamed I could be."

"I'm glad to hear it. Can you stand another surprise?"

She frowned with a sideways grin. "What are you up to? Who's with you?"

He went to the door, opened it and spoke to someone out front. "Come in, the lady will see you now."

Lisette saw him stand aside, her mouth dropping open when she recognized her parents. "*Maman*, Papa, you came all this way."

Celeste enfolded her daughter in her arms as Sheridan smiled at the two of them.

"You could not keep us away."

Lisette finished embracing her mother and turned to her father. "It is so good to see both of you."

"You, too, my little one." He smiled down at her.

"Papa I'm a grown woman now, don't you know that?" She laughed.

"You will always be my little girl, no matter how old you grow."

Celeste glanced around the reception area, smiling at the women seated in chairs. "Are you permitted to leave? I don't want to interfere with your work."

"Don't worry, *Maman*, Caroline is upstairs. I'll get her to take the reception area. She won't mind."

After Caroline greeted the visitors, Celeste and Sheridan took their daughter to a small teashop in the vicinity.

"This is quite nice." Celeste looked at the small establishment.

"I know it isn't like the ones at home, but these Americans are becoming civilized," Lisette teased, laughing as she looked at her parents. "So what news is there from London, anything of interest?"

Sheridan cleared his throat. "Lady Afton sold her Mayfair home as well as the country estate. She disappeared into some country shire. If anyone knows where she went, they are not telling. I think we're shed of her for good."

Lisette nodded at the attendant as she brought their order. Sitting in silence while they were served, she waited until the young woman finished and walked away from their table. "I feel sorry for Lady Afton to lose her son, but with his behavior it was inevitable."

She savored the aromatic tea in her cup. "Let us talk of more pleasant times. How is William doing these days? Is he still terrifying the *Ton* with his pronouncements?"

Celeste looked at Sheridan with a raised eyebrow. He nodded.

"William retired to Parkfield with his son."

Lisette choked, spewing tea into her napkin. "When did William acquire a son?"

Her mother told Lisette the story of Lady Aimsley, Frankie, and their hurried wedding.

"William never suspected?"

Sheridan shook his head. "They both were numbed from drinking during their rendezvous. He never remembered much of the incident at all."

"How terrible for him, does he recognize the boy as his?"

"It's hard not to know who Frankie's father is. He's the image of William at that age. The worst part is *Jolie Madame* wrote several columns about the story. William decided to return to Parkfield away from the uproar."

"Poor Uncle William exiled to the country with a seven-year-old." Lisette attempted to maintain a somber expression but her giggles broke through her resolve. "How is he coping?"

"He's finding his way." Drake smiled at her. "He's learning to be a good father. The last time I saw him William appeared to be content."

"What about his absent wife?"

"Neither he nor Frankie seem to miss her, in fact they never mention her."

Celeste took a last sip of her tea. "The one person William misses and regrets losing is Caroline."

"How do you know?"

"We chatted together before he left for the country. He blames himself for being cold to her when they parted."

"He should regret cutting her like he did. She cried for days during the voyage, at least her eyes were red. She made up some excuse about the salt air bothering her."

Lisette stopped a moment. "Oh dear, Caroline doesn't know, does she? William's news will demolish her hopes." She looked from her mother to her father and to her brother. "Which one of you is going to tell her?"

Celeste sighed. "I will tell her. He's my brother. I should be the one to bring the news."

William sat in his study, Frankie by his side.

"Why should I wanna read? I'd rather work with the 'orses."

"So, now you like the horses, do you?" He smiled at his son. "Remember when you began your lessons? You were not too enthused about riding then. Now you love to ride. Perhaps the same thing will happen when you read a book you like."

He snorted. "That'll never 'appen. Who wants to be stuck inside all the time?"

"I think you'll change."

"Beg pardon, Baron Hargreaves." His major domo, a slight individual named Fyffe, burst through the door, red-faced and out of breath

"I would never disturb you, but the Baroness—"

Susanna elbowed the shaking man aside. "Is here to see you and our child. Oh do leave us, little man. You're disrupting our family reunion."

Fyffe glanced at William who nodded. The harried servant hurried away, shutting the door behind him.

What the devil does she want?

She moved to Frankie, taking his chin none too gently in her hand as she peered at him. "You've cleaned up better than I thought you would, I must say." She let go of his chin leaving white fingertip pressure marks on his skin and sat without invitation.

"Why are you here?" William asked when she spoke no more.

With a sly smile, she looked at her husband. "Now that's what I like about you, Will, no nonsense, always right to the point." She looked down into her elaborate beaded reticule and withdrew a piece of paper. "It seems Father has disinherited me. He is displeased with me. Oh no, it was not enough that I marry my son's father. Now he objects to my, how did he put it? Ah yes, my 'whoring ways'. He always did have a puritanical sense of expression."

"Frankie." William turned to his son. "Why don't you go ask Cook if you can have some of the cookies she baked this morning. Tell her I sent you."

The boy looked from his father to his mother. "Ye sure ye won't need me?"

"I can handle this. After you get your cookies you may go to the stables and visit the horses, if you like."

"Don't mind if I do, thank ye, Father." He raced out of the room.

"You've done well with the boy. I wouldn't recognize him as the scruffy waif you brought home. Who knew you had such a way with brats?"

He sighed as he looked at her. "What do you want?"

"I want to live here with my husband and son." She smiled at him, her eyes flirtatious.

"Cut the subterfuge, Susanna, we both know there's nothing between us. What do you need? Money?"

She cocked her head. "It doesn't hurt to try. All right, Father not only cut me off from my funds, he ejected me from his home. I don't have anywhere else to go."

"I'm surprised you didn't ask to stay at Brenham House in London. At least there you would be able to attend social events."

She held up the piece of paper. "I am no longer welcome at social events, thanks to this."

"What is it?"

"It's a column from the witch. She's made me a pariah. No one wants me at their gatherings now." She handed the page to him.

He frowned and read the column.

Excerpt from the *London Standard*—column of *Jolie Madame*:

My Darlings, a word of warning from your dearest advisor. Baroness H has gone beyond the pale. Cast out by her father after he disinherited her, she is hoping her friends will assist her. The few friends she still possessed rejected her. No one knows where she has gone. With no money and the gossip about her infamous behavior, she is no longer received in any of the best homes. If she should appeal to you for assistance in her time of need, turn her away. She is a cold, vicious woman whose lovers touch most of the highest ranked families in the aristocracy. Devoid of conscience, she cares nothing about whose marriage she ruins. Do not, under any circumstances, offer her charity. She will destroy your happiness if you do. If you must pity someone in this sordid tale, pity Baron H, the once proud authority of all things elegant. He never deserved to be brought low by such an evil woman.

His lips pursed as he finished reading, he looked at his wife. "It sounds to me as if you slept with her husband. This is much too personal to be casual observation."

"Who knows, I suppose it's possible." She shrugged. "Whoever she is I'd like a few minutes with her."

"A confrontation would only end up in another column. The best thing is to let it die down. People have short memories, often forgetting a scandal when something new comes along."

"But what am I to do in the meantime?"

He sighed. "You can live here at Parkfield with us."

"I don't know. I'd perish here in the country with no society." She looked at him. "I hoped you'd finance a trip for me to Europe. I would be away from you and the little monster, free to pursue my own life."

"Free to pursue new lovers, you mean." *It is the best solution for all of us, though I won't let her bankrupt me. I can finance a grand tour for her.*

"As if you care who I see. Besides, you will be free to go after your American actress, Caroline isn't it?"

"Miss Burgess and I were only friends. We've lost touch with each other. She is back at home with her American set."

Susanna smiled. "You don't fool me. I know you prefer her to any other woman you ever met."

I won't allow you into my private life. "Whatever I thought of her we will not see each other again. I don't plan to travel to America."

"Pity, you don't know what you are missing."

"And you do, I suppose, with all your lovers."

She shrugged. "At least I am experienced."

If you think your salvo reached its target, you are mistaken. "Where would you like to go on your continental sojourn?"

She smiled in apparent satisfaction. "Oh France and Italy, I suppose, they are so much more broad-minded about love than the stuffy English are."

"Very well, shall I have my man of business book your tickets and hotels?"

"Yes, please, the sooner I depart the better it will be."

I agree. He stood. "If you will excuse me, I'll have the servants show you to your room."

She giggled with intended irony. "We won't be sharing a bedchamber?"

He inclined his head. "No, we will not."

William walked out the door in search of Fyffe.

Chapter Nine

"What a lovely meal, thank you for inviting us to dinner." Celeste smiled at her hostess. "I see Americans enjoy the same social habits as the English."

"I don't know what you mean."

"The men all retired for their brandy and cigars."

"Yes, they did, my father is particularly fond of the practice. It isn't often these days we have several gentlemen included in the dinner party. I'm sure he's making the most of his opportunity to entertain and share his best cigars."

Jayne stood. "Caroline, do you mind if I retire early? I'm tired tonight."

"Of course I don't mind, you've worked very hard in the last couple of weeks. Go on and get a good night's sleep for once."

"Lady, uh, Viscountess Brenham, it's been a pleasure to meet you. We're very fond of your daughter." Jayne made a jerked bow.

"Mrs. Lowell, it isn't necessary for you to bow or call me by a title, I'm Celeste St John. It is a pleasure to meet you as well. My daughter tells me good things about you."

Jayne's face tinged pink. "We're all happy Lisette is here with us. She's an asset at the settlement house. Goodnight." She hurried out of the room.

"Did I do something to frighten her?" Celeste watched her exit with a frown. "I didn't mean to."

"It's all right, *Maman*." Lisette touched her mother's arm from the chair next to her. "Jayne is a bit skittish around English aristocrats."

"Why would she be?"

Caroline glanced at Lisette before answering. "Jayne worked for the Aftons when I hired her. She was subject to Everett's . . . proclivities."

"He raped her, *Maman*, repeatedly, laughing when she begged him to

229

stop."

"The poor child, she seems to be doing well over here."

"She is." Caroline smiled, "Jack Lowell worships her and treats her gently. They both work for me at my new theater. He supervised the building of the stage and audience areas. Now he will stage the plays. Jayne designs the costumes and supervises the seamstresses who make them."

"It sounds as if you are busy as well, with the women at the *Sisters of Mercy*, and your new theater."

Caroline nodded. "Would you like more tea?"

"No, thank you." Celeste looked at her daughter, who nodded. "I bring news of William for you. He has experienced some major changes in his life."

"Oh really, I hope it's nothing dire." *Don't let him be ill, please let him be all right.*

As Celeste related the tale of William's new family, Caroline sat still, trying to show no emotion on her face. Inside, she grew cold.

How could such a thing be possible? Did he not have any inkling he was a father? Oh dear, William as a father. The poor child, I hope William will be able to open up to his son. If not, the boy will suffer.

"Caroline, you're so quiet, are you unwell?" Celeste looked at her hostess.

Pull it together. Don't show them how much you care. "I'm fine." Caroline's smile stretched her lips until they ached. "What a surprise. I hope William and his new wife will be very happy."

Hearing footsteps approaching the parlor door, she looked toward her salvation. "I'd say the men had their fill of brandy and cigars."

When Sheridan appeared in the doorway, she smiled. "Come in, gentlemen, I hope you enjoyed your time together."

"It's been a pleasant evening." He looked at her with kind eyes. "Thank you for your gracious hospitality."

"I'm glad you took pleasure in our company."

Drake bowed to her. "I'm afraid we need to get back to the ship. It's a bit of a drive back to the dock."

Caroline continued smiling with only her lips. "Such a pity you must leave early. I hope you will all come back while you're in town."

"We would love to." Sheridan offered his arm to his wife. "You must let us entertain you as well."

"I look forward to it. Good evening." Sheridan led his wife and son out of the room.

"I'll see them out." Lisette looked at her friend. "We can talk later."

"Thanks, but I'm tired. I think I'll go right to bed."

"All right, sleep well." Lisette turned and rushed after her parents.

Caroline dropped the smile she wore and stood in the same position, breathing harder. *I don't want anyone but William. It took me so long to find him and now he may as well be dead to me. I hope his wife appreciates him. Dear Lord, how will I face all the coming years alone?*

She did not realize she was crying until the tears dripped down her chin. With a shaking hand, she reached up and wiped them away. Seeing nothing beyond her pain, she staggered up the staircase to her room.

Inside, she locked the door and sank down on the bed.

Maybe I was wrong. He never cared for me. He couldn't, and marry someone else. It's true, then, I never measured up to his high standards. I would never fit in his world. I'm never meant to marry nor have my own children . . . .

Long after the house rested in silence, Caroline finally slept. On the bright dawning of the day, she woke with a new resolve. As she dressed and prepared to resume her activities, she glanced in the mirror at her red-rimmed eyes.

Last night was an indulgence I can no longer afford. The past is gone. I must take my life as it comes, no more pining after the baron.

With a final pat to her hair, she turned to exit the room. *I will not occupy my time in self-pity. I have work to do. If I cannot have love, I will make myself useful.*

"Jayne, the costume is perfect." Caroline stood back from the stage and admired the dark-haired actress dressed in the lovely dark red gown. "You've captured just the look I want for the character Sylvia."

"I'm glad you like it. Do you want to see the finished costume for Julia?"

"Of course, I'd love to see it."

"All right, Agnes, please come onstage."

The blonde moved with assurance, holding the skirts of a sapphire-colored gown.

Caroline sighed in satisfaction. "Jayne you are a wonder. Who knew you carried such visions in your mind?"

"I always liked pretty clothes. It was the best part of working for the aristocracy, seeing all the gowns and ensembles the ladies wore."

"Thank you." Caroline dismissed the actresses. "You may go change now." She walked up to Jayne and put her arm around her shoulders. "Thank you for giving us such beautiful designs. How are the rest of the costumes coming along? Will they be ready for the costume parade next week?"

"Yes, they should be. Our seamstresses work very well together. They're so happy to have jobs to support their families."

"We're doing it, Jayne, giving women jobs as well as entertaining people. I think our theater will be very successful."

"Excuse me, Miss Caroline." Aidan stood glancing around in nervous agitation. "May I speak to you?"

Jayne waved at the man. "I need to get back to the sewing room." She left and walked backstage.

"Now, what can I do for you?" Caroline smiled at her new manager.

"I've been going over the accounts. If you'll pardon me for saying so, there is an enormous outlay of cash. I can't see how you could hope to make back your investment with the current production."

"I won't. I'll be lucky if I make back half of it at the end of the season."

He frowned at her. "This doesn't seem to be a practical venture. How can it continue?"

She laughed. "The theater is never a practical venture. People work in the business out of love. If they are able to make a living, it's a bonus."

He frowned. "I'm looking out for your interests. I am concerned this venture will falter and cost you the entire investment."

Caroline looked at him for a moment. "Are you worried your position might not be permanent?"

He would not meet her eyes. "Well, I have Josie to think about. I don't want to uproot her again. She's happy here, making friends at school."

"Are you happy with the house you've rented?"

"Oh yes, it's the nicest place we've ever lived. Thank you for sending Mrs. Muller to us. She's a wonder, Josie already loves her."

"Don't worry about the theater, it will either last or it won't. Whatever happens, you will still have a position, I guarantee it."

His expression changed to one of relief. "Thank you, I've worried about losing this job."

"You won't. If the theater fails, I'll keep you on. I have several other investments you could manage."

He smiled at her. "I'm grateful for all you've done for us."

"You're welcome. How is the search going for your wife?"

He shook his head. "She's disappeared. I don't know where she is or if she's even still in Philadelphia."

"Have you spoken to the police? They are familiar with the area where she was living with Mr. Meacham. They might know something."

"Thank you, I'll go to the station and make an inquiry."

"I hope you find her. I'm sure Josie misses her mother."

"She does. Let's hope we can bring my wife back home."

Chapter Ten

"I cannot believe Father is so interested in Independence Hall." Lisette stood next to her brother and shivered in the cold.

Drake shrugged. "His father supported the King during the war against the colonies. His uncle left to come to the colonies and never returned. I imagine he's heard about those events most of his life."

"I don't want to stand here freezing. Why can't we at least sit in the coach?"

"We can, Sprout. Let me lead the way." He walked with her to the coach parked on the road and helped her into the vehicle. Stepping up he sat beside her and shut the door. "There, is that better?"

"At least we're out of the wind." She rubbed her gloved hands to warm them.

"You had a good idea. I was cold, too."

She snorted. "I should mark the date. You said my idea was a good one."

"Very funny." Her brother leaned toward her. "How are you doing, really?"

"I'm much better than I was. Many of the women at the settlement house endured worse situations than I did. I learned to understand what happened and why. Aside from the naiveté of a sheltered young woman, I did nothing to cause my shame."

"You've grown into a strong woman. I'm proud of you, little sister."

She elbowed him in the ribs. "You know better than to call me such a thing."

"I give up." He laughed with his hands in the air.

"That's better. Now why don't you tell me what has gone on between you and Bridget O'Halloran while I've been gone. Have you seen her?"

The smile disappeared from his face. "No." His voice was clipped.

"What happened?"

"I'd rather not discuss it, if you don't mind." His cold, flat tone sounded alien to her.

"All right." She reached across and touched his knee. "I won't ask any more questions about her." She leaned back against the cushions. "Instead, why don't you tell me about Frankie?"

Drake grinned. "There's a lot I can tell you about Frankie. You wouldn't believe how much he looks like Uncle William."

"So he really is the boy's father?"

"When you see him, you'll have no doubt." He chuckled. "What's more, he's an imp, completely undisciplined, and says whatever he wants."

"I bet Uncle William is exhausted."

"Actually, a strong bond is growing between them."

She smiled at him. "I'm glad they found each other. Frankie could be the spark to turn his father away from his haughty baron persona."

Drake glanced at her. "How is Caroline, do you think she's gotten over him?"

"No, she hasn't. I think the news of William's marriage overwhelmed her. She retired when you left. I didn't see her until the next morning. Her face was pale, her eyes red from weeping when she came downstairs. Since then, she's been efficient at her duties but keeps an emotional distance from all of us."

"I understand how she feels." His voice sounded restrained as if he said the words unwillingly.

Lisette watched him.

I wish I knew what happened with Bridget. He'll tell me when he's ready.

Caroline wrapped her cape tighter around her, shivering in the frigid night. She pulled up the hood to protect her head from the falling snow.

Aidan appeared beside her. "Shall I escort you to your coach?"

"No thanks, you go on home. Nobody should be out in this weather. I'll see you tomorrow." She watched him wave as he turned and disappeared into the night.

As she neared her conveyance, she could not see her coachman. *That's odd, I sent him out just before I locked the building.*

"Obadiah, are you out here?"

She walked to the coach in silence, her senses alarmed.

"Obadiah?" She found the driver's seat empty, the reins slack. The horses still sported their blankets. She moved to the animals, looking around them and on the ground beneath. A crumpled mass lay on the street beyond.

Hurrying into the street, she knelt down. Her coachman, an elderly man, sprawled on the bricks, already white with falling snow. An ominous dark patch welled from the side of his head, staining the frost. She touched his chest. *Thank goodness, he's breathing. I've got to get him inside the coach.*

Moving to lift him under his arms, she dragged him even with the door. *How am I going to get him inside? I can't lift him up to the entrance, he's too heavy.*

"Caroline, is everything all right?" Aidan called through the rising wind.

"Aidan, I'm over here on the street. My driver's been hurt."

He appeared and knelt beside the stricken man. "What's happened?"

"I think he's been attacked, though why someone would attack him is a mystery to me."

"We need to get him out of the cold." He grasped the older man's hands and hoisted him up over his shoulder. "Can you get the door?"

She rushed to open it and stood back while Aidan put the unconscious man on the seat.

"If you will get in, I'll drive you home."

"It's not necessary. I can drive the team. You should get home to Josie."

"She's already asleep. Mrs. Muller is with her. Let me drive you. I wouldn't feel right about leaving you to deal with this alone."

Caroline smiled. "This is very kind of you."

He stood aside and gestured for her to get into the vehicle. "Nonsense, it's what friends do for each other."

When she was seated, he closed the door. "Roll down the window covers, the snow is falling harder."

"I will."

He walked toward the front of the vehicle.

She let down the heavy curtains and leaned across to check Obadiah. A jolt rocked the coach.

He's on the driver's seat.

"Here we go," Aidan called. "Hold on, we may have a slippery ride."

The coach started forward as the animals jerked a bit. Their pace evened out as they went forward.

In the darkness, she steadied her coachman's body on the bench. Her hand brushed something on his chest. *What is this? It feels like paper.*

She spread her fingers over the substance and crumpled it with her exploration. Pushing the curtain back, she leaned toward the meager light from outside, hoping for enough to see the paper.

Crude block letters appeared briefly as they passed a streetlamp. Squinting, she read the note.

YUR NEXT

She let out a shuddering breath and watched the frosted exhalation float out into the night.

Oh, dear Lord.

Horace, red-faced and blustering, glared at his daughter. "Of course I sent Marcus after a police officer. Someone threatened my only child."

Caroline sighed. "I'm safe here at home. It could wait until morning."

"No it cannot, I will decide when you are safe, young lady." He put out his palm. "Now don't give me the lecture on being an independent woman. I know you're capable of taking care of yourself. But I am still your father."

She looked at Aidan. "Why don't you go home? It's late."

"I should stay in case the police want to question me."

Horace clapped him on the shoulder. "Sound thinking. I knew I liked you."

Aidan ducked his head. "I understand what being a father is like, especially with a daughter."

Mrs. Arnold bustled in with a tray of tea and cups. "You drink this." She handed a full cup to Caroline. "You almost froze to death."

"I don't want any tea."

"You drink it anyway. It will warm you." Mrs. Arnold stood and glared down at her.

"Oh very well." She sipped the tea. *It does feel good.* She drank more.

"Would you gentlemen like tea?"

"No, thank you, Mrs. Arnold." Horace's voice boomed. "I think Aidan and I will have brandy instead. How about it, son?"

"Sounds good, Mr. Burgess."

He winked at him. "Now, none of that 'Mr. Burgess' business. Call me Horace."

The knocker on the double front doors rapped. "I'll see who it is." Mrs. Arnold hurried out of the room.

Caroline concentrated on her tea. *I suppose it's best to get this over with. But I don't know what I can tell them.*

Mrs. Arnold entered the room, her face dour. "Mr. Burgess, the police are here."

"Why do we have to go with her back to London?" Frankie whined on the upholstered seat of the barouche.

"It's the right thing to do, proper behavior. No matter the circumstance, we must always be correct. It's expected of men in our position."

The boy slumped in his seat and picked at his velvet trousers.

"Baldersash," he murmured, almost under his breath.

"What was that you said?" William tried not to laugh.

Frankie raised his face, his mouth in a straight line, his eyes defiant.

"I said *baldersash*. What's the matter, didn't I say it right?"

His father looked down and covered his chuckle with a cough.

"I believe you mean *balderdash*."

"Balderdash, then." The seven-year-old folded his arms across his skinny chest. "Ye know what I mean."

"Yes, I do and you're lucky your mother didn't hear you. It might hurt her feelings."

He slumped further down into the seat. "That one ain't got any feelings, what difference does it make to her what I say?"

In a great flurry of noise and activity, Baroness Hargreaves entered the barouche.

"See that box is particularly well tied on top. It would not do to have it bouncing off and disappearing into the woods en route. I'd be positively bereft if such a mishap were to occur." She sat beside her son.

Frankie jumped up as if shot and sat beside his father, "Wouldn't do for me to wrinkle yer dress."

William elbowed him gently in the ribs, frowned and shook his head.

"Well it wouldn't, ye know, we can't have her arrivin' all de-shoveled." He gave a swift nod.

Out of the side of his mouth, with twinkling eyes, his father whispered, "I believe you mean *disheveled*."

"Whatever ye say." The boy grimaced. "Ye know what I mean."

"Well, I think your concern for my state of dress is most refreshing. You see, William, I was right. You're having a most positive effect on our son."

"Somebody has to." Frankie rolled his eyes as he whispered to himself.

Chapter Eleven

"Are you certain you won't come back with us?" Celeste looked at her daughter with tears in her eyes.

Lisette hugged her. "*Maman*, you said yourself, it's only two weeks journey now from Philadelphia to London. Besides I want to stay here."

"I wish you'd reconsider."

Lisette dropped her arms from around her mother. "We'll see each other in a few months when you come back in the spring." She looked at her father, pleading without words.

"Come, my Celeste, it's time to board the ship." He stepped in and embraced his daughter. "Write to us, tell us all the new things you learn, the new people you meet."

"I will, Papa. Take care of *Maman* and of yourself."

He nodded and put his arm around his wife. "We mustn't hold up the sailing. Captain St John will be displeased," he teased with his sideways smile.

Lisette smiled as she watched them walk up the gangplank and board the ship. She waved when they reached the deck and turned to look at her.

"Goodbye, tell everyone hello for me."

"We will." Celeste waved back at her daughter.

The ship's bell rang. "All ashore that's going ashore."

Lisette waved once more, turned, and walked back down the dock. *I can't watch them depart.*

She arrived back at *Sisters of Mercy* to find the place in an uproar. Several of the women residents were standing in groups, crying, talking, or looking lost. She saw Caroline at the reception desk deep in conversation with a police officer. She rushed to join them.

"Are you sure it's her? She's been positively identified?"

"Yes, ma'am, her husband identified her an hour ago."

Caroline shook her head. "It's terrible."

The officer nodded. "Quite a shame. And her leaving a nice husband and a little girl."

"Indeed, thank you for coming here to tell us." Caroline looked at Lisette. "Mrs. Arnold, please see the officer to the door."

The officer tipped his hat and turned to follow the older woman.

"Caroline, was it Josie's mother?"

"Yes, they found her near the park. They think she was out there overnight."

Lisette looked at the other women staring back at her. "They're all afraid again, aren't they?"

"Of course, they all think it could have been any one of them or any one of their husbands."

"Does Aidan know?"

"Yes, he identified her body. The cause of death hasn't been determined. It could be she passed out in the cold and never woke up. There are signs of fresh bruises on her skin, but not enough to kill her."

Lisette looked around before whispering. "Do they think it was Mr. Meacham?"

"He is certainly a suspect, but they don't have enough information about how she died to know for sure."

Lisette sighed and folded her cape. "How sad for her, no one may ever know the truth of how or why she died."

"Don't take this on. None of it is your fault. She chose to go with him and leave her daughter here. Women make the wrong choices every day and spend the rest of their lives living with their mistake. Don't you be like that."

"Me? Listen to your own advice, Caroline. Don't you live that way, either."

"Hello, Aunt CeCe!" Frankie ran into his aunt's arms, almost knocking her to the floor in his enthusiasm. "Ye're my favorite aunt." He wrapped his bony arms around her.

She smiled at him and ruffled his hair. "I'm the only aunt you know, you rascal. It's so good to have you and your father back with us."

"I wondered if you meant to include me in your welcome." William leaned over his son and kissed her cheek.

"You both are always welcome here."

"Aunt CeCe." Frankie tugged at her skirt and stepped back, "D'ye like my new garb?" He strutted back and forth, fingering the frill on his shirtfront and tracing the lapels on his waistcoat. "Do I look posh or what?"

"You're quite the gentleman, Franklin." She curtsied to him.

"Ye bet I am. I look as good as any gent in Mayfair." His cocky grin brought smiles to his aunt and his father.

"What have we here?" Sheridan walked into the room. "Who is this elegant young man?" His eyes twinkled with mischief.

"Aw, ye know it's me, Uncle Sheri. I'm wearin' my new *fash'in'able* duds my pa got for me." He turned around to show off his clothes. "Ain't I a sight?"

Sheridan raised his eyebrow as he looked at William who shrugged suppressing his grin.

"I even got on ridin' boots, see here." He stuck out one leg. "We were about to go for a ride in the park."

Sheridan smiled at the boy. "One of these days I will go with you on your ride and tell you the tale of your father riding my warhorse."

"He didn't!"

"Oh, yes he did and he wasn't much older than you are now."

Sheridan touched Frankie's shoulder. "Would you like to hear it?"

"Yes, please, tell me, don't make me wait."

"Very well, William, we'll walk to the stables and await you there." He led the boy away.

"How could Pa – err, Father, ride a warhorse?"

"He only held on for . . . ." Their voices faded down the hall.

Celeste smiled at William. "You've done very well with him. He's come so far in only a short time."

"He has a way to go until he will be acceptable to society."

"You remember some of the boys you grew up around. They were perfect terrors, arrogant and full of themselves. Frankie is learning to speak better and to appreciate the finer things without arrogance."

"He doesn't have time to cultivate arrogance. Everything is new to him."

"I remember how you were when we came back to society. You were twelve, angry, belligerent with your tutors. At first it was a task to teach you anything new."

He sighed. "I don't want my son to grow up all muddled about what is proper and what is good."

"You needn't worry, he won't be confused. He's got a fine example in his father."

"I'm not so sure about the example I set."

The London Standard – excerpt from the column of *Jolie Madame:*
My dears, have any of you seen Baron H out and about with his newly discovered son? They make a dashing pair, if a seven-year-old could be called dashing. Though still hampered with speech of the lower classes, F has adopted the fashion sense of his father, along with observing the proprieties at every turn. He is a most impressive young gentleman. I am certain his speech will improve with time.

As to his wicked mother, little has been heard of her since she left to pursue other interests on the Continent. Rumors abound but no facts are in evidence. It is whispered she took up with a French Duc, spending time with him at his estates in Bordeaux. She is rumored to be aligned with an Italian Count, as well as a scandalously handsome Spanish Matador. Who can say who gives her shelter these days?

Wherever she may be, it is for the best she remains there. Such a woman does not belong among our exalted ranks in England. Baron H and his handsome little son most certainly do not need her. Bravo Baron H, you are raising a wonderful son who will be the toast of the aristocracy one day.

Susanna stretched on the chaise and curled her bare toes as she looked out over the Mediterranean. "Such a lovely villa and such pleasant company, why would I ever want to go back to cold, damp England?"

"Why indeed?" Her host smiled, his white teeth a brilliant contrast to his deeply tanned skin. He took her hand, holding it as he lounged on the chaise next to hers.

"Baroness." The turbaned servant bowed beside her. "I bring the post for you."

With a frown, she took a letter from him. "Who even knows I am here?" She opened the envelope and a page of paper fell to the terrace floor.

The servant hurried and picked up the paper, presenting it to her.

She nodded and began to read. "It's from that witch. I never was able to discover her true identity, though she apparently had little difficulty finding me." She frowned as her eyes moved over the page.

"Is it bad news, my darling?"

"No, Carlos, it's just the awful woman trying to upset me once more."

He shrugged. "What do you care what they say in England? You are not there anymore. If I have my way, you will never return." He reached for her hand once more and brought it to his lips.

"I don't plan to go back there, unless we run out of money." She smiled at him, her eyes calculating. "I'm glad she sent this to me. It will give me the impetus for blackmail, should I need it."

With a panther's grace, he moved over her and pressed her down on the chaise. "Such an ugly word," he murmured as he trailed kisses down her skin bared by the dressing gown she wore.

"Yes, but such a lovely concept, darling." Laughing, she wrapped her arms around him and drew him closer.

Chapter Twelve

Josie clung to Caroline's hand as the strong wind buffeted her small body.

The minister droned on with the graveside service. Caroline opened her cape and drew the shivering little girl closer, wrapping the cape around her.

"Ashes to ashes, dust to dust . . . ."

Aidan choked back tears beside her.

Poor Josie and her father having to endure this. Such a shame the little girl lost her mother and Aidan lost his wife. I didn't need the doctor's examination to know she was likely murdered. When they find Meacham, his hand should match the huge bruise on the back of her neck that caused her death.

"In the name of the Father, and the Son, and the Holy Ghost . . ."

The minister's words drew Caroline's attention back to the funeral service. Many of the women from the settlement house were present, most of them pale, their tears already dried on their cheeks.

At last, the service concluded. Aidan stood holding his daughter's hand with Caroline holding Josie's other one. The small group of people in attendance lined up to murmur condolences to the bereaved husband and his little girl.

Later the guests returned to the Burgess home where luncheon was served. People spoke in the hushed tones of polite bereavement. Josie did not let go of Caroline's hand.

"Come now, Josie, Miss Caroline is tired. Let me take you upstairs where you can rest." Mrs. Arnold reached out to the little girl.

"No." She held Caroline's hand harder. "I want to stay here."

Mrs. Arnold shrugged and went to answer the doorbell.

Aidan bent to her. "Sweetheart, it has been a difficult day for all of us. Wouldn't you like to rest a bit?"

245

"No, Daddy, I don't want to leave Miss Caroline." Josie nestled deeper into her friend's skirts.

"She's all right with me."

Aidan frowned. "At least sit down before you fall. You look exhausted. Josie can sit beside you."

Caroline nodded and led the little girl to a settee. She sat and pulled the child on her lap. "There now, are you comfortable?"

Her eyes, closing as she snuggled against her benefactor, the child nodded before she drifted off to sleep.

"Poor little mite." She stroked the brown curls.

Mrs. Arnold came up to Aidan. "There's a police officer here asking for you, Mr. Cavanaugh."

He frowned. "I wonder what he could want. Excuse me, please." He hurried out of the room.

"Would you like a glass of sherry?" Mrs. Arnold frowned at Caroline.

"No, thank you, it would surely put me to sleep."

"How about some tea, then, you look as if you're going to collapse from fatigue."

"I suppose tea would be nice. If nothing else it should keep you and Aidan from worrying over me for a bit."

"Don't you sass me, young lady." The long-time servant grinned at her and went to fetch the tea.

When Aidan returned, he found the crowd gone and Caroline asleep holding Josie in her arms.

Moving with care, he eased his daughter into his own arms without waking her.

"What are you doing?" Caroline blinked up at him.

"I'm taking her home. The coach is waiting for us."

"You're welcome to stay here tonight, if you like." She rubbed her eyes as she struggled to an upright position.

"It's kind of you to suggest it, but we'll go back home. I think it would be better for her to wake in her own bed." He wrapped the woolen cape around his sleeping child. "We'll see you tomorrow, I expect."

She nodded as she stifled a yawn. "Oh, what did the police officer want? Did he have some more information on the case?"

Aidan hesitated as he glanced at his sleeping daughter.

"They found Meacham."

"They did? Well, that's wonderful, did he confess?"

"I'm afraid not." He turned to carry his child out of the house.

"But why not?" Caroline hurried after him. "Surely he's not claiming he's innocent."

Aidan looked at her before responding. "No, he's not claiming anything. He's dead. They found him tonight. Someone cracked open his skull."

"Where is everybody?" Lisette leaned on the reception desk. "It's so quiet here today." She looked all around at the empty space.

Caroline bustled through the door, tossing back her cape.

"Well, it's time you got here," Lisette greeted her with a teasing smile. "I was about to send the cavalry out after you. Nobody else is here and I was worried. You didn't even come down for breakfast at home."

"Didn't someone tell you?" Caroline hung her cape on a hook on the back wall. "I had an errand this morning."

"Oh la la." The English woman's eyes lit with mischief. "Were you meeting a man, perchance?"

"Yes I met a man."

"I knew it! I'm so glad you're finally seeing someone." With a grin, Lisette watched her friend. "Tell me all about him, where did you meet?"

"You've reverted to the debutante, haven't you?" Caroline sighed. "I met a man, a police officer. I wanted to ask him what they knew about Meacham's death."

"Oh, I'm sorry. I misunderstood." She looked down for a moment and took a deep breath. "What did you learn about Mr. Meacham's demise?"

Glancing around the entry area and finding it empty, Caroline finally answered. "He was killed before Aidan's wife. He could not have murdered her."

"Then who could have done it?"

"No one knows at this time. They're still looking for clues in the area where he was found. It is evident he was out in the elements since before the last snowstorm, a good three days, perhaps."

"But that means . . . ." she looked at Caroline in horror. "He could not have been the one who attacked Obadiah, either."

Caroline leaned close to Lisette to whisper into her ear. "We're not to discuss these findings with anyone until the police discover the truth. Do you understand?"

"Yes, of course. Are the women staying away from here because they're afraid?"

"No, they've all gotten jobs. They're at work."

"How did you manage to get positions for eight women?"

Caroline sighed. "It took some finagling, but I was able to persuade several business men and women to find places for them. Three were placed with merchants. Two now work for the archdiocese helping with the foundlings. The remaining three are sewing for my theater company. We still need to finish the costumes, the curtains, and the hangings for the stage."

"You're a wonder. Why didn't I know about all of this?"

"You were busy with your family. Don't worry, you can help with the next group."

Lisette glanced around the empty space. "It doesn't feel right for no one to be here. What will we do?"

"We need to document the progress for each woman in the ledgers. It's a tedious task but should keep us occupied for a bit."

"I don't like being here alone. It feels different, menacing somehow."

"Working on the ledgers will take your mind off the solitude."

"What about the unknown killer out there after you? What if he comes here?"

"Quit worrying, we'll be just fine."

Chapter Thirteen

"Explain yourself, young man." William stared at his son, frowning at the ripped coat, soil streaked breeches, and muddied boots.

"I got in a fight, but 'twasn't my fault, I tell ye. I was pro . . . pro . . . ."

"Provoked?" He took Frankie's chin in his hand. "You've got a bruise forming on your eye. Who hit you?"

Frankie ducked his head. "Don't matter. I took care of it." He refused to look at his father.

William took the boy's hand. "Come with me." He pulled him through the house and out onto the grounds.

"Where're ye takin' me?" Frankie stumbled trying to match his father's stride.

At last they reached the rose garden. William walked to the benches and gestured for Frankie to sit.

He looked at the bare plants pruned for the winter. "Why'd ye bring me here?"

William sat beside him. "Because out here, we can be sure no one will hear what we say to each other."

"Oh, so ye're gonna yell at me, are ye?"

He wrapped his arms around his slight body, his expression resembling a bulldog.

"No, I'm not. I thought it best we talk in private, so you are more comfortable telling me what happened today."

Frankie paused and then mumbled. "Nothin' for ye to do about it."

"Why don't you let me decide what I can and cannot do?" He leaned closer to his son. "Come on tell me who did this to you."

Heaving a loud sigh, Frankie began to speak. "I was walkin' down the street when I passed Lord High Snot Nose goin' to his coach."

"I presume you mean Viscount Lindsey?" *I must not laugh.*

"How'd ye know?"

William shrugged. "His father's home is the nearest to ours. It follows you would see him boarding his coach."

"Makes sense. Anyways, I passed him by, not wantin' any trouble, and he started in again . . . ." Frankie looked away. "The toff says 'well look here what we've got—a guttersnipe disguised as a gent'. I kept walkin' but he came after me."

This reminds me of the fights I used to get into. "What did he do then?"

Frankie shrugged. "I don't like to say."

"Tell me. It's all right."

The boy took a deep breath. "He said I was a dirty little beggar dressin' up like quality, only I wasn't. He laughed and said I was the son of a whore and . . . ." He looked away.

"And?" William prompted him.

"He called you a no-class popinjay, taken in by a schemin' woman. I couldn't help it. I had to hit him after that."

"Then he hit you?"

Frankie grinned. "No, he was down on the ground screamin' by then."

Sounds like something I'd do back in the day. "Isn't Viscount Lindsey older than you are?"

"He's twelve and he's bigger, but he fights like a girl."

I mustn't smile, mustn't encourage such behavior, but how I would've liked to see the fight. "Then how did you get so dirty?"

Frankie shrugged. "He sent his stable boy after me. We had a real fight we did, rollin' in the dirt and all."

"Who won?"

"Well, I'd say it was a draw."

"Is he as dirty as you are?"

The boy stuck out his chest. "Hard to tell, he was dirty already. But I got him down and got in a punch or two."

William put his arm around his son's shoulders. "We need to talk."

The lad deflated, slumping down on the bench. "I knew it, 'ere it comes."

"No, I'm not going to lecture you. This isn't really your fault." *You've got to fight the identical battles I did.*

Frankie looked up at him, one eyebrow lifted. "Then whose fault is it?"

It's like looking in a mirror. "I was exactly the same as you when I was a boy. I was twelve when we came back to London. Until then I grew up in the country running with the rough lads in the village. We got into some great brawls."

"Tell me about 'em." The boy looked up at his father with eager eyes.

"I will someday, I promise. Now I'd like you to understand something. It's hard to go from one world to another."

"I can handle it."

"Yes, you can take on anything that comes your way. You will live in this world from now on. You must learn how to live with these people."

"What if I don't wanna?"

William grinned at him. "What if I teach you the proper way to fight? I will hire a boxing tutor for you. Would you like that?"

"Yeah, I would." Frankie's eyes danced with excitement as he looked up at his father.

"I'll tell you a secret, Son. Once you learn how to move through this world, you'll have no more trouble. The most important thing is always be yourself. You don't need to put on fancy affectations. They'll respect you more if you don't."

I learned the lesson the hard way by driving away the woman I love. At least my son will benefit from my experience.

"The first act went well." Caroline smiled at the assembled cast. "We will begin the next act after a respite of fifteen minutes. Tomorrow night we will run through the production like a performance. Remember, there are only three more rehearsals until opening night. Thank you, everyone."

Accompanied by the sound of the cast departing the wooden stage, she turned and sighed.

Everything is going fine. I thought I'd be happy at this point.

Walking into the lobby, she glanced out the side windows by the entrance. The street was empty of pedestrians and quiet. She leaned against the frame and watched her breath fog up the chilled glass. *I wonder if the weather is as cold in London as it is here. I wonder what William is doing?*

She twisted her lips in a self-deprecating grin. *No doubt he's asleep, likely with his wife. Don't be an idiot. He's lost to you and nothing can be done.*

Turning to go, movement in the street made her look out the window once more. A tall figure wrapped in a hooded black cape with a slouch hat on his head moved with no difficulty through the icy February night.

What are you up to?

She moved farther from the glass, not wanting to reveal her position. The person kept walking toward the door, glancing from side to side as he approached.

Caroline backed away from the door, hurrying into the alcove where the patrons would check their coats. Her back to the wall, she heard the outer door open with careful stealth.

Dear Lord, he's inside. Her panting breath sounded loud in her ears. She put her hand over her mouth to muffle the noise.

He's walking, is he coming this way?

With an effort, she stifled a gulp and waited.

The footsteps, deadened by the expensive new carpets in the lobby, continued.

With a shaking breath, she eased her way to the edge of the sheltering wall.

I have to see what he's doing . . . one, two, three . . . . She turned her head, leaned her neck out, and glimpsed the figure, his back to her, as he stuck a note on the door to the auditorium with a knife. He stopped as if to admire his work.

Her mouth dropped open as she gasped. She drew back quickly into her sanctuary.

Please don't let him find me please . . . . She covered her mouth with both hands.

She heard no sound.

Where is he? Why isn't he moving?

Her breath came faster than before, until she panted her fright.

The footsteps started coming toward the alcove where she hid.

She froze, awaiting the inevitable discovery, incapable of thought in her panic. There was nowhere to hide. She was trapped.

"Caroline?" Jack's voice was muffled. "We're ready to start the next act. Where are you?"

Quiet footsteps rushed away from her, ending with the sound of the outer door opening and slamming shut.

"Caroline." Jack's voice followed the smooth sound of the well-oiled inner door opening. "Where are you?"

She leaned over, trying to breathe. "I'm coming."

"What are you doing in here?" He appeared in the alcove entrance.

"Hiding—somebody slipped in here and put a note on the door."

Jack took her hand. "You need to sit down. Let's go into the theater."

She pulled back. "Not until I see the note." With determination, she moved to the door. "There, you see?" She gestured to the paper and knife on the door.

Her hands trembled and she took the knife out of the door and grabbed the note before it fell.

Oh no, I was hoping it wasn't meant for me . . . .

"What does it say?" Jack leaned over her to look at the paper.

Without a word, she handed it to him.

I'll git you bitch. He read aloud and looked at her. "Did you see who left this?"

"Only from the back." She gasped for breath.

He gave the note back to her and rolled up his sleeves. "If he's still out there, I'll teach him some better manners." He started for the door.

She grabbed his arm. "No, don't go out there. He's dangerous. He might well be the same man who attacked Obadiah."

"Do you have your gun with you?"

She shook her head. "I don't like carrying it since . . . Gareth."

He looked out the window at the street. "Nobody's out there." He turned back to her. "I suggest you carry your gun with you whenever you leave your house until the man is caught."

She nodded. "Let's get back to rehearsal. Jack, I'd rather you don't say anything to Jayne or the cast about what happened."

"They all need to know if they're in danger. This man could hurt anyone here."

"I'll hire guards for the theater. It makes sense. We'll be opening on Friday night."

He took her arm and led her into the theater. "I'd feel better if you hired a bodyguard to accompany you wherever you go."

"I will, and guards for the theater as well. Are you satisfied?"

"If there's any other trouble, I'll go straight to Mr. Burgess." He frowned down at her. "You don't understand how dangerous this man could be."

"I saw his handiwork on Obadiah, remember? I promise I'll be careful, take no more chances, and carry my gun."

Chapter Fourteen

"Father." Franklin ran up to him. "Look at what I can do." He ran over to Seamus O'Malley. "Can we show him?"

"Right ye are, Master Franklin." The burly boxing coach winked at William and got down on his knees.

Holding his hands palm out in front of his body, O'Malley, barked his orders. "Very well, begin . . . uppercut—nice one, right jab—good, left jab—that's the spirit, you've got the hang of it."

"See me? I can do it . . . ." Frankie bobbed and weaved back to his parent.

"You're doing well, Son, and it's only your first lesson."

"All right, give me a right cross." O'Malley drew the attention back to the lesson.

The boy complied. "And here's one from the left."

"Good one!" O'Malley grinned at his student.

Sheridan stood in the doorway smiling as he watched. "Nice job. Did you learn the roundhouse punch yet?"

The boy shook his head. "What kind of punch is that?"

"It's one you didn't learn today."

"'ow do ye do it?" The boy smiled at his uncle.

The Viscount Brenham stroked his chin and pretended to contemplate. "Well, as I remember, you wind up by moving your arm backward like a pinwheel. Do you know what that is?"

"O'course I do," Frankie scoffed. "I bet I can do it . . . ." He faced O'Malley.

"Master Franklin, ye shouldna try to do a punch ye havena practiced."

"I can do it." He tossed his head and rotated his arm backward over and over gaining momentum. He punched his teacher's upraised palm with great force.

O'Malley remained still, a stone facing a child.

255

The force of the punch hitting the man's palm and meeting resistance knocked Frankie backward. He dropped hard to the floor.

"What happened?" He shook his head, still jarred from the experience.

William lifted him to a standing position. "Are you hurt, Son?" Looking up at Sheridan who tried to suppress his grin, William warned him with a scowl.

Quickly composing a contrite expression, Sheridan looked at his nephew. "I'm sorry, Frankie. I wasn't clear in my instructions. You must wind up the arm once and then punch. Do you understand?"

The boy nodded and cocked his head. "I get it. Just once around and then ye hit."

"Very good." O'Malley moved beside him. "With yer permission, Baron Hargreaves, I believe Master Franklin should practice and we'll resume our lessons tomorrow afternoon."

"Yes, thank you, I'll see he practices this evening." William nodded to the instructor. "You are dismissed until tomorrow."

"Thank ye." The muscled boxer bowed and walked out the door.

"Would you like to see if Cook has a treat for you? I think you deserve something special today. Why don't you run along, I'll join you in the kitchen." He looked at Sheridan, his lips twisted. "After I speak to Uncle Sheri."

"Yes, sir." Frankie ran out the door, "But there might not be anything left when I get through." The sound of his feet pattered across the polished floor.

His father sighed and looked at his brother-in-law. "What were you doing? Frankie has been battered enough. How could you embarrass him like that?"

Sheridan smiled and put his hand on William's shoulder. "He's fine. Don't you remember? I pulled the same trick on you when you were twelve. There's no harm in teasing him."

"I don't want him ridiculed by his family. He'll get enough of it among the members of the gentry."

"A little gentle teasing by the family won't hurt him. It will make him feel part of us, bring him closer. Did you resent it when I teased you?"

"No, but I was older than he is and I remembered my family, the way it was."

"Frankie will adapt and fit right in with us. Drake will tease him, you can be sure of it. Your son isn't used to being part of a family. The teasing and roughhousing is part of the relationships. You watch, in a few months it will be like he was always with us."

"I hope you're right."

Sheridan guided him to the door. "I'm right. I raised a son of my own, didn't I? Go on and catch up with yours. Tell him how well he did today."

William nodded and disappeared down the corridor.

"Dispensing your fatherly wisdom, my love?" Celeste stood watching him.

"How long have you been there?"

"Long enough." She smiled up at him and she slipped her arm around his waist. "You make me remember why I fell in love with you so long ago."

He smiled down at her as he gathered her in his arms. "Remind me of the reason, won't you?"

"Well." She grinned as she picked at the buttons on his waistcoat. "You were handsome."

"Only handsome, not very handsome?" his eyes danced with suppressed laughter.

"Don't press your luck, Viscount Brenham." Her hand stopped to rest on his chest.

"What else did you like about me?"

She cocked her head as she pursed her lips. "You owned a great horse."

"What a thing to say. Don't you want to praise my eyes, or my physique, or my commanding manner?"

She sighed as she hugged him. "You are my match in every way and I always knew it even when I hated you."

He kissed the top of her curls. "CeCe, you are my life. I hate to think how empty my days would be without you and our children."

They stood together noting only their closeness, not the passage of the moments.

Finally she pulled back and gazed up at him. "You're good for William, you always were. He'll learn how to be a good father from you."

"I hope so. He's been stunned by recent events. Does he know where his wife is?"

"No, she's gone somewhere on the continent. *Jolie Madame* seems to know much more about his wife than he does." She sighed. "I hate it that he'll never know what we have together. It's such a shame he's saddled with such an awful wife."

Sheridan sighed. "We must hope his situation changes, although it isn't likely."

"He misses Caroline. I've watched his eyes when we read her letters. They should be together."

He hugged her once more. "If they are meant to be together, they will find a way."

Chapter Fifteen
Opening Night

Caroline inhaled a deep breath of the crisp air. The stars glimmered above in the clear night sky. *Thank heaven it stopped snowing.*

With a nod to Obadiah, she left the coach and walked to the theater entrance. The back of her neck tingled and she frowned as she glanced behind her.

I must be imagining things. It's probably opening night jitters. Still, I'm glad Obadiah has Heston with him, wouldn't do to have him injured again.

Shaking off the feeling, she walked into the theater, smiling at the guards stationed inside on either side of the entrance.

Aidan greeted her in the lobby. "We've sold out the house. Do you know how much money comes in with a filled house?"

She smiled at him and touched his arm. "I expect it won't cover the expenses but it's a good start." She started to walk down to the stage entrance.

"Oh, I almost forgot, someone left a note for you." He searched his pockets until he found the envelope. "Ah, here it is." He held it out to her.

"Where did you find it?" Her voice shook.

"I believe Jack found it when he came to open up for the actors. Why, is there a problem?"

"No." She stretched her lips in a fake grin. "I'm sure it's fine, likely someone offering best wishes."

"I'm surprised no one delivered flowers for you. Isn't it expected on opening night?"

She shook her head. "Not for the owner, only for the actresses, besides flowers are rare in the winter, far too expensive. Well, I'd best get backstage and see how our cast members are." She turned and walked away. "Thank you for the note," she called over her shoulder.

In the theater, lit only by the stage lights, she made her way down the center aisle. When she reached a pool of light spilling from the stage, she stopped. With trembling hands, she opened the envelope.

I ain't forgot. I'll come fer ye when ye ain't lookin'. Enjoy the little show. Ye won't be doin' no more.

Caroline glanced around the silent auditorium. Shadows leapt from the flickering gaslights onstage, causing shapes to dance about the walls and between the rows of seats.

Don't be silly, you're safe in here. Heston is outside watching the entrance. The inside is guarded. The whole cast is here. No one would dare try anything.

With a stubborn jut to her chin, she stuffed the note into her reticule. *I'll deal with this later. I've got to greet the actors and give them the opening night speech. And then, we've got a show to do.*

Walking up the steps to the stage, she headed backstage through the curtains and side hangings. She walked straight through and down the stairs to the dressing rooms.

Three hours later, she sat in the audience as they erupted in thunderous applause. Around her everyone stood, the men shouting, "Well done." The ladies cried "Bravo! Brava!"

Caroline smiled so much her cheeks hurt. When the chandeliers were lowered over the audience, she clapped and called for quiet.

"Thank you, ladies and gentlemen, for your wonderful response to our efforts. If you'd like to exit to the reception area off the lobby, you will find champagne and dainties being served for your enjoyment. Please take care as you exit the auditorium." *At least I can still project my voice.*

The evening was a great success. Caroline grinned at Aidan. "I understand we have reservations booked throughout the run of the play."

"Indeed we do. I am most pleased about the outcome of tonight's success. This could be a profitable venture, after all." He ducked his head for a moment and then took her hand.

"Miss Caroline, I must tell you how grateful I am you were kind enough to offer me the position. You made it possible for Josie to live in a stable home and go to school like other little girls. I cannot thank you enough."

She patted his hand. "Nonsense, I should thank you. I seized the opportunity to hire a skilled manager for my theater. We both win. I don't know what we would do without you."

"Let us say we benefitted from our mutual society."

His eyes darkened as he looked at her. His voice dropped. "Perhaps we could benefit in other ways from this association." He leaned closer to her.

Caroline put her hand on his chest. "I should tell you my heart is given elsewhere. I'm not the kind of woman who enjoys dallying with men." She stepped back from him. "I'm sorry if I gave you the wrong impression."

He coughed and looked away, avoiding her eyes. "No, you did nothing wrong. I assumed a connection where none exists. For that I must apologize."

"Shall we agree to be friends?" She thrust out her hand.

He eyed her offered hand and took it in his own, shaking it with confidence. "Friends, it is. May I see you home?"

"No, thank you, my coachman and my guard are waiting outside for me. I'll be fine."

"If you're sure, I will lock up and close the building. I'll see you tomorrow night."

"Yes. Thank you for your hard work in bringing this production together. Don't dismiss the guards until you're ready to leave." She put on her cape with his help and pulled up her hood.

"You're welcome. I look forward to tomorrow night." He turned to go back to his office.

Caroline pulled on her gloves and watched him go. *He's such a nice fellow. I shall look for a lady for him. I know he'd be happier with a wife as well as a good mother for Josie. I wonder if I know someone.*

She walked out into the frigid night.

"I was coming to fetch you." Heston took her arm. "It's late and time for you to be at home." He helped her mount the step into the carriage.

She leaned out to tease him. "Really Heston, you're like an old woman."

As she glanced at him, she saw someone standing down the street out of the meager lamplight—tall, garbed in a long cloak, hood, mask, and a slouch hat, all in black. The figure executed a mocking bow in her direction.

Dear Lord, he is so close. She put her hand to her throat to calm her racing heartbeat.

"What is it, Miss Caroline, what's wrong?" She looked down at Heston.

"Didn't you notice the man?"

"What man?" He looked around. "I don't see anyone."

Where did he go? "I tell you he was right there on the next corner, just out of the range of the streetlamp."

"There's no one now. It's time for you to go home. You've had too much excitement." He gestured for her to retreat inside the coach.

"But I saw him, I know I did."

"I'm sure you thought you did, Miss Caroline. In any case, we must get you safely home." He shut the door and peered in the open window.

"Obadiah will get us home in no time. You rest. It's been a long night."

She sat back against the squabs. The carriage lurched forward, the team trotting over the cobbled streets.

I know someone was out there. I saw him.

"*Querida.*" Carlos leaned over her. "Are you feeling better?" His hand stroked her back as she turned her face away.

"Go away." Her voice was muffled. "I've been sick. I'm not fit for company."

"I am not a stranger. I am the man who loves you." He brushed his lips over her bare shoulder. "What can I bring you to make you feel better?"

Susanna groaned. "I don't want anything, even the thought of food makes me want to retch."

He continued to stroke her back. "I know what ails you."

"Did we have bad food last night? Did you get sick, too?"

Turning her over to face him, Carlos smiled. "I think you are carrying my child."

"But I can't be. I'm too old." *Dear Lord, what would I do with another brat?*

He hugged her to his warm chest. "You are not too old. I am certain you will deliver our baby in the autumn. The signs are all there."

"How would you know the signs?"

"My mother had eight children after I was born. Believe me, I know what happens." He smiled down at her. "I've been hoping we would have a child together."

She pulled back and sat against the pillows, drawing the sheet up over her bare breasts. "Well, I haven't. You don't know what having a child is like for a woman. I never intended to have another one."

"Like it or not, you are having another one. We need to make plans."

"Plans for what?" She fussed with the covers and scowled at him. *I hope he doesn't plan to set me up somewhere for his convenience.*

"We will marry as soon as the Church sanctions our union."

"Hello? I am already married, remember?" *He must be delusional, thoughts of being a father completely turned his head.*

"Yes, but you were married in England, outside the sanctity of the Catholic Church. I am certain we can arrange to have a ceremony here in Spain once the church accepts the annulment of your English marriage."

Confident, aren't you? "What if I don't want to be married to anyone, even you?"

"I will claim you and our child. You will never want for anything. We will live an exciting life."

She snorted. "You mean you will live an exciting life, while I'll be stuck in the hacienda with the brat and all the brats to follow. It's not the way I pictured my life."

"I'm already a wealthy man, younger than your baron, and in love with you. What more could you want? I will give you everything you ask. You will live like a queen in a palace worthy of you."

Susanna cocked her head and looked at him.

He has far more wealth than most of the English aristocracy, including William. He's the best lover I've ever known.

She smiled at him as she pondered his proposal. *If I get bored, he's so besotted I will be able to control him. There will be nurses and dueñas for the children. I won't have to do a thing. This could work to my advantage.*

She reached out and ran her long-nailed fingers up his leg. "Carlos, you make perfect sense. If you can obtain an annulment for me, I will marry you."

"There. It was not a difficult decision for you, was it? I will make you very happy, you'll see. I will provide for you and our children."

Gulping, she stared at him. "How many children do you want to have?"

"As many as come to us. We might best my mother's record." He laughed, his eyes twinkling.

That's easy for you to say. You're not the one who has to give birth. She drew an unsteady breath.

"*Querida.*" He pulled her into a deep embrace. "You will never regret your decision."

Feeling her gorge about to rise, she pulled back. *I regret it already.*

"Carlos, I'm about to be sick once more, please leave me. I don't want you to see me like this."

He moved off the bed and went to the door. "Alma, come quickly, your lady is ill."

"Carlos, please leave now. I don't want to be sick in front of you."

He moved back to the bedside and took her hand. "I will never leave you."

He brought her hand to his lips. "Ah, here is Alma. See to your mistress, she is ill this morning."

Chapter Sixteen
Parkfield - March, 1843

Fyffe scurried down the hall, out of breath. "Baron Hargreaves, a post rider delivered a message for you." He stood panting in William's study. "I thought you would want this right away."

"Thank you, Fyffe, for your consideration." *It's likely something from Drake or Mimi, nothing of great importance.* "You are dismissed."

The man bowed before him and made a hasty exit from the room, as if to avoid any conflict.

I suppose he thinks this is something upsetting. Perhaps he's right.

William looked at the outside of the paper bundle. *This is from Spain, Andalusia. Who do I know in . . . oh, Susanna must want more money. I don't know if I'm at all disposed to finance her voyages forever.* Breaking the seal, he opened the letter and began to read.

Fyffe had just caught his breath and walked in a proper sedate manner back to the kitchen.

Suddenly a loud shout echoed through the house.

"Huzzah!"

The scrawny butler jumped, barely containing his anxious shriek. He ran to aid the Baron. "Sir, what is it? Is something amiss?"

William capered in the middle of the room, bubbling laughter surrounding him like froth. "Nothing is wrong, nothing will ever be wrong again." He grabbed the man's slight shoulders. "You brought me the best news I ever received. I should kiss you." He leaned toward his servant.

Fyffe jumped back. "Oh, please don't do that, Sir. It . . . it isn't necessary, truly."

"I tell you, my good man, you brought a miracle to me this day."

Still eying his employer with suspicion, the smaller man backed away a bit. "Think nothing of it, nothing at all."

"Bring Frankie to me, will you?"

"Of course, Sir, right away." Eager to be out of the Baron's effusive company, his servant hurried to fetch the boy.

William watched him disappear down the long corridor, a smile on his face. *I wonder, what is the best way to tell your son we're about to be annulled?*

Jayne frowned down at her best friend. "You're working too hard, Caroline. You haven't stopped since before Christmas. Wouldn't you like a rest?"

Caroline sighed and put down her quill.

"I must manage the settlement house as well as work on the next production at the theater. Besides, what else would you have me do, find some nice man and get married because it's expected of me?"

Without ceremony, Jayne sat in front of the desk. "Is your father badgering you again?"

"He means well, I believe, but he doesn't let up on the lectures. Father will not listen to me. He thinks I should marry and is becoming more concerned about my status, which makes him less likely to listen to my protests."

"You're in a difficult position, to be sure. I don't envy you. Still, what could it hurt to start seeing one of the men he brings to dinner?"

"I don't want to give anyone, including my father, false hope of an eventuality which will never occur."

Jayne reached across the desk and put her hand on Caroline's. "I realize you still pine for the opinionated cold fish we left back in England."

"He's not—"

"Oh yes, he is. Has he sent you any letters or messages since we've been here?"

"No, of course not, he married someone else."

"And the fact he married her doesn't give you pause, give you a glimpse of reality? Face it. William Hargreaves will never come for you.

He'd be a cad if he did. He is married to the mother of his son. He is lost to you. Accept it as fact and invite someone else to dinner. What about Patrick Harris? He's interested in you and approved of by your father."

Caroline withdrew her hand and wiped a tear from her eye. "I can't forget William. I've tried but it's useless."

"You must face the truth. He is no longer available. You should see other men and move on with your life."

She's right. I can't keep waiting for someone who will never come. Wiping her face, she sighed. "So you like Patrick Harris, do you?"

"What's not to like? He's handsome with his black hair and dark eyes. He's also wealthy therefore not interested in your fortune."

Caroline snorted. "He may still be interested in my fortune. For some men acquiring more wealth is a lifelong goal."

"You will never know what kind of man he is unless you spend time with him."

"All right, I'll send an invitation for dinner on Friday."

Jayne smiled and clapped her hands together. "Good. Now, what will you wear?"

"I don't know. I'll select something, it's not important."

"I'll remind you of what you just said on the day you get married."

"You're looking forward to a day I may never see."

Jayne stood, "Oh I think you will most definitely marry. I can see it."

"Go on with you, I must finish my work." Caroline smiled as she shooed her friend out the door.

Jayne laughed as she left the room. "Write a nice invitation so Patrick will accept."

It doesn't matter what kind of invitation I write, he'll come. Jayne's right, he is handsome. Somehow, he leaves me cold though, they all do. I bet he's never skipped a stone in his entire life.

She picked up the next letter.

Wonderful, Heston reports no more sightings of the stalker since February. Excellent. I'm glad to be able to put those incidents behind me.

Shaking her head, she recalled the last time the man threatened her.

I don't know why he stopped tormenting me, but I'm glad he did. I was beginning to think it was my imagination.

Drake strode into the offices of Foster Shipping in Norfolk, Virginia.

"Captain St John," Cooper greeted him with a smile. "I haven't seen you in months. How are you?"

"I'm well, thank you. Is Elijah here?"

"He's gone to a meeting but should be back soon. Haven't you gone to the house?"

Drake shook his head. "I have personal business to discuss with him. I'd rather Aunt Mimi doesn't get wind of it."

Cooper nodded. "I understand. Elijah should be back within the hour. You can wait here if you like. We have the blueprints for the next steamer. Would you like to see them?"

"Sounds good, yes, I'll take a look."

When Elijah arrived, he found Drake poring over the plans.

"She'll be a beauty, won't she?"

Drake looked up. "I didn't hear you come in. The plans look fantastic. When will this one be launched?"

Elijah put his hat on the hall tree and sat at his desk. "The keel is already laid and riveted. We anticipate the ship will be ready in the autumn of this year."

"It's amazing how much faster ships are built now, not to mention how much quicker their voyages can be."

"Speaking of quick voyages, I didn't expect you until next week. Were there any problems on your crossing?"

Drake shook his head. "No, I was anxious to get here, and return to England for the next scheduled voyage."

"Why are you in such a hurry?" Elijah looked at him.

Drake looked away. "After the next voyages scheduled are completed, I want leave to travel to Ireland on personal business."

"Let me guess. You want to see Bridget."

"Her father intercepted my last letter and returned it. I have to see her to determine if she still feels . . . well, if—"

"If she still loves you." Elijah looked at him with understanding.

"Yes. I can't let her go if there's any hope for us. If she doesn't feel the same way, at least I'll be able to stop pining for her."

Nodding, Elijah rose. "I tell you what, we'll get the *American Eagle* unloaded and prepared for the return voyage to England. I don't think any passengers booked her for the trip. If not, we can get you loaded and you can leave in, say, four days. Will it be satisfactory?"

"Yes it will." Drake shook Elijah's hand. "Thank you for doing this."

Elijah clapped him on the shoulder. "Your lady must be your priority."

"I'm not sure she is my lady or even wants to be."

"Don't look so downtrodden. If what I saw of you on the voyage back from Casablanca is any indication, you should not worry."

"I hope you're right."

"I am." Elijah smiled, "But don't tell Mimi I said so. Now, let's get you home to your aunt. If she knows we kept her waiting she'll skin us both."

Drake grinned in return. "She doesn't even know I'm in port."

"This is Mimi we're talking about. Do you think it will make any difference in her reaction?"

"You made your point."

Chapter Seventeen

Excerpt from the *London Standard*—column of *Jolie Madame*:

My dears, you will positively swoon with the latest escapade of the notorious Baroness H. Not only did she leave her husband Baron H and their young son to go traipsing about the Continent, it seems she fell in love with El Matador. Can you credit it? I scarcely can. Apparently, he has connections in Rome. Baroness H was granted an annulment, thanks to the intercession of a highly placed Bishop. Word is by the time you read this she will no longer be Baroness H but El Matador's Señora. It does help to have influence, dontchaknow.

Poor Baron H never deserved such a wife. He is well rid of the harridan. No doubt he will instruct his son to become a fine upstanding gentleman. It is a most refreshing turn of events to find the good Baron once again on the matrimonial market. Add him to your guest lists, ladies, he remains a superb catch.

"You don't understand. I must sail on your next voyage." William's face grew warm as he argued with Drake.

"Me, too," piped Frankie. "We got to get to Philadelphia for the rock-skippin' lady."

Drake looked at his uncle. "What is he talking about?"

William put his arm around Frankie's shoulders. "I realized long ago what a mistake I made in rejecting Caroline. I want to win her back."

"Yeah, she sounds like a right 'un. I want her for my new mama." The boy nodded his head with incisive speed.

"Surely there are other ships traveling to America."

"Yes, but not as fast as the *American Eagle*. Please, Drake, I'll book full passage for both of us."

"Look, Uncle William, I'd like to help you, but I won't be staying. We're due to sail back three days after arrival. I don't know when I'll be returning to Philadelphia. How will you sail back to England?"

I've got to make him understand. "Wouldn't you be desperate to find your lady if you were in my position?"

"I understand your predicament, but—"

"Suppose I absolve you of the responsibility of carrying us back to England? Will you allow us to travel with you to Philadelphia?"

"Why are you in such a hurry to get there?"

Frankie elbowed his way in front of his father.

"We got a letter from my cousin Lisette. She says Miss Caroline is about to marry another gent. We ain't gonna let it happen. Now d'ye understand the gra, uh, grav, uh—"

"Gravity?" Drake suppressed a smile.

"Yeah, that's the word, well d'ye know what I mean?"

"I see you're most interested in reuniting your father with Miss Caroline."

Frankie frowned up at him. "He says she's as good at rock-skippin' as he is. Who wouldn't want a mama like that?"

"Indeed." Drake grinned at the boy.

"Very well, Uncle William, between you and my cousin Frankie, you won your case. Be packed and ready to leave tomorrow morning."

"Aye, Aye, Cap'n." Frankie saluted, then frowned at the smiles on the faces of the adults. "Well, it's what them sailors do, ain't it?"

Caroline sat and watched the rehearsal for the curtain call of *Love's Labour's Lost*. She sighed. *Of all the plays I could have picked to stage now . . . .*

She wiped a tear from her eye. *I hope nobody noticed.*

Footsteps sounded behind her coming nearer. "What is it, dearest?"

Willing her face to smile, she turned and greeted her fiancé.

"Patrick, I did not expect you so early. How was your meeting?"

He brought her to her feet and kissed her. "The meeting was dull. I kept thinking of my beautiful lady toiling at her theater." He smiled down at her, his dark eyes fathomless in the limited light from the stage.

"Sitting through a rehearsal run by the director is hardly what I consider toiling." She smiled at him with a simple stretching of her lips.

"I know you better than you think. Tell me what made you cry and I will make it go away."

Sighing, she looked up into his eyes. *You cannot fix my sadness. Even though I accepted your proposal, I cannot forget William. I doubt I ever will. It isn't fair to you. I don't love you. But we get along together and Father wants it for me.*

"You alarm me, my love. Won't you tell me what made you weep?"

She turned away wiping her eyes once more. "It's nothing. The play does not end well, that's all. There is no true resolution to the story, no happy ending."

He gathered her into his arms from behind and rested his head on her shoulder. "So you crave a happy ending, do you?"

"All women do, you must know how we think." She gently worked out of his embrace. "We'll do something a bit lighter next time, perhaps *A Midsummer Night's Dream*. The way our audiences are growing we can justify the expense of such a grand production."

He took her arm without asking. "You've done enough this evening. I'm taking you home."

"But I've got to speak to Jack and the cast members before I leave."

"Now, now." His ingratiating smile was firmly in place, "I know what's best for my lady. You can speak to everyone tomorrow." He led her up the aisle and out the auditorium door.

I don't care if he is my father's choice. Let him marry Patrick. I'd wager they'd do well together.

At the absurdity of the manifestation of her thoughts, she began to giggle.

"You see, there you have it." He clicked his tongue and walked her out of the building. "You're so tired, you are giddy. Perhaps you should give up this silly theater notion. I know it makes a tidy profit, but you should turn it over to someone else."

"I can't do any such thing. The theater is my creation, one for which I worked hard and long to realize. It is unthinkable for me to give it away."

As they neared the carriage, he patted her arm. "You'll see, when the babies start coming you will not have time for such foolery." He nodded to the footman as he handed her off to the servant's assistance.

She sat on the seat, watching as Patrick boarded, sitting opposite her.

How did I get into this mess? The wedding looms, everything is planned down to the last detail. Everyone else seems to be happy for me. Why am I so unhappy at the prospect of marrying this man?

She looked up at the starlit sky.

What am I going to do?

"Jayne." Lisette tugged her friend's sleeve and spoke in a whisper. "Are you available now for a bit of a chat?"

Jayne looked around the empty lobby. "No one is here seeking help. They don't usually come at this time of night. I suppose we could talk in the side office so I can see if anyone comes in."

Once they were settled in chairs in the small office, Lisette glanced out the open door before speaking.

"I've done something I may come to regret."

"What could you possibly do?"

Lisette looked down. "I couldn't help noticing how sad Caroline is." She glanced up. "I don't think she wants to marry Mr. Harris."

Jayne shrugged. "She knows her own mind. Perhaps she is ready to marry and he's the most pleasing prospect."

"Perhaps, he is handsome enough and wealthy as well. Mr. Burgess seems to like him."

"He's thrilled at the prospect of having Mr. Harris for a son-in-law. I've heard him say as much."

"What have you heard Caroline say on the matter? Anything?"

Jayne's eyes narrowed as she appeared to consider. "Come to think of it, she hasn't said much about her marriage at all. She's very busy with the play opening in a few days. She might only be distracted."

"Nobody is so distracted by other matters, when she's about to wed. I don't think she's happy."

"Now you mention it, she hasn't talked about the wedding plans. Her discussions have been about the production or the settlement house. What do you suppose it all means?"

"Nothing good, I'm sure, but I've done something to help the situation."

"Lisette, what did you do? You didn't meddle in her business, did you?"

"I didn't do too much. I only wrote my mother about Caroline's upcoming marriage."

Jayne stared at her friend. "Tell me you didn't do it."

Lisette tossed her blond curls. "I did nothing wrong. I simply set things in motion for Caroline and Uncle William to have another chance."

"Oh, you didn't, how could you? Why would you torment them both with what can never be?"

"Humph." She crossed her arms. "If I know my uncle William, he'll find a way to make his wishes all come true. You wait and see."

Chapter Eighteen
Aboard the American Eagle

Frankie stood on a chair looking over the prow of the ship as it cut through the sea.

"Your perch is a bit precarious, don't you think?" William walked up to him. *Good Lord, he could fall overboard.*

"I ain't never seen nothin' like this. There's only water as far as I can see." Frankie turned and looked at his father.

William smiled as he reached for the boy and lifted him off the chair on to the deck. "It's beautiful, but you could fall into it. Let's talk awhile, all right?"

"What'd I do now?" Frankie's face became sullen.

"You didn't do anything. I want to tell you about my family, how I grew up. Let's sit in the deck chairs instead of standing on them." He guided his son to a seat and took the next one for himself. "You already know about my father, how he was executed, and we were banished from society."

"Uh huh."

"I liked living in the small town in the country. Nobody tried to make me into something I didn't want to be. But when we were brought back to live with the duke and his family, everything changed. All of a sudden, there were all these rules and ways to behave. I didn't like it and I was twelve, not seven like you."

Frankie looked at him, a quizzical eyebrow raised.

I'm making a muck of this.

"I want you to understand I made mistakes. Some of the snobs laughed at me, made fun of me. When I'd decided I'd make them stop laughing, I resolved to outdo them in the manners department." He shook his head. "I withdrew into myself and never let anybody else know the real

276

me. Can you understand?"

"It's when ye became so hoity-toity."

"Exactly, and it was the wrong thing to do. By retreating into a shell, I hurt a lot of people."

"Had to be a big shell for ye to fit into it. Where'd ye ever find it?"

William subdued his laugh. *He's only seven. He's bound to take everything literally.* He smiled at the boy.

"I didn't mean I climbed into an actual seashell. I meant I hid my real feelings and pretended to be somebody else."

"Now ye're makin' sense."

"The pretense cost me my friends as well as Miss Caroline. I hurt her by acting like a prejudiced aristocrat. Now I know better and I hope it's not too late to win her back."

Frankie pursed his lips and looked at his father. "I hope ye learned yer lesson. I don't want to miss out on a lady who can skip rocks."

"I did learn my lesson, the hard way. Now I want you to learn from it, too. Always be yourself, you'll learn proper grammar and better speech, but don't change who you are."

The boy frowned up at him. "What d'ye mean?"

"You're a bright lad, full of energy and spunk. I want you to always stand up for yourself and your family. I want you to grow to be a good man, not hiding under the mask of a cold aristocrat."

"Kin ye show me how to be a good man?"

William smiled with relief. "It's my job to do just that." He looked around for a moment and spied the chair Frankie dragged to the prow. "All right, here is your first lesson. See the chair you moved over there?"

"Yeah." Frankie's eyes were puzzled. "What about it?"

"The men on this ship all work very hard. There're lots of chores for them to do. Sometimes they don't watch where they're going. So what could happen with the chair in the way?"

"They might fall over it?"

"Yes and what else might happen?"

Frankie looked at the chair and back to his father, his expression alarmed. "They could fall in the water."

"So what should you do?" The boy jumped up.

"I gotta move the chair outta the way, back where I found it." He dragged the chair back into the row of chairs.

William followed his son and touched his shoulder. "Well done. You must always be considerate of others. Your second lesson is this: you must always be concerned for other people, no matter who they are. They're human beings like us."

"Did ye learn that from yer father?"

William led his son across the deck. "My father, your grandfather, was a kind, caring man. It made the travesty of his death even worse. I want you to honor his memory. He would have loved you very much. I'll always remember what he taught me. And now I'm teaching you."

Caroline frowned at her reflection in the glass. "Do you like this?" She glanced at Lisette and Jayne, who had come to her fitting.

"It's a lovely dress. Who wouldn't like it?" Jayne smiled at her, though her eyes were troubled.

"What do you think, Lisette?"

"It's a wonderful gown and looks very nice on you."

Caroline turned this way and that, looking at her reflection. "I don't know what it is, but something isn't right."

Lisette sighed and looked at her friend. "There's nothing wrong with the dress. You seem to have doubts about your upcoming marriage."

Jayne, frowning, poked Lisette in the ribs with her elbow and shook her head.

"I will say what I think. Caroline, if you don't want to marry Patrick, don't do it."

"But . . . what else can I do? I don't want to live without children. I must marry someday, why not please my father?"

Jayne bit her lip. "I never thought I'd say this, but don't marry Patrick or anyone else to please your father. It's all very well for him to like the groom, but he doesn't have to…well, you know what I mean."

Lisette leaned toward the blushing English woman. "He doesn't have to share a bed with Patrick."

Caroline looked at her friends.

"I suppose we could postpone it for a while. There's no need to rush into anything. The plans will keep."

If I do change my mind, my biggest problem will be telling Father and Patrick.

"You can do whatever you wish. It is your wedding, not your father's. Remember my experience. I'm not saying Patrick would beat you, but you should be certain you will not regret joining your life with his."

"Caroline, you're a strong woman. Look at what you do for the women who come to the settlement house. Don't get trapped into marriage. You know well the pitfalls of such an arrangement."

"Thank you, Lisette and Jayne, for reminding me I'm more than a daughter or a wife. I'm a strong person in my own right. I've been walking around in a haze." *I will tell Patrick and my father tonight that the wedding is off.*

"Good." Lisette smiled. "You never know what surprises might come to you."

"Horace, it was an excellent meal, as usual." Patrick gestured to the divan, indicating to Caroline she was to sit there. But she didn't.

Her father laughed and rubbed his rounded stomach covered in a waistcoat of the finest brocade. "We eat very well, don't we, daughter?"

"Hmmmmm? Oh yes, I suppose we do." Caroline began to pace.

"Dearest, come sit." Her fiancé patted the seat beside him.

"No, thank you, I want to talk to you both. I prefer to do it standing."

Horace glanced at her. "I hope you don't mind if we sit. I've had a long day."

"Yes, please sit, both of you. What I want to say shouldn't take too long."

Both men looked at each other in minor puzzlement as they sat.

Caroline steepled her hands in front of her and took a deep breath.

"Come now, dearest." Patrick laughed. "Nothing could be so serious. What is it? Can't you get the posies you want for the wedding?" He looked at Horace in camaraderie. "Leave it to a woman to be upset by trivialities."

She looked at him, all semblance of amiability gone from her face. *If I had any misgivings about calling off the marriage, they are gone now.*

"I've decided not to marry you."

Horace sat up straighter, alarm on his face.

Patrick chortled. "What's wrong now, didn't I include you in my dinner conversation? Or was it my critique of your little theatrical work? Either way, it's not serious."

"Yes, it is serious. I do not want to marry you, not now, not ever."

Horace frowned. "Are you certain you will not change your mind?"

"Yes, Father, I am. I've been sleepwalking through life since the incident in London with Gareth, healing perhaps. But I realize Patrick and I would never suit. We would be miserable with each other."

"Well, if you do not want to marry him, I won't make you."

Red faced and blustering, Patrick jumped to his feet. "I will not release you. You must marry me."

Caroline raised an eyebrow and observed him. *Now we see the real man, the one he concealed from all of us. I must remember to thank Lisette.*

The jilted suitor lunged toward her. Horace leapt to his feet with speed astonishing in a large man. He stopped Patrick by blocking him.

"If my daughter does not want you, I will honor her wishes. Get out of my house."

"But what about our business matters? Surely those will go forward even if she won't marry me."

"I will consider the merger, but for now it is best you leave."

Running his fingers through his hair, Patrick made a visible effort to calm down.

"Very well, I will go. But don't think this is over, either of you. Horace, I'll be back in the morning. Caroline, I will talk to you later."

She stripped the garish diamond from her finger. "Here is your ring back. I don't want to keep it."

He flashed angry eyes at her, "Very well, if you insist."

"I do. You can get your money back or give it to someone else. I wish you happiness. I'm sure there are many young ladies who would welcome your attention."

He bowed without speaking and left.

Caroline let go of a breath, she did not realize she held.

Horace walked to her and hugged her. "Are you sure you did the right thing?"

She nodded. "I couldn't do anything else. Marriage between us would be a disaster."

He pulled back and smiled at her. "I'm glad you were sensible enough to see it and avoid a painful mistake."

Her eyes were weary. "You mean not make another mistake, don't you? My record with men is awful."

"Don't worry, Caro, you'll find the right one." He chucked her under her chin. "After all the excitement, I think I'll retire for the evening."

She kissed his cheek. "Goodnight and sleep well."

After he went upstairs, she went to the window and moved aside the heavy drapes to look out on the midsummer evening. Sighing, she leaned her head against the window casement.

I already found the right one, but he doesn't want me.

Patrick waited in front of his house until his carriage drove out of sight. He walked down two blocks and caught a hansom. Bounding up into the seat, he pulled his hat low over his eyes.

"Drive me past Seventh Street, I'll tell you where to stop."

"Are you sure you want to go down there, Sir?"

"I'll pay double. Just drive me where I tell you."

"Whatever you say, Sir." The driver flicked the reins over the horse's back.

Patrick sighed and folded his arms across his chest. The streets grew more narrow and redolent with the smells of waste and molding cabbage.

I don't care what happens, I will never live here again.

"You, there, driver, stop here."

The driver reined in the horse.

Patrick handed him a handful of coins and jumped out of the cab.

"Will you want me to wait, Sir?"

"I wouldn't advise it in this neighborhood. I'll find my way back."

He waited until the vehicle disappeared into the night. Looking around, he walked to the third tenement down the street. Opening the outer door, he went to the last apartment on the corridor. Knocking on the door, he put his ear to the flimsy wood.

"Who is it?" An elderly voice asked.

"'Tis Patrick, *Maimeó*."

The door opened without hesitation. A tiny white-haired sprite of a woman rushed to hug him.

"Oh Patrick, 'tis been so long . . . ."

He smiled as he embraced her. "Is Morag here?"

"She's just come in for a visit. Morag, Patrick's home."

His sister walked into the cramped room. "What brings the wealthy man to visit his poor family?" A giant of a woman as tall as her brother, she smiled and hugged him.

"She broke off the engagement tonight."

Morag shook her head. "I told you it was a bad plan. She's stubborn."

"I've thought of a way to get her back."

His sister smiled. "You don't mean—"

"Yes, that's exactly what I mean. After she's frightened into compliance, we'll have no more trouble with the likes of her."

Chapter Nineteen
Sisters of Mercy

The door opened and Drake strode into the lobby. Grinning, he walked to his sister, "How are you doing?"

She ran to him, smiling as she hugged him.

"I didn't expect you back so soon. I thought you were just going to Norfolk this trip."

"I brought a special delivery." He pulled back from her and gestured for the person behind him to come forward.

"Lisette St John, may I introduce you to our newest cousin, Franklin Henry Hargreaves?"

The little red haired boy looked up at her with a grimace on his face. "I've told 'im over and over, m'name's not ever gonna be 'enry."

"I'm pleased to make your acquaintance, Cousin Franklin." She held out her hand to him.

He took her hand and showed her a gap-toothed grin. "Likewise, I'm sure, but most people call me Frankie."

"You're the image of your father, do you know it?"

He lifted his palm and made a downward motion. "Everybody says that. I don't see it myself, 'course we both got ginger hair." He preened, apparently relishing the attention from his pretty cousin.

"Where is Uncle William, isn't he with you?"

Drake turned and looked toward the door. "We left him paying the cabbie. I wonder what . . . ."

The door opened and William smiled as he walked into the lobby. "I see you've met my son." He reached Lisette and hugged her. "It's so good to see you."

She cleared her throat. "Perhaps this isn't the most tactful question, but did you bring Baroness Hargreaves with you?"

"Nah," piped Frankie. "She didn't come 'cause we got annulled."

"Oh, I'm sorry, I shouldn't have mentioned it."

"Don't be," continued the boy. "Ye ever meet her?"

"Sadly, no." smiled Lisette.

"Ye wouldn't think it was sad not to have her here, if ye had."

William appeared to be struggling to curtail his laugh. "Frankie still has some lessons to learn about polite conversation."

"Ah, I do all right." The boy looked at Lisette with adoring eyes. "Ye sure are pretty." He sidled up beside her. "Can ye skip stones?"

"No, I leave such things to Caroline. She's much better than I would ever be."

Frankie nodded. "That's what I hear. Where is she?"

"She's at the theater. Her new play opens tomorrow night. I'm sure I can get a ticket for you and your father if you'd like to go."

The child wrinkled his nose. "Never seen a play. Don't think I'd like it."

"Uncle William, would you like to go?"

He smiled, his eyes lit with happiness. "I would, but we have to make arrangements for accommodations. Where is the best hotel?"

She pulled Frankie against her and tousled his hair. "Nonsense, I'm sure Mr. Burgess would be glad to have you staying with me at his house. He should be home now. Why don't we go ask him?"

"Lisette, do you think it's wise for us to stay at Burgess House?"

"Why wouldn't you? It's better than any hotel. Besides, Mrs. Arnold loves children. Frankie will have the time of his life."

Later in the evening, they all sat with Horace at his spacious dining table. Even Frankie was allowed to dine with them.

"We don't stand much on ceremony here, Frankie. As long as you don't throw food or pitch a wall-eyed fit, you'll be welcome at the table."

"Thank you." William looked at his son. "Do you know what Mr. Burgess means by a 'wall-eyed fit'?"

"No." The boy's eager eyes shone, "But why doncha teach me about it?"

Horace tossed back his head and roared. "You've got a fine boy, there, Baron. He's no spoiled little aristocrat."

"I don't want him to be like them. I want him to be a boy within reason. His behavior will improve as he learns, but I never want him to be an affected prig."

"Like someone we used to know?" Lisette spoke out of the side of her mouth.

William joined in the laughter from the other diners. "If you want to know the truth of it, Frankie is teaching me more than I teach him."

"What's all the laughter?" called Caroline from the hallway. "I'm glad I got off early so I could join you. I could use a good—" She walked into the room, freezing in place when she saw William at the table.

Is he really here?

"Hello, Caroline." His voice was soft, a marked contrast to the previous laughter.

"William," she whispered. "How . . . why . . . are you here?"

"We came," Frankie stood and gazed at her with adoring eyes, "because my mum annulled us."

"She did?" Caroline still didn't move. She couldn't.

"Father." Frankie's voice echoed through the dining room. "Is she the rock-skippin' lady?"

"She is indeed." William kept his gaze on hers.

Frankie stood and ran to her, taking her hand in his. "It's about time ye got here. We came all the way cross the water to meet ye." He tugged her with him to the table and the chair next to his. He pulled out the chair for her.

Caroline sank onto it, her mouth forming a perfect "O."

Across the table, Lisette caught her brother's glance and grinned at him.

He nodded in response.

"Mrs. Arnold!" Horace's roar filled the room. "Please set another place for my daughter."

The servants entered and bustled about the table, setting a place for Caroline and serving the first course.

Accompanied by the sounds of the clinking of china plates and the pouring of beverages, Frankie tugged on her sleeve. "How did ye learn to skip rocks?"

Shaking off her emotional stupor, she smiled at him. "My father taught me first and then your father gave me some valuable pointers." *He looks so like William.*

"Your father did? How'd he know?"

She leaned down to the boy. "He wasn't always such a prosperous gentleman, you know. When I was your age, he was a coal miner. We lived in the town near the mine. I spent those years usually covered in black dust."

"Cor, go on, he worked in the mines?"

"Yes. He spent as much time as he could with me. On those days, he'd teach me interesting things. You'd be surprised what all I know."

Mrs. Arnold placed a full plate in front of Frankie.

"I hope you enjoy it, young man."

He leaned toward the food and sniffed with appreciation. "It smells good."

Caroline grinned at the sight and glanced up to find William smiling at her from across the table. The tension of the day fell away from her shoulders. She relaxed, taking a deep breath.

I can't believe he came all this way. It's the best surprise I ever remember.

Horace sat, observing Patrick Harris seated across from him.

Look at him sweat. Caro's right. He wouldn't be a good husband for her. He's more interested in her money. I wonder why?

Patrick leaned forward. "I hope the end of my engagement does not mean the end of our business together."

"I believe in being practical in money matters. If you bring me more capital, I will gladly work with you."

The younger man sank back in the wing chair. "I'm happy to hear it."

They continued to discuss their proposed merger and came to agreement.

When he rose to leave, Patrick suddenly stopped. "How is Caroline? I suppose she is excited about her opening night."

"I don't think it crossed her mind. We are entertaining unexpected visitors from London."

"Oh, whom, if I may ask? Is it anyone I know?"

You're not very subtle when you're looking for an advantage, are you? "Baron William Hargreaves and his son are staying with us. They are great friends of ours. Caroline is delighted to see them."

His expression rigid, Patrick picked up his hat and turned to go. "I will see you tonight at the performance." Nodding, he hurried out of the office.

Horace frowned as he watched Patrick leave. *He doesn't take rejection well. I will instruct Heston to double the guards tonight just to be prepared.*

Chapter Twenty
Another Opening Night

"Oy." Frankie whistled in appreciation. "Ye look like a lady, or a queen, Miss Caro. Are ye sure ye can skip rocks?"

She bent over to him, her gold satin skirts dragging the floor. "You wait, tomorrow we'll drive over by the Schuylkill River and I'll prove it to you."

"I'll 'old ye to yer promise."

She kissed his forehead. "I'll remember. Good night and sleep well." She grinned at him once more before turning to descend the stairs.

William followed her down. "He doesn't understand why he can't go to the play."

"We could get a seat for him, but he'd be bored in a few minutes. Perhaps if you return next spring, he can come to see *A Midsummer Night's Dream*."

"I'll keep it in mind." He put his hand on her arm. "Are you certain you don't want me to escort you now?"

She patted his hand. "No, you can wait and come with Father's group. I'm well-guarded going to and from the theater. Thank you for the offer. Besides, I'll be working until the play begins." *He's so different than he was in London. Frankie worked a miracle.*

"I worry about you. Are you carrying a gun?"

"Of course I am, don't be concerned. Between Heston and my pistol, I am all but invincible."

He kissed her hand. "Later after the performance, I'd like to have a serious talk with you."

Her breath caught. *Don't get too excited, you don't know what he's going to say.*

"I look forward to it." She canted her head. "Sorry, but I must leave now if I am to talk to the business manager, the director, and the cast before we open."

In the darkening twilight, she got in her coach, rolling up the window shades.

I smell the first roses from the garden. It's going to be a lovely evening. I wonder what William wants to speak to me about?

Riding over the cobblestones, she sat staring at the sky out the window. When they arrived at the theater, she snapped back to the present. *You've got a lot to do, Caroline, get going.*

She got out of the coach without help. Turning to Heston who approached her, she saw something behind him disappear around the corner of the building.

What was that? Was it a cape?

No, don't be silly, that man never returned.

I'm sure he's long gone.

She shook her head.

"Heston, I'm late for my meeting with Aidan. Let's go." With one last glance at the darkened corner, she sniffed and hurried up the steps into the building.

Hours later, Caroline smiled with grace and accepted the applause and cheers the audience members gave her.

"Thank you." She held up her hands asking for quiet. "We are so happy you like the work of our gifted actors. The response to our first two productions is so great, we will continue the season through December." She paused as she looked over the crowd.

"If you have a favorite among Shakespeare's plays, we'd like to hear about it. Please use the suggestion box in the lobby to tell us what play you would most like to see."

She bowed once more. "Thank you again for your applause. We've set up a champagne reception in the lobby, please join us. The cast will be out there. Enjoy your evening." She left the stage.

Aidan awaited her backstage. He had to raise his voice to be heard over the departing audience. "We had another good house tonight. If we keep making money like this, our theater will be open for years."

She touched his arm. "Thank you for your diligence. I'm confident the management of this group is in wonderful hands. How is Josie? I rarely see her these days."

"She's fine, very happy in her new school, thanks to you."

"I'm glad—" Footsteps sounded behind her on the wooden planking of the stage. She turned to find William approaching.

"There you are." He smiled at her, his eyes narrowing as he saw Aidan. "I don't believe we've been introduced."

"William, this is Aidan Cavanaugh, our business manager. Aidan, may I introduce Baron William Hargreaves, my friend from London."

She watched as they greeted each other with nods and eyes that judged. *They're like two stallions taking the measure of the competition.*

"William, I wouldn't be able to run this theater group without Aidan's assistance. He brought the necessary experience I lacked. He tells me we're doing well."

"If the quality of the production is any indication, I would say you're doing a splendid job. Many of my peers would be surprised at the excellence of the performance."

"Being Irish," Aidan spoke with a brogue Caroline never heard before, "I'd say the English will continue to be surprised by what former colonials can do."

What's he doing? William hasn't said anything wrong.

"I agree." William smiled. "I predict great things in the future for you and this theater company." He inclined his head. "Caroline I sought you because everyone at the reception is asking for you." He offered his arm. "May I escort you to the lobby?"

She took his arm. "Aidan, please come out and join us when you're finished."

"I will for a few minutes, but I want to get home to Josie."

"I understand. William, Aidan's daughter is a wonderful little girl. Perhaps she can meet Frankie while you're here."

"I'm sure he'd like to meet her."

"Josie would like it, too." Aidan cocked his head. "I'll be out in a few minutes." He walked away through the side curtains.

William watched him disappear. "I'm afraid I upset him. Is he more than a friend?"

So that's what you're worried about. Caroline moved closer to him. "We're just friends. He suggested a closer relationship once, but I declined. He recently lost his wife. He and his daughter need a woman in their lives. I'm looking for some likely candidates."

William's posture relaxed. "So you're a matchmaker now?"

She poked him in the ribs as they walked. "Only for the right people." She grinned at him.

After everyone was gone, William stayed to escort her home, while Heston left to make sure no one waited on the route.

"We are going the same way. It's foolish for me to let you leave alone." They walked to her coach.

"I'm hardly alone. Heston is with me and my driver, Obadiah." She leaned against him. "But you are very welcome."

"I'm happy you said that." He stopped their progress to look at her by the dim streetlamp. "I wasn't sure what my reception would be."

"Your visit surprised me but I'm delighted to see you." She looked up at him. "The last year must have been difficult for you."

He shrugged. "It was hard at times. The gossips were relentless, loving the story of the oh-so-correct Baron being brought to his knees by an old acquaintance and the son she concealed from him."

"You married her for your son's sake, didn't you?"

He smiled at her. "I was worried I'd have to tell you the whole sordid tale, and you guessed it."

"I know you, the real you. Hidden under the patrician sneer, I could see the real man."

He hugged her. "I'm amazed. I thought the aristocrat was the real man."

"Oh no, he was the façade, used for years by a frightened boy who never felt part of the world he'd been tossed into. What brought you back to reality?"

"Frankie, of course. He doesn't accept pretense. If I played the charade with him, he'd laugh at me before he walked away."

"You've become a wiser man and a good father."

"I try, although at times I don't know what to do, how to answer him."

"From what I've seen, most parents are insecure to some degree. You're doing very well with him."

Holding hands, they arrived at her coach. Heston opened the door for them. "I was about to walk back to the theater."

"We're fine, just catching up on our lives since we last met." Caroline smiled as he handed her into the coach.

William entered when she was settled, and sat across from her. "I haven't enjoyed an outing so much since you left London." He leaned toward her. "I missed you."

She grinned at him. "And here I thought you came here to escape Lady Morehouse."

He grinned at her. "Well, I must admit fleeing from her determination to have me for her daughter's spouse was another incentive."

"Ha, you admit it!" Caroline giggled. "I bet she was furious when she heard you were gone. She's likely planning your welcome home party." Laughing harder, she bounced on the seat and reached down to grip the edge.

"What is this?" Her hilarity ended with a jolt.

Is this a knife stuck in the seat? She explored more with her fingers.

It is a knife.

Pulling it out of the lower cushion, she found a note it had pinned to the seat. Hands shaking, she held the note up in an attempt to read it. Her mouth dropped open when the simple block letters became clear in the limited light.

I'M BACK DIDJA MISS ME?

"Oh dear Lord . . . he's back." She looked at William sitting across from her.

"Caroline." William's voice was urgent. "What is it, what's wrong?"

Chapter Twenty-One
Sisters of Mercy

"Miss St John, just the lady I sought." Aidan walked toward her, carrying his hat.

"Mr. Cavanaugh." She looked at him. "I'm surprised to see you. Is something wrong?"

"I . . . ." He glanced around at the women in the waiting room. "Might I speak to you in private for a few moments?"

"Of course, I hope nothing is wrong with you or Josie." She led him to an empty office.

"No, we're both fine. I wanted to ask you about Miss Caroline."

Lisette sat at the desk and waited until he sat in the chair reserved for clients. "She is happy these days. What did you want to know?"

He chewed his lower lip for a moment. "Who is this Hargreaves fellow visiting at her house? Is he a trustworthy person?"

She barely managed to curtail her smile. "I've always found him to be a righteous man."

"Oh." The corners of his mouth turned down as he looked at his hands in his lap. "What is his relationship to Caroline?"

"I've long believed them to be in love, though certain obstacles kept them apart."

He scowled. "How could she be in love with a married man with a son? Where is his wife?"

Oh, so that's how it is. I long suspected him of having a penchant for Caroline.

"Mr. Cavanaugh." Her voice and smile were gentle. "Caroline and William fell in love in London, long before he knew about his son or married the boy's mother."

"Outrageous. The arrogant cad does not deserve a woman like

Caroline. I've seen his like before. Worthless, every one of them."

Taking a deep breath, Lisette met his eyes. "Please be aware Baron William Hargreaves is my uncle, the younger brother of my *Maman*. He is a fine man who never knew he had a son. Frankie's mother waited to tell him until it was to her advantage."

"How scandalous, using a woman like Caroline. I should . . . ." His hands fisted in his lap.

"You should mind your own business. The former Baroness Hargreaves never lived with either my uncle William or their son. She was recently granted an annulment to dissolve the marriage. She has since married another man."

"Oh." He looked down. "There is no hope for me, is there?"

"I'm afraid not with Caroline. But I know many fine women. I would be happy to introduce you to some of them."

He stood and shook his head. "I'm sorry I bothered you, Miss St John." He walked out the door without looking back.

She sighed. *Poor man.*

"Miss Caroline, you beat my father! I never saw a lady skip stones like you. I never saw a lady skip 'em at all." He smiled up at her, clearly in a lofty state of hero worship.

"She didn't beat me by much. Besides I taught her everything she knows." William laughed and picked up his son, spinning him around. He brought him down with merciless tickling.

"Oy, no fair," cried Frankie. "Miss Caro, help me!" His words were almost altered by his continual giggles.

"I know when not to interfere." She smiled as she backed away from the grappling duo.

William stopped and looked at her. "Frankie, don't you think we should find out if Miss Caroline is ticklish?"

"Yeah, I do." He ran toward her, flanked by his father.

Caroline shrieked in mock horror and ran up the bank, only to trip on a protruding stone. She crashed to the ground.

Frankie and his father were at her side immediately. "I'm sorry, I didn't mean to make you fall." The boy hovered around her, tears beginning to drop down his cheeks.

"It's all right. I'm not hurt, just jarred a bit." She rose and dusted off her skirt. Putting her arm around him, she smiled. "Are you hungry?"

He nodded.

"He's always hungry." William looked at his son with a warm smile.

"I tell you what." Caroline looked at the boy. 'Why don't you and your father lay out the blanket and put the food on it, while I wash my hands in the river? Then we'll eat."

Frankie ran for the blanket while his father picked up the basket of food. She smiled as she watched them and turned toward the water. *It's a lovely day.*

After they finished the meal, Frankie curled up on the blanket and fell asleep in the sunshine.

William drew Caroline to her feet and walked with her to the water's edge. "We need to talk."

I know what he's going to say.

She licked her lips and waited for his questions.

"When do you plan to tell me what happened last night?"

"What do you mean?" She looked away from him.

"You know what I mean. Who is the man who left you the message with his calling card?"

"I don't know. He left threatening notes for me over a two-month period last winter. Then he stopped. I don't know why."

"And now he's back?"

She nodded. "It's the same writing. I thought I saw him last night as I went into the theater."

"Why didn't you say anything to Heston or to me?"

"I wasn't certain I'd seen him. There was no reason to mention it. He didn't reappear."

"He left you the note." William raised his voice and then glanced at

Frankie, awake now and listening. "He's threatening you." His voice dropped to a whisper.

"I'm through living in fear. If he wants to come after me, let him come."

"You're carrying your gun again, aren't you?"

"Yes, what of it? I'm a good shot. I can take care of myself if necessary."

"Ye have a gun?" Frankie raised his head and looked from her to his father.

"Yes, I do."

"Kin I see it?"

"It's not a plaything." William's tone was harsh.

"Your father is right. How about I show you how well I shoot?"

"Please, I'd like to see ye do it."

She chucked him under his chin. "Go stand over there, by the big rocks."

When the boy was in position, she turned to William.

"Please toss each one of the stones you carry into the air one at a time on my mark.

He nodded.

"I'm ready when you are," she called, pointing her pistol in the air.

William tossed the rocks in quick succession.

Caroline aimed at each one, shattering two of them and nicking the third.

"Cor," cried Frankie running to throw his arms around her legs. "I never seen nothing like that." He hugged her. "Anybody who tries to hurt you is gonna get a big surprise."

She leaned down and hugged him tight. "I hope so, Frankie."

Caroline arrived at the theater on time. She carefully looked up and down the street as she exited her coach.

"Did you see any signs of the intruder tonight?"

Heston smiled. "No, and there is no news of anyone bent on mischief this evening."

"Good, I'm glad to hear it. I just want the performance to go well. It's been a long week."

"Don't worry, Miss Caroline, I'm at the ready should trouble occur." He took her arm and escorted her to the door.

"Now, then, go inside and enjoy your evening. I'll be waiting to take you home. Enjoy the performance."

"Thank you."

I want to trust him but something is niggling at my mind.

As she stood in the open doorway, she glanced once more looking for any traces of the stalking man. *I don't see him anywhere.*

With a relieved smile, she turned and went into the building.

The performance went well. After the final curtain, surrounded by people all talking at once, she caught glimpses of faces in the crowd. Someone tapped her shoulder from behind. She turned to find Patrick Harris smiling down at her.

"Looks like you staged another hit. I'm proud of you, Caroline."

"Thank you, Patrick. It's kind of you to say so." *You were never this nice about my work before. What do you really want?*

He took her hand. "Nonsense, I'm speaking the truth." His eyes shifted left and right as he glanced over the crowd. "Would you like to find a place where we can talk?"

She managed not to frown. *Absolutely not, my friend.* "Another time, perhaps, I'm tired this evening."

Bowing over her hand, his eyes gleamed in triumph. "As you wish, we will speak later."

She nodded, chills running down her spine.

His eyes disturb me. Something in his expression is threatening. Why won't he forget about me? He has to know he'll never get my fortune.

"Miss Caroline?" Aidan walked up behind her. "I have the total for the ticket sales this evening. Would you like to go over the figures now or wait until tomorrow?"

Sighing she turned to him.

Let's get this over for tonight.

"I'm in no hurry. Why don't we go over the receipts for everything now?"

An hour later, she left Aidan in his office and headed for the door. *At least we got it done this evening so I don't have to come back early tomorrow.*

She saw her coach parked in front of the building. *Poor Obadiah is probably sleeping on the coachman's seat.*

The street was silent, empty as she walked down toward the coach.

I wonder where Heston is.

She stopped to look down the street. A gloved hand covered her mouth from behind, while her assailant's other hand held a knife against her throat.

"Ye're comin' with me, bitch," whispered a grating voice in her ear. "Make no trouble and ye're likely to live through this."

No, I will not be taken. You'll regret this more than I will. She dropped her hand from where she had gripped the arm holding the knife at her throat. Sagging, she pretended to feel faint.

"Skeert, are ye, bitch? Good. Ye should be." The hand holding the knife eased the pressure against her throat.

Beneath her light evening wrap, she dropped her hand to her reticule and pulled out her pistol, primed and ready.

"Faintin' won't help ye none." The attacker laughed at her supposed apprehension.

Without a word, Caroline raised the pistol and fired directly into the shoulder of the person behind her.

With a surprising, high-pitched scream, her mugger fell to the ground.

Caroline stood over him, her foot on his chest and the gun at the ready.

She leaned to rip off the face mask. "Let's see who you really are."

She pulled off the mask to reveal not a man, but a woman, screaming, "Curse ye, well-heeled she-devil!"

"Who are you?"

"I'll never tell ye." An ominous pool of blood spread on the ground from the woman's shoulder wound.

"Miss Burgess, what's happened?" Heston ran from the direction of the alley.

"Where were you, why weren't you waiting for me?"

He looked at the woman on the ground and back to Caroline. "I saw the man in the cape, just as you described. I chased him but he disappeared. I ran back as soon as I heard the shot."

"It appears there were two people stalking me in capes. This woman held a knife to my throat until I shot her."

Heston grabbed the woman's hands and tied them together. "What shall we do with her?"

Caroline returned her gun to her reticule. "Let's take her back to my home and question her there. Mrs. Arnold can staunch the blood from the wound."

Heston pulled the woman to her feet. "Come along, you." He dragged her to the coach. "What did you do to Obadiah?"

"I don't know who you mean." The injured woman's lips grew whiter as the color leached from them.

"You will tell us what happened to the coachman. You'll face charges for harming him both this time and the time before."

Caroline shook her head. "I doubt she'll tell us anything."

Entering the coach unassisted, she turned back to Heston. "I'll send some of my father's men to search for him once we get home. Put her up top with you."

She closed the door and listened to the sounds of the woman being pushed and prodded into place.

Who is she and what did I possibly do to her? She was never helped at the settlement house. I would recognize her if she'd been there.

Lying back against the soft cushions, she stared out the window.

I'm tired of all this. I just want to be left alone to live my life. Is this too much to ask?

Chapter Twenty-Two

"I knew it. I should have insisted on accompanying you home last evening." William paced back and forth.

"It's all right. I came through the incident unharmed." Caroline stifled a yawn as she watched him.

"You should rest today. You're exhausted from the ordeal." He stopped to caress her face. "You're so pale, like parchment. Should we call Mrs. Arnold to bring you some tea?"

She patted his arm. "I'm fine. I didn't sleep much last night. I waited until Obadiah was found. How is he this morning?"

"He's awake and talking, though he's got a knot on his head."

"I should have inquired about him sooner."

No, you're dealing with your own attack. You should never be exposed to such violence."

Caroline looked up at him. "I caused most of the bloodshed, remember?"

"You mustn't constantly be put in the position of protecting yourself." He began to pace the room once more.

She slumped against the back of the chair. "Please stop moving, you make me dizzy. Sit down, can't you?" Her voice held a petulant note.

"I'm sorry, my dear. I didn't mean to upset you."

The door opened behind him. William jumped at the unexpected sound.

Mrs. Arnold entered the room carrying a tray loaded with tea and cakes. "I thought you might want something." She stared at Caroline, "Especially since you didn't eat anything this morning." She set the tray on the table beside Caroline's chair. "Now don't give me your stubborn look. I am here on specific orders from your father. You are to eat something and drink some tea." She folded her arms in front of her and glared at her charge. "I will brook no refusal, young lady."

301

"Oh all right, I recognize your tone. No sense in trying to refuse. Thank you." Caroline reached for a scone filled with plump raisins and smelling of cinnamon.

Mrs. Arnold poured her a cup of tea. "Here you go, be sure to drink it all."

Caroline nodded her thanks, her mouth filled with the delicious pastry.

"Baron Hargreaves." Mrs. Arnold smiled at him. "Would you care for tea?"

"Yes, thank you." He returned her smile.

She filled his cup, handing him the sugar tongs and cream pitcher.

"Please help yourself to cakes. If you need anything else, please ring for me." She bobbed her head and left the room.

Caroline didn't acknowledge her departure. *I was hungry and didn't realize it.* She sighed and reached for another scone.

"Your color is coming back." William smiled at her over his teacup.

"I admit it, you were right. I forgot to eat this morning."

"Do you feel up to discussing the progress of the investigation?"

"Yes. What have we learned about the woman?" She wiped her mouth with the linen napkin and set it aside.

"She's Irish by her accent, and claims not to know you."

"Is that all we've learned? I knew as much last night." She took one last sip of the cooling tea. "Did she say anything else?"

"Only you have more money than you need, or some such drivel."

"Well, it's something, I guess. At least we know she and her compatriot were after my money. Do you suppose they thought to hold me for ransom?"

William sighed. "It would seem to be their motive."

"Any thoughts of where her companion might be?"

"No, he's disappeared. He's a clever fellow, I must say. Wearing the mask and obscuring his features, we have no clues to his identity."

Caroline leaned on the table beside her chair. Her elbow on the table, she stroked her chin. "I wonder he'd take the trouble to be anonymous."

She looked at William. "He's got to be someone I know, someone I could identify. Why else would he wear such a disguise?"

"I believe you're right. You must be acquainted with him. Can you think of anyone who might wish you harm?"

She shook her head, "No one who would be serious about it. Patrick wasn't happy I broke our engagement, but he doesn't need my money. He's wealthy in his own right."

"Some men always want more wealth, more power. Are you certain it couldn't be him?"

"Yes, he's not the nicest man I ever knew, but he doesn't wish me any ill. Besides he and Father are merging two of their companies. Patrick does not need my fortune."

"I will accept your judgment. From now on, we must take every precaution and guard your safety at all times. The villain will doubtless come after you once more. We cannot take any chances."

Oh, so he's taking charge now is he? "We are in league with each other now? When did we form our alliance?"

William took her hand. "I was awful to you in London, afraid of the *Ton's* censure. I let you leave when I should beg you to stay with me. I won't make the same mistake this time."

"Why, Baron Hargreaves, are you, the oh-so-correct aristocrat, actually offering me an apology? After all, I am the daughter of a coal miner, dontchaknow." She bit her lip to keep from smiling as she teased him.

He stood, pulling her up into his arms. "I don't care if your father was a dockhand. You're the woman I love. I hope one day you can forgive me for my actions."

Running her fingers through his hair, at last she smiled at him. "I forgave you long ago. Once I saw you with your son, I knew you'd discarded your arrogant baron persona for all time."

As his lips moved down to hers, she whispered. "I love you, too, always have."

Jayne bustled into the lobby of the settlement house. "Did you know Caroline was attacked last night?"

"Yes." Lisette tallied the figures in the ledger before her. "I spoke to her this morning. She's exhausted but otherwise well."

"Why didn't you tell me?" Jayne banged on the desk.

Lisette frowned and looked up at her friend. "Because this is the first time I've seen you today."

"I'm sorry." Jayne sat in the side chair. "Jack went to the theater earlier and rushed home to tell me about it. You know how men are. He didn't get all the details. Can you tell me what happened?"

Lisette put down the pen. "She was accosted on the way to her carriage. The person was masked and cloaked like before. Caroline didn't know the assailant was behind her until she felt a knife at her throat. She pulled out her gun and aimed for the shoulder."

"How awful for her, I'm glad she carried her pistol."

"Her attacker was a woman, which they only found out when she was unmasked."

"Does Caroline know her?"

Lisette shook her head. "She said she doesn't. I couldn't help wondering if it was some woman we'd seen here."

"What is her name?"

"Last I heard she refused to give it."

"Why not? What's she hiding?"

"Who knows? Perhaps she thinks her punishment will be lessened if they don't know what she's done in the past."

"Drat." Jayne chewed her lip. "Now I'm going to be wondering about this woman all day."

Chapter Twenty-Three

Frankie tugged on Caroline's hand leading her toward the riverbank. "Come on, Miss Caro." He panted with the effort. "Let's go toss some rocks."

"I thought you were hungry." She laughed as she ran with him.

"Cor, we kin always eat!"

"You're right. Everything must be done in the proper order." She dropped his hand. "Let's find some stones. We can't have a competition with nothing to throw."

He scrambled over the sparse vegetation, picking up stones here and there. She watched him smiling at his frown of concentration. *He's such a spirited boy. I'm glad his father found him. He deserves the best possible life.*

William walked up to her. "Where've you been, Slow Poke? We've been here collecting stones."

She grinned at him as he took her in his arms. "Someone had to secure the horses and bring the picnic basket. You two scampered off in wild abandon."

"First of all, I never scamper. Second, I'd hardly call a brisk run a moment of wild abandon."

"I got all my rocks. Are ye ready for the contest?" Frankie's voice sounded far away.

"How'd he get all the way over there?"

"He's faster than you can imagine, particularly when he's intent on something." William took Caroline's hand and led her toward the bank. "Franklin, what did I tell you about running off when we're out?"

"I'm sorry, I wanted to get started." The boy kicked a stone at his feet and peered up at them from under the red fringe of hair dusting his forehead.

Caroline struggled not to smile. *The little scamp isn't a bit sorry.*

305

She looked at William and saw his mouth stretched tightly as he fought to maintain a stern expression. She elbowed him in the ribs. "Let's get on with the contest, shall we?"

After an hour of competition, during which they paused only once to find more rocks, Caroline put her hands up. "I yield to the two of you. I don't think I can toss another stone. How about eating lunch? Who's hungry?"

"I am." Frankie danced toward her, his face a picture of triumph. "I won! I never won before."

She hugged him. "You learn very well. I'm proud of you. Let's go set out our lunch." She took his hand and led him back to the buggy.

Soon the blanket was spread and the food brought out of the basket. William and Frankie watered the horses before sitting down to eat.

"What is this?" Frankie held up a chicken leg crisp with batter.

"We call that fried chicken. It's popular in the southern parts of America. Mrs. Arnold says it's the best food for picnics."

"It's good," he mumbled, his mouth full.

Between the three of them, they ate all of the chicken and half a loaf of fresh bread with apple butter.

"Oh, this was so good." Frankie leaned back on his elbows. "Can we have more fried chicken while we're here?"

"I'm sure Mrs. Arnold will make it special for you if you tell her how much you like it."

William yawned. "It's warmer today than I expected it to be. Is it always this warm in the Pennsylvania summer?"

Caroline nodded as she packed away the remnants of their meal. She wiped her hands on the tea towel, tossing it in the back of the buggy. She dropped beside William and looked at the blue sky. "Some days are even warmer."

"Shocking." He grinned at her, putting his arm around her. "I shall make sure we will spend more of the summer in England from now on."

He kissed her forehead. She put her head on his chest. In the warmth of the afternoon, the three of them drifted off to sleep.

Later, Frankie stirred first, woke and looked at his father. *I'm glad he's not mad at Miss Caro anymore. I like her.*

Glancing at the sparkling river and back at the sleeping couple, he nodded. *They'll not miss me.* Rising to his feet, he picked up his remaining pile of stones and ran toward the shining water. *I kin toss some more rocks.*

When he reached the bank, a dark figure loomed from behind a tree. "Who are ye?"

But Frankie's voice was muffled by the large hand that covered his mouth. Unable to make a sound, he kicked his legs as hard as he could, but his captor did not release him.

Caroline awoke and stretched, refreshed. *I haven't slept so well in days.* Looking around, she saw the sun dropping toward the horizon. *Good grief, I wonder what time it is?*

"William, wake up." She touched him gently. "I've got to get back. I'll be late for the theater."

"What? What time is it?" He ran a hand through his hair.

"I don't know." She stood and offered her hand to him.

"Today's been wonderful."

"Yes, it has." She smiled at him. "I hate for it to end."

"There will be other such days, I promise you."

"I'll remember your promise."

He took her into his arms and kissed her.

Sighing in contentment, she leaned against him.

Their reverie lasted only moments, before William frowned. "Where's Frankie? Did you see him when you woke?"

"Perhaps he's asleep in the buggy." Caroline ran to the vehicle and found it empty.

"I'll search around the riverbank."

"Good idea, maybe he skipped some more rocks." She scanned the horizon as best she could through the trees. *Where could he be?* "Frankie? Now isn't the time to tease us. Come out, please. Frankie?"

"Caroline!" William's anguished cry sounded from the riverbank.

Oh no, please . . . don't let him be floating in the water.

She picked up her heavy skirts and ran over the rocky ground. "I'm coming."

Stumbling twice, she finally reached him. "What is it, what did you find?"

He turned back to look at her. "Look." His voice shook as he pointed to the ground.

She looked where he indicated and her mouth dropped open.

On the riverbank was a black full-face mask with a dagger plunged through one of the eye holes. On the side was a small pile of rocks, Frankie's rocks.

"It's from him," she whispered. "The man who stalked me . . . ."

"Ye ain't so tough." Frankie slipped from his captor.

The tall man rubbed his knee kicked with gusto by his hostage. He glared at the boy. "I don't think you appreciate your situation here."

Frankie snorted as he looked around the darkened warehouse stacked with barrels. "I 'preciate it just fine, thank ye very much." He turned back to look at the masked man. "Ye're the one in trouble. My father and Miss Caro will find me. She'll shoot ye for yer crimes, too. What d'ye think about that?"

The stranger moved to one of the stacks of barrels, pulling a candle and a flint from beneath his cape. Striking the flint, he lit the candle. "There now, that's better at least I can get a good look at you."

"Look all ye want for all the good it'll do."

"I want to describe you and your clothes in my note." He took out a book and began to write.

"Why?"

The man looked up at him, the mask he wore obscuring not only his face, but any light from his eyes.

"I'll use the description as proof I have you when I send the ransom note." He continued to write and sighed in apparent satisfaction when he put down the pen.

"There now, I'm ready." He swung toward Frankie. "It's time for me to leave you."

Taking a large coil of rope from beneath his cape, he strode toward his captive as his hands uncoiled the rope.

Frankie looked left and right. *There's nowhere to go.* He backed up until he hit the wall. "What're ye goin' to do?"

"That's a stupid question, I must say. But not unexpected given your background."

He grabbed Frankie's wrists in his gloved hands, tying them together without wasted motion. Testing the strength of the binding, he nodded his satisfaction. "You'll never get out of these knots."

"Why are ye doin' this to me?"

The man took the end of the rope and reached high above his captive, "Because your Miss Caroline has more money than she'll ever need. So by kidnapping you, I'll get a goodly share for myself." Humming a tune, he tied the other end of the rope to a metal ring nailed to the wall high above his own head.

He looked down at Frankie and spoke with laughter in his voice.

"I tied you to the wall with sailors' knots. You'll never escape. Be good while I'm gone and you'll survive. If you don't, well . . . ." He shrugged his shoulders.

"Miss Caroline will shoot ye, just ye wait."

He laughed once more. "I'm not worried. The rope is long enough so you can move about a bit. Scream all you want, no one will hear you."

He chucked Frankie under the chin. "This is easier than I thought it would be." Turning, he ran up the stairs, taking two at a time. His footsteps sounded all the way out of sight and into the darkness beyond.

Frankie squinted to try to see what was at the top of the stairs. A door slammed above him. He swallowed the panic squeezing his chest.

Think, why don't ye? Listen. What d'ye hear?

He discovered a distant sound of lapping water. *I'm still somewhere by the river. He didn't carry me long when he caught me. I must still be close by where we ate.*

"'Ello, is anybody out there?" His voice echoed through the musty space.

Don't 'ear anybody, probably 'cause nobody's 'ere.

He took a deep breath and a thought occurred to him. "Wait a minute, did he take my rocks?" He touched the pocket of his pants. "No, there they are."

I can't toss 'em with both hands tied. I gotta find something to cut this rope. Guess it's time to find out if there's anything 'ere I can use.

Chapter Twenty-Four

"Heston!" Horace roared at the top of his voice. "Where the devil are you?"

"I'm coming, Mr. Burgess." The bodyguard hurried into the room.

"Did you find anything?"

"No, Sir, my men searched the area for anything from the boy. We even looked for footprints but most of the ground is covered with meadow.

"Oh dear." Lisette sniffed into her handkerchief. "How will we ever find poor Frankie?"

"We'll find him, no matter what it takes." William fisted his hand on the back of Lisette's chair. "I'll make the ones who took him pay."

Caroline looked at the faces of those she loved. *This is all my fault.*

I should have said something about the man who kept appearing around me. I knew it was a man, and not a woman. Drat, we don't even know who she is. Where do we start? Perhaps I should pay the prisoner a visit.

"Pardon me, Miss Caroline." Mrs. Arnold bustled in with an envelope in her hand. "This was delivered by a boy."

Caroline took the envelope addressed to her in an educated hand.

"Let me see." William jerked the envelope from her. Breaking the seal, he opened the letter and read it. "Damn, look at this." He handed the note back to her. "It's a ransom note. They've got him."

"How can you tell?" Lisette broke in between Caroline and William.

Oh dear Lord, it's true. Tears started their path down Caroline's cheeks. "They've described what he was wearing, where he was found, even the rocks in his pocket."

"What do they want?"

Caroline sniffed. "They want money, what else?"

Horace frowned at his daughter. "How much are they asking?"

"Fifty thousand dollars." She wiped her eyes with a lace-trimmed linen handkerchief.

He rubbed his chin. "Well that's not much. We can afford it."

Lisette looked at her uncle with wide eyes.

William shrugged.

"Pardon me, Sir." Heston moved to stand next to Horace. "If you pay them what they ask, there is no guarantee they'll bring back the boy. They might keep asking for more."

"What do you suggest we do?" Caroline looked at the man who protected her. "I'm willing to take the payment to them."

"Absolutely not." William's face turned redder than his hair. "I won't have both you and my son in the hands of these blackguards."

"I didn't say I would go unarmed." She put a placating hand on his arm. "I'll be prepared. He won't."

"Oh yes, he will. He knows you shot his partner. He will expect you to carry your gun."

"I hadn't thought of that. You're right."

Heston spoke. "If I may, I have an idea."

William looked at him. "What do you want to say?"

"It struck me when we searched the area by the river there were no other carriage tracks than yours and no horse tracks, either. Wherever they took your son, they carried him on foot. I think they stashed him in one of the warehouses along the river."

"A warehouse would be a perfect place to hide him." Horace nodded.

"No one would be back to the building until Monday. With no other business near and no residential area, no one would hear him, much less find him."

"Yes, it could work." William looked at Horace. "What should we do?"

"Caroline, the note says you're to be back at the picnic site, alone, in—" Horace stopped to pull out his pocket watch, "two hours. I'll get the cash from my safe. Are you willing to do it?"

"Yes, and I thought of a way I could carry my gun."

"They know you keep it in your reticule. Are you certain they wouldn't find it?" William looked at her.

"Yes, I'm certain. If I'm not needed right now, I'll go and arrange my hiding place for the pistol."

"Go ahead, my dear." Horace gazed at his daughter with love. "You're the bravest woman I've ever known."

"I get it from my father." She smiled back and left the room.

Frankie's exploration proved fruitful. He found a crowbar among the barrels, and a curved baling pick with a wooden handle.

"This oughtta do it." Using the curved pick, he worked the knots loose on his wrists until he could slip out of the rope. "There ye go, ye better not mess with a Hargreaves, no sir."

He tugged on the rope still tied to the metal ring on the wall. *It should hold me.* Tying the pick and the crowbar tight on the open end of the rope, he climbed up the wall using the rope. "It's a good thing I use'ta do this at the old place in the country."

Working hand over hand, he made it into the storage loft above the floor. He pulled up until he stood looking down into the warehouse. Nodding, he looked at his surroundings. More barrels and crates were stacked there. He untied the pick and crowbar from the rope and let it fall to the floor below.

"Now, they'll think I got outta the rope and ran away. Boy will they get a surprise!"

As he inspected the crates and barrels, he found a box hidden behind one of the crates filled with funny rocks with bits of shiny yellow in all shapes and sizes.

More rocks! I kin pelt 'em all day and all night.

He tugged the heavy box and gathered his treasures, moving over to the corner of the loft nearest the edge. He piled his weapons around him and sat to wait for the return of his kidnapper.

Nothin' ta do now but wait. Come on, ye blighter, I already waited a long time.

Caroline moistened her lips as she pulled the reins to halt the horse. Looking around, she saw no one in evidence. *Either I'm early or he's hiding in the trees.* She straightened her spine. *No time like the present.*

Stepping down from the buggy, she grabbed her reticule and moved to stand beside the mare.

A familiar figure clad in black emerged from the tree line. She watched him walk toward her. *His gait is easy, as if he's already won. If our men aren't in place in the warehouse district, he may well win.*

She straightened and looked at the mask hiding his face. *I'll have the advantage if he thinks I'm not intimidated by him. I won't play the victim.*

"You're right on time, Miss Burgess, how gracious of you." He bowed, his cape pooling on the ground around his booted feet.

I know that voice . . . .

Her mouth dropped open. "Nice complement from you, Patrick. Why go to the pretense of concealing your identity?"

With a laugh, he removed the mask with a flourish. "I knew you'd figure it out eventually. That's what I always liked about you, Caroline, your quick brain . . . and your fortune, of course." He grabbed her arm. "Too bad you broke our engagement. I would enjoy matching wits with you."

"Take me to Frankie. If you hurt him, I will—"

"You'll do nothing or I'll kill him the next time. You must know there will always be a next time. You're going to fund my endeavors for the rest of your life, my dear. And just think, I didn't have to chain myself to an unnatural woman like you to reap the benefits." His snide smile turned his handsome features ugly.

He caught her wrist roughly in one hand. "Now before we go another step, I want to be assured you didn't bring one of your toy guns with you."

Grabbing her purse, he grinned. "This is heavy but not heavy enough for a pistol." Spreading the drawstring top, he peered inside. "Well, my, my, you brought the ransom." His eyes widened. "And apparently all of it."

"It's all there." She strained against his confining hand on her wrist. "Count it if you like."

"Don't worry, I will, when we reach our destination." He flipped the reticule and closed it by pulling the drawstring. Slipping it over his own wrist, he leered down at her. "I know not to trust you. I will make certain you aren't concealing a gun on your person."

He dropped her wrist, swept aside her short cape, and ran insolent fingers over her breasts and waist. "Nothing here."

His mouth twisted into a sneer as he patted down her hips and lower abdomen. His hand lingered lower. "You appear to be a woman of your word, but I want to see for myself."

Caroline gritted her teeth and forced herself to remain still as he lifted her skirt, pulled it up to her waist, and held it in place with one hand. He knelt and stroked each of her pantalets-clad legs in turn. "My dear, you should never deprive the theater-going public the sight of your beautiful legs."

When he finished touching each leg, he cupped her at the joining. "No gun here." Still on his knee, he reached around her and caressed her derriere with both hands. "No gun here, either." He licked his lips. "I will regret never having a taste of your charms."

She forced herself to stay motionless, wouldn't allow him to feel her trembling.

He got to his feet and let her skirt drop back into place. "You seem to obey instructions well. I find no evidence of a gun. Congratulations, Caroline, for understanding when you are outdone."

She spoke through a stiff jaw. "If we're through here, will you please take me to Frankie? I'm anxious to see him."

"Of course, my dear, I am at your service." He extended his arm, "This way, if you please." He led her through a tree-lined path following the river.

Farther down the river, Heston's men were positioned on roofs of the warehouses lining the water's edge.

One of them spotted the couple emerging from the trees and watched to see which warehouse they entered. He made it to the ground and ran to where the men waited.

"He took her to the building two doors south of us."

Heston clapped the man on the shoulder.

"Good work, Stevens."

He turned to William. "Milord, if you're ready, we will surround the place and await your signal to move forward."

"Thank you, I'll take it from here." With a look of resolution, he stuck a pistol in his belt and, keeping to the shadows, hurried to the building.

Caroline peered into the darkness below. "You kept him in the dark? How could you do such a thing?"

Patrick shrugged. "He'll get over it. You baby him too much."

A voice rang out from the bottom of the stairs. "Is that you, Patrick? I can't find the little shite. He got away, I'm thinking."

"What do you mean he got away? He couldn't have. I tied the ropes myself."

Rapid footsteps sounded on the stairs. "Well then he had help, because he's gone, look for yourself, if you don't believe me." He appeared out of the darkness. "Hello Caroline."

"Aidan, what are you doing here?"

He grinned at her. "I'm getting my share of your generous contribution. Then I'm headed west."

"But what about Josie?"

"What about her? Now her mother's dead, she'll be better off with the nuns. They'll teach her to honor her father at least."

"You look confused, Darling." Patrick laughed. "Aidan and I are cousins. We hadn't seen each other since we were boys, but we ran into each other a few years ago. We learned about you and your fortune from the newspapers. Together we planned to woo you in the hope one of us could win your favor. When our plan didn't work out, we came up with the alternative of taking the English whelp."

"Aidan, are you embezzling money from the theater company?"

His grin was ugly. "And what if I am? You don't need it." He took the lantern from the sconce on the wall. "But what I need now is to find your little friend." He started down the stairs, light held high.

Patrick prodded her in the back. "Go on, don't dawdle, we don't want to keep the lad in the dark any longer, now do we?"

You're the one who will be living in the dark, if you survive. I'll see you thrown into the deepest hole in the worst prison in this state.

She followed Aidan without saying a word. As they reached the bottom, Caroline glanced at her surroundings.

Surely he wasn't left tied to that rope hanging from the wall.

"I swear I tied him tight." Aidan groveled before his dominant cousin. "I don't see how he could escape. Where would he go? He couldn't get out the front door. I locked it."

"Locked it? Like you tied the brat?" Patrick's voice held scorn. "If he's escaped, he'll blab to his father and Mr. Burgess. Where do you think we'll be when they finish with us?"

"I didn't mean to—"

"Shut it, we need to come up with another plan."

No, you fools. I'm the one with another plan. Caroline slid her right hand up her left arm. "It's cold in here," she whined.

"Yeah, well Princess, you'll need to get used to being uncomfortable. If we don't have the kid to make you give us our money, I'll hold you and let your father pay the ransom."

As her hand reached under the belled sleeve on her left arm, she looked up at her captor.

"He'll pay it, I know he will."

"Yes, he will, and he'll keep paying. Of course we'll have to hold you for a bit to milk him for more."

He scratched his cheek with the barrel of his gun. "I need to plan, to think how to best approach him." He stared off into the warehouse.

Good boy, forget about me, believe you've won.

She felt under the sleeve for the pocket she'd sewn into the lining.

With careful fingers, she grabbed her pistol and slid it down into the fold of her skirt.

"We could cut off some of her hair." Aidan approached his cousin. "You know, as proof we have her."

"Yes, we could, but I'd much rather send her dress." Patrick leered at her, "Then the rest of her garments, one at a time. We could have a bit of sport for our trouble."

Caroline gripped her gun. *They're too close together. I have to take them by surprise.* Her fingers curled into place. *Move apart, why don't you? I need more room to work.*

Her hand pulsed on her weapon, still hidden in her skirt.

"I like your idea, Cousin." Aidan brayed coarse laughter. "We can share. She's got charms enough for both of us . . . OW!" He reached up and felt his head, a trickle of blood flowing down by his ear. "What the hell?"

"Why are you yelling, wha—?" Patrick staggered backward after a shining rock hit between his eyes. Two more rocks pelted Patrick in quick succession. He stared in disbelief at the stones on the floor by his feet. "It's my gold. He's throwing my nuggets at us."

"What gold?" Aidan ducked and looked toward the loft. "You have gold and didn't tell me?" Another stone hit his hand as he protected his ear. "Ouch, that hurts."

"I got more o' these to toss. Why don't ye give up? Nobody kin beat us Hargreaves." Frankie's little-boy voice sing-songed off the rafters.

"You little bugger." Patrick charged forward toward the loft, only to be hit by four nuggets in quick succession. "Cease at once!" Another nugget grazed his eyelid. He raised his gun. "I'll stop you."

"Put your weapon down." Caroline held her pistol aimed at his heart. "You know I am not afraid to use this."

Patrick grinned with insolence at her, never lowering his weapon. *What is he doing?*

"Miss Caro, look out, behind you!" Frankie's scream carried from the loft.

Damn, it must be Aidan, how could I forget him? Because I'm too focused on saving Frankie, that's how.

Starting to turn, she felt the muzzle of a gun jammed into her temple.

"Now, now Caroline, I'm ashamed of you." Patrick moved toward her. "Next time I shall have to strip you to make sure you're unarmed."

He held out his hand. "Give me your gun, slowly, please."

There's got to be some way out of this mess. I must help Frankie.

"I said, give me the gun. Do it now." Patrick's voice shook with rage. "Do it!"

I must give Frankie time to get away. With a sigh, she dropped her gun into his outstretched hand.

He pocketed the gun, smiled, and backhanded her across the face. "You will learn to obey me or I'll kill the boy. Do you understand?"

Nodding, she kept her gaze on the floor.

"He'll have ta ketch me first, Miss Caro."

Another, larger missile sailed from the loft, hitting Aidan in the middle of his forehead. He fell unconscious to the floor, his gun clattering across the wooden slats.

Caroline tried to grab the fleeing weapon. Patrick reached it first, kicking it to the back of the warehouse.

"Naughty, naughty, Caro. Looks like I'll have my hands full teaching you some necessary lessons."

"Leave 'er alone," Frankie yelled as he tossed another nugget. It sailed past Patrick by a wide margin.

"Getting tired, lad? I can understand. Why don't you come down here with your friend? I promise I won't hurt you."

William crept down the stairs, reaching the landing in time to overhear Frankie's reply.

Frankie leaned down from the loft, taunting Patrick. "Why don't ye come and git me? Like young boys, do ye? I heard stories about men like ye."

"You filthy little beggar, I'll teach you to talk to your betters in such a way." Patrick aimed the gun and cocked the trigger.

"Harris!" William's voice rang out from the landing, "Put down your gun or I'll shoot you."

"I'm not afraid of an English baron, you weak-willed twit." Patrick took aim and shot at William.

The Baron ducked the shot. "So be it." He fired and hit Caroline's stalker in the center of his forehead.

The Irishman fell to the floor, his lifeless eyes staring at the beams above.

"Well done, Milord." Heston ran down the steps two at a time. Ignoring the body, he moved to Caroline. "Miss Burgess, are you all right?"

She looked at him a moment. "How did you find us?"

He took her arm. "Come with me, Miss. I'll take you home."

"I can't go until I'm sure Frankie is safe." She broke away and hurried to the wall beneath the loft.

"Frankie, are you up there? Did he hurt you?"

A bright red head appeared. "I'm right as rain, Miss Caro. Move back. I'll be down in a minute."

Shaking her head, she backed away from the wall. *What is he up to?*

"Watch out, below." A wooden box half filled with gold nuggets dropped to the floor, breaking apart on impact. "Those're mine, nobody touch 'em," he called.

"Be careful!" Caroline watched him. *He's likely to break his neck.*

He reached down with the bailing hook and caught the rope, pulling it up. Then he stepped over the edge of the loft and shimmied down to the floor.

"I told ye it was easy." He grinned and ran to her.

"You scared the life out of me." Caroline hugged him.

"'Twasn't anythin for ye to worry about. I wasn't in danger." He smiled up at her and winked. "Ye know we Hargreaves men are strong."

"Yes, you are." She hugged him once more.

"Miss Caro, don't you think it's time you married us?" Frankie's bright eyes gazed up at her.

William hurried over to take his son's arm. "Franklin, it isn't appropriate for you to ask such a question. Come along. Find another box for the gold nuggets you discovered. We'll take them back to Burgess House." With a short nod to Caroline, he turned and followed his son.

"I don't unnerstand what's wrong askin Miss Caro to marry us? My mother annulled us. Why can't we marry Miss Caro?"

"Franklin, please be quiet and pick up the nuggets." William guided his son away.

Caroline sighed.

Why did he come here, then?

Why did he tell me how remorseful he was?

What did I do to make him reject me?

He's still hiding behind the arbiter of all things proper.

Chapter Twenty-Five
Sisters of Mercy

"Caroline, you shouldn't be here. You should be home resting after your ordeal." Lisette gently scolded her friend.

"I'm not staying. I came to get Josie and take her home with me. She lost her mother and now her father will go to prison for the rest of his life. If she's willing, I'll adopt her and raise her as my own." Caroline walked to the stairs. "Is she in her room?"

"I don't know where she is. Don't you think it would be better to wait and not make such decisions when you're upset? Josie will be fine here."

Give me strength, if my friend reacts this way, we will find obstacles at every turn.

"This matter isn't open to discussion. My decision is made. Excuse me." she started up the stairs.

"Miss Caroline?" a small voice called to her. Josie came down from the landing. "I heard your voice. Did you really come to take me with you?"

"Yes, if you want to come. Do you?"

The little girl ran to her. "Oh yes, please."

Caroline hugged the child. "Then you will come live with me. Mrs. Arnold made molasses cookies this morning. Let's go see if there are any left, shall we?"

Josie grinned up at her and took her hand, skipping as they walked out the door.

"Why is everybody so quiet?" Frankie looked up and down the long dinner table. "Why isn't anybody talking?"

"Eat your dinner. We'll speak in private later," William snapped.

"Why can't we talk now? We rescued her. I'm proud I helped."

"If you can't hold your tongue, you must leave the table."

"I did a good thing, beanin' Aidan with the rock. I knocked him out. The coppers took him away forever."

Caroline sighed as Josie began to weep beside her. "Come along, dearest, let's go wash your face."

She glared at William as they left the table. *You're to blame for this. Baiting your son in front of her.*

Frankie shook his head. "Ye made a fine mess o' things, this time." He spoke out of the side of his mouth to his father.

William rose and tossed down his napkin. "If you will excuse me, I believe I am finished." He walked toward the back entrance and disappeared from sight.

With one last glance at the table, Caroline escorted Josie out the opposite entrance to the room.

In the darkness of the garden, William lit a cigar and blew smoke rings toward the stars. *How did it all go so wrong? We were so happy. Why couldn't I leave things alone, rejoice my son and the woman I love are finally safe? Why did I spoil it? From the look on Caroline's face just now, she will never forgive me. I have no right to expect it of her.*

Sighing he looked toward the East, the darkest part of the sky. *Perhaps it is time to return to England. Caroline will never forgive me now. Frankie and I should go home to Parkfield. We can live a quiet life in the country.*

The crickets chirped as the moon made its nightly journey. William sat keeping his own counsel. *I wanted a love like Sheridan and Celeste or Mimi and Elijah. I know it is possible, but it never happened for me. Now it never will.*

Deep inside him, the little orphaned boy wept, his unhealed wound filling him with pain.

I wanted the love Papa had with Maman.

"I want to talk to you." Caroline strode across the dew-covered grass.

William jumped to his feet, his hand raking through his hair. "Of

323

course, is something wrong with Frankie?"

"No, your son is in much better shape than you are." She sat on the opposite bench.

"I don't know what you mean." His voice sounded pompous even to him, as he grabbed his lapels and stood straight.

"Yes, there he is, the stodgy baron. I wondered where he was. Lately, he's been absent and we're the better for it."

He raised a supercilious brow in her direction. "If I upset you, of course I shall withdraw from your presence. In fact I think it best for Franklin and me to return to England at our first opportunity." He bowed and turned to go.

"Oh yes, that's right. Run away, why don't you? Isn't it your usual tactic when someone gets too close to the truth or too close to you?"

"Madam, I take offense—"

"Go ahead. At least you're showing a bit of real emotion for once."

"Whatever I did to cause your outburst, I most sincerely apologize." He turned away once more and started up the path to the house.

Caroline jumped to her feet. "I never took you for a coward."

He stiffened but did not stop his trek to safety.

"You're a typical spoiled English aristocrat, with no care for anyone beyond your small inbred circle of friends. I don't know why I ever loved you."

William stopped, his fists clenched at his sides. "Love me? You could not love me and speak to me this way." He turned to face her.

"You think so? Well, this is me loving you, Baron Hargreaves. I love you enough to tell you the truth. It isn't my fault you can't bear to hear it."

He charged her, stopping immediately in front of her, his face dark with rage in the moonlight.

"You think I am a coward, eh? Why do you think I rushed into the blasted warehouse alone to save you and my son?"

I mustn't smile. He's almost ready to break. She pursed her lips. "I don't know. Why did you rush in to save Frankie and me, Will?"

"Because I love you both, dash it." He grabbed her shoulders and pulled her to his chest in a fierce embrace. "I was in torment trying to decide which of you to save first."

"About time you admitted it." Caroline snuggled against him and sighed when she felt the movement of his chest. His heartbeat slowed against her as he calmed.

She waited for him to breathe deeply, to relax.

"Have you ever killed a man before?"

"Certainly not, what do you take me for?" His arms tightened around her.

"My darling what you're experiencing is normal. I went through the same thing when I shot Gareth. It's a traumatic experience."

When he held her without words, she pulled back and looked at him. "It is all well. You saved Frankie and you saved me when I made a mistake. You showed me no one is invincible, not even a wicked American pistol-packing actress."

William's lips twitched. "I've never met anyone like you." He dipped his head and then looked into her eyes. "I love you."

"You're not going back to England for a while."

"I'm not?"

She shook her head. "I want to be married here in Philadelphia."

His lips twitched with the ghost of a smile. "Oh you do, do you?"

"Yes, I want a big wedding with all our friends and available family. Do you think your sister Mimi might be willing to come?"

"If I know my younger sister, she'll want to manage the whole affair."

"She'll have to battle Lisette and Jayne for the honor."

For the first time that night, William laughed, a genuine expression of joy. "You are right in your estimation of Mimi and Lisette. I'll bow to your superior knowledge of Jayne. You may invite anyone you wish."

She picked at the buttons of his waistcoat. "There is one person who will not be welcome at our wedding."

"And who is that?"

She shook her head. "The stuffy Baron Hargreaves. He'd better not be there. In fact, I don't ever want to see him again."

He inhaled sharply and stiffened against her.

"No, darling, it isn't what I meant. His persona is your defense mechanism when you are uncertain or afraid. I realize that now. You don't need to hide behind him any longer."

He relaxed once more. "You know me very well, don't you?"

"Let's say I recognize a kindred spirit. Neither one of us will ever need to fear being abandoned. We are already a family."

He touched his forehead to hers. "I'll hold you to the promise." He kissed her once more. "I never proposed marriage to you." He pulled back to sink to one knee. "Shall I do it now?"

Laughing, she helped him rise to his feet. "Frankie already proposed, don't you remember?"

He offered his arm to her and she accepted it. Together they walked toward the house. "I must remember to thank Frankie for proposing to you."

She stopped. "When you speak to him, you might advise him not to mention Aidan in front of Josie. He's still her father, even though she'll live with us."

"Good idea, but will Josie accept me? I don't know how to be a father to a little girl."

"You'll learn. You've done a splendid job with Frankie."

"You mean he's done a splendid job training me to be a father."

"I'm so glad you found each other. Besides, you need practice. We may one day have another daughter or a son, perhaps two. You never know."

"Zounds, I'm to be leg-shackled at last . . . ." He used his cold Baron voice.

She laughed in delight. "If you don't behave I'll put you onstage for everyone to see."

He pulled her close as they reached the door. "Who would ever believe I would love and marry such a wicked lady?"

"I would," she whispered, as she kissed him on the doorstep.

Excerpt from the *London Standard* - column of *Jolie Madame*:

My dears, there is lovely news to share. I learned of a wedding that took place in Philadelphia in the United States. Baron William Hargreaves married his longtime ladylove in a large and exquisite ceremony. By all reports, the new Baroness Hargreaves née Caroline Burgess glowed with a beauty worthy of a Botticelli. I do so love to see a happy ending for such a splendid couple. I am told they will divide their time between England and America. I cannot wait to see them in person when they return to London. They will be the undisputed hit of the season .
. . .

Afterword

On the September day William married Caroline in Pennsylvania, Drake traveled as a passenger on a ship bound from Liverpool to Dublin. Pulling the lapels of his captain's coat tight against the damp cold of the Irish Sea, he stood at the railing.

"I'm coming for you, Bridget O'Halloran. No one, not your father, nor the Queen herself will stand in my way."

His eyes focused on the land rising out of the sea on the horizon as he used his chilled breath to warm his hands.

About the Author

Sharon Drane first set foot on a stage at the age of six. For the next 54 years she acted in productions. In her early 20s she began directing, a second career which lasted over forty years. Employed by various agencies with the State of Texas, she worked for over 35years as a social worker in the field, and then as a manager of contracts. She worked first at the regional level and then was promoted to Austin and management of statewide contracts.

She began writing short stories and poetry in high school. During her tenure in the field of social work Sharon began writing love stories, completing two novels in spite of her hectic schedule. She retired in 2009 and moved to Florida on family business. It was here she rediscovered her love of writing. During her time in the Sunshine State, she has completed two published novels, with the third in the series due out late in 2016. Her fourth novel is currently in progress and slated to be published in 2017.

www.ingramcontent.com/pod-product-compliance
Lightning Source LLC
Chambersburg PA
CBHW051949240626
47153CB00005B/1690

You need to share them, a voice whispered. Henry's, maybe. Or Janey's. But I didn't feel like arguing with it. I felt... peaceful, almost.

"Janey's on break, but she'll be back in a minute and Danielle's at the desk." As if he sensed my reluctance to part with the box, he placed it carefully on the floor outside the office. "I'll leave this right here, and be back with the cart."

I thanked him and walked into the office, bracing myself for the memories that waited inside. Same filing cabinets. Same mauve carpet. Same couch, sagging a little lower. Only the walls were different—the screens replaced by an enormous mural of flowers that looped around the room gracefully, like a tattoo covering a scar.

Danielle sat at the desk, filing her nails. *She and Janey must get along*, I thought. She jumped when she saw me, curls bouncing with the movement. "I'm here to get my file, and my brother's file," I said, after enduring a few minutes of awkward small talk as she tried to work up the courage to ask me for a picture.

"Right!" She opened a filing cabinet and shuffled through it while I tried to look like a person who was "moving forward."

The guard returned with a cart as Danielle pulled my file. "So, here's yours." She held out a CD. "Doesn't look like much, I know, but all the old paper files got scanned and shredded. There's a box of personal things downstairs, too. And then there's a cross reference for your brother—David?—but someone already picked that one up."

"That's not possible. I'm his only family." I wasn't worried. Janey filed these papers. How organized could they be?

"Hm. Well, it says here it was picked up by someone named Robert Rocca."

Robert. *Bobby*. His name sucked all the air out of the room, stealing the peace I found in my box of journals.

"He left a note for you. And one of your brother's personal items—a guitar. He also left that. Downstairs." She scribbled something on a piece of paper and handed it to the guard, who promised to find the guitar and my box and bring them back. The note, she tried to hand to me.

How dare he, I thought. *How dare he come here, and take David's things. How dare he leave the guitar for me like a gift. He had no right.* I didn't take the note. I couldn't. I was trembling. Furious. Ready to explode.

"Um, Janey?" Danielle called, sounding nervous enough that I knew I must look how I felt. "I'll just leave the note on the counter," she said, backing away from me.

Janey rushed in, big hair and strawberry perfume and glitter. She grabbed my arm and then pulled her hand back like it burned. "I'm so sorry, I didn't think you'd be here before I got back…" She took in the CD and the note, wilting as she realized she couldn't do much damage control at this point. I wondered what she would have done if she'd gotten to me first. Lied, probably. "Come on, say something. You look scary right now."

The guard clattered back with a cart full of things I wasn't sure I wanted, and I hurried to it, grabbing the note off the counter as I passed.

"You don't have to read it right now," Janey called, rushing after me, but I could hardly hear her through my anger. "We'll go through it all together, later. How's that?"

I picked up my pace, afraid of what would happen if I stayed still for too long, feeling like this. I pushed my notebooks, my box, and David's guitar, moving as fast as the pain would let me go. I heard Janey behind me, offering reasonable suggestions—I could wait for the end of her shift and go home with her, or she could clock out early and come with me, or we could just go sit somewhere quietly and talk—but I didn't stop.

I had to get away.

I shoved the journals, my box from the basement, and David's guitar into the trunk of the car, angry with them and with myself. Whatever peace I felt in the hallway was gone, replaced by red-hot anger. It was stupid to expect anything else from that place.

I tried to toss the note away, but the anger needed to be fed. I flattened it.

"Grace," it said, in blocky capital letters. "I'm so sorry. For everything. I left David's guitar for you. He'd want you to have it. Please call me—I want to talk. And to visit his grave, but I can't find the lake house—I guess no one can, except you."

His phone number, bold and underlined, ran across the bottom of the page like an order. Blood rushed in my ears. The numbers swam in front of me. *Damn right I'm the only one who can find it*, I thought. I crumpled the note and screeched out of the parking lot, so angry I could hardly see the road.

Sky Lake belonged to me. David's grave belonged to me. Bobby couldn't have it.

I knew I shouldn't be driving, but I was afraid to stop with all those feeling chasing me. I rolled the windows down, breathless no matter how much air I gulped. Hot, even with the wind whipping around me.

I was furious. Scared. Trapped, because no matter how fast I drove, Bobby's note was already burned into my eyes.

Bobby can't go to Sky Lake, I thought, and my breathing eased a little.

But maybe I can.

My heart pounded. Maybe I *could*.

I flew onto the highway. I could feel my old fears, poking and whispering and gnawing, but they were far away. The anger, on the other hand, was close. Hot and raging right underneath my skin.

I would find Sky Lake. I would prove that it belonged to me.

It was easy, until I got off the highway. Everything looked the same at first—the ice cream stand that had been there since I could remember, the dirt parking areas at the hiking trails, the thick forest disappearing into darkness on both sides of the road. But the path twisted and turned, stretching out forever in all the wrong directions.

My fear got louder. What if I couldn't find Sky Lake? What if it really wasn't mine anymore? I gripped the steering wheel so tight that my knuckles ached, eyes boring holes in every tree. Looking for something—anything— I remembered.

And then, I felt it. The riptide pull that terrified me at the karaoke bar. The cutting swirl that sliced me open when I kissed Chris. My heart, prying my ribs apart to get out. It didn't feel like home. But it did feel familiar, and I let it pull me.

It hurt. But when I thought about how Bobby felt—rejected, cast out, grieving—resolve flowed through me again. I could go to Sky Lake, and he couldn't, and I didn't need anything more than that. If I cut myself open in that moment, I hate to think what would have gushed out.

How's that for moving forward? I asked an imaginary Henry, and I could see him making that face that he made when I completely missed the point. But it didn't matter. No one else could find Sky Lake. It was mine. I would never let Bobby near it.

I felt the right spot but didn't see it—nature had healed over the driveway long ago, and a less desperate person would not have turned the wheel on memory alone. But I could feel it, smell it, taste it at that point—*home*. I would have driven straight through the forest if I had to.

I tried not to notice the leafless trees, reaching. The deep potholes, grabbing my tires. The clouds gathering like mourners over the house. I needed to be home. And I needed home to be glad to see me.

I stepped out of the car and into the perfumed air of the place I loved most in the world. As I took my first breath—roses, pine trees, water, earth—I wondered how I ever could have accepted the false, one-dimensional smell of the Sky Lake in my mind. The real Sky Lake wrapped around me, cool and fresh and thick and *layered*. Every cell in my body sucked it in.

Home. How had I lived without it for so long?

To my right, a path led up to the rose garden, and, beyond that, the cemetery, but I couldn't see the glow through the trees. To the left, the house loomed like a huge, neglected dog. Peeling and faded and overgrown with weeds. I felt sick with sorrow. It had been this way for years. Alone. The dining room table stood at a slant, sinking in the lawn. A shipwreck washed up on shore.

"I'm sorry," I whispered to the ruined house. The beached table. "I'm going to fix this." The clouds lowered like eyebrows. Not believing me. I didn't blame them.

Overwhelmed by the house and its needs and the table slowly returning to the earth, I walked to the edge of the water and took off my shoes. I crunched over pebbles—the same ones I used to stuff into my suitcase by the handful—and into cold mud. I closed my eyes. *Please*, I thought, *let it be like I remember.*

For a few, beautiful seconds, peace rose up through my legs, into my belly, filling my chest and sliding smoothly down my arms. The pain faded into background noise. My anger cooled. I remembered my grandmother telling me that Sky Lake could heal anything.

Anything you were ready to be free of.

The peace flowed back into the lake, where it belonged. The pain throbbed to life. My mind resumed its sad, angry circles. Sky Lake wasn't going to save me this time, either. I turned my back on it, hurt and angry and more surprised than I should have been.

I left the water and walked, barefoot, to the front door. Sharp rocks bit the soft soles of my feet and mosquitos stung my ankles and I was ten years old again, locking up with David for the last time. Me with my suitcase full of rocks and David with his half-empty backpack that somehow contained everything he needed for weeks.

I could almost see him there, full of talent and love and life. He'd tell me Henry was right and Janey did her best. He would beg me to let go of what was hurting me, and he'd be right.

I felt him, pushing those thoughts into me. Wishing I'd give Bobby a rock from the lake.

Hot needles of anger pierced my heart again. David was dead. What could he possibly know about my life?

At the door, I hesitated. The second-floor window screens hung like loose teeth above me. A pile of leaves waited on the doormat. The knob turned easily—unlocked. Going inside the house would only give me more sad things to remember about it. But the clouds were pressing down, dark and electric, and I knew better than to try to leave while they were like that.

I had to go in. I wasn't done with my penance yet.

Inside, I found chaos. Chairs and couches from every room gathered in a rough semi-circle in the living room. Dishes overflowed the sink. The air was hot and as stale as an attic. My feet stirred tornadoes of dust with every step.

Beer bottles and cereal boxes clustered on counters, connected by nets of cobwebs. Pizza boxes in various states of decay were stacked precariously. Loose piles of shredded cardboard marked the corners where animals nested over the years. I flipped over the graying receipt still taped to the top of a pizza box and it crumbled between my fingers. It looked like a group of teenagers took the place over for a month and then left in a hurry.

I'm so sorry, I whispered. But the air inside the house felt light, not heavy, and the rumble of thunder that responded to my apology sounded more like laughter than anything else.

I wandered through the ruined kitchen and into the dining room. An old boombox sat on a milk crate next to the piano David and I put in the center of the room so long ago. An expensive microphone on a stand dominated one corner, a bright blue drum set claimed another. Old comforters and cardboard hung on the walls and over the windows to reduce the echo in the room.

Musicians, I thought. *Appropriate.*

The thunder rumbled its approval.

A heavy antique desk, taken from the downstairs office, held stacks of brittle paper covered in scribbled notes, and a dusty red guitar leaned against a chair. I trailed my fingers over the surface of the desk, resisting the urge to sit down and read the words written there. I would have time for that later. Right now, I needed to assess the damage.

Explore, a voice in the back of my mind corrected, like the house itself objected to my characterization of its condition.

Upstairs, I found the bedrooms in similar disarray, with beds unmade and crumpled clothes littering the floors. In one room, a tall stack of science fiction books teetered on a bedside table. In another, junk food wrappers spilled over the trash can. In the third, I found more scribbled pages and my own face on the bed, unsmiling on the cover of a magazine.

Who were you? I asked, and I'm not sure if I was talking to the person who stayed in this room, or the girl in the picture.

Back downstairs, I sat at the piano for a long time. Janey would tell me to choose something—pizza boxes, beer bottles—fill a trash bag with it, and go from there. She could get through this mess in a few hours, because she knew how to start somewhere and keep moving. But I didn't want to put the bottles in the trash. I didn't want to move the desk or wash the dishes or gather all the paper into a neat pile.

The house sang with the energy of these mystery guests, and I didn't want to erase it. I liked it. It felt like home.

I turned to the piano. It was so out-of-tune that I cringed at the sound, but I played a song David taught me, and then another, trying to feel him in the room. What would he say if he saw me now?

He wouldn't even recognize me, I thought. *He'd want me to pull myself together and live the life he didn't get a chance to live.*

My hands pulled toward another song. A sad one that I wrote and never played, because Johnathan's team edited it so brutally that I couldn't bring myself to look at it again. I let my fingers find it, enjoying the painful clank of the bad keys. I never imagined it as a piano song, but it would probably work.

As I played, I felt the excitement of the previous inhabitants around me, encouraging. "Who were you?" I asked again. It felt important, suddenly, for me to know.

I went to the desk and flipped through the papers. They were lyrics, mostly illegible from water damage. But something coursed through the pages—something I recognized. I could feel it in my fingertips. "Who were you," I asked again, half-convinced that the walls themselves would answer me. I grasped at the words and phrases still visible on the muddied pages. They were familiar. And they made me burn with that strange longing that didn't quite belong to me.

And then, I realized that I didn't have to wonder. Damia would know.

How long had it been since I talked to Damia? Guilt pulled me out of my thoughts, back into the mess. She only wanted to help me, and I pushed her away. I wished I had given her a chance to explain. *Better late than never*, I thought, and dialed, crossing my fingers because the signal in the house was so weak.

I thought she might ignore me after my months of silence, but she answered on the second ring. "I'm at Sky Lake," I told her, even though I knew I should be apologizing. "And I'm so curious about what happened here." Curious didn't begin to describe it. I needed to know. The phone crackled, then smoothed, and I imagined the trees stretching their arms to steady the connection.

She was quiet for a few seconds. Then, cautiously, "It's a long story. And I'm not sure you want to hear it. Last time, you ran away and didn't speak to me for a year, remember?"

"Last time you wanted to talk about Bobby," I reminded her. His name stung—I was still glad he didn't have a map or a pebble. "I want to hear about the lake house. About who you helped."

"Yes," she said. "I understand. But to talk about that, we have to talk about Bobby."

My heart stuttered and I pressed the heel of one hand against it. I wanted to hear about the people we helped, who filled this house with so much music that it still seeped out of the walls. The person who wrote the lyrics I could feel in my fingertips. I didn't want that story contaminated with bad memories.

I couldn't face it. Just like I couldn't face calling Damia, or having an honest conversation with Janey, or doing a single thing Henry suggested. Static crackled in my ear. If I didn't want to hear this, I didn't have to.

I ran my fingers over the piano keys, remembering the Sky Lake in my mind, where the piano stayed in tune and never got dusty and I couldn't hit a wrong note. And how it changed—went bad—when I tried to keep it. I didn't want to be there. I wanted to be where I was. I wanted to be real.

And real me needed to start facing things.

"What does he have to do with this place?" I asked.

"He came back for you," Damia said, gently. "That's where the story starts."

Pain shot up my neck and flashed in my eyes. I gripped the piano for balance, and the keys moaned tunelessly under my fingers. "He left me," I said, my vision swimming. "That's where the story started."

"Your story started there, yes. If you want to look at it that way. But this story isn't about you. It's about the people we helped."

We. Damia and me? Or Damia and Bobby? I wanted to keep him in my past, frozen in his worst moment, a one-dimensional villain. I wanted to *blame* him. "I don't think I'm ready to hear this."

"Ok," she said, and the bad connection sizzled over her voice. "I'll respect that, if you mean it."

Henry's voice came back, telling me I chose to be a victim. David hovered nearby, loving me but also loving Bobby. I felt Janey's hand on my arm and heard Greg and Brad's worried voices on the phone. The people who made music in this room whispered encouragement from the walls. My fingers glowed lightly where they touched the papers on the desk.

If the lake itself could talk, I knew what its watery voice would say—*listen*. I braced myself. "I didn't mean it. Tell me."

Damia took a deep breath. I could see her, settling in a soft chair, leaning forward to give me her full attention even though I wasn't sitting across from her. The static faded and her voice came through, strong and clear, carried by the wind or the trees or my willingness to hear it. "Well, it's like I said. He came back. You'd just left for Charlie's second tour, and he was looking for a lost kid. I couldn't get in touch with you, and what could he do for you, anyway? So… I made a decision."

Tears sprang into my eyes. *He came back.* "What kind of decision?" I asked, struggling to speak past the ball of emotion in my throat.

"I gave him a chance to redeem himself."

31

DAMIA

The man in my office was tall and broad shouldered, with a beer gut and the pale, waxy skin of someone who doesn't take care of himself. His shoes were visibly worn out. An old bruise darkened one eye, and a cut ran along the knuckles of his right hand. He hunched in one of my chairs, waiting, when I returned from lunch.

"Can I help you?" I asked, hoping he had the wrong office. I didn't feel like dealing with a surprise, and this man didn't look like a good surprise.

The past two weeks had been a whirlwind as we prepared Charlie for her second tour, and my guilt made it even more exhausting. Johnathan pushed the poor kid into the studio the second she got back from the first tour, and then he pushed her back out like her fame would go bad if he didn't use it. He insisted she'd be fine. "She's born to perform," he said. "She loves it. She'll be happier on stage."

He might have been right to send her away. She certainly couldn't be happy in that sad little dorm room, living whatever life she lived with us. But she looked thin and pale when she left this time. Small. Like Grace had to shrink in order for Charlie to grow.

Once Johnathan saw how much money Charlotte London could make for him, he stopped leaving things to chance. Every detail required a meeting and a decision. Every song demanded review and revision and more review. I had a bad feeling that she wasn't going to have fun this time, and it weighed on me. *She* weighed on me. Ever since I brought her to bury her brother, I felt responsible for her.

Responsible is the wrong word. When you're responsible, you can do your best and then sleep at night. But I lost my chance to help Grace when I didn't leave her at that house. And now she was Charlotte London, and I couldn't protect her. She was an aching regret that I carried on my back and heard every day on the radio.

In just a few hours, Kit's son and his friends would arrive. I would pick them up at the airport and bring them to ERC and they'd be in Johnathan's clutches, too. It would be Charlie all over again. Worse, maybe. Johnathan saw Charlie's value. Who knew what he would do to those kids?

They were just pawns.

And I was going to deliver them to him. Because that was my job. My life. That's who I *was*.

The man sat between me and my desk, where the map to Sky Lake sat in a locked drawer. When I felt like this, I opened the drawer and looked at it, and the possibility that I might help someone someday made me feel better even though I knew I'd never have the courage to do it. I wanted the man to go away and leave me in peace with my map.

And then, I recognized him.

Bobby.

I almost called him a piece of shit and sent him away. He shouldn't have been able to get in to begin with, with his expired security credentials. But he was probably the only other person on earth who knew how I felt about what happened to that little girl. Part of me wanted to hug him.

"Please, just tell me where she is," he begged, without introduction, because our guilt had already reached out and shaken hands. He stood and took off his baseball cap, revealing a shiny bald spot that wasn't there before. I had never seen anyone age so much in so little time. "I have to see her. I have to…" He glanced up at the camera in the corner and lowered his voice, "I have to get her out of here."

It was heartbreaking, how much he wanted to help her. How could he, though? Even if she'd been in the building, there was no way out. Not for anyone, but especially not for her.

"She isn't here," I said. "And even if she was, he wouldn't let her leave." I tried to be gentle, but I saw the words sting him.

"Tell me where she is, then," he begged.

My top lip twitched—nervous—and I bit it to keep it still. Bobby was desperate. He would do something crazy if I didn't think of something. He'd get himself killed. And maybe her, too.

"I never should have left her here. I don't know what got into me… I have to save her." He rubbed his hands back and forth over his head. He looked like he wanted to climb out of the bad dream he was living in. "Please," he said.

I started to tell him the truth—that Johnathan wouldn't have let him take her then, either—but stopped. It wouldn't make any difference. If anyone knew that, I did. I couldn't absolve him of his guilt.

But I might be able to give him a way to make amends.

Before I could have second thoughts, I wrote down the address of a late-night diner and told him to wait for me there.

If not for Bobby, I wouldn't have had the courage to take the kids to Sky Lake. I was a little bit angry with Kit at that point, to be honest. What did she think she was doing, walking into Johnathan's office asking to go home? Of all people, she should have known it would only provoke him. *I* knew, and I don't have a psychic bone in my body.

By the time I left for the airport, I'd talked myself out of all my sympathy.

But then I saw the kids. They stood in a loose group on the curb, duffle bags hanging casually from their shoulders, joking around, looking hopeful every time a car slowed down because it was a cold day and none of them were dressed for it.

I stopped and they tumbled in, a rush of noise and energy that made my head or my heart hurt—I couldn't tell which. Kit's son—Nic—introduced himself to me. Polite and friendly and glowing from the inside. The others jostled for space in the back seat, teasing each other.

They were awful, cocky teenagers, drenched in cheap cologne, making fun of Kit's son for having a crush on Charlie London, of all people. But they were good, underneath. Overflowing with life. Full of potential.

So *young*. Delivering them to Johnathan, I knew, would be a crime.

Another, to add to my list. And I would have done it, if not for Bobby.

If not for Bobby, I only would have *considered* saving them. And then I would have thought it through, realized it was a suicide mission, and put the map back in the drawer for next time. And there never would have been a next time, just a map to gaze at when I slid too close to despair.

But Bobby seized the opportunity to make up for what happened to Grace, and he carried me along on his enthusiasm until bringing them back to the hotel would have been the same thing as murder.

I left them at Sky Lake and went back to face the consequences.

And I returned three weeks later with Kit's ashes in a box. I remember it, so vividly. A light, crunchy layer of snow under my shoes as I walked across the driveway. A thin coating of ice sparkling on the lake. Roses in the air, even in the middle of the winter.

The weight of the box in my arms. Hard and sharp. Not like Kit at all.

Nic opened the door and I choked on the words I planned to say. How to you tell a teenager that his mother is in this box?

They'd moved all the furniture. Every surface seemed to have a takeout container on it. There was a concerning amount of beer, considering that Bobby was the only adult in the house. But they were bouncing off the walls—happy and free and inspired. I only brought them to Sky Lake to hide them, but they'd breathed life into it. It was beautiful but also sad—a temporary place, turned into a home.

They cleared a space on the couch and gave me cold pizza on a paper plate like chefs presenting a gourmet meal. I balanced the plate on Kit and pulled the crust apart. I couldn't have swallowed a bite if my life depended on it.

The kids tripped over each other telling me about the place—the rose garden, the hot springs, the strange way the lake glowed at night. They played the new song that was going to make them famous.

And the whole time, Kit's box sat there like a bomb.

Bobby's eyes kept flicking to it, and then to Nic, anticipating the pain to come. He cared about those kids, and I knew I had done a good thing by giving him this. I clung to that—he was doing a good thing, which meant I had done a good thing. Maybe Kit was right to save me.

But it didn't feel that way. It felt like she should be pulling the pizza apart, and I should be in the box.

When we first arrived at Sky Lake, I wasn't sure about leaving Bobby in charge. He disappeared for a long time that day, and when I found him up in the cemetery, I thought he might not be able to handle the memories.

"It has to be one of these," he said, pointing at the three stones that glowed, "but I don't know which one."

I showed him which rock little Grace dragged out of the lake that afternoon. The memory made me cold.

"She got this... from there?" he asked, shivering at the idea of her little body in that deep black water.

I nodded but didn't elaborate. Nothing I said about that day would make him feel better.

Bobby knelt next to David's stone, big hands cupped around it, head bowed. He stayed that way for a long time while his pain soaked into the ground and peace took its place. I hoped little Grace felt something like that when she buried her brother, but I knew in my heart that she didn't. I didn't give her the chance.

That's why I brought Kit's box to the house with me—to give Nic peace. But we couldn't bury her until I told him she was dead, and it felt wrong to bring death into a place so full of *life*.

When I couldn't delay any longer, I told them the lies I'd prepared—*an accident, no one's fault, she didn't feel any pain*—and we trudged up to the cemetery, where the ground was soft in spite of the snow.

Nic knew the truth—I could see it in his eyes—but he didn't push for it. We buried her in soil that should have been frozen solid, but wasn't, and Nic found a big stone at the edge of the lake to mark the spot.

"It doesn't glow," he said, and Bobby assured him it would, eventually.

I didn't think that was true, but I also didn't want anyone to jump into that water, so I kept my mouth shut.

They stayed at Sky Lake for months, and I checked on them when I could safely get away. I remembered the warnings about the map, but Bobby seemed to have no trouble running errands and returning, so I stopped worrying about it. They went out to a show, and then another, and found their way back.

After a while, I stopped being so careful. By the time I spilled the coffee, Grace's swiftly drawn lines were already smudged, the paper tearing at the edges. I didn't think anything of it until I tried to drive back.

At first, it was all just like I remembered. The wide swath of highway, the long, sharply curved exit, the ice cream stand with the plywood sign. Winding roads cutting through forest so thick you could only see two trees in. But an hour flew under my tires, and then two, and my heart started to race—*lost*.

I wasn't lost. I could find my way back to the highway easily. I just couldn't find Sky Lake.

I searched for weeks, always sure the half-hidden driveway lurked around the next bend, but Sky Lake might as well have been on another planet. Nothing I did made any difference. I tried to clean the map with lemon juice and water. I drew over the faded lines. I squinted at regular maps until my eyes burned. It hollowed me out until I felt as thin as an eggshell, but I kept searching. Sniffing the air for roses. Losing hope, because that map had been my hope.

The next time Bobby and the kids left, they couldn't find their way back, either.

Sky Lake was gone. I took it from them—broke the map and broke the spell and it was lost to all of us.

I told myself it didn't really matter. Johnathan lost interest in the kids after Kit died, and their careers took right off—they couldn't have stayed at Sky Lake anyway. But there was something special about that place, and something special about all of them in that place. And it was my fault that they lost it.

Something else for me to carry.

Bobby sent a postcard every so often. He didn't write anything personal, but I read his slow, steady healing between the lines and I put the cards in the drawer where I used to keep the map. He turned the ugliest thing he ever did into something good, and I held onto him as an example for a long time before Mallory Harmon approached me for help.

I didn't get many chances to do things that mattered, and I grabbed that one like a life raft. But Johnathan saw right through me, and, instead of Kit coming to rescue me, Charlie did.

Little Grace, trying to trade her life for mine, after everything.

The day they closed ERC, they herded us into a huge warehouse with rows of cots and police at the exits. They put high ranking people, like me, in private cubicles so we couldn't make our stories match before questioning. My cubicle contained a metal table, two chairs, and a fake potted plant. It didn't have proper walls, just dividers, and I could hear the constant, urgent clamor of activity outside. People came in and out all night. They wanted to know my name, age, social security number, where I went to school, how I met Johnathan, what I did for him. One person asked questions, and then left, and then someone else came in and started from the top. I got lost in my own story.

This, I thought, *is how they get confessions from innocent people.*

But I wasn't an innocent person, and I deserved every sleepless, disorienting minute of it.

Mallory arrived at four in the morning, gulping coffee and apologizing. No one else knew I was supposed to be the informant, so I hadn't received special treatment. I waved her apologies away.

"Forget about me," I told her. "I'm fine. Tell me what happened to Charlie." I desperately wanted to hear that she was in another little room like mine, answering questions. I didn't want the rumors to be true. "Tell me they didn't shoot her." I clutched my throat and wrapped an arm around my middle, protecting myself from the answer.

"They did, and she's in bad shape." Mallory spoke slowly—she knew the impact of her words. "But the best doctors are working on her. I'm making sure of that. She's going to be ok."

I started to explain that treatment could only prolong her suffering, but the words caught in my throat. Charlie—little Grace—couldn't give her life for mine. They had to *save* her. I nodded, not trusting myself to speak without breaking down.

"I need your help." Mallory sat in the other chair and gripped my wrist, pulling my attention back into the room. "Charlie's in too much pain to talk, but she was yelling names when she first got to us. She called for Janey—

that's Johnathan's niece, it looks like—and for you, and for someone named Bobby, who was in her brother's file. I'm getting Janey over to the hospital to be with her now, and I have people tracking Bobby down. But if you have information on her next of kin, it would be helpful."

"Janey is her best friend," I said. "Closest thing she has to family. Her brother was her only blood relative, as far as I know, and he's dead." I started to explain that she wouldn't want Bobby at her bedside, but something stopped me—an icy finger on my lips, warning the words back down my throat. "I'd like to see her," I said.

"I'll arrange that," Mallory promised. "And I'll get you into a room with a bed. You must be exhausted."

I was, but I couldn't sleep. Johnathan's eyes had been on me for so long that I didn't know how to hold myself together without them.

When Mallory returned late the next morning to grant me my freedom, I was surprised. I don't know what I expected, but I did not expect to be sent out into the world. The ground felt slippery under my feet.

Mallory gave me a piece of paper with phone numbers and websites. She promised that I'd be able to access whatever support services I needed. The car I drove for Johnathan was, miraculously, in my name, and she gave me the keys, along with a debit card so I could book a hotel room and feed myself for a few weeks.

I know, now, that she pulled strings for me, and many were not so lucky.

"That guy— Bobby—he should buy himself a lottery ticket," she said, as she filled out my release paperwork. "If Charlie hadn't been yelling for him yesterday, he'd be dead." A sick, dizzy feeling came over me. First Charlie, now Bobby. "My people found him just in time. Overdose. Suicide note said *I'm so sorry, Grace.*"

Suicide note. Poor Bobby. I felt Mallory's hand on my elbow, holding me up. And I felt Bobby settling on me—another rock in a basket already too heavy to carry.

When Bobby asked, all those years ago, if Johnathan would hurt Charlie, I held up the glossy magazine version of her life like a courtroom exhibit. "She's beautiful and successful. The whole world is in love with her. She's safe."

I knew it wasn't true. But he couldn't help her—it seemed like the kind thing to say. I never really thought he believed me.

But he must have. He built his fragile mental health on my lies, and it came tumbling down in an instant when he found out what happened.

If only I told the truth, and let him get used to the pain gradually, instead of all at once. If only I hadn't spilled coffee on the map, and taken his peace away from him. If only I'd tried to stay in touch, when the postcards stopped.

"Can you contact someone for him?" I asked, trying to pull myself together. I couldn't afford to fall apart—not now, with Mallory about to toss me out on my own. I gave her Nic's name. He was a good kid, and they were close. He wouldn't leave Bobby alone, like I did.

Mallory gave me Charlie's room number and the code I'd need to get past the guard at the door. "We didn't find any family," she said. "You and Janey are all she's got."

"We'll take care of her," I promised, but I had a hard time believing it. I didn't even know how to take care of myself. I'd saved my pennies, but for all I knew our accounts would be seized, and no one would hire a psychiatrist who worked for Johnathan Everett for twenty years. If I hadn't been so worried about Charlie, I might have collapsed under my own uncertain future.

I needed sleep and food and a plan for the rest of my life, which suddenly and unexpectedly belonged to me, but all I could think of was Sky Lake. The snow crunching under my feet. The lake sparkling with ice. The air smelling of roses in the winter. The way it felt to stand under the sky there—like the stars themselves were singing to me. Like if I opened my mouth wide enough, they'd rush right down my throat.

I drove and drove, making tighter and tighter circles around the spot where it had to be, thinking if only I could find it, I could bring healing back to Charlie. Back to Bobby. If I found it, I could make amends.

But it wouldn't reveal itself to me. It was like Sky Lake never existed.

32

CHARLOTTE

Damia stopped and waited, but I couldn't speak—my memories were shifting and I could hardly breathe. So, she went on, rearranging my past like furniture. "Bobby looked out for Kit's son, the way he didn't look out for you," she said, her voice heavy with regret.

I felt Bobby's eyes, blaming. I heard the door slamming behind him as he left. I felt my own little-girl heart breaking all over again. He couldn't take it back. But, maybe, the wound didn't have to bleed forever.

"The kid ended up doing pretty well, got really popular in Europe, less here. You've probably never heard of him."

She paused again. I sat there, eyes closed, hand frozen painfully around the phone, dust thick in my nose. I wanted Sky Lake to help people, but I wanted it for my own reasons. To balance my debt. Confronted with Damia's story, rich and important even though it had nothing to do with me, I wondered what else I'd missed.

"The song they played for me," she said, looking for the words that would make me forgive myself, "was a love song, not like their usual loud stuff. And years later I heard it on the radio. What was it called?" I could hear her clicking a pen as she tried to remember. "It was sad..." She blew out a frustrated breath, like the name of the song was the thing standing between me and my future. "Something about a woman with eyes like fireflies and arms like the night sky. It was wonderful..."

Damia kept muttering about the song, but I could hardly hear her. I was in a bubble again—past pressing, future pulling, the present about to pop—and she sounded far away. Muffled. My fingers picked out a melody on the piano and I heard it from a distance. *Fireflies... night sky...*

It couldn't be. I must have misunderstood.

"Soul shine eyes," Damia said, triumphantly. "That was it."

My mouth went dry. I *knew* that song.

Impossible, I thought, but even if I didn't believe my ears, I couldn't deny my fingers, glowing faintly against the piano keys. *They* knew the song.

Just like they knew the lyrics scribbled all over the desk. Just like I knew the energy in this room, beating right along with my heart. Of course it was familiar. It—*he*—had been with me for years.

I slid back on the bench, dazed. Everything—the dust sparkling in the air, the smooth wood of the bench, the gentle tap of branches against the windows—was heightened, like someone turned the volume up inside my head. My heart beat in time with the walls. My feet bounced impatiently. Longing swelled my chest like a balloon. Mine, but not only mine.

My eyes slid over the drums, the guitar, the drifts of dust and leaves and shredded paper on the floor. I let my fingers find the keys again—they knew where the song was, even though the rest of me hadn't quite accepted it yet.

"I still can't remember the name," Damia said, giving up. "But you'd like it."

I was almost afraid to say it, but the word was already in my mouth. *Please be true*, I thought, and it slipped out on a breath.

The song was "Witch." Kit's son was Nicolas Bell.

Damia was right—I did like it. I *loved* it. It saved my life.

I breathed deeply for the first time all day, opening my chest and tipping my head back. It felt like someone took bricks off my shoulders and replaced them with flowers.

"Yes!" Damia cried. "I always thought that was a funny title for a love song." She chuckled at the memory, and I wished I could see them—see Nic—in this room, like she did. "When they played it for me," she said, "they called it 'Priestess.'"

I sat up straight and grabbed the piano for balance—I couldn't have been more startled if Kit's tarot card fell out of the phone and landed on the keys. I was back in her office, the air warm with tea and pastry, the cards spread out on the table, Kit's hand holding the marker out. I was drawn to the tied-up lady, but I chose the High Priestess with her flowing robes and inner wisdom. I wanted to be like her, and not like me.

Goosebumps rushed up and down my arms. I felt the sharp, eye-watering sting of the permanent marker. I heard it squeak across the shiny surface of the slippery new card that I signed for Kit's son. For *Nicolas Bell*.

"He wrote it for you," Damia clarified. "I mean, for Charlie. Like I said, he had a huge crush. It was cute."

Heat rose into my cheeks and I leaned on the piano to ground myself. It was impossible. But I could feel the warmth of Nic's hands on the keys, composing the song that saved my life. *For me.* Tension melted out of my face, down my back, into the floor. My fingers found the melody again, but it was too much. I pushed myself away from the piano.

Damia stopped, still searching for magic words. She didn't realize she'd already said them. "Saving him...was good, ok? You helped me do something good."

I couldn't argue with that—saving Nicolas Bell *was* good. "I know," I said. "Thank you for using the map to help him."

"Thank you," she said, "for giving me a way to help someone."

We sat silently, lost in all the things we didn't have words for.

"Can I say one more thing?" Damia asked, after a while.

I could hear her pen clicking again—nervous—but I wasn't afraid. Whatever she had to say, I could take it. I smiled down at the piano. I had come a long way in a year. A long way in an hour. "Sure," I said.

"Go a little easier on Janey. She isn't perfect, but she was trying to keep you safe. There was no good way to do it."

I could feel Damia bracing herself for my reaction, but I felt more relieved than anything else. *No good way to do it.* Those words rang with truth—how many times had I found myself backed into a corner with no good options? I wanted to be angry with Janey, but I didn't want to let her go—maybe, I was the one who needed to make a choice. *Stay or go.*

She was my oldest friend. We'd been through hell together. I didn't want to go. "Ok," I said. "I will." It felt good to make a promise like that, and to mean it.

I touched the piano again, looking for the first notes of *Witch*. My heart swelled with gratitude. One good thing. Enough, maybe, after all.

Damia took another big breath and I thought *what more could you possibly have to say?* I said it out loud, and we both laughed, and it felt good. A relief, after such a heavy conversation. "It's nothing big. Just that Kit left you something. Tarot cards. They were in her office with a note after she…" Damia trailed off, Kit's death still too painful for words. "I filed them with your things."

I shook my head slowly, unable to make sense of this news. "She left me something? And I didn't know?" Memories flooded in—Kit shuffling her cards, pouring our tea, turning away from me. The grooves her table left in the floor. How could a message from Kit have been in a box, all this time?

"It didn't seem important," Damia explained. "You hardly knew her."

"That's not true! I saw Kit every day." I pulled the memories around me—cards, tea, the pulsing glow of the machine lighting her face—they were real. They had to be real.

"You must be remembering wrong."

Damia sounded so sure that I almost believed her. I saw a fortune-teller in a movie. I drank tea in the cafeteria. Janey told me about the machine. Kit was nothing but my imaginary friend.

"I scheduled all of your appointments. You met with Kit once."

My grip on the piano bench tightened, cutting off the circulation to my baby finger. It didn't make any sense.

And then, suddenly, it made all the sense in the world. Kit scheduled our daily sessions herself. She spent time with me that she could have spent on her research, on the phone with her family, plotting her escape. She wasn't testing me. She was spending time with me. Because she *wanted* to.

Those last months, when she was so distant, had nothing to do with me— Johnathan threatened to hurt her son. I bit back a sob—Kit was in so much pain. And all I thought about was myself. Grief rolled over me, long and slow. But something else filtered through it. A little bit of light, shining through a crack.

Our friendship was *real*.

The past shifted again, slick and slithering in my belly. Johnathan orchestrated my life, but that didn't make it meaningless. *Maybe*, I thought, heart lightening, there were things worth salvaging from the wreckage of my past, after all.

Kit might as well have been there, twinkling at me as I figured out the answer to the riddle. *See, little one, you didn't even need the cards*, she would have said.

But I *did* need the cards. Every time I returned to ERC, I went to Kit's storage closet and tried to feel her presence. I would have given anything for the weight of her cards in my hands. And now, I could have them.

Kit's final message was waiting in the trunk of my car.

"I have to go." Then, before hanging up, "Thank you, Damia. For everything. I mean it."

I sat for another long moment, my fingers crawling across the piano, imagining Nic's hands there. And then, I pushed myself up. Out the door. Toward the future, maybe.

My bare feet crunched over the sharp gravel of the overgrown driveway. I arrived vengeful and broken, convinced that this place—*home*—would cast me out again. But hope spun in my chest now, spitting sparks.

Kit left me a message—an answer, I hoped.

I opened the trunk, feet cold in the damp weeds, hands clumsy with nerves and exhaustion. Kit's cards were right there, held together by a brittle rubber band, reaching out like a hand waving.

I went to grab them, but the air pushed back, as cold and firm as ice cream. My stomach dropped when I touched it. *Not air*, I thought, *time*. It felt like the edge of a cliff—steep and exhilarating—and it smelled like black pepper. I thrust my hand through it. Sneezed. And then, with a wet, sucking pop, it let go.

I stumbled forward, half-expecting someone to catch me, and grasped the cards. I could feel the softness of Kit's palm on mine, the scrape of one of her big rings against my thumb. For a moment, I felt seen in that way that only Kit ever saw me.

The feeling faded, but it left something. A residue. A *gift*.

The cards were warm, like she'd just put them down, and heavy with meaning. Kit used to call them "little worlds." I gasped as her voice rang in my ears. *Turn around, little one*, it said.

The roses blazed through the trees and I sucked their perfume in like medicine.

I wanted to stay with the roses, but the cards pulsed in my hands. In the trunk, my journals and David's guitar gleamed with promise. I hoisted the whole awkward load into my arms, although my broken body longed to run to the garden and bury itself in petals. There would be time for that.

First, I needed to read Kit's message.

My heart sank as I turned back toward the crumbling house. It looked worse, somehow, than it did when I arrived—dining room table sinking in the lawn, windows as dark and sightless as they were the day I buried my brother.

The day I wasn't allowed to stay.

Bitterness boiled up, acidic and surprising in the back of my throat, curling me over the box. The roses faded. I searched for Kit's voice, or David's. But I was alone with the erratic hammer of my heart.

They can't reach me, I thought, *when I feel like this.*

As if the house heard my thoughts, a weak light came on upstairs. It was just like the one I saw the day I buried David. But it looked different to me now, as an adult, than it looked to the lost little girl I was.

It was a hello. An acknowledgment. And it could have been burning in my heart all this time, if I hadn't worked so hard to push it away. I closed my eyes and found the light still glowing behind them. *Mine.*

Sky Lake never abandoned me. It couldn't. We were connected.

The roses caught on fire again, filling the air with their perfume. The box grew lighter in my arms. I felt David next to me, looking up at the house the way we did at the start of every summer—home, finally.

As I stood barefoot in the driveway, the house blurred. Paint smoothed and weeds receded. Lights ignited in every window. The faint outline of a Christmas wreath appeared on the door. I knew, without knowing how, that Damia, Janey, Brad, Henry, and Greg waited inside. All the love I never quite believed in, wrapped like a present in the home I loved.

A fantasy, I thought, but it didn't feel like a fantasy.

I held my breath and the vision with it, trying to keep it whole and glowing. But the house—the real, abandoned one—came back in pieces. The wreath faded. The windows dimmed. The paint peeled and the weeds grew and there was the table again, half-buried in the yard.

But the feeling stayed. Warm and full. A gift from the future, this time.

I stopped in the doorway and pressed my palm against the spot where the wreath hung a moment before. Not yet. But someday.

Inside, I cleared a space on the kitchen table, shoving dusty beer bottles and crusty plates to one side and gathering a stack of paper. Scribbles. Nic's scribbles, and the idea sent an embarrassing shiver of excitement through me.

I wiped the wood as clean as I could with the sleeve of my shirt and spread Kit's cards. It was her old, worn-out deck, not the slippery new one I played with the day I signed The High Priestess for Nicolas Bell.

I spread the cards. They still meant nothing to me—just pictures—but one faced the wrong way. Its white and gold side faced up, marred by a message in permanent marker. I flipped it over—*The Empress*—and then turned my attention to Kit's note, my vision blurred by tears.

It was true. Kit left me a message. An *answer*.

Part of me wanted to stay where I was—eyes full of tears, Kit's message in my hand. But if I'd learned one thing, I'd learned that you can't stay in the "before." "After" always comes for you.

Hope strained against my ribs and a breeze blew through a broken window, filling the kitchen with roses. The Empress warmed between my fingers. But I knew, before I even processed the words, that Kit didn't leave me what I needed.

She left me a list. One through three. Short and to-the-point with no I-love-you at the end. *Not enough to change my life,* I thought, a wave of weariness washing over me. Kit was dead, and I was alone, and it was stupid to think her note would make a difference. It was stupid to imagine Christmas wreaths on the door and Henry, who hadn't spoken to me in weeks, inside my house.

It was stupid to think that one good thing—saving Nicolas Bell—could paint my whole life over.

But then Kit appeared in my mind, eyes half closed, hand gripping a permanent marker, the universe whispering in her ear. I could feel her love. Her worry. Her rush to get these words out before it was too late.

No matter what she wrote, she wrote it for me. Her little Grace, who she didn't want to leave, after all.

The list sat patiently in my hands, waiting:

Share your songs.
Mark my grave.
Complete the set.

And in bolder, underlined writing, ***mistakes are an illusion of time.***

I ran my thumb over each word, searching for meaning beyond them. But I couldn't find any. Just cryptic instructions and one of Kit's favorite pieces of wisdom, repeated so often that I could hear her saying it. *No accidents, no mistakes, no beginnings, no endings.* Kit thought everything fit into a big, beautiful picture, and it was just a matter of zooming out enough to see it.

It didn't ring any truer now than it did when I was fourteen years old.

I slumped over the table. The jumble of cards stared up at me—waiting to see what I'd do next, or for Kit's capable hands to shuffle them back together. I felt sorry for them, sitting in that box for all those years. Missing Kit. Stuck with me, instead.

My eyes caught the pinned man in the ten of swords. His broken body, under all those blades. She should have written on that card, because she didn't have the answers, either.

And then the whisper, in my ear, so soft I could have missed it—*are you sure, little one?*

Mistakes are an illusion of time. It was a stupid saying. Kit probably got it out of a fortune-cookie. I felt angry and resentful and tired enough to curl up on the dusty, mouse-infested couch and sleep. But I could just see Kit, shaking her head and chuckling—nothing ever shook her belief. *Just wait,* she would have said. *You'll see when you get there.*

But I *was* there, looking back at a pile of mistakes. Bobby, leaving me at the mercy of Johnathan Everett. My songs, butchered by people who only cared about money and power. Me, giving a monster my voice.

And now I'd lost it all—my friends, my music, half of my life.

But Kit was still there, shaking her head, waiting for me to catch up. "Just give me the answer," I begged, talking to the scarred table now. I needed advice and guidance. Not a phrase that belonged on the wall of a yoga studio.

The Wheel of Fortune came into focus, intricate and mysterious, and Kit's voice came with it. *Our destinies are entwined.* I was so young when she said that, but I still felt it, warming me—the idea that our lives were tangled up together. *Someday,* she said, *it will be clear.*

I imagined that "someday" so many times. Johnathan let Kit go home, and I went with her. Destinies, entwined. But here I was, sitting in my real someday. Our destinies couldn't have been more entwined if I tied them together myself, but I didn't want to be connected like this—by pain and sadness and loss.

Kit would have chuckled at that, too. She would have asked what would have become of Nic, without Bobby's mistake. What would have become of me, without Nic's song. How Nic could have written that song, without the tarot card I signed. *Zoom out,* she would have said, *and you will see that it is perfect.*

I could see the story, as Kit would tell it. Bobby left me, but he saved Nic's life, and Nic saved mine. Johnathan stole years from me, but I shut down ERC and changed the world. Grief rolled through me again—I couldn't have destroyed ERC if Kit hadn't sacrificed herself for Damia.

A painful sob forced its way out, making way for more. I left hundreds of donuts outside that empty storage closet, but I never let myself face the loss head-on. Kit *died*. Johnathan *killed* her. I kept that knowledge tucked away, a grain of sand that became a pebble and then a rock and then a huge, choking boulder.

I couldn't face it and still look him in the eye.

But I didn't have to look Johnathan Everett in the eye anymore. Relief coursed through me, still mixed up with pain. Kit was gone. Johnathan was gone. They both hurt, even though I wished I could make it simple—hate him, love her. It *wasn't* simple, and that was part of what felt so unfair.

None of this should have happened to me, or to Kit. Nicolas Bell shouldn't have grown up without his mother and Damia shouldn't have spent most of her life at ERC. What happened to us was not perfect and I couldn't—wouldn't—see it that way. But it was hard to look at the story Damia told and not see meaning shining out of the muck.

I slid the Wheel of Fortune forward and ran my finger around the Wheel. Arguing with the past wasn't getting me anywhere. I didn't have to think it was perfect. But I couldn't stay in-between forever.

I am here for reasons, Kit said that day, banging her fist on the table to show me how much it mattered.

She was. And so was I.

The past loosened its grip just enough to let me sit up straight. I was weak from crying, but it felt good. My muscles twitched and cramped as they relaxed. I didn't realize how much I had relied on pain and anger to hold myself together until I started to let go. I felt weak. Fragile.

Tension crept back into my body as I looked around the kitchen. I was exhausted. Mice rustled in the walls of my ruined house. Back in the city, my relationships were in tatters.

I didn't even know where to start.

The card vibrated between my fingers. My eyes caught the word "grave" and I shivered—Kit was buried in the cemetery past the rose garden. Her grave was dark, and my broken body couldn't swim to the bottom of Sky Lake for a stone.

The card buzzed against my fingernails again, demanding my attention, and I could feel Kit over my shoulder. Proud, but impatient. *Enough thinking, little one—start at the top.*

My shoulders pulled themselves back and my tears dried up. I had things to *do*.

Kit didn't leave me an answer.

She left me a map, and I was going to follow it. My songs had been trapped between pages for too long. It was time to give them their freedom—and claim my own.

I reached into the box of journals, hands steady, headache receding, throat thick with roses. But it was more than roses. It was my voice swelling inside me.

I chose the plain brown book—*Sky Lake Lost*.

I might not be strong enough, I thought, touching my throat lightly. But I could feel Sky Lake knitting me back together. And the forest getting ready to lend me its voice.

I picked up David's guitar and went back to the piano room, where the walls were alive with music.

It scared me to sing at Sky Lake without David. But I could feel him mingling with the energy that lingered from Nic's long ago visit. *I can always delete it*, I thought, *if it's really bad*. But I knew as soon as the first notes came that it wouldn't be bad. I forgot the magic of singing at Sky Lake right up until the moment the magic started pouring out of me.

I sang, and I wasn't scared little Grace, or charming Charlie London, or the in-between person I turned into after the hospital. I was the girl who sang on the rickety stage in the yard, joyful and unselfconscious. The one who sang David away from his pain. The one who stood on stages all over the world and made people feel something bigger or better or more real than they thought they could—Charlie didn't do that. *I* did. It was *real*.

All that time thinking I didn't know myself, and here I was.

I sang through the brown notebook, and then the red one, and then pulled them out at random, recording whatever jumped out and said *my turn.* I worked until the spell broke, shattered by hunger, thirst, and that feeling past tired where you don't even want to sleep anymore.

I drooped over the piano. It hurt to swallow. I could feel my headache trying to come back. But I wasn't done yet.

I sent the files to Henry without listening, hoping he would open my message. "I miss you, Henry. Please accept this as a peace offering. Go easy on me, I did it on a phone and didn't delete the ugly bits."

I did not say *I'm sorry. You were right. Once I started, I didn't want to stop.* He'd have to hear it in the music.

I sat for a long, quiet moment, hoping for the little dots to start dancing under the message—Henry, answering me. But I had a feeling I wasn't going to get any answers until I finished my tasks. And the second one loomed so heavily that I could hardly lift myself off the bench.

Kit's grave.

She was buried without a rock from the lake. Without the glow of somebody remembering her.

I dragged myself to the desk, where Nic's scribbled lyrics brimmed with energy and inspiration. I wanted to sift through them and find "Priestess." But it felt intrusive to reach into his past, uninvited. And I wasn't sure I was ready to see those words, written for me. *Written for Charlie,* I reminded myself, *not for me.*

I forced myself to step back. He left his mother here, without a stone, and I could set that right.

I walked slowly on the overgrown trail, made dark by clouds in the middle of the afternoon. I didn't know it by heart anymore. At the rose garden, I had to stop and adjust to the light—the roses glowed so brightly that I could see all the way up to the graves. I lifted my arm and waved, slowly, like I did at the other Sky Lake. But the air didn't fight back this time. I was awake. And alone.

The graves weren't arranged in rows, but there was a logic to their placement that the newest one didn't follow. I knelt in front of it, thinking the stone might light at my touch. But it didn't, no matter how hard I tried to pull Kit's essence out of my memory.

She didn't need my memories. She needed a stone from the bottom of Sky Lake.

"I can do this," I said, looking into the deep well of reflected branches. But the desperate courage that propelled me into the water for David's stone belonged to a younger, braver person. I felt sick as I took off my clothes. I remembered the cold indifference of the lake pressing down on me. The angry thrust as it pushed me out.

I unbuttoned my shirt slowly. *I don't want to do this*, I thought, willing the stone to light itself. The lake stretched out like glass, dark and uninviting. The stone didn't even flicker.

I breathed slowly to fully inflate my lungs, still praying for a reprieve. But the stone and the lake remained dark. I could get the stone, or I could walk away. But there were no other options.

I wobbled to the edge of the big rock like a prisoner walking the plank. I felt cold and exposed and I did not want to disappear under that dark water. But the forest was holding its breath and the clouds were watching and Kit's rock was at the bottom of the lake, calling out to me.

I tipped toward the cold darkness and dove before I could change my mind.

The water was colder than I remembered, and darker. The breath I took before I jumped didn't feel like enough, and I wanted to pop up for another, but I needed the momentum to carry me to the bottom. I kicked, keeping my arms straight and my core tight like an arrow sailing through the water.

I'd get one chance.

Reeds brushed my bare legs, slimy and alarming in the dark. Fear screamed *get out get out get out.* My hands hit leaves and sticks and the slippery bodies of slow fish. The darkness deepened one shade, then two, and the water turned so murky that I couldn't see my own pale fingers piercing the water ahead of me.

I hit the bottom gently, bouncing, Sky Lake's watery arms wrapped around me.

Kit's stone was right there, pulsing with her unmistakable energy.

I pried it out of the silt. The silent, peaceful water felt like a being, bearing witness. And when I lifted the stone, I felt it—not pressing or pushing or spitting me out, but lifting with me. The stone would be heavy once I reached the shore, but for now, Sky Lake would hold it with me.

I surfaced just as my lungs forced me to breathe, a split-second separating water and air. My lungs heaved. The rock sat lightly on my chest. The clouds parted to let the sun in.

Sky Lake couldn't hold the stone once I left the water. I stumbled up the steep bank and dropped it with a graceless thump, then knelt and pressed my hands against it. *Please*, I thought. *Please let this be enough.* When it didn't glow, I put my forehead against it and remembered more, remembered harder.

Still nothing.

I looked down at The Empress, lying on the ground near the grave. The third instruction waited for me—*complete the set*—and it was just like Kit not to cooperate until I finished the job. I leaned on the stone, shaking with cold and adrenaline. "Please, Kit," I begged. "Give me a break." But the stone stayed dark, and my teeth kept chattering, and I knew, without looking, that Kit removed the High Priestess from her deck before she left it for me.

Nothing was going to change. Not until I changed it, anyway. Nicolas Bell had the High Priestess, and she was the missing card. I'd have to track him down and have a very strange conversation.

A conversation with Nicolas Bell—a blush bloomed in my cheeks. It was a ridiculous idea. But then I looked down at the Empress, smiling her motherly, all-knowing smile. I had to do it. For Kit.

I pulled my clothes on over my wet bra and underpants, wishing I'd had the courage to go in naked—at least then I'd have a full set of dry clothes. My dying phone blinked with messages and missed calls, but I already knew what they would say. They loved me, and were worried about me, and wanted me to come home.

It was time to go back and claim my life.

Before I left Sky Lake, I went to the edge of the water. It glowed silver under the clouds, as still and shiny as a skating rink. "I missed you," I said, and a breeze rippled over the water, answering me.

I bent and selected two pebbles.

One for Nicolas Bell, because he should be able to visit his mother's grave.

And one for Bobby. None of us came out of ERC unscathed. We all did things we weren't proud of. But I wouldn't trade my pain for his guilt—if Kit was right, and it all worked out like it was supposed to, he might have played the hardest part.

I settled the little rocks in my pocket, feeling like the grudge I'd been carrying was a mountain, and I'd just traded it in for that tiny pebble.

33

NIC

"Are you writing anything?"

Brad rarely asked questions I didn't want to answer, and when he did, he asked gently and let me change the subject. But he stopped being shy about that question after a while. He asked it in his office and on the street and in the middle of crowded restaurants. When I avoided it, he just asked again, louder.

I always said no, and he never believed me.

He wouldn't let me off the hook.

I was and I wasn't writing. Sometimes, as I drove in circles searching for that damn lake, a few lyrics or a line of melody floated around the car. I hummed along. Drummed the steering wheel. But I never tried to keep it—what was the point? I knew the song would fall apart before I got halfway through.

One, though, wouldn't leave me alone. It sat in the back seat and jumped out of my closet and haunted my dreams. It reminded me of the song I wrote at the lake house—that song didn't care if I felt like writing it down or not. It would have burned itself through my skin if I refused to let it out. This one was the same. And I would have grabbed it with both hands if I wasn't so afraid of losing it.

"I have some ideas," I admitted, reluctantly, over lunch one day.

"And have you discussed these ideas with anyone? Thomas, maybe?" Brad peered at me over his glasses, eyebrows raised, eyes dancing. He knew he was saving my ass. "I suspect the band would like to be included in the process."

Brad left the rest—that I was treating my oldest friends like obedient sidekicks again—unspoken, but I heard it loud and clear. If I wanted things to work out differently this time, *I* needed to be different.

"I'm not saying you have to share anything you aren't ready to share," he clarified. "Just that we might have a meeting. A little update, you know? To keep them involved."

Brad went back to his salad, letting me take or leave the advice even though we both knew he was saving me from myself.

I could have cried, I was so grateful.

I let Brad schedule the meeting. Eventually, I hummed the melody into my phone, typed the lyrics into an email, and shared it. Thomas responded with a song of his own. Ben hated it. I made peace between them, surprising everybody.

We moved forward.

But privately, I was still driving in circles.

"You have to let that place go," Bobby said, whenever I saw him. "Trust me. If anyone knows, I know."

Bobby had gone to ERC to collect David's file, and he wanted me to collect my mother's things. *Closure*, he called it. But I knew David's box didn't make him feel any better, just like my mother's mindreading machine wouldn't bring her back to me. Bobby thought he'd find something more—a key, a map, a magic word. That's what I would have been looking for. But you never find things like that—you only hope for them.

Bobby told me I was wasting my time, and he was probably right, but I felt my mother's presence every time I set out on another pointless search. She urged me this way and that way, nudged me to go a little farther, begged me not to give up.

It sounds crazy, but there was something at that house that I needed.

I didn't tell Brad any of that, because he would have questioned my sanity, but he knew something wasn't right, and his questions got a little closer to the truth every time we talked.

"Would you just tell me what's wrong?" he asked, late one afternoon, fed up with my evasive answers.

I was driving back from another day of not finding the lake. Not just any day—my last day. It came to me all at once, like a toothache or the start of a cold. I was done searching. I'd go out one more time, and then I'd put the lake in a drawer and move on.

The band was making progress by then, and I could feel the momentum pulling me out of the past and into the future. I would have to stop looking for the lake soon, because my life would require me to stop, just like it did the first time we lost it.

I didn't want to be carried along again, toward this, away from that, never fully responsible for where I ended up. I wanted to choose. I wanted to take one last ride down those winding roads to nowhere, knowing it was the last one. *Feeling* it. Apologizing, maybe, to my mother's restless ghost. But I couldn't even find her nervous energy in the car that day. It was just me and the radio and the wind rushing through the wide-open windows.

I felt like a sleepwalker waking up.

"I'm serious, Nic. It's not writer's block anymore, because you're writing. It's not your voice, that's for damn sure. It's not the band. Things are going *well*. But you're still holding back. Just tell me the problem so I can solve it. That's my job."

"There's no problem," I said.

"You're lying."

I was and I wasn't. Everything *was* going well. When we were kids, we gave up the search to go on to bigger and better things, and it felt appropriate to be doing the same now. On purpose this time—choosing the future. "I'm not lying," I said. "I'm on board with all the plans, I swear."

I was. And I knew it would all work out fine. And I couldn't shake the feeling that something important was still missing.

"Hang on," Brad said. "Janey keeps calling, I have to see what she wants. Don't hang up."

As I waited, I searched for the anxious, nagging voice that told me to keep looking for the lake, but only heard the open phone line and the rumble of uneven pavement under my tires. My mother's ghost seemed, for the moment, to be elsewhere. *Where did you go?* I asked, not sure if I felt relieved or sad.

The car was peaceful. I was peaceful. And I was so unused to that feeling that it made me itchy.

"You still there?"

Brad sounded excited, and I hoped his conversation with Janey distracted him from the interrogation we were in the middle of. "Still here," I confirmed. "Hey, why don't I come in tomorrow? We can finish this conversation over lunch."

"No," he said. "How far from the office are you?"

"I don't know. Forty minutes? Longer if there's traffic." I was almost at the motel, and the last thing I felt like doing was turning the other way and heading to Brad's office. "I'll come by first thing tomorrow."

"No. Now."

"Come on. I'm exhausted." But I wasn't, not anymore. The glittering, restless energy that used to flit around the car was in my chest now, spinning and sparking and spreading. My foot was pressing the gas, my hand clicking the turn signal up. I was already on my way.

If the car broke down in that moment, I think I would have gotten out of it and run.

"Do you remember when I met you, and I said you needed to come to my office because it felt like destiny but it was probably just the punch?"

I did remember that. If he had said anything less ridiculous, I probably wouldn't have gone.

"It wasn't the punch. You need to come straight here."

34

JANEY

I told her to pick a new name.

When she stopped being Grace and started being Charlie, she got a whole new identity. But she woke up in that hospital with nothing. She needed to mark "before" and "after." A ritual. Like burning your ex's letters or turning into a butterfly.

On a practical level, I just didn't know what to call her. Grace didn't feel right, because she wasn't a kid anymore. But calling her by a name Johnathan chose... that gave me the *creeps*. Every time I said "Charlie" I felt a little sick.

But when I tried to say "Grace" I got tears in my eyes, remembering.

A new name made a lot of sense. Damia thought so, too. So, I suggested it, and she shot me right down. She was done getting new names, she said, and whatever I wanted to call her would be fine.

It wasn't fine—I could see it all over her face every time I said "Charlie." And Charlotte wasn't any better, since that was *his* special name for her. But she wouldn't even discuss it.

I called her Grace sometimes and Charlie sometimes and *hey you* sometimes and wondered why we never came up with nicknames. We'd been friends for so long. Weren't friends supposed to have nicknames?

It took a while for me to realize how angry she was. I mean, at first, she was basically in a coma. I sat with her every single day, and I always had to stop outside her door and brace myself for it—her fragile, broken body with all those tubes coming out of it. The angry purple bruises that followed her veins like infections. Sometimes, I'd pick up her cold, limp little hand and it was all I could do not to gag.

She was like a corpse. Except when she struggled, and that was worse.

And then, she woke up. I didn't think she would, at that point. I was starting to wonder what we were doing to her, keeping her alive like that. It was hard not to look at her strapped to the bed and not think *prisoner*. And that brought up a lot of feelings, for me. Some days, I'd just stand outside the elevators, frozen.

And then her eyes opened and I thought *ok, this is why we didn't give up*. Because she was going to live.

For those first few weeks, I was just happy to have her back. She was sitting up in bed with her eyes open—shooting daggers at me, sure, but that was easy to blame on the pain, or the shock, or the people poking her with needles all the time. I figured she was tired and hurting. Adjusting, like we all had to. But her blood pressure shot up every time I came in the room, and I wasn't poking her.

She was angry. She *blamed* me. It would have hurt less if she stabbed me, to be honest.

She must have thought I was smacking my gum so loud that I missed the elephant in the room. But that's not it. It honestly never occurred to me that she'd be angry. By the time I figured out that she was holding me responsible for the whole thing, it was too late. She didn't want to talk about it.

And I didn't make her. I was so used to taking care of her that it felt natural to just do what she needed.

She'd be fucking shocked if I told her I got into Harvard. I never told her, and I wouldn't now—she'd feel terrible and try to fix it, and it can't be fixed. But it was a big deal, back then.

It was supposed to be my way out.

She thought I liked working for my uncle. Or at least that I wasn't trying to stop him, and that's not true. I had a plan before she even knew me. I studied and got a perfect SAT score. I made Johnathan's researchers give me projects I could write essays about. I took every single AP course online. It was actually pretty impressive.

But school wasn't the point. Getting out was the point.

I collected so much dirt on Johnathan—more, maybe, than Charlie even had—and I knew I could shut him down if I got away for a few years. I *knew*. And it all went exactly like I planned.

I remember the day I got the acceptance letter—a thick packet, so I knew it was a yes before I even opened it. I was so proud. And Johnathan was proud of me too, in his way. Not many people managed to surprise him. He called me into his office and told me there was nothing that fancy school could teach me that I couldn't learn right where I was, but if I wanted the bragging rights, he could spare me for four years.

But I stayed. I had to.

She needed someone to look out for her, and she didn't have anyone but me.

I stayed to protect her. And I guess she stayed to protect me.

And the difference is that I thought it was a fair trade, and she thought she got duped.

She'd say I lied to her. Controlled her. And, ok, I did, but only because she wouldn't have believed the truth. Johnathan visited her, talked to her, took her out to dinner, gave her gifts. She thought she was special to him. She *was* special to him. But I knew that wouldn't matter if she betrayed him. She didn't believe he would hurt her. And then, after a while, I don't think she cared if she got hurt. Telling her he would hurt me was the only way to keep her safe. And it wasn't a lie—if she ran, he would have killed her, and that would have wrecked me.

That's what I would have explained if we talked about it, but she didn't want to talk. She just wanted to grunt at my questions and pretend to fall asleep ten minutes into my visits and make snarky comments about my job, because she thought I liked being in my old office every day when really, I had to go outside sometimes just to breathe.

That was fine—I could wait it out. But it was hard to be in the room with her. Her anger and assumptions took up so much space that I didn't know where to sit. And then she left the hospital and I would have given anything to have her back in that bed, glaring at me. *Safe.*

After that, I was always chasing her and she was always avoiding me. And every time I caught her for a minute, I wondered why I kept trying to be near her when it hurt so much.

History. History is why. We'd been through hell together, and come out the other side, and you don't just throw that away.

I saw Grace the day she arrived at ERC with her brother. I wasn't supposed to be in the public area, but I was small and fast and young enough that people didn't pay attention to me. Usually, I just stole cake from break rooms and spied on people's private conversations. But, when I saw Grace come in, everything changed.

She was young. Not so much younger than me in years, maybe, but her eyes belonged on a baby. *This place is going to eat her*, I thought, and made a point of noticing where they went. I don't know why. I was just a kid, too, and couldn't do anything. But helping her felt like something *important*.

When I saw the psychic a few days later, I had an idea. She seemed to exist just outside of Johnathan's authority, wandering around like she had every right to be wherever she was. She talked to people and dressed funny and didn't look at the floor when she walked, and I thought she might be able to help.

I wasn't supposed to talk to anyone without permission, and I knew enough not to disobey direct orders, but there were plenty of things Johnathan never even thought about telling me not to do. I kept track of the psychic, and the day she headed toward the hospital, I grabbed a mop and bucket and all the "caution" and "wet floor" signs from the supply closet and set them up so she couldn't help going to the right place.

I don't know what I expected to happen. Maybe I thought she was really psychic, and she'd take one look at Grace and see exactly what needed to be done. Wave her magic wand, or something. Or maybe I just hoped a grownup would do the right thing, for once. But she never walked that way again, so I was back where I started.

When I found Grace on the couch in my office I thought *shit, there she is, don't screw this up.* I never knew what it meant in a book when it said someone looked haunted, but that girl was *haunted.* She wasn't even the same kid. A baby's face with thousand-year-old eyes in it. Kind of spooky, actually. But I treated her like a regular kid because that's what I would want, if I got stuck in a nightmare.

I tried to give her things she needed—food, company, a place to sleep. I warned her about Johnathan and how closely he watched her. She was never going to fly under the radar, though, no matter how many trashy magazines she read. She might as well have had a flashing neon sign on her that said "Look at me." And everyone looked, that's for sure. It was like she had her own gravity.

Everyone is still looking at her. She's hard *not* to look at.

Having a famous best friend is weird. I didn't actually know that until after, because all the time I spent with her before was at ERC, where she wore a disguise. Once she got out, it became a thing we had to think about.

Where could we go without gathering a crowd, who could I invite to my dinner party who wouldn't be weird about it, that kind of thing.

Not that she wanted to spend any time with me. She thought I didn't notice how she was—quiet, polite, counting down the minutes until she could leave. But I did notice. And I hated it. And I made her come to dinner anyway, because seeing her upright and breathing on her own let *me* breathe for a few days. But her desire to be just about anywhere else came off her in waves.

I took it personally at first, and then I realized she didn't want to see anyone.

Things got a little better after she hired Henry. She had people, at least. But it wasn't much of a life, and she left me out of it completely. Even when I managed to get into a room with her, she was a thousand miles away. She didn't want her old life, and she didn't want a new one, either. It was like her body got out of the hospital bed, but the rest of her stayed behind, and I didn't know how to help her. And then Henry invited me to his party and it was like finding her in my office all over again—*shit, don't screw this up.*

I changed my outfit ten times and couldn't get my hair right and spent about an hour choosing the wine. I told myself I would be a perfect guest. A perfect friend. And then I got there, and she wished I would leave, and it *hurt.*

I almost left. I would have, if not for Brad. But he smiled like I was a treasure and I forgot about taking care of her for the first time since we were teenagers.

Brad didn't even think it was my *job* to take care of Charlie London. I disagreed, but I liked his perspective, because it meant he cared about me more than he cared about her. I loved that, and him, and who I became with him.

But the relationship gave me a permanent window into her life, and I hated what I saw. She was stuck in the mud, and she didn't want to be pulled out. I don't know if she was punishing herself or traumatized or just insecure, but she needed something. And I was lucky to get her over for dinner once a week.

It seemed hopeless, until Brad said the magic words.

We were drinking wine on my patio, which had an excellent view into the apartments across from me and could be quite entertaining. But he hardly said a word all night. He reminded me of Charlie, actually, the way he sat there, all wrapped up in himself, and the longer it went on the more nervous I got. *What could I have done*, I wondered, *to screw this up?*

I must have been worrying openly, because he apologized for being bad company. "I have a client I don't know what to do with," he explained. "He's in his own head... not going anywhere... searching for something, I guess. I thought I could help him, but I feel like I'm failing."

I'm not the best listener, but I could relate to those feelings. I felt the same way about Charlie. I refilled our glasses and leaned in.

Brad told me about his client, who was talented and amazing and incredible, *blah blah blah*—there were a lot of adjectives—but had low self-esteem or writer's block or some other vague, self-absorbed problem. I nodded and smiled and tried to think of something wise to say when it was my turn to talk.

And then he dropped the guy's name into the story.

Nicolas Bell. *Holy Shit.* Charlie's Nicolas Bell.

She'd been in love with that guy since she was what, eighteen?

"I wanted to introduce him to Charlie," Brad said, plucking the idea right out of my head. "I don't know why, I just feel like they'd get along. Be good for each other, somehow. But she's stubborn." He shook his head, marveling over Charlie's talent for not cooperating. "I even tried to coordinate with Henry to get them into the office at the same time, but she changes her appointments at the last minute. It's like she can hear me scheming."

He did something funny with his hands on the word "scheming" and I fell a little more in love with him.

"She's got a sixth sense," he said.

She didn't sense anything. She just spent so much of her life under the thumb of a madman that evasive maneuvers came naturally. I knew something about that. I also knew I couldn't explain life after Johnathan Everett to Brad. No one outside of that place could understand what we went through. And no one from inside wanted to talk about it. It was lonely.

"You know Charlie," he said. "Anyway, I just don't know what to do with this guy…"

Brad went on about Nicolas Bell and his wasted talent, but I wasn't thinking about him anymore. At least, not for his own sake. I was thinking about her.

She could be stubborn, but I could be even more stubborn.

From then on, it became my mission to put them in that office at the same time. It felt right, with Brad saying he wanted them to meet at the same time that my brain screamed the exact same thing a little less politely. It made my heart tingle, like a movie with a really good ending. *Fate.*

But even if it wasn't fate, it was something unexpected. A jolt. And she needed that to move her forward, even if moving forward meant moving farther away from me.

Tricking her, though, was as impossible for me as it was for Brad. She dodged me like an annoying, overprotective mother. I'd call her when I knew she was in Brad's office, and she'd still claim to be at the coffee shop or in the hotel or some other place. She knew I knew she was lying, and she did it anyway. It was kind of our thing.

Once I started trying to figure out her schedule, she really pulled back. It took three or four calls from me to get one back. If I said "what are you up to today?" she didn't even lie, she just asked why I wanted to know. She knew I was up to something. But, like I said, I'm stubborn. And I waited.

I thought I stumbled into my chance the night of Henry's birthday party. I was late, and I felt awful about it—she had a wig on and makeup and she looked so nervous that I wished I'd arrived earlier to give her a hug before she went on. But when I met Brad at the office and found Nic still there, I seized the opportunity. He rejected Brad's invitation, but he was no match for me. I dragged him along and crossed my fingers.

Henry thought he'd just throw her on stage and she'd love it and all would be well, but I knew better. I told him she needed to do this in baby steps, not all at once. But Henry said karaoke with his friends *was* a baby step for a woman who regularly sang in front of thousands of people, and Brad told me to let it go. But when I walked in and saw the look on her face I thought, *oh shit, this is going to be a disaster.* She was scared. And there I was, late, with Nicolas Bell, of all people.

And then she started to sing. Charlie London burst out and the room belonged to her. I thought, *maybe Henry had it right,* and then I glanced at Nic and forgot all about Henry. Nic didn't even know who the woman on stage *was,* but she was pulling him across that room. I could feel the force of it, like a drink hitting me too hard even though I'd only had a sip of my wine. And she was leaning like she felt it, too.

They were like something out of a romance novel or a fairy tale. And then she ran out like someone was chasing her. If she lost a shoe, it would have been perfect.

But she kept her shoes, and then she and Henry had that stupid fight, and I took my lunch break at the worst possible time, and she saw Bobby's note before I could get to her. A perfect storm. She ran away and I didn't even blame her.

Charlie finally called from her car after hiding out in that lake house overnight. I figured that's where she'd go, but no one can actually find the place and she might as well have been on the moon. I'd been calling and calling and practically having a heart attack, because anything could have happened and none of us would have known and I seemed to be the only person who considered it an emergency.

"She's a big girl," Brad soothed. "She can take care of herself. She'll come back when she's ready." But that was the thing—she wouldn't take care of herself, not necessarily. And it was exhausting, trying to do it for her.

Henry was no use at all. He just left a few messages and told me that calling the police would be "an overreaction." They left me alone to dial and re-dial and pace around my kitchen, certain that she fell down the steps or into the water or worse.

"I'm sure she didn't have an accident," Brad kept saying, "she's very responsible." But it wasn't accidents I worried about. She thought I didn't know what she was doing when she ran out of ERC that day, but I knew. She was killing herself. And I couldn't stop worrying that if she tried again, she'd get it right. So, I paced and called and paced and called and when her face finally popped up on the screen, I pounced so fast that I almost hung up on her.

"Hey," she said, "it's me."

I was relieved, and then furious. "How could you run away and disappear and not even send a text? I was the last person who saw you. If something happened to you…"

If something happened to her, I would have carried that burden for the rest of my life. But I stopped short of saying it, because nothing happened. She was ok. I flashed back to her eyes opening in the hospital.

"I'm fine," she said, and I sank down on my kitchen floor. It reminded me of the conversations we used to have as teenagers, when she was on tour and I was supposed to be working and I had to hide behind the counter where the cameras couldn't see me.

"I was so worried," I said, tears threatening. If I let them start, they wouldn't stop, so I squeezed my eyes shut and bit my tongue. I could cry later.

She didn't answer, but I didn't hear the usual brick wall of silence that surrounded our conversations. It was a soft, thoughtful silence, and after a minute she let a lot of air out. "I'm sorry," she said, her voice barely above a whisper, and I told her it was ok because she sounded like she ripped that apology out of her chest.

"No," she said. "It's really not ok. I'm a crap friend. You deserve better."

"What does that mean?" *Don't break up with me*, I thought, heart pounding. *You're my best friend. We've been through so much together. I don't care if you hate me, just don't leave.*

"It means I took a lot of things out on you, and it wasn't fair. You've always taken care of me, and I don't love all the ways you do it, but I know you always tried to protect me. I've never thanked you for it. So... thank you. For saving my life. If you hadn't looked out for me... Well, I don't know what would have happened, but it probably wouldn't have been good."

"You don't need to thank me." I didn't mean it. That thank you felt like water in the desert, and I filed it away for later. "I'm sorry, too. I was so focused on keeping you safe... I didn't let myself think about how hard it was for you."

"I think we were both guilty of that," she said, and we were quiet for a while, remembering. "I don't know what's next," she said, finally, and a wave of empathy almost flattened me on the floor. How could she know what was next, when she'd never had the freedom to make a single decision?

"Baby steps," I said, because that's how I got through it. "Maybe you could start coming to dinner again?"

"That, I can do." I heard tears in her voice, and that old instinct—to protect her at all costs—urged me to fix it. To fill the silence with comfort or plans or solutions. But then I remembered Brad saying it's not my job to take care of her, and I stayed quiet, which turned out to be harder than jumping in and making things better. I didn't realize how much I clung to my role as her savior—the one good thing I could do in that place.

She took another big breath. "It's more than that. I need to figure out how to be a better friend. How to be more... open. And... trusting. And I will, but based on the progress I've made on cooking and driving, you better be patient, because I learn slowly."

Relief and affection spilled out of me in a giggle, and soon we were both laughing so hard that she had to pull over. It wasn't funny, not exactly, but all those feelings had to come out somewhere. I was red and gasping. Tears streaming down my cheeks. But not crying the way I expected to at the end of that call.

She's going to be happy, I thought, *and I don't have to do anything to make it happen.* But then she calmed herself down and started the car and said she needed to go straight to Henry's office to try to win him back, and the first thing I thought was *she called me before she called Henry*, and the second thing I thought was *here's my chance.*

Brad must have been on the other line. I called seven times before he finally switched over, and every time I dialed, I was thinking *too late too late too late.* But he finally picked up. Annoyed with me for calling seven times. But it didn't matter. This was my chance. I wasn't going to screw it up.

"I don't care what you have to do," I told him. "Get Nic into your office, right now. She's on her way."

Charlotte London is my best friend.

She calls me her oldest friend, and she doesn't think I notice the difference.

I do. I just don't think it matters. After what we went through together, "best" and "oldest" might as well be the same thing.

35

CHARLOTTE

I wouldn't have been brave enough to go in on my own. But Sky Lake was inside me, singing. Its music wrapped around my fingers and whispered in my ears and tried to keep me warm all the way back. It parked my car at Henry's office and pushed me inside before my fear could drag me to the hotel.

In the elevator, it rushed inside me. Smoke, but not dark or bitter anymore. Light and sweet and lifting me, like Sky Lake. I was the stone now. Not glowing yet, but close.

The doors opened, and the music started to spin. *Something*, I thought, *is coming*. And I wasn't going to run away from it this time. I thought I might be done running.

I didn't realize how I looked until I saw it reflected in Brad's face. "Charlie!" he cried, hurrying toward me as I walked into the office. "You're... wet."

I touched my hair, still damp from the lake. "Oh. Right." My voice felt rough—I wouldn't be able to sing again for days, and I didn't want to wait.

"I… didn't have time to dry it." Brad needed a better explanation, but I couldn't fit the past twenty-four hours inside the office.

Brad pulled something—a weed or a leaf—out of my hair, but didn't argue with me. "Henry called," he said, gently.

Too gently, and my heart squeezed. What if Henry didn't forgive me? What if he didn't like my songs? There was safety in being someone else. Now, Henry could reject *me*. But the music throbbed under my skin. Mine. Whether or not Henry liked it.

"He's on his way. Go sit. I'm getting you… coffee." Brad looked me up and down again, like I definitely needed more than coffee but he didn't know what to offer. "Sit," he ordered, and waited until I was settled on the couch to go to the kitchen.

He kept one eye on me while the coffee brewed. I huddled on the couch, wet and cold. Anxious about what Henry would say when he got there. But peaceful, too, because I'd done everything I could. It was out of my hands now.

Not everything, I thought. Kit's cards sat heavily in my pocket. I still needed to find Nicolas Bell. My breathing quickened, and the air seemed to pull itself tight. *Something isn't right,* I thought, as the energy shifted around me. My skin tingled, responding to it.

Brad handed me a mug and I curled around it to steady myself. "I called Janey," I said, surprised that it wasn't his first question. "She knows I'm ok." My voice pinged against the tense atmosphere in the office.

Brad smiled. "I heard." He gave me a searching look, and I wondered how much Janey said.

"I was at… my house," I explained, trying to ease my nerves with conversation. But the words felt too small. How could I explain Sky Lake to Brad? I remembered the way I saw it for that one, beautiful moment, glowing with Christmas lights and full of people. It felt like a glimpse of the future. Maybe Brad would experience it for himself, someday. "It's in the woods. My phone didn't work very well." My excuses were thin. No match for the electric thrum around me.

Brad nodded, but he had one eye on the door, and a nervous flutter went through my belly. It was going to be bad, with Henry. There was no other reason for Brad to be so jumpy, or for the air itself to be trembling. The main door clicked open. My heart pounded, hard, like it wanted to get away. I closed my eyes and took a slow, careful breath.

Brad was talking, fast and loud, trying to distract me. "What condition is the house in, after all that time?"

Lovely Brad, always ready with an easy, practical question. Except that it wasn't easy. I hated to think of how I left the house. I would need to go back with trash bags and bleach and those gloves that go all the way up to your elbows. And I'd have to decide what to do with all of Nicolas Bell's things. I clutched my mug tightly, feeling the weight of Kit's cards against my hip again. "I don't really know," I said. "Bad."

The lights flickered and I smelled roses. Something was definitely coming. I could feel it. And it didn't feel like Henry.

I waited for Brad to tell me he knew someone who could sort the house out in a week, because that was Brad—the problem solver. But he wasn't looking at me. His eyes were on the door.

A shadow fell into the room.

My heart threw itself against my ribs, making me gasp. I felt hot and claustrophobic and I thought *not now*. I took another breath of roses—stronger, now—and braced myself as Brad turned to the person in the doorway.

It wasn't Henry.

My heart lurched. Sputtered. Crashed into the front of my chest so hard that I jerked forward. *Not now*, I thought again, harder. But my heart kept flinging itself against its walls. It didn't want to be on the couch.

And whatever it did want was *here*.

Nowhere to run this time, I thought, but I still didn't want to run. I wanted to let my heart take the lead, and see where we ended up.

A man leaned in the doorway, arms folded. Black boots. Jeans. Leather jacket. Dark eyes and dark hair and the easy, confident posture of a person who likes being looked at. And all around him, the glow of the roses. Recognition bloomed in my chest and a lightbulb blew out on Brad's desk and the man stepped back, surprised.

It couldn't be—but it was. I would have known him anywhere.

As I took him in, he tipped his head, mouth on the verge of smiling, eyes crinkled with interest. His arms relaxed down to his sides. He squinted like he was trying to get a better look at something surprising and wonderful.

And he was looking at me.

Nicolas Bell.

Looking at *me*.

The room tilted—reality rearranging itself again—and I fought to keep my composure. This was the man whose voice woke me up, put me to sleep, made me happy or sad or angry or whatever I needed to feel for so many years. Who saved my life on that balcony, and again in the hospital. The man who wrote my favorite song... for me.

My face heated. I wished I had Charlie's makeup on.

"Charlie," Brad said, his voice tight enough to snap, "this is Nicolas Bell."

Nicolas Bell, who left pizza boxes and beer bottles and crumpled pages all over my house. Just hours before, I stood in the middle of a mess he made as a teenager, and now he stood four feet away from me, all grown up.

I felt like a time traveler.

Nic hung back, his smile not sure of itself, one hand on the doorframe like he needed it for support. I felt my own mouth wobble. My heart was still ramming my chest—if it went on that way much longer, I would faint. In front of Nicolas Bell. I felt myself go a shade redder.

Nic took half a step forward and stopped, still holding onto the doorframe. He looked exactly like I expected him to, from the toes of his beat-up black boots to the shaggy dark hair falling into his eyes. He could have stepped off the cover of one of his albums.

And I was a mess.

"Nic, this is, obviously, Charlie London."

Nic shot Brad a funny look—there was a whole paragraph embedded in it, and I felt like I should give them a minute. But he was hovering like he wasn't sure if he should stay or leave, and I couldn't let him leave. Not with his scribbled lyrics all over my house and the pebbles burning holes in my pocket and Kit's tarot deck still incomplete.

Kit's stone, dark.

And my heart, pounding. Trying to throw itself through my chest. *Vines,* I thought. Reaching for him as he looked out of his soul, and into mine.

Soul shine eyes.

I forgot about the leaves in my hair. Nicolas Bell wasn't looking at my hair.

Nic was searching me for something, and it startled me back into my body. Back into the room, where I was wet and exhausted and he looked like a rock star. *Charlie,* I thought. *He's looking for Charlie.* I tried to bring her to the surface. She fizzed over my skin just long enough to give me hope. But even she couldn't fix my stringy hair, red face, and shaky voice.

I stepped forward, even though the couch felt like safety and my body wanted to stay near it. I was on my own. Kit's cards warmed in my pocket— *no you're not, little one.*

We met in the middle of the room. The cards trembled in anticipation. I searched for Charlie, but she was hanging back. Watching.

Nic wiped his palms on his jeans and stuck out his hand. "It's nice to meet you," he said, and I got the funny feeling that he wasn't looking for Charlie, after all. I let her go and gave him my hand and he held it, gently. Not squeezing or shaking. Just holding. The lake water warmed on my skin, responding to him.

"It's nice to meet you, too," I said. The words were not enough. But I couldn't say *I was going to jump off a balcony once and your voice saved my life.* "I'm a huge fan of yours."

He raised a skeptical eyebrow. The air vibrated.

"Really," I said. "I saw you in Los Angeles. It was a great show." *I knew your mother. She saved my life, too.* I would have to tell him that much, at least, in order to complete the deck of cards. But I couldn't imagine this conversation ever getting there.

Nic shook his head, remembering. "That show was terrible. I owe you forty bucks and an apology. But it's incredibly cool that you were there. I'm a big fan of yours, too." I swallowed a laugh, remembering how Damia described his teenage crush. "Like, a really big fan," he said, sheepishly. "I can't believe you know who I am."

"The show wasn't terrible. I loved it." I remembered his voice in that room, singing me home. Like it always did.

Nic was red now, shuffling from foot to foot. The energy in the office turned fast and restless. Kit's cards grew heavier in my pocket. *Where do I go from here?* I asked, but my ghosts were only watching now. I touched the cards, but whatever strength I hoped to draw from them eluded me. Nothing could make this conversation easy. "I knew your mom," I said, finally. "She had me sign one of her tarot cards for you. A million years ago, before anyone ever heard of me. She was... a really special person."

His smile reached full strength—beautiful and open. It wasn't a stage smile, and I wondered if he hid another person underneath, too. "She must have loved you," he said, and the words felt like a hug, reaching through time.

And then Kit's voice in my ear. *Not reaching, little one. You're in someday, now.* I smiled. *Someday.* The one Kit saw coming, even when I couldn't imagine it.

Brad raised his hands to stop our conversation. "Janey didn't tell me you two actually knew each other," he said, confused.

Janey. Of course—who else could have orchestrated a meeting like this? Brad wasn't nervous about Henry. He was nervous about whatever scheme

Janey cooked up to get Nic and me into this office at once. My heart warmed—all this time, Janey was trying to give me *this*.

"We don't," I said, but it didn't feel like the truth. I knew him. And he knew me—I could feel it. The tension wasn't in the room at all. It was between us. Pulling.

The main door clicked again—Henry, walking into a moment so thick I expected it to trap him in the doorway. But he ran straight in and scooped me into a hug that lifted me right off the floor. "I knew you could do it!" he said, uniting Brad and Nic in confusion. "You just needed a little push."

I laughed, weak with relief. Henry forgave me. I found Nicolas Bell. The music was tickling my cheeks and ruffling my hair—not leaving me. It was all working out. *Too easy*, I thought, holding onto Henry. But then Kit's voice came again, firm. *Someday.*

"A little push?" I asked, because Henry was waiting for me to say something. "I take it you're not going to apologize for dumping me?"

I could feel Nic's eyes. Warm and interested and just for me. The music swirled around me.

Around Nic, like the voice of Sky Lake belonged to him, too.

"Nope," Henry said. "It was exactly what you needed. And it hurt me more than it hurt you."

"That's true," Brad offered. "He's been a mess."

I gave Henry another, tighter hug. "Thank you."

I meant it. He did what I needed, even though it hurt. Not many people were strong enough for that.

Henry held me away from him. "So, what did I miss? Let's start with where you've been. Janey's been trying to make us call the police."

Brad jumped in, glad to have more information than someone. "She went to her house in the woods," he offered. "Big mess. No reception."

Nic went very still. Something inside me went still with him. *Connected*, I thought. Destinies, entwined.

Kit would have loved this story.

"Ok," Henry said. "That's not so bad. Next time, though, maybe tell someone where you're going?"

"Of course I will," I said. "I promise." I tried to look sorry, but I knew I did the right thing, going there by myself. I found Nic's eyes, and for a moment we were alone in the room.

Henry turned to Nic. "And you are…"

Nic started to answer, but I interrupted, feeling lighter and more playful than I had in years. Nicolas Bell was the boy who made a mess of my house and couldn't find his way back. I could feel him, hoping. Smelling the roses and not understanding why. I was about to give him a gift, and part of me wanted to draw the moment out. Keep him in *before* just a little longer. But the lake water was hot on my skin. It wanted him back.

"I'm pretty sure this is the guy who left a drum set in my dining room," I said. I could feel myself sparkling. Me, not Charlie. And I could feel Sky Lake in the room, deep and dark and full of mysteries.

Nic's eyes widened. Part of him knew, but most of him didn't believe it, and the truth knocked him back. "Wait," he said, hands flexing like he could grab the rest of the sentence. He sat down, hard, on the couch, never taking his eyes off mine. "Your house," he breathed. Then, so quiet I almost didn't hear him, "You."

Me. Part of Sky Lake. Just like David said.

Nic was searching for Sky Lake. Nic was searching for me.

I found Sky Lake. And I found him.

I felt it—the click click click of puzzle pieces snapping into place. The air cooled and shifted and I heard birds, somewhere in the distance.

"By the lake," he said, like he still didn't quite believe it. "With the roses."

"Yes," I said. "By the lake. With the roses." The room seemed to twist—it was Brad's office, but not *just* Brad's office anymore.

Nic shook his head like he should have seen this coming, but didn't. "I dreamed of you, there," he said, and the office filled with the sweet, spicy smell of home as I remembered my own dream—the man who wasn't David.

"We dreamed of each other," I said, my voice choked with roses and feelings. The scent intensified, cool and damp and pulling me. Henry sneezed.

"I've been searching," Nic said, his voice rough. "For the lake. For... Something." He released a long, slow breath. "I stopped. Today."

Of course he did. He had to. Sky Lake couldn't heal something you're not ready to let go of. The room swirled, floor softening, walls turning to smoke. I felt the breeze off the lake and heard the whisper of wind through the trees. My feet sank into mud and the ceiling became a well of stars. But I resisted it, pulling myself back into Brad's office.

When I stood at Sky Lake with Nic, I wanted it to be real.

I steadied my breathing and sat down next to Nic on the couch. I could feel the music, wrapping its arms around us both. The room shimmered. Brad was rubbing his eyes. Henry was blowing his nose. Nic's shoulder was warm and solid against mine—he wasn't just a voice, or a picture on a screen anymore—and I felt shy. He was real. I was real. *What next?* I asked, but my ghosts were quiet.

I pulled the pebbles out of my pocket and held them, feeling the hum of home against my palm. They were smooth and buzzing on my skin and I wanted to hold onto them. But that was not the way forward. "You need one of these." I held them out—both pebbles, because he would know how to get the other one to Bobby.

The rocks looked ordinary at the lake, but in Brad's office, they glittered like moonlit water—holding onto the place they came from. Silencing any questions about their power.

Nic's hand hovered over mine, the pebbles sparking between us, ringing like bells as Sky Lake waited for his decision. His fingers closed over them cautiously, like they might burn, and I felt the jolt of a melody flow between us. "They're like the map?" he asked, and I nodded. I wished I had told

Damia to pick up a pebble, back then. And I was glad that I didn't, because then I wouldn't be here, Nic's shoulder warm against mine.

What's next? I asked, but my ghosts didn't answer. I was on my own. *Stay or go,* I thought. *Danger or safety.* But I could never tell which was which. "If you want," I said, and then stopped myself. *Risky.* But where did safe choices ever get me? I took a deep breath. "If you want, you could come back with me."

It would have been safer not to ask. Safer not to want more.

But I *did* want more. I wanted us to buy trash bags and bleach and drive those winding roads together, heading toward something real. I wanted Nic to read the lyrics to Priestess over my shoulder. I wanted to stand with him, knee-deep in the lake, under a full moon.

I did not want to do all those things alone, after he said no.

But I wasn't afraid of his answer. No matter what he said, Sky Lake ran through my veins, just like David promised. Its voice belonged to me, and I would always find my way back to it.

But I still held my breath, hoping. I wanted the *someday* Kit imagined.

The one where Nic and I found our way back together, and Sky Lake's voice belonged to both of us.

36

KIT

They buried my cards.

Such a deliciously dramatic interpretation of my instructions. I only meant for them to find each other.

I waited in the woods for them that day. I would have liked to be in the car, overhearing their conversation as they drove to me, and in the house, watching them prepare to walk out to the cemetery, and next to them on the path as they picked their way through the forest in the dark. But wandering became difficult once the rock from the lake covered my grave. It made me heavy. An anchor.

I couldn't go far, but I could hear them. For weeks, the music of their sweet voices carried on the wind as they cleaned up the old house. It warmed me to imagine them putting the place they both loved back together again, but I couldn't even go that far for more than a minute or two.

I saw them in brief, beautiful, entirely inadequate snapshots.

I saw Grace filling a trash bag with bottles while Nic cleared the counters. The mess looked overwhelming to me, but they seemed happy in the middle of it.

She shivered. He peeled off his sweatshirt and offered it with that boyish smile he never grew out of. She hesitated, but took it. Pulled it over her head. His eyes lingered, watching her hands find their way out of the sleeves. And then I was gone, sucked back to the cemetery.

I saw Nic dragging furniture out of the way so Grace could sweep underneath. They moved in careful sync, like people dancing without touching. He watched her so closely that I thought she must be able to feel it, but her eyes stayed on the great drifts of dust she pushed with her broom. And then, the pull of the stone became too great, and I floated back.

I watched their beautiful, shining faces come into focus through the big kitchen window as they washed the dirt away and let the sun in. He said something and she giggled and I leaned closer, wishing I could share their joke, but I felt the stone calling me back.

I watched them laugh at things I couldn't see, dance to songs I couldn't hear, and tell each other stories I would never know. Tiny sips, when I wanted deep, greedy gulps.

I worried that they wouldn't come back once they finished cleaning, but they did. They measured the walls in the dining room, and even though I could only stay for a moment, I saw Grace's concentration face break into a smile in response to something Nic said.

The next day, I caught them replacing the cardboard on the walls with panels. They carried the big ones in together, moving like one person. Nic tuned the piano, and I wondered where on earth he picked up a skill like that.

I saw him puzzling over the electrical outlets with fancy equipment all around him on the floor. I saw Grace assembling furniture. I saw the walls gradually disappear underneath more panels and hope grew like a flower in the place where my chest should have been, because they wouldn't turn that room into a recording studio together if they planned to go their separate ways.

But my glimpses never gave me enough to be *sure*.

Seeing them made me sad and happy at the same time. I wanted to stay forever, a little bird hovering at the edges of their lives. But the dirt and trees and water and the wonderful blanket of stone made me slow and comfortable. Every evening, as the sun sank and the fireflies came out, I thought *I could stay here.*

But I knew I couldn't stay under the rock forever. There was somewhere better to go, and I would go there soon.

Soon, but not yet.

When Grace first placed the stone on top of me, it took every ounce of strength I had to prevent it from lighting. I could see her, wet from the lake, breathing hard, struggling but *fierce.* My little Grace—not the princess anymore. The lion.

I wanted to give her the light, but I couldn't, not yet. Not when she hadn't found my Nic. I clenched and squeezed and pressed with all the strength in my invisible body to keep it dark. She cried, and it broke my heart, but she needed another push, if she was ever going to get to *someday.*

After that, I experimented, letting the light out and squeezing it back in, until I could play the stone like a flute. I thought, *if only I found a way to make my machine do this while I was alive.* And then I thought *oh, but now I have found the way,* and the swell of pride threatened the weak boundaries of my not-body, making the light intense and uncontrollable. It burst out like an explosion of love. I thought *this is the part where I'm supposed to let go.*

I would have, except that I needed to see the ending. Or the beginning, depending on how you look at it.

As they walked up the path toward me that day, their serious little faces pointed at my grave instead of at each other, I wondered if I might have misjudged things. Maybe wishful thinking, not intuition, made me see them together from the moment little Grace showed me her sunrise smile. Maybe I was only comforting myself by imagining that my little ones wouldn't be alone. Telling myself bedtime stories.

They walked silently, side by side, and I analyzed their movements. Were they in sync with each other? I couldn't tell, with the uneven ground and the frequent interruption of tree stumps and overhanging branches. I couldn't quite think of how a couple in love looked while hiking in the dark. Like this, maybe?

Nic pushed a branch out of the way so she could pass. She pointed out a vine for him to step over. But they were lost in their thoughts, not in each other.

Don't look at the stone, look at her, I urged. *She's right there. See her.* But he focused on the stone and not on her pretty hand, pointing the way.

Take his hand, I begged, when they stopped in front of my grave, both hesitating like they didn't know what to do next. But her hands remained stubbornly by her sides.

They were on a mission to bury those cards and nothing more. My disappointment turned the leaves on all the trees over, like rain was coming.

Grace—*Charlotte*, he called her *Charlotte*—knelt and my Nic knelt next to her, both of them still so serious that I wished I could tickle them silly. It seemed unfair that I understood what mattered and they didn't, when they were the ones who could still *do* something about it.

Forget the cards, I urged, and they didn't, but Charlotte didn't pull back when his shoulder brushed hers. I felt a hopeful little flutter where my belly should have been.

This isn't a funeral, I shouted, *I'm here, I see you, I love you, I want you to be happy, please be happy, for me.* But I didn't have a voice. I didn't even have the restless energy that used to let me annoy Nic. I was too sleepy. Too comfortable. Too close to floating away. *Listen to me*, I screamed silently. The shriek caught in my phantom throat—painful and pointless.

And then Charlotte tilted one ear up, listening.

You can hear me, I cried, overjoyed, and then cursed myself for wasting words. Who knew how long I had? *Enjoy this,* I told her. Her head tilted a little more. *I know this moment is perfect, because I can see the whole story.* Tears brightened her eyes, and I couldn't tell if they were happy tears. So, I thought of a chocolate glazed donut. *You never failed me, little one.*

She smiled, and their futures crackled to life around them, a single, shining, *tangled* thing. The spot that used to hold my heart lifted. The rest of me tried to fly away with it.

But I held onto the stone. I wasn't done yet.

They worked together to make a little hole on top of me. Charlotte placed the deck of cards inside it, and Nic placed his one card on top, and their hands lingered together just a little longer than they needed to. Eventually, Charlotte put her palms down on my stone while Nic pushed dirt over the cards.

Such a waste, I thought, but Charlotte had no talent for reading them, anyway.

Charlotte made her serious face and Nic took his time with the dirt and I thought *hurry up, hurry up, hurry up* because I could only keep that stone from glowing for a few more seconds before the effort would become too much.

Charlotte was crying. Nic was being brave, but I could see the little-boy tremble in his chin. "She'll be able to rest now," Charlotte said—reassuring him, like I wished I could. He swallowed hard and brushed a tear off her cheek. Finally, they stood back, his arm around her shoulders, hers around his waist.

I relaxed.

The light bloomed around me, warm and bright, pouring like water. I exhaled. Stretched. Floated.

Not weightless, exactly—*pulled.*

It was beautiful, the way their memories lit up the night. But the real beauty was in their hands—laced together—as they walked away.

Into the future. Into their *lives.*

THE END

About the Author

Leigh Chandler lives in Los Angeles with her husband and a talking bird who thinks he is a dragon. Sky Lake Lost is her first novel. You can contact Leigh at Leigh.Chandler@gmail.com.